Elisabeth Carpenter lives in Preston with her family. She completed a BA in English Literature and Language with the Open University in 2011. Elisabeth was awarded a Northern Writers' New Fiction award, and was longlisted for the Yeovil Literary Prize (2015 and 2016) and the MsLexia Women's Novel award (2015). She loves living in the north of England and sets most of her stories in the area. She currently works as a bookkeeper. Her debut novel, *99 Red Balloons*, became a bestseller in 2017 and received widespread acclaim from both reviewers and readers.

You can follow Elisabeth @LibbyCPT.

By the same author:

99 Red Balloons

ELISABETH CARPENTER

11 MISSED CALLS

avon.

Published by AVON
A division of HarperCollins*Publishers*
1 London Bridge Street,
London SE1 9GF

www.harpercollins.co.uk

A Paperback Original 2018

1

A catalogue record for this book is
available from the British Library

ISBN-13: 978-0-00-822354-0

This novel is entirely a work of fiction.
The names, characters and incidents portrayed in it are
the work of the author's imagination. Any resemblance to
actual persons, living or dead, events or localities is
entirely coincidental.

Set in Bembo by Palimpsest Book Production Limited,
Falkirk, Stirlingshire

Printed and bound in Great Britain by
CPI Group (UK) Ltd, Croydon CR0 4YY

MIX
Paper from
responsible sources
FSC™ C007454

This book is produced from independently certified FSC™ paper
to ensure responsible forest management.

For more information visit: www.harpercollins.co.uk/green

In memory of:

Daniel and Dorothy Sweeney
Patricia and Stanley Carpenter
Michael Carpenter
Julia Thorn

Prologue

Monday, 28 July 1986

Tenerife, Canary Islands

Debbie

The rock I'm standing on is only twelve inches long – just a foot stopping me falling into the water nearly five hundred feet below. The stone is cool under my bare feet.

It's quiet; there aren't many cars going past behind me. It must be late, or early. There's a lovely warm breeze, one you don't get in England when it's dark. If it gets stronger, it might push me over the edge. Hitting water from this height is meant to be like landing on tarmac.

I've always been afraid of heights. What a strange time to conquer my fear. Nathan said this part of the cliffs is called La Gran Caída. Perhaps the name will be imprinted on my soul, alongside Bobby's and Annie's. I thought that when I had children, I'd become a better person. I think I've always had a badness, a sadness, inside me.

Why are my thoughts everywhere? They need to be here. I'm ridiculous, silly; my mother's right. She's always right. I'm useless to everyone. Everyone will be happier without me. Especially the children.

Oh God, no.

I can't think about the children.

They have Peter. I'd only let them down again. What if I were left on my own with Annie again? I might kill her.

They'll forget me soon enough. They're young enough to erase me from their memory.

Breathe, breathe.

I'm surprised by how calm I am.

It's like my mind was coated in tar, but now it's been wiped clean.

I close my eyes.

So, this is how it ends.

I thought I'd be scared if ever I fell from such a height, but if I jump there'll be nothing I can do about it.

The warm breeze skims my face again. I should be with my children right now, lying next to them, watching them sleep.

But I can't. I'm not good enough for them. They'll end up hating me.

Bobby, Annie, you were the loves of my life.

'Debbie! For God's sake, what are you doing?'

Is that the voice inside my head again?

I close my eyes. I don't want anyone to stop me. I just want darkness.

Don't look back. I can't look back.

'Debbie, come away from there!'

Before I have time to think, I'm turning around.

'Oh,' I say. 'It's you.'

Chapter One

Present Day

Anna

My mother, Debbie, has been missing for thirty years, ten months and twenty-seven days. It's her birthday the day after tomorrow – two days after mine. I'm three years older than she was when she was last seen. She disappeared so long ago, that my father doesn't talk about her any more. I have always taken scraps of information from my stepmother, Monica, and my grandfather, who will *never give up hope.*

But they have run out of new things to say about her. I was just over one month old when she left. I have no memories of my own, but I have a box. Inside it are random objects, music records, and photographs that belonged to her. There's also a scrapbook with pages and pages of facts I wrote about her: *She had dark hair, like mine. She was five foot five (two inches taller than me). She had her ears pierced twice in each ear. (Gran didn't like it and had no idea where she got the money, at fifteen, to do that.) She liked The Beatles and Blondie. She wasn't very happy at the end.*

I started the list when I was eleven, so my first entries are naive and in the past tense. What I would like to know now is: *What made you leave?* and *Do you ever think of us?* But of course, no one can answer those questions but her.

The letterbox rattles, shaking me out of my thoughts. Sophie runs to the front door. The envelopes look huge in her little hands.

'There are loads more cards for you, Mummy,' she says.

She hands me the three pastel-coloured envelopes. I examine the handwriting on each one to see if I recognise it. I don't know why I do it to myself every year. If the writing is unfamiliar, I get butterflies and a feeling of anticipation. What if this is the day she contacts me? What if it is today that I find out that she's not dead – that she did something so terrible she had to protect us from the truth?

It is wishful thinking. I have made up so many stories in my head over the years. They get more absurd every time: she died the night she disappeared; she's in prison for drug smuggling; she's living in a South American village after suffering from amnesia.

I place the birthday cards on the table.

'Are you not going to open them?' asks Sophie.

'We'll wait till Grandad arrives. He'll be here in a minute.'

Birthdays make me think of her even more. I often wonder what my mother would look like now if she were alive. I try not to look out for her any more. Not after it got me into so much trouble last time.

A few months ago, I told Sophie she was dead. It was the worst thing I could have said, but I didn't want her thinking she had a grandmother out there in the world that wasn't interested in her. I hadn't meant to say it.

'When are you going to leave *me*, Mummy?' Sophie had said.

'Never,' I said.

'But Granny Debbie left you and Uncle Robert.'

'Not on purpose.'

'Did you lose her?'

4

'I suppose we did,' I said, stroking her hair to take the sting out of it.

'Is she in heaven, then? That's what my friend Lila said about her nana. She had to go to church and then after the singing and the crying, they went outside and the wooden box she was in went into the ground. At least three metres under the grass, she said. But she wasn't allowed to watch that bit – it was what her cousin told her. He's twelve so he saw everything. Is that what happened to Granny?'

'Yes,' I said. 'I'm sorry about your friend Lila.'

Sophie shrugged. 'She's okay. She's on the gold step now. But we all don't mind. It was her first time. She might be naughty again next week.'

'Everyone's naughty sometimes, Sophie. But be kind to her, will you?'

'Yeah.'

She's sitting at the kitchen table now, making her own birthday card for me.

Sometimes I worry I might have the same thoughts as Debbie – that I will abandon everyone, leave in the middle of the night without being able to stop myself.

I hear Dad's car pull up outside.

'Grandad!' shouts Sophie, as the car door slams shut.

Just the one door: Monica's not with him.

They usually do everything together now they're both retired.

I open the front door, and Sophie squeezes between me and the door frame as we watch Dad walk down the front path. He's tall, but he always keeps his head down, like he wants to blend in with the background.

He looks up before the step.

'I didn't realise there'd be a welcoming committee!' he says, bowing slightly.

He's trying to look happy for Sophie and me, but the smile

is only present on his lips. It's a manner so familiar to me that it's almost normal.

'Happy Birthday, love,' he says, before kissing my cheek, and stepping inside.

He ties a silver balloon to the end of the bannister and places a gift bag on the floor.

'Am I allowed to play with it?' Sophie says, standing on the bottom stair, and blowing the balloon sideways.

'Maybe later,' I say. 'I'll put the kettle on.'

Dad and Sophie follow me into the kitchen.

'But it's your birthday,' says Dad, 'and it's a Saturday. Let's have a drop of fizz.'

Sophie sits back at the table.

'Why's Grandad talking posh?'

'I don't know.'

Dad pulls out a bottle of champagne from my gift bag and hands it to me. It's already chilled. He nudges me aside and reaches into the cupboard for three wine glasses. It's like he can't stop moving.

'You know how I feel about birthdays, Dad. I don't want a fuss.'

'Course you do – it's your thirtieth! We had champagne on your twenty-first, remember? I take it Jack's at work . . . on a Saturday? I've never known a conveyancing solicitor work a weekend in my entire life.' Dad glances at me and raises his eyebrows. 'Anyway, your brother should be here any minute.'

I don't say that Robert probably won't drink either. Robert would think that ordering a taxi so he can enjoy a few glasses of champagne during the day is one step towards anarchy, lack of self-control, and being on the verge of a nervous breakdown.

He has always been the same. Robert was six when Debbie

disappeared. Everyone says it's harder for him, because he remembers. When I was little, Robert told me that Dad was arrested after we came back to England – that, for a few days, it was like he had lost two parents. He probably doesn't remember telling me; he's barely mentioned it since. He hates talking about her now. He couldn't understand why, until only a few years ago, I had pictures of her everywhere. Most of those photographs are in the loft now.

'Where's Monica?' I say. 'Is she ill again?'

He fills the glasses halfway, waiting for the bubbles to melt before he tops them up. We're not usually the champagne kind of family.

'No – well, not physically – it's just . . . we've had an email. I can't tell you what was in it until Robert gets here. He won't be long.'

'An email? Why didn't you just forward it to me, or tell me over the phone? Does Leo know?'

Leo is our stepbrother – Monica's son – but he lives in America with his father.

'No, no. We wouldn't tell him without you two knowing first.' He paces along the small space between the sink and the kitchen table. 'I did wonder whether it was the right day to do this, but I couldn't face you today without telling you.'

'What does it say?'

He narrows his eyes and purses his lips.

'Is it about Debbie?' I say.

He nods slowly.

My legs start to shake. It feels like the blood has run cold in my face. I lean against the back of a chair.

What could an email say about her? If her remains had been found, or if she were still alive – it wouldn't be in a casual email. Maybe this is how it's done these days – especially if she were found in Tenerife. Has a dog found her while searching

7

for a bone? Or has she been discovered in a hospital somewhere – her memory wiped by an accident?

I must stop thinking.

Dad wouldn't open champagne if it were bad news, would he?

I open my mouth; I almost don't want to say it out loud.

'Is she dead?' I whisper, so Sophie doesn't hear.

'Anna, love, just be patient. Please. He'll be here soon.'

Why did he not just say no – put me out of my misery?

My stomach is churning. Deep breath. Breathe, breathe.

He looks at his watch and we stand wordlessly, with only the sound of the wine bubbling, losing its fizz. Briefly, the mask slips from his face when he thinks I'm not looking – I have seen it often over the years: the sadness of remembering something lost.

'Sophie,' I say. 'I'll put a film on for you while we wait for Uncle Robert. Then we can have some cake.'

'Cake?'

'Yes, love.'

She takes my hand, and we go into the living room. I flick on the television, but it takes too long to find a film – my hands are shaking.

'Just put the kids' channel on,' she says, her head tilted to the side as she looks at me.

'Good plan. Thanks, sweetheart.'

She's only six, but she can be so perceptive at times. I pull the living-room door closed as much as I can without her panicking that I am going to abandon her.

Dad's looking at the clock when I walk back into the kitchen.

'It's not like Robert to be ten minutes late,' he says. 'Why don't you open your present? Monica's so excited about it.'

'Why isn't she here then?'

8

'She thought she'd give us some space while I tell you the news.'

'That's very understanding of her.'

Dad narrows his eyes for a second. Perhaps I was too sarcastic. Monica has been married to my father since I was eleven, but she has always been in my life. My mother is *presumed dead* in the eyes of the law.

'She hasn't taken it well,' he says. 'She didn't even want me to read it.'

'What? Wasn't it addressed to you?'

I follow him as he walks out of the kitchen and into the hall. He peers through the window next to the front door.

'Dad?'

He is saved by the bell. I open the door to Robert.

'Happy Birthday, Anna,' he says, unwrapping his scarf – he's never without one. 'Hotter than I thought it'd be today. Should've gone with the cotton.'

Robert hands me a birthday card, which will contain fifteen pounds.

'Come on through to the kitchen, you two,' says Dad, walking straight there.

'What's going on?' says Robert, draping his jacket along the stairs. He glances at the balloon on the end of the bannister. 'You really should get a coat stand or something.'

'He's got an email,' I say, 'about Debbie.'

Robert's shoulders slump; he lowers his head, his eyes scanning the wooden floor of the hall.

'Is it good news or bad?' he says, finally looking up at me.

'I don't know. But he opened champagne.'

'That could mean anything.'

He links his arm through mine and guides me through to the kitchen.

'What do you mean by that?' I hiss.

Dad's leaning against the kitchen cupboards – he's already pulled out two chairs.

'Ssh,' Robert says to me, sitting on the chair nearest Dad.

'Okay.' Dad clasps his hands together. 'Sorry about this, Anna – it being on your birthday and all.'

'She hates birthdays anyway,' says Robert.

'This came through yesterday.' He picks up a brown envelope from the kitchen counter behind him, and takes out two sheets of A4. 'Well, Monica received it a few days ago – I only saw it yesterday. I've done a copy for both of you.'

'Why didn't she show it to you straight away?' I say to Dad. He just shrugs.

My brother snatches one of the sheets from Dad's hand.

'Robert!' I say, taking the other.

I glance down quickly. There are only a few lines.

I read it properly.

Dear Monica,
It's time to tell the truth.
Debbie x
The memories of shells and sweet things are sometimes all we have left.

'Is this it?' says Robert, standing up. 'It's a crank letter. You've had them before, haven't you, Dad?'

'What?' I say. 'No one said anything to me.'

'I suppose they didn't want to upset you,' Robert says.

I frown at him, making a note in my mind to ask Monica about it next time I see her.

'But what if it's not?' I say quietly. 'My memory box is covered in shells.'

Robert tuts. 'That could mean anything. You're just making it significant because it means something to you. It's like these

10

charlatan psychics. If Debbie were alive, why would she make contact now after so long?'

'Something might've happened,' I say to Dad. 'It says *it's time.* Why did she address it to Monica and not you?'

Dad shakes his head.

'I've no idea what it means,' he says. 'Neither does Monica. We'll just have to wait and see if she sends something else.'

'If it's even a *she* who wrote it,' says Robert. 'It could be anyone.'

'Did you reply?' I say.

We both look up at Dad.

'I . . . I think Monica might have. I've been a bit shaken by it all, to be honest.'

'It sounds a bit sinister,' I say. 'What does Monica think it means?'

Dad takes one of the glasses of champagne and takes a large sip.

'Like I said, she doesn't know.'

Robert looks at me and shrugs.

'That's because it's a load of crap.'

'Uncle Robert!' Sophie runs into the kitchen and jumps onto Robert's lap. 'Did you just say *crap*?'

'Of course not!' says Robert. 'I said *slap*.'

'Which isn't much better,' says Dad, rubbing the top of Sophie's head.

I walk into the living room and switch off the television. I look down at the email again. Monica received it days ago, yet didn't show Dad. I look out of the window, leaning against the glass. I don't know what I expect to see outside. But a thought strikes me.

Monica knows more than she is letting on.

Chapter Two

3 a.m. Thursday, 26 June 1986

Debbie

I've been looking at the same page of this stupid magazine for over an hour, trying to read the words under the crappy night-light above my head, but I keep daydreaming. The article's about making the perfect chocolate roulade, and getting the timings right for all the 'trimmings' on Christmas day. It's from one of the women's magazines Mum has been saving for months – or maybe years, judging by the state of them. She's still trying to convince me that *Good Housekeeping* will make me a more fulfilled person and a better mum. But there's nothing more depressing than reading about Christmas in June. I don't know why she thinks I'd be interested in things like this – she's not the best cook herself. I'm nearly twenty-seven, not forty-seven. I should be reading about George Michael or the G spot.

I throw it onto the bed tray, but it slips off. The sound is amplified by a rare moment of silence on the maternity ward. I hold my breath in the hope that it cancels out the splat of the magazine onto the floor. Please, no one wake up. This peace is mine right now, and I don't want anyone else to ruin it. My normal life is far from peaceful.

Annie looks like a little doll; she's been so quiet. It must be the pethidine. She's got the same podgy fingers that Bobby had – they're like tiny tree trunks. I didn't think she'd suit the name. I'd suggested Gemma or Rebecca, but Peter wanted to call her Anna after his late mother. It's just right for her.

I've lost track of time and I've only been here for one night. The sky is purple; is it nearly morning or is it still dusk?

It's hardly ever quiet in here, but they're all asleep now. The new mothers try to feed as quietly as possible, but they're amateurs, all three of them. And it's never completely dark. They like to keep the light on above their heads. Perhaps they're afraid that if it goes out, their babies will disappear.

I pick up the magazine, as quickly as I can with damn painful stitches, and place it on my cabinet. There are seven birthday cards, still in their envelopes, ready for me to open tomorrow, or is it today? Is it terrible that I'm glad I'm not sharing my birthday – to be relieved that Annie arrived two days earlier than her due date? It probably is, but I'll keep that selfish thought in my head. It's one of many, anyway.

'Debbie.'

My mind wakes up, but I leave my eyes closed. It's so hot. I'm on a beach, lying on sand in a cove that only I know about.

'Debbie.'

Was that a voice in my head? I open one eye to find a nurse bending over me.

'Oh God,' I say. 'The baby.'

I sit up as quickly as I can. How could I be so careless falling asleep so heavily? The nurse rests a cold hand on my wrist.

'Baby's fine,' she says. 'There's a phone call for you.'

I swing my legs so they're dangling over the side of the bed. The nurse pushes the payphone towards me and gives me the handset.

'Debs, it's me.' It's Peter. 'How's Annie? Did she wake much in the night? I wish I could be there. Shall I ask if you can come home early?'

It takes a few moments to digest Peter's words. He must've thought of them during the night, to be saying them all at once. Being with children does that; makes you go over things in your mind, with no adult to talk to. He's not used to it being just Bobby and him.

'No, no,' I say. 'It's fine. She's being as good as gold.'

Good as gold? I sound like my mother.

'I can't make the afternoon visiting times today,' he says, 'but I'll be there at seven tonight. I'll drop Bobby off at school, then I'll work straight through. Is that all right? I have to make sure I can spend at least a week at home when you both come out.'

'That's fine. Monica's visiting this afternoon.'

'Good, good.'

'I have to go now, though. They're bringing lunch round.'

'Really?'

'Bye, Peter.'

I place the handset back into the cradle. I hate making small talk, especially while a whole maternity ward can hear me shouting down the payphone. The nurse doesn't say anything, even though when I look at the clock on the wall it's only eight in the morning, and four hours from lunchtime. I suppose she's seen everything, so I don't feel as embarrassed as I should. I've spent so long lying to Peter – *Yes, I'm fine* and *Yes, I've always wanted two children* – that it comes naturally to me.

Why is he taking a whole week off? He's branch manager now at Woolies – surely they can't be without him for that long. I'm sure he didn't with Bobby, though that time is a blur. I don't think I can remember anything – I might've forgotten how to look after a tiny baby.

14

The woman in the bed next to me is snoring so loudly, it's like being at home. A silver chain her boyfriend bought her is dangling off the hospital bed. 'I can't wear necklaces at night,' she said yesterday, 'in case they strangle me in my sleep.' I was about to tell her that I was afraid of spiders to make her feel better, but I remembered Mum saying I shouldn't make everything about me. 'It's called empathy,' I said. 'Ego,' she said. She's too humble for her own good. I blame Jesus – she loves him more than life itself.

Yesterday, she whispered, 'Mothers are so much older these days.' (Some of her opinions aren't as Christian as they should be.) 'Women want everything now,' she said. 'They all want to be men.'

It was, of course, a stupid thing to say in a maternity ward. And she was an older mother herself.

An assistant is coming round to change the water jugs.

'It's good that you're dressed,' she says to me. 'Makes you feel a bit more together, doesn't it?'

I look down at my *Frankie Says Relax* T-shirt and red tartan pyjama bottoms. My mouth is already open when I say, 'Yes.'

She looks at my birthday cards, displayed on the cabinet. I can't even remember opening them.

'Happy Birthday, lovey,' she says.

It's only then I realise that Peter forgot my birthday.

At last, Annie makes a feeble sound as though she can't be bothered.

'I know, little girl,' I say. 'Sometimes it's more effort than it's worth, waking up.'

I pick her up and out of the plastic fish tank (that's what Bobby called it when he visited yesterday) and put the ready-prepared bottle to her lips, settling back into the pillows. She suckles on it – probably going too fast, too much air – but I let her. She's going to be a feisty little thing, I can tell.

Everyone else wanted me to have a girl. No one believed me when I said I didn't mind, that healthy was all that mattered. But I would've been happy with two boys, I'm sure. It seems longer than nearly six years since I had Bobby – I was only twenty-one, but I felt so grown-up. He's so loving, so sensitive. 'Perfect little family now,' said Mum. 'One of each.' And I should feel that, shouldn't I?

But I don't.

Chapter Three

Anna

I used to have dreams that Debbie was dead and had come back to life. Sometimes she would be rotting, sometimes she would be an unwelcome guest as the family was sitting around the table for Sunday lunch. I don't remember seeing her happy in my dreams. When I was eight, I used to have the same nightmare, over and over. I still remember it now. Our house was burning down, and a woman stood at my bedroom doorway screaming. Robert came to my side that night and sang 'Hush, Little Baby'. I thought it childish the morning after, but at the time it soothed me. He said that Debbie sang it to me in the middle of the night a few times when I wouldn't sleep.

I can't sleep now. My mind won't be still.

If Debbie were alive, then it would mean it was my fault that she left. She was fine until I came into the world. Not that anyone has said as much, but Dad, Robert – they all probably think it is down to me that she isn't here any more. Perhaps I was a mistake.

I can't stop thinking about her. I wish I hadn't put all of Debbie's photographs in the loft. Jack would call me crazy if I got the ladder down at three o'clock in the morning.

What would she look like now? Would she still hate me?

Random thoughts like these always come into my head when I try not to think of her.

A few years after we married, Jack told me I was obsessed with her.

'I know,' I said.

'It's not enough that you're aware of it,' he said. 'You have to change it.'

Yesterday, he came home after Dad and Robert had left, and Sophie had gone to bed. Dad asked why a conveyancer would be called out to work on a Saturday, but I've stopped probing Jack about it. He must be so busy at work that he forgot my birthday. He knows I hate birthdays, which is his usual excuse. I should tell him that *it's not enough that you're aware of it*.

We met when I was twenty-two and Jack was twenty-four, at a Spanish evening class. I only went on Monica's suggestion. 'You're too young to be stuck in all day on your own, love,' she said. 'I don't like seeing you so lonely.'

I had been desperate to meet someone, perhaps have children – a family of my own. I'm not sure I would be in so much of a rush, had I the chance to start again; I was far too young, but I had no friends and hardly ever went out. I had just finished university and was applying for at least twenty jobs a week.

Before the first class, Monica took me into Boots to have a makeover.

'Could you do something with her eyebrows?' she said to the lady dressed in white – plastered in thick foundation and bright-red lipstick. 'They've gone a bit wild.'

'Monica!' I said through gritted teeth, as I sat on a pedestal for everyone in the shop to see.

'We might as well, while we're here.'

After my face had been transformed, Monica took me to the hairdressers: my first visit for several years.

'She has beautiful hair,' Monica said to the stylist, 'but perhaps we could put some highlights at the front . . . to frame her lovely face.'

On the way home, I caught sight of myself in her car's vanity mirror and got a fright. I didn't look like me any more.

When I walked into the classroom that evening, I thought Jack was the teacher. He was standing at the front, talking to the students with such confidence. But when he opened his mouth, he spoke with a broad Yorkshire accent and was worse at Spanish than I was. I learned that he'd stayed in Lancashire after university, after his parents *abandoned* him to go and live in Brighton.

Jack said I wasn't like other women he met. 'You're an innocent, Anna. It's like you've been sheltered from the world.'

But that was my act – the character I chose to present to others at that time. Self-preservation. I didn't even look like the real me. I could act like I had no silly fears – of heights, swimming pools, and other irrational things. But I couldn't pretend forever. When I confessed my greatest fears three months later, Jack hadn't laughed at me. 'They're perfectly reasonable phobias,' he'd said. 'But life's about risk sometimes.'

Jack's parents moved away so long ago – Sophie has only met them six times. They think it's enough to send my daughter ten pounds in a card for her birthday and Christmas.

I think because Jack isn't close to *his* parents, there's no love lost between him and *my* dad. When he's drunk, Jack often ponders out loud whether my dad had anything to do with my mother's disappearance, and rolls off the possible ways in which it could have happened.

'Why else,' he said one night, 'would he end up married to Debbie's best friend?'

I switch off when he starts talking like that. He has stopped saying sorry about it in the morning – if he remembers saying it at all. I console myself that he's only so boorish when he's had a drink.

'Dad . . . well, Monica . . . got an email from someone saying they're my mother,' I said to him when he got in last night. I was sitting at the kitchen table – the champagne, which had long gone flat, still in three glasses.

'Is that why you've taken to drink?' he said, shrugging off his suit jacket and hanging it on the back of a chair.

'It's not funny,' I said.

I thought he would be more surprised. It was like his mind was elsewhere.

He grabbed the glass with the most wine in, and downed half of it. He winced.

'It's flat.' He pulled out a chair and sat down. 'Do you think it's really her? It can't be, surely. It must be some lunatic wanting a bit of attention.'

'I've no idea if it is or isn't. How would I know that?'

Jack raised his eyebrows. He hates anything that borders on histrionic.

'If it is,' I said, 'then it means she left us . . . That she left me.'

I saw the briefest flicker of irritation on his face. He gets like that when I talk about Debbie in that way. He hates people with a *poor me* attitude. It's bad enough that I have a fear of swimming pools and spiders. I don't want to be a victim. I have tried to overcome that feeling all my life.

He pulled off his tie, in the way he always does: wrenching it off with one hand, while grimacing as though he were being strangled. Who's the victim now, eh? I thought to myself.

'What a day,' he said, as usual. 'Have you got a copy of the email?'

'Yes. Dad gave me and Robert a print-out. I wonder if we could trace the email address. Do you think I should ring Leo?'

'Will he care?'

'Course he'll care . . . he grew up with us. At least, until I was ten.'

'Sharing a bedroom with *your* brother would make anyone want to flee the country.'

I don't laugh.

'I'll look at the email later,' he said. 'I've had a really long day. Is there anything in for tea?'

I looked at him for a few seconds, waiting for him to realise. But he didn't. Sophie had claimed the balloon my dad gave me; it was floating from her bedpost. My cards were on top of the fridge, but Jack hadn't noticed them.

I stood.

'I'm going to bed,' I said. 'There's a new volunteer starting tomorrow.'

He snorted. 'Ah, the ex-con. And on a Sunday as well.' He made the sign of the cross with his left hand. 'Lock up your handbag.'

'Yes, very funny,' I said as I walked towards the door. 'It's part of the offender-rehabilitation programme Isobel's been going on about.'

His chair scraped on the stone floor as he stood.

'Guess I'll just stick a pizza in the oven then.'

I tried to stomp up the stairs, but failed in bare feet. *Happy sodding Birthday, Anna.*

I look at him next to me in bed now, jealous of his ability to sleep soundly at this hour. He's never had anything big to worry about. It's 3.45 a.m. If I get up now, I'll be a wreck later, but I can't lie here with only my thoughts.

I manage to avoid all the creaking floorboards and make it quietly downstairs to the kitchen. The ticking of the clock is too loud. On the table, Jack's plate is covered with pizza crusts, and crumbs litter the floor under the chair.

The three wine glasses are now empty. Why the hell did he want to drink flat champagne? I go to the fridge to count the bottles of beer left: there were six, and now there are none. No wonder he's sleeping so soundly. I don't know why he's drinking so much when he's looking after Sophie tomorrow. He's usually the sensible one.

I sit opposite his empty chair. It's wearing the jacket that Jack was earlier. His right pocket is slightly open, and the top of his wallet is peeking out.

Before I know it, I'm out of my seat.

The wallet slips out of Jack's pocket so easily, it's like it was waiting for me. Inside is a picture of Sophie and me. It's old – from Sophie's first birthday. I look quite together in the photo, which is surprising considering what I was going through. There are some receipts – the usual expenses he claims: newspapers, dinner. I scan the food he ate at lunchtime yesterday: steak, crème brûlée, and one small glass of pinot noir. Only one meal, but quite an extravagant one – on my birthday. I almost give up searching, but I feel like I am missing something.

There is a compartment I've not noticed before: to the side and underneath his cards. I wedge my fingers inside it. There's something there. I grasp it, using my fingers as tweezers, and pull it out.

It's a note. The paper is blue, with black lines – like the old-fashioned Basildon Bond writing pad my grandmother used. The creases are crisp; it's not been read many times. I unfold it and look straight to the name at the bottom: Francesca.

I read the rest of the letter.

This woman definitely knows my husband.

Chapter Four

Friday, 27 June 1986

Debbie

Peter's holding Annie while I pack. I almost don't want to leave the hospital. With Bobby, I wanted to go home straight away, but regretted it as soon as I got back.

Ever since I gave birth to him, I've been scared that I'll die any minute. I go to bed and, most nights, I think I won't wake up. Sometimes I'm exhausted, but when my mind feels sleep begin – it's like I'm slipping from life, and I'm jolted awake. I can't sleep for hours after.

At least in hospital I'm safe. Plus, people give you food to eat, and you don't have to worry about housework. As much as Peter said he'd become one of these New Men who help tidy up and change nappies, it didn't happen. Now I know what's waiting for me when I get home.

I had a little routine here. I got to know Stacy in the next bed. Actually . . . *know* is exaggerating it a bit. We watched *Coronation Street* together, and both our babies decided to sleep through it, which was a miracle in itself. Stacy couldn't get over Bet Lynch being in the Rovers when it was on fire. I told her that it's not real life, but she was having none of it. I put a cushion between us when she said she fancied Brian Tilsley – it still gives me shivers thinking about it.

'Was it horrible spending the whole of your birthday in hospital?' says Peter.

'It wasn't too bad,' I say.

I smile at him, so he'll probably think it's because of Annie that I didn't mind, because she's enough of a present. He gives me a smile back. He thinks he can read my mind. I look at him and he's the same lovely-looking man I've been with for years. I love him. Why are my thoughts telling me different? It's like they're betraying me.

I zip up my suitcase; the clothes inside'll smell of hospital when I open it up. I'll probably feel sentimental about it.

'It's too warm in here,' I say.

He smiles again. Perhaps he likes the fact I'm suffering for our child – even after being pregnant and giving birth. Perhaps he's right. It was a relatively quick labour – I've not endured enough to deserve the life I'll go back to: swanning about the house all day watching *Sons and Daughters*, *The Sullivans*, and all the other soaps he reckons I watched during those long weeks when my maternity leave started.

'Good luck,' says Stacy, lying in the next bed, baby fast asleep in her arms – her only child.

'Good luck,' I say, to be friendly. 'Not that you'll need it.'

'We should meet up for coffee sometime,' she says.

'Yes, we should.'

I pick the baby up from the bed and Peter and I leave the ward. I didn't give Stacy my telephone number because we'll never get together. People suggest it all the time and they never mean it. I'm not sure if I'll regret it or not.

Annie's wrapped up in the shawl we used for Bobby on his first day out into the world. We're in the lift and Annie's not opened her eyes since leaving the ward. She's going to miss her first proper glimpse of sky if she's not careful.

'There, there,' I say, stroking her soft, plump cheek.

'Don't wake her, Debs,' says Peter. 'The bright light might startle her.'

'Don't be silly. She's got to see it some time.'

The lift doors open and there are people everywhere.

'Can we pop into the shop to get a souvenir?' I say.

I don't wait for Peter.

'Is Annie not souvenir enough?'

I pretend I didn't hear. I want something to put in her little keepsake box, like I did for Bobby. Someday she'll look at it and know that I cared enough.

On the counter, there's a selection of pens. I pick one up that has a boat sailing up and down. She'll like that, I know she will. I'd have loved my mum to have bought me anything that wasn't on a birthday or Christmas, even if it were practical.

'A pen's got nothing to do with hospitals,' says Peter.

'They're hardly going to sell stethoscopes and hypodermic needles.'

I smile at the lady behind the counter, but she doesn't smile back. She's not amused. I'm used to it. Peter's always telling me not to be so honest in public.

I wind the window down because it's as hot in the car as it was in the hospital. I'm holding on to Annie tightly on the back seat. Peter's driving at about ten miles an hour. It's a good job our house is only five minutes away.

I'm staring at Annie, willing her eyes to open, and it seems she's telepathic: her eyes don't even squint in the daylight.

'Welcome to the world, little girl.'

I say it quietly, so Peter doesn't hear. I'm keeping this moment for me.

They're due here at three. The house looks okay; I have the baby as an excuse not to bother about it so much. If it were my mum visiting, I'd make it a bit messier – if only to give her something to do. She likes to feel useful.

Bobby's waiting by the window. His little hands are around the cat's neck as it lies on the back of the settee. Annie's in the pram next to him by the window – the midwife said it's the best way to get the jaundice out of her.

'Are you sure you don't mind Monica and Nathan coming round?' says Peter. 'I tried to put them off, but she wouldn't listen.'

'It's fine, it's fine.'

Sometimes I think Peter knows about my secret, but he doesn't seem to let on.

He says I look good, *considering*, but I don't feel it. I can't move quickly with these damn painful stitches; I walk like I've drenched my trousers in starch. I'd planned what to wear when they came round, but my blouse gaped too much at the front. I'm like a cow that needed milking two days ago, and my breasts are leaking so much. So now, I'm wearing a jumper, in June, with two green paper towels from the hospital stuffed in each cup of my bra.

'They're here,' shouts Bobby, jumping down from the settee, scaring the cat.

'I'll go,' says Peter, as though he's doing me a huge favour by answering the door.

I hear them in the hallway – Monica's whispering in case Annie's asleep, but Peter's talking normally because *we've* decided to talk at a regular volume during the day so as not to make the baby used to silence. It took Bobby three years to learn that there didn't have to be quiet in order to sleep.

I'm not the first person Nathan looks at when he walks in the room. His eyes are on the floor until his gaze reaches the pram wheels, and only then does he look up. He almost tiptoes, which isn't really necessary on the carpet.

'Well aren't you a pretty little thing?' he says.

Monica's in my face and I almost jump, until I realise she's kissing my cheek.

'I know I saw you in the hospital,' she says, 'but bloody well done, you.'

She hands me a Marks & Sparks carrier bag that she's filled with magazines, Ferrero Rocher, and a mini bottle of Snowball. Is it too early to open it?

'You don't need to whisper, everyone,' shouts Peter, as though there were a crowd in the room. 'We're doing this thing . . .'

I let him explain. It's embarrassing. It's like we're pretending to be New Age parents when we're probably the opposite. Does Nathan think I'm boring now – worrying about babies and what sort of noise is acceptable?

'Did you see the match on Sunday?' Peter says to Nathan.

'Oh God, don't mention it,' says Monica. 'He's not stopped moaning about it all week.'

'Bloody hand of God,' says Nathan. 'I'm not watching any more World Cup. I just can't believe . . .' He shakes his head.

Monica sits and pulls Nathan down towards the settee by his hand; he lands next to her. Peter goes to the kitchen, and Monica leans towards me, her hands on her knees.

'Peter's so good, isn't he?'

I glance at Nathan; he's still not looking at me.

'He is,' I say. 'He's the best.'

Monica tilts her head. They've left Leo at his friend's so they can have a *proper visit*. She's so nice to me, she's been such a good friend. I suddenly have this sense of remorse and a crushing

27

feeling of shame about the thoughts I've been having. She gets down onto her knees and reaches into her pocket for a rectangular tissue.

'It's only normal,' she says. 'I cried for days after I had Leo.'

I hadn't realised I was crying.

I pat my face dry and look at Nathan above the tissue.

He narrows his eyes when he looks at me.

Was that hatred? Does he think I'm weird? I've always been inappropriate. I feel like I'm in the wrong life. I should be with Nathan, not Peter. He was with me first, after all.

There was a girl in my class at school who died in a car crash when she was fourteen. I'll always remember her name: Leslie Pickering. It's terrible that I think about her at times like this, and I don't know why I do. I think to myself: *she never has to go through this*, and I wish I were her. These thoughts scare me.

'It's just . . . just . . .'

I think of poor Leslie Pickering's parents. I bet they wish *I* were dead instead of her, too.

My face is in my hands. Why am I doing this in front of them?

Monica pats my knees and rubs them like I need warming.

'We need to arrange a night out,' she says.

I look up. Nathan wrinkles his nose.

'Don't be stupid, Monica,' he says. 'She's just had a baby – why the hell would she want a night out?'

I sit up a bit straighter and stuff the tissue up my sleeve.

'Mind your language in front of Bobby,' says Monica. 'What about Lytham Club Day tomorrow instead? We could let the boys go on a few rides.'

'Actually, that doesn't seem such a bad idea,' I say, pretending I want to go outside – that I wouldn't care if everyone saw me walking like I've a horse missing between my legs. I could take

28

some painkillers. 'I've been in the house for too long. I could do with getting out.'

I try to make eye contact with Nathan, but after a few minutes, it gets silly. I'm ridiculous. Because it's all in my head. Why would he want me? A mother who's just given birth to her second child, and a wife who's supposed to be in love with her husband. I'm a joke.

Chapter Five

Anna

Sheila, the volunteer who comes in nearly every day, is in the back room of the bookshop, filling the kettle and sighing to herself. I don't want to be here either. I need to be investigating the address that Debbie sent the email from.

It was at the end of primary school that I started the scrapbook filled with facts about her. I thought if I kept a list, then it would keep her alive – it was something tangible. As soon as I learned something new, I would write it down. There must be over a hundred snippets of information in there. Sometimes things would slip out of Dad or Robert's mouth and I would repeat it again and again in my head till I could find a pen and paper. Grandad never said much about Debbie, though. I never had to carry a notebook when I went to his house. Perhaps he thought he was being kind.

Grandad usually comes into the bookshop on a Sunday after the ten o'clock Mass. He sits at the counter if he can wrestle Sheila out of the way. He said he wasn't really into religion until Gran died nearly twenty years ago. He's been to church every Sunday since.

My grandmother was sixty-nine when she had her first, fatal

heart attack. I was ten, nearly eleven. She used to talk about my mother all the time. 'I want you to remember all the little bits,' she said, 'in case I'm not around for long enough.' It was as though she'd predicted her own death. She was the one who helped me create the scrapbook. 'Your brother's still too hurt to hear all of this. I don't see that changing any time soon, Lord help him,' she said. 'But I'm glad you want to know. Frank can't talk about her for long . . . He hides in his office.'

Grandad's office is a little wooden shed he built in their back yard.

I wonder how he is taking the news about the note from Debbie. Dad must have told him by now, yet Grandad's not answering his telephone or replying to his emails or texts. My messages are coming up as *read*, so I know he's okay. But it's not like him to ignore anything. He loves technology – he was the person who explained the workings of the Internet to me. 'We are all closer together because of this,' he said. 'Though sometimes it makes us realise we're worlds apart.'

The new volunteer is five minutes late. How can she expect to be taken seriously if she's not punctual? She's meant to be embarking on a new start. That's what my boss, Isobel, said. I might be the manager of this bookshop, but sometimes Isobel sends volunteers here because she wants to appear more Christian than she really is.

At least it takes my mind off the letter for five minutes. Or rather, letters: plural. Why are different aspects of my life falling apart at exactly the same time? Can't things go well for more than one day?

I put Jack's letter back in his wallet last night, but only after I had taken a photo of it on my mobile phone. *To the love of my life*. That's what she called him. It wasn't dated, so I can't tell if it is old or new. There were no references to any events past or present. I try to think back to when Jack and I got together, to remember names of past girlfriends, but I can't. I don't think we even mentioned our exes; it didn't seem important once we found each other.

If the volunteer isn't here in three minutes, I'll look at the letter on my phone ag—

'Annie Donnelly?'

I didn't even hear the door open. A woman is standing in front of me. She is taller than me and in her late fifties, at a guess. She's without make-up and her face looks weather-beaten and tanned, as though she spends her weekends outdoors. Her hair is dark, and her skin has a healthy glow that I will never have, being in this bookshop all the time.

'It's Anna,' I say, a little more harshly than I intended.

I slide off the stool behind the counter.

'Sorry.' Her voice is quiet, but she returns my gaze. 'I'm Ellen.'

'It's eight minutes past.'

I'm not usually so spiky, but already I get the impression she doesn't want to be here. She glances at the clock behind me, then looks at her wrist.

'My watch is behind . . . since the clocks went forward. I must've set it wrong.'

'Right.' I try not to waver from her gaze.

The clocks went forward nearly three months ago, but I don't mention it.

'Follow me into the back,' I say, leading her into the small stockroom. Every spare space on the twenty-three long shelves is crammed with books.

'I'll get to my spot behind the counter,' says Sheila, carrying her cup of tea.

'Do you want to see my CV?' asks Ellen, blinking so much now, it's like there is something in her eyes. She reaches into her handbag before I reply, and hands me a brown envelope. 'It sounds worse than it was.'

'Excuse me?'

'What they say I did. Did Isobel tell you?'

She means her criminal record. I've seen enough crime dramas to know that everyone says, *I didn't do it.*

'No. Isobel has this thing about confidentiality – she takes it seriously. If you want to tell me when you're ready, then that's up to you. As Isobel took it upon herself to get your references, you don't have to tell me anything.'

I really want to ask what she was in prison for, but the words won't come out. I'm the manager – I can't engage in gossip.

'Oh,' says Ellen.

I've said too much, mentioning Isobel and her *confidentiality*, which I over exaggerated. She goes on about data protection, but she's the biggest gossip I know.

We look at each other as I wait for Ellen to tell me all about it. She breaks my stare, looking instead at all the books on the shelves.

'What do you want me to do?' she says.

I try not to look disappointed – it might be on her CV. Though I doubt most people would count being in prison as an occupation.

I point to the table, which has three huge boxes of books on it.

'These need sorting into categories and putting on the shelves, which are labelled with different genres, and fiction and non-fiction. Would you like a cup of tea first? My grandmother always used to say . . .'

I walk towards the kitchenette, not bothering to finish my sentence. Ellen's already unpacking the books. I was boring myself anyway.

The sound of the kettle masks my opening her envelope. There is only one thing I want to check. If my mother were alive, she would be fifty-eight tomorrow. I look at the back of

Ellen's head. There is a photo of Robert in one of our old albums, where he's gluing plane parts together; Debbie is sitting with her back to the camera – her long dark hair is pulled into a bun, so it looks like it's shorter. Ellen looks just like her from behind.

I peek at the top of her CV. I see it.

I read it again to make sure.

Ellen has the same date of birth as my mother.

Sheila sniffs and remains on her perch behind the till.

'I don't *have* to go in the back if I don't want to,' she says. 'If she wants to say hello, she'll have to come in here.' She leans forward. 'She could be a murderess for all we know.' She whispers as quietly as a church bell.

I could argue that Ellen probably isn't a convicted killer, and that being the veteran volunteer of the bookshop with twelve years' service, Sheila should make an effort to welcome her, but I don't. It will fall on deaf ears, as things like this usually do with her – she pretends, at times convenient to her, that she's hard of hearing.

Instead, I say, 'How many people do you know that have the same birth date as you?'

It's like I can hear the index cards sifting in her mind as her eyes drift away into the past.

'Mavis Brierly,' she says. 'Fattest girl at school, though I don't know how; no one had much money to buy so much food. After that, I met a woman in the maternity ward when I was expecting Timothy – can't remember her name . . . began with a "C", if I remember rightly. So, two people. Though they're probably dead now. Most people I know are.'

I shouldn't have asked her; I shouldn't be thinking like this.

The last time it happened was six years ago. It was the woman who used to work in the bakery a few doors down from the shop I used to work in. If it hadn't been for Jack, I'd have a restraining order against me.

'Okay,' I say. 'So, it's not as unusual as I thought.'

'Obviously not. There are only three hundred and sixty-five days in a year, and millions of people in this world.' She leans towards me again. 'Why do you ask? Has Tenko in there got the same birthday as you?'

'Sheila! You must stop talking like that. Everyone deserves a second chance.'

Ellen clears her throat. She's standing at the doorway.

'This book,' she says. 'I think it might be valuable. It's a *Harry Potter* first edition.'

Sheila picks up a pen and writes on the notepad next to the till on the counter. She pushes it towards me when she's finished. *She's probably a thief.*

My face grows hot as I rip the sheet from the pad. I screw it up and drop it into the bin, before ushering Ellen back into the storeroom. She can't have seen what Sheila wrote, but she will have noticed the whispering, and the silence that followed her presence.

'I'm so sorry about that,' I say, in case she read it. 'I'll give Sheila a warning. I don't want you to feel uncomfortable.'

Ellen sits at the table and places the book in front of her.

'It's okay. I'm used to it,' she says. 'There was one person in particular who targeted me when I was inside: Jackie Annand. She never liked me. But that's another life. I'm here now.'

She looks up at me and smiles. She has the same eyes as Sophie.

35

Chapter Six

Wednesday, 2 July 1986

Debbie

We need to bin this digital alarm clock. Even when I close my eyes, I can still see the angry red numbers reminding me I'm not asleep. It's one fifteen in the morning. If I go by her previous feeds, Annie'll be waking again at three thirty. I could go and heat a bottle ready, in case she wakes early.

I keep checking she's still breathing. She's only a foot away, in her basket. What if I fall asleep too deeply, roll off the bed and crush her? No, no that couldn't happen – I've not fallen out of bed since I was a child. But you never know. I shuffle away from the edge a bit.

I close my eyes, but my mind is busy with too much crap. My body's exhausted – why won't my brain listen to it? It's no good. The memory of last Saturday keeps coming back to me. I wish I'd never gone with them to Lytham Club Day. There were too many people around – everyone stared at me. *You shouldn't be outside.* I bet that's what they were thinking.

I watched Bobby and Leo on the little rides, while Nathan, Monica and Peter went on the waltzers. It was too warm. The children's rollercoaster went round and round and round, hundreds of times. I had to sit on the grass.

Peter and the others came over, swaying.

'That was amazing,' said Monica. 'I haven't been on one of those since I was a teenager.'

'You have to go on something, Debs,' said Peter.

I ended up climbing onto the lorry that had been converted into a two-storey 'fun' house with the boys. Bobby took me by the hand and pulled me up the stairs.

'You'll love it, Mummy,' he said.

Halfway up the stairs, my legs started to shake. Why hadn't I realised how high it would be up there? The eyes on the faces painted on the walls watched me. I tried to cover them with my hands as I walked past, but there were too many. Their gaze followed me until we reached the outside part of the upper level.

I held the rail opposite.

Peter and Monica stood waving at us; I couldn't let go to wave back.

It was too high. I couldn't breathe. A cold sweat covered my body.

Oh God, I thought. I'm going to die.

I kneeled on the metal floor. The ringing in my ears got louder.

'Mummy? Mummy? Are you okay?'

Breathe, breathe.

I put my head close to my chest, closing my eyes.

I don't know how many minutes passed before Bobby's hand touched my shoulder.

'Is it too high for you, Mummy?' he said. 'Don't worry. I'll help you down. I used to be like this when I was four.'

He reached down for my hand; I looked up at him.

My breathing gradually slowed.

'I'm sorry, Bobby.' I looked around, relieved I could get the words out of my mouth. The sound in my ears faded. 'Come on, love. Let's find something fun for you to go on next.'

I don't know what happened to me that day.

Am I dying? I feel numb and my body doesn't feel like mine any more. That day, I could barely breathe – there must be something wrong with me. My mind might be shutting down first.

1.23 a.m.

Oh God. I might go insane with tiredness. In an article in one of Mum's magazines, it said if you can't get to sleep, get up and make a milky drink, but I can't find the energy.

After counting three hundred and fifty-six sheep, I turn onto my back and look up to the ceiling. This is torture. I bet Monica never had this.

I can't believe I was trying to catch Nathan's eye on Friday. What was I hoping to achieve? My face feels hot with the memory of it. He doesn't even know how I feel – *I* don't even know how I feel. Monica wouldn't have noticed anyway. She was too busy being amazed by how great Peter is.

'We should get a microwave too, Nath,' she'd said. 'We could have jacket potatoes every day, then.'

He'd rolled his eyes at her back, but frowned when he realised that I saw him.

Go away, Nathan, I'd thought to myself, fully aware that – as always – my feelings were as fickle as Preston sunshine. There'd been a smash of china in the kitchen, and Monica had jumped up immediately.

'Are you all right, Peter?'

It was my turn to roll my eyes. I glanced at Nathan, but he was looking at the impression Monica had left on the settee. I wondered, then – as I do now, in the darkness – if he'd had the same thought that I did. That perhaps Monica was in love with my husband.

'Get up! Get up!'

I sit up quickly.

'I'm coming, Uncle Charlie,' I say without thinking.

But there's no one here. The bedroom is semi-lit by daylight filtering through the curtains. Annie's basket is empty – so is Peter's side of the bed.

Why did I call out for Uncle Charlie? My mum's brother has been dead for years.

I battle with the cover, tangled in my legs, almost tripping out of bed.

Bobby's duvet is made up as though he's not slept in it.

'Peter!' I shout as I run down the stairs. I push open the living-room door, and there, sitting in the armchair holding Annie, is my mother.

Bobby's sitting on the floor, eating dry Rice Krispies, and watching *Picture Box* on the telly. That's not right – it can't be after nine thirty.

'Is this on tape?' I ask Mum.

She looks to the heavens.

'Course not, love. Since when have you seen me operating machinery? And shouldn't your first question be why Bobby's not at school?' She doesn't wait for me to reply. 'He said he wasn't feeling very well. The baby must've kept him up all night.'

'What? No, that can't be right. Where's Peter?' I'm still standing at the door in my nightie; she'll tell me to get dressed any minute now. 'Has he popped to the corner shop?'

'He's at work.'

'Really? Has a week passed already? That went quickly.'

Mum's eyes widen, and she shakes her head a little.

'I do wonder about you sometimes,' she says. 'You have not been asleep for a whole week. He popped into work for an emergency – said he wanted you to catch up on your rest.'

She sits Annie up, rubbing her little back.

She knows I didn't mean that, but she's doing me a favour by being here, so I don't argue with her. Part of me wishes I *had* slept for a week. 3.15–9.30 a.m. – that means I've had six hours and fifteen minutes' sleep. A record. I haven't slept that long since I was four months pregnant.

'I was just joking about sleeping that long,' I say.

I know she doesn't believe me. She probably thinks I'm not coping. It's family legend that the day after I was born, she was up and about doing housework, or sheafing wheat in the fields or whatever.

'Do you know what'll do you some good?'

I glance at the ceiling. 'What?'

'Getting a bit of exercise. I've been doing it every morning with what's-her-name on TV-am.'

'You mean Mad Lizzie? Have you heck been doing aerobics, Mum.'

'Well, I watch her do it while I have a cup of tea. Her energy's infectious.'

'She'd make me feel worse,' I whisper, turning to look at myself in the hall mirror. Before Mum has a chance to mention it, I say, 'I'll just have a quick wash and get dressed.'

As I put my foot on the first stair, she hollers, 'Best run a bath, Deborah. You look like you could do with one.'

I stare at my face in the bathroom mirror until it becomes a boring collection of features that could belong to a stranger. My body has been hijacked for so long, it's going to be months before I feel like it's mine again.

Mum thought I believed I'd slept for a whole week. I have my moments, but I'm not that ditzy. She probably remembers the time I swallowed an apple seed when I was pregnant with Bobby. I telephoned her in a panic that it might harm him – everything scared me then.

'What do you think will happen, Deborah? That an apple tree will grow inside you?'

I've since learned that apple seeds contain cyanide, so I'll be sure to tell her that if she brings it up again.

The steam from the bath starts to blur the glass.

'You know it's not meant to be like this.'

A man's voice. It sounded like Uncle Charlie again. But what if it's not him – what if it's God trying to speak to me?

I open the bathroom door.

'Mum? Is that you?'

Silence.

There's nobody upstairs. What's happening to me?

I dress quickly, putting on whatever's on the back of the chair in the bedroom.

Downstairs, Mum has dressed Bobby, and a sleeping Annie is in her pram under the window. Mum looks up at me as I loiter at the living-room door again, as though it's not my house.

'Are you all right?' says Mum. 'You look as though you've forgotten something.'

'I'm fine.'

I walk straight to the kitchen without saying another word. After the *sleeping for a week* conversation, I can't tell her what's actually worrying me; she wouldn't understand. The voice I heard sounded as though it was outside of my head, but there was no one there. I feel like someone's watching me all the time.

I don't know what's real and what's not any more.

Chapter Seven

Anna

It has been five days since I read the email and I still can't find the right words to write back. I searched the loft for the box of Debbie's things, but I couldn't find it anywhere. This morning, Jack suggested it might be in the storage unit with the rest of the belongings we haven't seen for years. I must not have looked at her things for over three years. Jack promised he would go over later to collect what he can find.

I pull up outside Dad and Monica's to collect Sophie. I haven't seen nor heard from Monica since last week. I should have brought her a box of chocolates or something to let her know I'm thinking of her – that I appreciate all that she's done for me.

Growing up, neither I nor Robert called her *Mum*. Robert had always known her as Monica, so I must have copied him. 'Why do you call your mum by her first name?' friends used to ask. 'She just likes it that way,' I'd say, too embarrassed to tell the truth.

Monica never treated us any differently to Leo. It must have annoyed him. I haven't heard from him in months – he's been living in America near his dad for almost ten years. It must be so hard for Monica, Leo being so far away.

Dad opens the door before I have the chance to ring the doorbell.

'Good day, love?' he asks, as though it is a normal, unremarkable day.

How can he act so nonchalant? My mother is alive! Perhaps he's worried about Monica. Leo's been gone for so long, and now my mother might be coming back to replace her. Like *she* did to Debbie.

I put my head around the living-room door. Sophie raises her hand in greeting, chewing something without taking her eyes off the television. There's a plate next to her with an unopened tangerine.

'Not bad, thanks,' I say. 'Is that chocolate she's eating?'

Dad's hovering in the hallway and doesn't answer my question.

'Do you want a cup of tea, or do you want to head straight off?'

'Are you trying to get rid of me?'

I follow him into the kitchen. He puts the kettle on and beckons me to stand closer to him. He waits until the water starts to hiss until he speaks.

'Monica's not feeling too well,' he says.

He points to the kettle, then up to the ceiling. What he means is that the walls are very thin in their three-bedroomed terraced house – you can hear next door sneezing, and I dread to think what else.

'Shall I take her up a drink?' I ask.

Making yourself heard whilst trying to be quiet is harder than it seems.

Dad shakes his head. 'Best leave her to it, love.'

'It's okay,' I say, pouring hot water into the teapot. 'I want to see Monica for myself. I'll take her up a digestive.'

Dad doesn't look happy, but what is he going to do? Wrestle me to the ground to stop me? I pour tea into a china cup, and milk into a little jug, and place them on a tray with a biscuit she probably won't eat. I carry them upstairs, everything rattling.

I balance the tray on the palm of one hand and knock on their bedroom door with the other. There's no reply. She used to do this a lot when she and Dad had arguments about the boys when they were teenagers. Robert and Leo didn't get on most of the time. They had to share a bedroom. Robert's side was reasonably tidy; Leo's not so much.

I knock again.

'Monica, it's me, Anna.'

Still no reply.

I open the door. My eyes go directly to their bed, but she's sitting in the chair that faces the window. I place the tray on the little table, and sit on the footstool next to her.

'Have you been crying?' I ask.

She blinks several times.

'Oh, hello, Anna. I'm sorry. I'm not with it today.'

'That's okay. Is it the news about Debbie?'

I can't call Debbie *my mother* in front of her. It feels disloyal to Monica; she has always been here for me.

'Yes, I suppose it is,' she says. 'It's all come as a bit of a shock.'

I pick up the cup of tea and offer it to her.

'I've put two sugars in it.'

She purses her lips in a smile. 'You're too good to me. I don't deserve it.'

'Of course you do. Who else would put up with Robert and me?'

There is an answer that hangs in the air that neither of us even jokes about: *Not my mother.*

'You know,' she says, 'I felt tremendous guilt getting together with your dad after your mother left. She was my best friend, you know. I met her in the third year of secondary school. I'd just moved up north, and spent the first couple of days sitting on my own at dinner time. Then Debbie came over to me – of course, she was Deborah, then. Her mum, you see, she always wanted her to be Deborah, never Debbie.'

I love hearing Monica talk about my mother like this. Grandad still calls her Deborah – when he talks about her, that is.

'Has Dad told Grandad about the email?'

Monica drops a splash of tea onto her skirt as she sips from her cup. She frowns, disorientated at being interrupted.

'I imagine so. You'll have to ask him.'

I take the tea cup away from her as she dabs at the blotch.

'Where was I? Oh yes, at school. She walked up to me, her dark, wavy hair flowing behind her – you've got her hair, you know, the exact same. She looked stunning. Who looks so beautiful while they're a schoolgirl? Back then it was different – kids weren't allowed to wear make-up to school, and I had terrible spots. Debbie thought she was hideous, but she was never hideous. She was a joy to be around . . . well, until the end . . . Anyway, when she met my eye that day, I was sitting on a bench near the Maths block. I had to turn around to check it was me she was talking to. "I hear you're from London," were her first words to me. "I'd love to go there," she said.'

'What did you two used to get up to?'

I have asked the question so many times, but Monica never complains. Sometimes, there will be something I've never heard before.

'We didn't get up to much really. In the first summer we spent together, we were fourteen. All we did was talk about boys, though the ones at our school could never compare to David Cassidy.' She smiles at me. 'He was famous in the seventies – Google him. We were so naive. We read about boys and sex from a book, for God's sake. *Forever* by Judy Blume – though we'd heard about most things by sixteen.' She returns her gaze to the window. 'We didn't spend much time at her house. I think she was ashamed, but she needn't have been – her parents were lovely.'

'Why would she feel ashamed?'

'Her parents sent her to a school in the next town – she mixed with other people than those on her estate.' She looks at me and places a hand on mine. 'I'm not saying that it's right or anything, for her to have felt like that. It's just how it was. Her parents were older than most when she was born. When she was growing up, they focused on what was best for her. I wish my parents had been like that, but Debbie felt embarrassed that they showed so much interest in her life. It made her lonely, I think. She didn't have many friends. She was like you, really.'

'A loner, you mean?'

'No, no. As if I'd say something like that to you.' She squeezes my hand, rubbing the top of it with her thumb. 'She chose her friends carefully . . . was wary of other people. Her parents sheltered her from the big bad world, protected her from the hardship they suffered.' Monica sighs. 'Time goes by too quickly. She was always there for me. Until the end. It was all my fault.'

My ears tingle with a new bit of the story – she has never mentioned any cross words between them.

'What do you mean it was your fault?'

'Has your dad never talked about the troubles we had?'

'He doesn't talk about her much at all, let alone any problems.'

'Thinking about it . . . I don't know if Peter would want me to say anything to you about it.' Monica's not looking at me any more. 'We haven't talked about it for such a long time, I don't know what he remembers. Memories can get distorted . . . hold you back, you know? Such a horrible time.'

Monica is staring out of the window again. It's like a mist

has covered her eyes, between the past and the present. I follow her gaze. Mr Flowers, from the house opposite, has dropped his keys; he's trying to pick them up using the end of his walking stick. I should go out and help him, but I want to hear what Monica has to say.

'I've said too much. Your father never wanted you to find out anything bad about Debbie. He blames himself, too, I imagine. There's a lot that's been airbrushed from Debbie's history.'

'What do you mean?'

She sits up and reaches for a tissue to wipe away the fresh tears.

Dad's heavy footsteps are on the stairs.

Monica leans over and puts a hand on my shoulder.

'Please don't tell your dad I told you anything, will you? He'd kill me if he found out I mentioned anything.'

'I'm sure he wouldn't mind. You've hardly said anything.'

She leans against the back of the chair.

'I loved her, you know. She was like a sister to me.'

Dad turns the handle of the bedroom door. I put a smile on my face, so that when he opens the door, he'll think everything is fine.

I put the key into our front door, and remember the letter hidden in Jack's wallet. I have spent the past week worrying about it, but barely thought of it today. Does that mean I don't care about him any more? I need to confront him, but that would mean admitting I was snooping again. I can't have him think I'm not coping. It can't be like last time. I nearly lost everything.

I let Sophie in through the door before me. She looks so small in her little grey school pinafore – her cute little legs. I can't lose my little girl; I must keep it together – pretend everything is okay. But I make a mental note to go through all of Jack's contacts on Facebook to see if there's anyone by that name – there can't be many. I have never met anyone called Francesca.

I reach into Sophie's school bag and take out her reading book. She skips through to the kitchen and sits at the table next to Jack. I place the book in front of Sophie and she begins reading quietly to herself.

'You're back early,' I say.

I glance around the kitchen. Jack's put all the dirty dishes into the dishwasher and the empty beer bottles into the recycling. The worktops have been wiped clean and the bin has been emptied.

There's a carrier bag of food on the counter. I peek inside: ingredients for a spaghetti bolognese and a bottle of red wine. I kiss the top of Jack's head and we almost clash as he jolts in surprise.

'Did you remember at last?' I say to him.

'Remember what?' He winks and walks out of the kitchen, coming back seconds later with a bouquet of flowers and a small gift bag.

'I'm so sorry, Anna,' he says. 'I've had the present in the boot of my car for days. I was mortified when I got to work this morning, saw it, and realised the date.' He hands me the bunch of roses. 'I got these as an extra – to say sorry.' He strokes my cheek. 'Are you going to open your present?'

'I might save it for later – when I can really appreciate it.'

He's smiling for the first time in weeks – I don't want to spoil it by mentioning anything about love letters from strange women. He's still looking at me, but his eyes glaze over.

'Are you all right?' I say.

He tilts his head to one side, blinking his thoughts away. 'I was about to ask you the same thing. After that email—'

48

'I'm fine.' I don't want to talk about it in front of Sophie. I nod in the direction of our daughter, her little head down in concentration.

'If you put Sophie to bed,' says Jack, 'I can nip out to the storage unit and get that box of things you were looking for the other day.'

'That would be great. Thank you.'

It seems I'm not the only one pretending we're all right. I know he's tried to make it better with the flowers, but I know there is something he's hiding from me.

It was four years ago when I first searched Jack's belongings. Sophie was asleep, and Jack had nipped to the bathroom. He'd just used his phone and the pin number wasn't needed so I picked it up. There were several texts from a woman.

Jack caught me looking, though I was hardly subtle. I was standing in the middle of the living room with his phone in my shaking hands.

'What are you doing, Anna?' he'd said.

'I was just borrowing your phone – mine's out of battery.'

I didn't look up. He walked towards me quickly, holding out his hand for me to give him the phone, but I held on to it.

'But we're at home,' he said. 'Use the landline.'

'Who's Samantha?'

'What? Give me the phone, Anna. You can't just go through people's things.'

He lifted his hand to grab it, but I put my hand behind my back.

'You're my husband, Jack. We shouldn't have secrets.'

He folded his arms slowly.

'There are boundaries, Anna. People have boundaries. Haven't you learned that from what happened with Gillian Crossley?'

'That's nothing like this. And you said we'd never mention it. It was two years ago.'

He tilted his head to the side.

'I know. But sometimes I get scared you'll do something like that again. She said you were stalking her. It's happened one too many times.'

'That's below the belt, Jack. You know I wasn't well. I had counselling. I know the signs, when to get help.'

He stared at me.

'You'd tell me if things were getting on top of you, wouldn't you? I love you. I'm not your enemy.'

I glanced at the photographs on the wall: of Jack and me, of Sophie.

'I know. I'm just tired.' I brought my hand round and handed him the phone. 'But who is Samantha? I'm sure any wife would want to know who the woman texting her husband is.'

He shook his head, grabbing the phone from my hands.

'A new solicitor at work. And if you'd read the texts properly you'd have seen that.'

My face burned.

Later, when he was asleep, I checked his firm's website and there she was: Samantha Webster, Solicitor – her arms folded in a serious pose for the camera.

I look at him now, listening to Sophie read, and you wouldn't think he was hiding something. If I were to admit I had searched his wallet, he would accuse me of *relapsing*. But what happened all those years ago has taught me one thing: two can play at that game.

Monica used to say that if a boy caused you so much heartache, then they weren't the right one for you. My first heartbreak was aged twelve. I lay on my bed, listening to LeAnn Rimes belting out 'How Do I Live' to drown out the sound of the boys arguing in the room next to my head. Monica knocked at the door.

'Are you okay, Anna? You've not come down for your tea.'

'Fine,' I shouted over the noise.

She walked in, closed the door, and opened the curtains and the window.

'A bit of fresh air is what's needed in here,' she said. She sat on the edge of my bed and swiped the hair from my face. 'What's wrong, love?'

'Nothing.'

'I've plated your dinner up. I'll leave it on the side. Just heat it up in the mike when you're ready to come down.'

She didn't move from the bed, was still stroking my hair.

'Thanks.'

'If you want to talk about it, I'm here.'

'Hmm.'

The song ended, but it started again because I'd put it on repeat.

'Is it your friends, Annie? Have they all ganged up on you again?'

I shook my head. That hadn't happened in months, but it wasn't them this time.

'A boy?'

I shrugged, my shoulders cushioned against the pillow.

'It's hard, isn't it?' she said.

'I suppose.'

I had to blink quickly so my tears didn't fall out of my eyes.

'Hannah said yes to a date with him. She knew I liked him.'

In the end, I couldn't stop the tears falling.

'Oh, love.'

I sobbed into the pillow. Monica lay down next to me, put her arms around me, and I cried into her jumper.

'Let it all out, sweetheart.'

We lay like that for ten minutes. The song played another two times, and I finally stopped crying.

'He wasn't the right one for you, that's all. The One will come along and he'll like you right back.' She stood up. 'Talk to me about it whenever you want. I've been there. School is tough, I know. It'll pass quickly enough.'

Now I blink away the tears that have formed in my eyes as I hear Jack's car pull up outside. I open the front door quietly and watch him open the boot and take out the box.

Is he being nice because he feels guilty, or because he genuinely wants to help me? Heartache sounds too indulgent when you've been with a person for years. I might not like Jack sometimes, but he's my family. I love him. Perhaps that's why I haven't confronted him: I don't want to hear the truth.

He's trying hard to be quiet, so he doesn't wake Sophie. I stand aside as he carries the box into the house as though it were a boulder. I shove my hands underneath and take it from him. It's not that heavy at all, but I pretend it is as I lower it to the ground.

'Careful – it's weighty,' he says.

'It's okay. I'm used to carrying boxes of books at the shop.'

It's fifty centimetres square and painted pale blue with hand-drawn flowers all over it. It has my writing in black marker: *Mother*. I don't remember writing that; it's been years since I've seen it. I want Jack to leave the room, so I can look at the contents alone.

'Well?' he says.

'Well?' I repeat, in the hope he'll take the hint, but he sits on the edge of the sofa.

I sit on the rug and lift the lid off. Straight away I see my scrapbook. It's decorated with pictures of beaches in Tenerife from holiday brochures, models from *Mizz* and *Woman's Own* who I thought might look like her, and The Beatles. Inside the box are the 45rpm singles Gran gave me: 'Norwegian Wood' and 'Heart of Glass'. Dad always switched the car radio off if one of those songs came on.

After Gran died, I began asking him more questions about Debbie. He gave me a telephone number, saying it was for Debbie's old mobile. At first, I rang it every day, but there was never a reply, obviously. I used to tell the answer machine my problems, what was happening at school, how much I missed her. It only dawned on me a few years later that it can't have been Debbie's – she wouldn't have had a mobile phone in 1986. It was probably one of Monica or Dad's old numbers; there must be at least a thousand missed calls on it. I don't want to imagine them listening to the messages I left.

'That's an unusual collection of pictures,' says Jack, making me jump.

I had forgotten he was here.

'I was a child when I decorated it.'

I shouldn't feel embarrassed in front of him, but I do.

'But why beaches?' he says.

'It's Tenerife. It was where she was last seen.'

'That's a bit macabre, isn't it? What if she was . . .'

He stops himself from saying what he usually says after he's been drinking.

'I just thought she must have really liked Tenerife,' I say, 'to have never come back.'

It's like my eleven-year-old self is saying the words.

Jack gets up and heads towards the door. Before he leaves, he turns around.

'Why didn't you just put a picture of Debbie on it – instead of models who look like her?'

He doesn't wait for me to answer. He looks away from me and tilts his head as though pondering. He hasn't seen the memories inside my shell box. He might have feigned interest when we first started going out, but he isn't bothered about the details of her as a person. He would rather pontificate at length about what happened to her – as though he were discussing a murder victim on the television.

I lay everything out on the floor as I take it out of the box. The records, the scrapbook, the old cigar box Debbie decorated with seashells – half of which are chipped. I know what's in it without opening it, but I flip the lid anyway. It's quite pathetic really, the number of things in there: my hospital wristband, a stick of Blackpool rock – now a mass of crumbled sugar held together by a cylinder of cellophane. There's also a pen with a moving ship and a silver pendant depicting the Virgin Mary with the words *Bless This Child*, threaded on a piece of pink string. Dad can't remember buying any of the items in the box, so I like to think Debbie chose them just for me.

I open my scrapbook.

> *She wore flip-flops in the summer and Doc Martens boots in the winter.*
> *She had a birthmark in the shape of Australia on the top of her leg.*
> *She 'couldn't take her drink' after having children.*

The front door shuts – I hadn't heard it open. Jack walks into the living room carrying a box the same size as my seashell one.

'I forgot this,' he says, placing it on the floor beside me.

It's decorated with what looks like real Liquorice Allsorts. I pick it up; it smells sugary, medicinal.

'They're real sweets,' I say. 'Where did this come from?'

He shrugs, and walks towards the door.

'It was packed next to your box. I'm going upstairs to make an important phone call. Don't just walk in, if that's okay? It'll seem unprofessional.'

I wave my hand in reply. His phone call might be far from professional, but I can't take my eyes off the box covered in sweets. It must be Robert's. It's an old King Edward cigar box like mine. I knew he must have had one, but I've never seen it before. I assumed he'd thrown it away. What was it doing in our storage?

I don't open it straight away. Like with presents, an unopened object is far more interesting than an unwrapped one. I turn it in my hands and hold it. She must have spent ages gluing them on like this.

I place it on the floor and slowly lift the lid.

There are more items in this one than in mine. Robert probably added some pieces himself. There's his conker that Grandad told him to bake in the oven for seven hours. After that, he painted it with five coats of Ronseal in mahogany. I would have been three or four years old. I bring it up to my nose – I remember the scent as he painted it, but it doesn't smell of anything now. The treatment was effective; it still looks as smooth and shiny as it did then.

I take out his other things: hospital wristband; a Pez dispenser, with a few rectangular sweets still inside; his first report from primary school; and birthday cards signed from *Mummy and Daddy*. I don't have any birthday cards with my mother's name inside. I run my fingers along the writing in one of them.

Underneath all of these is an old photo processing envelope. It lists different sizes and finishes of photographs – our old home address is scrawled on the form in childish handwriting. It's dated 20 February 1987 – nearly seven months after my mother disappeared. There is a cylinder inside it. I stick my hand in and pull out a black plastic container. I peel the cap off it, praying there's something inside.

There is.

A whole roll of film that might contain pictures of my mother that I've never seen before.

Chapter Eight

Friday, 4 July 1986

Debbie

The sun on my face is delicious. I feel like I haven't been outside for weeks, when it's only been days. Being inside feels so oppressive, like there are a hundred faces watching every move I make.

Outside, I feel free, away from prying eyes. Annie's sleeping in her pram, and even though I've only had two hours' sleep I feel calm for the first time in days.

Peter's finally back at work (I didn't tell him it was silly starting back on a Friday) and Bobby's at school until half three so I've over two hours of freedom. I park the pram outside the newsagents and pull the hood up.

The bell dings as I push the door.

'Is it okay if I leave it open? The baby's asleep outside.'

'Right you are, love,' says Mrs Abernathy.

There's that new song on the radio playing: 'The Lady in Red'. It's not like Mrs Abernathy to have the radio on. For a love song, it sounds pretty dreary – it's no 'Addicted to Love', that's for sure. I can't remember it on *Top of the Pops* last Thursday, but then I can't remember what I had for breakfast this morning. I *do* remember the 'Spirit in the Sky' video though, because it cheered me up. Mum wouldn't approve. She keeps harping on about Bobby being baptised so he can go to a better secondary school. I told her that's hardly the Christian way of thinking about things, but she just spouted her usual words of eternal damnation. I'll probably be waiting for my children in the burning fires of hell, if my mother's prediction comes true. It'll be more fun there anyway. Though the temperature might get a bit much; it's far too hot today.

Under the window is a giant freezer. I used to love picking an ice cream out of those as a kid – when Mum and Dad could afford one, that is.

I choose a lemonade ice lolly and, as I close the lid, I see him outside.

He's getting out of his car across the road. I quickly pay for the ice and dash out of the shop. He's walking in the opposite direction; he hasn't seen me. I've never been an attractive runner, so I try to walk a little faster. He's still a fair distance away from me. My flip-flops are smacking my heels – I'm surprised he can't hear me. I look around; there aren't many people.

'Nathan!'

He stops and turns around. I stop trotting just in time, and the breeze blows my long dress so it clings to my legs. He's still looking at it when I reach him.

'Hi, Debs.' He lifts his sunglasses and puts them on the top of his head. 'Pete let you out of the house, did he?'

I just nod. There are tiny freckles on his nose.

'Are you all right?' he says. 'Fancy a quick coffee?'

'Okay.' It seems the ability to think and speak has abandoned me.

He takes me by the hand and doesn't let go as we cross the road. I should be worried that someone we know might see us, but I'm not. He only lets go of my hand when he pushes the door of the café.

There are at least six tables free, but he chooses one at the back next to the door to the toilets. He pulls a chair out for me, and I sit. I feel like my head's out of my body – this whole situation feels so weird. We've not been alone since we were an item ten years ago.

That summer was so intense. We were sixteen, and secondary school had finished. We had no distractions from each other. Both of his parents went out to work, and we'd spend lazy days lying on his bed, listening to records and smoking cigarettes.

'Promise you'll never leave me for someone else,' he said to me one hot afternoon.

We'd closed the curtains for shade and they blew gently in the breeze.

'I'm not going anywhere,' I said, staring at the ceiling.

He rested his hand on my tummy and I placed my hand on his.

'Good,' he said. 'I don't know what I'd do if you did.'

He's still as good-looking now – better even. He's holding the menu, but staring into my eyes. I know, without glancing in the mirror, that my chest and neck will be red and blotchy.

'I'm sorry I was a bit quiet at yours the other day,' he says.

'I didn't notice.'

He laughs. 'You didn't notice? You were giving me evils.' He leans forward and puts his hand on mine. 'You won't tell Monica you've seen me today, will you? It's just—'

The waitress clears her throat – she's standing at the side of the table. How long has she been there? I swipe my hand from under Nathan's. I don't recognise her, but then, I'm not the best with faces these days. She's holding a notepad, a pen poised in her other hand.

'What can I get you?' she says.

I look down at my skirt. The top of my leg feels cold and wet. I grab a serviette, but it's no good. Something must've fallen from the table. I reach into my pocket and there's a wrapper. I take it out.

'Oh God.'

The ice lolly. From the paper shop.

I run out of the café without saying goodbye, and sprint down the street.

How could I have forgotten my little Annie? What if Mrs Abernathy tells the police and they're waiting for me. They might send me to prison.

I'm only seconds away. I can hear Nathan shouting my name, but I don't turn around.

What if Annie's not where I left her?

It'll be my punishment. What would I do without her?

As I cross the side street, I see the hood of her pram outside the shop.

Please be in there, please be in there.

I reach it, and push the hood of the pram down.

'Oh, thank God.'

I bend over to catch my breath.

Annie's still fast asleep. My beautiful, sleeping baby is where I left her.

Mrs Abernathy comes to the doorway. 'Did you get what you went for?'

I try to work out if there's a hidden meaning in what she's asking, but when I look at her face, I realise there's no agenda behind her words. She's not as dishonest as I am.

I can never see Nathan again.

'Yes,' I say to her. 'Thanks for keeping an eye on her.'

'Anytime, dear.' She turns and walks back into the shop.

I'm nearly at my house when the tears start streaming down my face. How could I have been so stupid? I reach under the pram for a tissue.

I see his shoes, his legs, walking towards me.

'Are you okay, Debbie?' Nathan can barely speak, he's breathing so hard. 'Did I say something to upset you? I didn't realise you had Annie with you.'

I'm still crouching near the floor, dabbing my face. I must look a right mess.

I stand to face him.

'I forgot about her . . . left her outside the shop. Please don't tell Peter.'

He frowns. Is he angry with me as well?

'What do you take me for, Debs? Course I won't tell him. What would I say? *Sorry, Pete, but while I took your wife for a sneaky coffee, she left the baby outside a shop?*'

I bury my face in the tissue. He strokes the top of my arm; I step away from him.

'I can't see you again,' I say, sniffing away the last of my tears.

'Why are you being so serious? We have to see each other. I'm married to your best friend.'

'What time is it?'

He looks at his watch. 'Ten to three.'

I turn around and walk away. I've forty minutes to get to Bobby's school. I can't forget another child. I dab my face to wipe away the remaining tears. I can't be seen crying at the school gates.

The phone's ringing as I open the front door. I back into the hallway, pulling the pram over the step and into the house.

If it's still ringing when I'm properly inside, then I'll answer it. I'm not in the mood to speak to anyone on the phone. Sometimes it can ring and ring and ring until the sound buries itself into the middle of my brain and I want to rip the cord from the socket.

I shut the front door and wheel Annie into the living room.

The phone's still ringing.

It might be Peter. I haven't spoken to him since this morning. The thought of him covers me in a warm hug. But I don't deserve that – not after the way I've behaved.

'Hello?'

'Debbie?'

Oh. It's Monica.

'Yes,' I say. 'It's me.' Who else would it be?

'You sound funny,' she says.

'No, I don't.'

'Hmm.' She says it in that disapproving way of hers. 'I've just seen you running up and down the high street in your bare feet – are you wearing a nightie?'

'What?'

My blood feels as though it's been replaced with antifreeze.

'Up and down the street. Are you okay? Do you need me to pop round? Is Annie all right – only I didn't see her with you.'

I don't understand what she's talking about.

'When?'

'Just now. I was driving back from work.'

'Oh,' I say. 'Did you see Nathan too? I saw him near the shops.'

'Debbie, are you sure you're okay? I can be there in five, no problem. I can watch Annie while you have a sleep.'

'I don't need a sleep. I'm getting Bobby at half three.'

'I know, but even half an hour might help.'

'Help? Are you sure you didn't see Nathan? He'll tell you I wasn't running around in my nightdress without my shoes on.'

I almost want to laugh at the image.

'Debbie, Nathan's at work. He's just telephoned me from his office.'

'Oh,' I say.

'I can come after school. Would that be better?'

'No,' I say, but I can't think straight. How could Nathan have phoned her from the street? I can't remember where the nearest phone box is . . . where is it? 'It's okay – Peter's coming home early today.'

He isn't, but it gets her off the phone.

Why the hell would she think I was running around without shoes? And in a nightie?

I feel the soft fabric of the carpet, underneath my toes.

I look down.

My flip-flops aren't on my feet any more.

Chapter Nine

Anna

The rain is battering against the bookshop window; it's going to be quiet today. Even though it's not Sunday, I'm hoping Grandad will come in today. I left him a message to say that Sheila's not coming in, so he can have free rein of the till, but I haven't heard back from him. Dad doesn't seem worried – perhaps he's been to see him. Maybe Grandad's angry with me. If I don't see him today, I'm going to bang on his door and sit on the doorstep until he opens it . . . or until I need to collect Sophie from after-school club.

Ellen's in the back room, pricing books that she thinks might be valuable. She said she has never used the Internet before, but I find that hard to believe. Prisons must have computers these days.

'Annie?' she says. 'Can you just help me again with this – the page is blank. I'm not sure it's connecting.'

I have given up trying to tell her that I don't like being called Annie, but it doesn't seem to register. I sit next to her, checking the side of the laptop. I click to slide a switch to the left.

'You must have put it into *airplane* mode by mistake,' I say.

'But why would I do that if I'm not on an aeroplane?'

I look at her as she stares at the screen, frowning. Surely she must know how laptops work. I click on the refresh button and the Amazon page loads. As I'm getting up, I notice there is another tab in the background. It's a site I'm familiar with: *Missing People*.

Ellen has been on the computer for nearly an hour. I keep trying to catch her looking at the missing persons' website again, but she's too quick, and both times I've gone into the storeroom she's minimised what she was looking at. I should warn her about using the Internet for personal use, but I haven't introduced a policy for that yet; we've only had the laptop in the bookshop for a fortnight. And once she's gone, I'll probably use it myself.

I'm still looking towards the back room when I smell a waft of Obsession.

'Anna?'

It's Isobel. Luckily, I have the accounts on the counter so at least I look busy. She glances at them and wrinkles her nose.

'I do hope you don't have those in view when we have clientele,' she says. 'It's highly confidential.'

I can't win.

'I was just having a quick check while the shop was empty.'

I slam the book shut and shove it under the counter.

'I've popped in to see how your new volunteer is getting on. Is she in?'

Isobel breezes past – the smell of her hairspray never fails to nauseate me.

I try to listen in, but they are talking too quietly. It's not like Isobel at all. Perhaps she knows Ellen more than she's letting on.

After nearly half an hour, all I have managed to overhear are the words 'vicar' and 'they might not want to know.' Now they're saying their goodbyes, I rush to the window so they don't think I've been listening. I move the elephant bookend a fraction, concentrating on it as though it were the most interesting thing in the world.

'See you soon, Anna,' says Isobel. She hesitates at the door, glancing at the window display. 'I must think of some other paperwork for you to do. We can't have you twiddling your thumbs all day.'

She hums to herself, putting sunglasses over her eyes before leaving the shop. That woman notices more than I thought. I wish I could tell her what I'm going through – that I can't concentrate on anything because the mother I can't remember has come back into our lives and, at the same time, my marriage might be falling apart. But I can't. She'll tell the whole of Lancashire.

'Annie.'

I turn quickly.

'Sorry,' says Ellen. She's already in her jacket. 'Isobel said it was okay if I left a bit early. I hope you don't mind, but I've got an interview for a new flat.'

'Oh, okay. Yes, I suppose that's all right.'

'Sorry. I hope you don't think I've gone above you . . . it was just she was asking about me finding a place to live and—'

'Don't worry about it. I know what she's like.'

'She told me about your mum.'

'Excuse me?'

'I'm sorry,' she says. She keeps saying sorry. 'I shouldn't have mentioned it.'

'I'm just surprised. I'm sure everyone knows about it anyway . . . it's not a big secret.'

'Do you still think about her?'

'What? I . . . Of course. Why?'

She shrugs. 'I'm getting too personal.' She looks at her watch. 'I've corrected my time now. I'd better go. See you next week.'

I watch her walk away until she disappears from view. I hurry into the back room and click on the Internet icon, then the 'History' button. Who was she looking for on that website?

I will never know: she's deleted today's history.

I've been standing outside Grandad's for five minutes. People walking past are looking at me. I have thirty minutes until I need to collect Sophie from school. The curtains are closed, but when I press my ear against the window, I can hear the television on low. Today's silver-top milk is still on the doorstep.

'I know you're in there, Grandad. Are you okay? Are you hurt?'

There's a shadow moving behind the curtains.

'Grandad! If you don't answer the door in a minute, I'll call the police – they'll break the door down, you know. Then everyone will come and have a nosy – even Yvonne from across the road. She's in, I can see her net curtains flapping. I've got my mobile right here, I *will* ring them.'

The left curtain flashes open.

Grandad's standing at the window. He hasn't shaved for days; he's still in his tartan dressing gown.

'Are you going to let me in?'

His shoulders rise and fall as he sighs. He rolls his eyes.

Moments later, he opens the door, but stands behind it so no one can see him.

'Well, come in then,' he says. 'Don't make a show of me.'

I do as he says and follow him down the hallway.

'I'll make you a cup of tea,' he says. 'Go through to the living room.'

'I didn't come here for a drink, Grandad. I came to see if you were all right.'

I sit on the sofa anyway. He always makes a drink for visitors, so at least I know he still has his senses. Dad said that when Gran, Debbie's mother, was alive, Grandad was never allowed to touch the kettle. Dad was probably exaggerating.

Diagnosis Murder is on the television, but it's barely audible. I look to the mantelpiece. There have always been three pictures of Debbie on there: one on her Christening day; a faded school photo, her hair flicked at the sides like a Charlie's Angel; and a third with Gran and Grandad – Debbie the only child.

Grandad comes into the living room carrying a tray of tea and biscuits. He's changed from his dressing gown into his usual beige cords and burgundy jumper over a checked shirt. He must have a wardrobe full of the same clothes. He places the tray on the coffee table. I wait until he's finished pouring the tea until I speak.

'I take it Dad's told you about the email.'

'He has.'

'At least we know she's alive, that's something isn't it?'

'Do we? How can we know if it's really her? Anyone could've written that. What we should be asking is *why*? If it is her, then why now?' He plucks a white cotton handkerchief from up his sleeve and presses it against his nose. 'I wish to God it were her. I'd give anything to see her face again. I just can't see her not picking up the phone, to tell us she was all right. She was our only child. A miracle, we called her at the time. She came to us later in life – we thought we'd never . . . I didn't believe in all that religious stuff before Marion died. But you have to believe they go somewhere, don't you?' He looks up to the ceiling. 'I hope to God we find out the truth about my girl.'

'I'm sorry, Grandad. This must be so hard for you. But I have to believe that she's out there. Perhaps she got into trouble? She might have been in prison. Or maybe she had an accident and has only just recovered her memory.'

He raises his eyebrows. 'You've been watching too many films, Anna.' He picks up his mug of tea and takes a sip. 'It can't be your mum. She'd have written to me, too.'

I stare at my cup on the tray.

'But no one could've known about the shells. It could only have come from her.'

'Hmm,' he says. 'Don't go getting your hopes up, love. At least one good thing may come from this: we might find out what happened to her.'

'I'm going to try and find her – or trace who wrote the email,' I say. 'If the police think it's a crank, then I'm going to get to the bottom of it.' I pull out the roll of film from my handbag. 'I found this in Robert's keepsake box. It might have some clues.'

Grandad shakes his head. 'This is only going to lead to heartache, Anna. The police will say it's some lunatic, obsessed with her or something – they won't even be interested, they weren't last time. It's been too long.'

'Last time? What happened last time?'

He flaps his hand.

'A letter, in strange writing. I took it to the police and they said it might be her, or it might not. They logged it and that was that. Said she was an adult – that she left of her own accord.'

My shoulders slump. Robert mentioned another letter the other day, and now Grandad. But I can't ask him more about it now – he looks exhausted. His eyes are bloodshot, even though he's tried to hide it with reading glasses. I shouldn't be talking to him like this. His only child. The bed she slept in upstairs still has the same duvet cover; her record player is still by the window.

'I'm sorry, Grandad.'

He doesn't look at me when he says, 'It's been hard for us all.'

The carriage clock chimes five.

'I have to go,' I say. 'The after-school club closes in half an hour.'

'They never had such things in my day.'

I smile a little as a tiny glimpse of the Grandad I know shows through. I lean over and kiss him on the cheek.

'I'll see myself out.'

I'm turning the roll of film in my hands, waiting in the queue. Who knew Max Spielmann would be so busy?

'What are we buying here?' says Sophie. 'I'm hungry.'

She says it like she's auditioning for *Oliver Twist*.

'Pictures.' I hold up the film. 'This shop can change this little thing into photographs.'

Her mouth drops open and her eyes widen. She steps closer to me.

'Is this a magic shop?'

'Yes.'

The man in front leaves, but the woman behind the counter is typing something into the computer. She has one long coarse hair growing from her chin and she's stroking it as though it were a beard.

'Is that woman a wizard?' says Sophie.

She hasn't got the hang of whispering yet. My cheeks are burning.

The woman looks up quickly; I've half a mind to run out of the shop.

'Not quite, young lady,' she says, looking up. 'I'm a witch. And you have to be good for your mum or you'll end up in my rabbit stew.' She smiles. 'How can I help you?'

I put the film on the counter.

'Can you develop this? I think it's nearly thirty years old.'

'That shouldn't be a problem. As long as it's been kept in its container.' She opens the lid and slides out the film. 'It looks intact. I'll have to send it off though – we don't do 34 mm

69

any more in store. No demand, you see. I'll post it off tonight and it should be back in two or three days.'

I fill out my details and she winks at Sophie as we leave. Sophie doesn't smile back.

Out on the street, I feel like celebrating. I thought they'd say it couldn't be done – that they didn't do things like that these days.

But the pictures might not even come out.

I take Sophie's hand and pull her away from the kerb.

'Is there a word for that?' she says.

'Word for what?'

'You always walk on the pavement near the cars.'

'I don't know. I've never thought about it.'

'What would happen if a car crashed into us and got you first? Who'd look after me?'

'Don't think like that.'

'But who would? Daddy's always working.'

'He's not *always* working. I work too. I'll think of the word.'

'What word?'

'For protecting you on the pavement. I'll Google it. And I'm glad you're thinking so practically.'

She starts skipping. My hands go up and down with hers. I wish I were in her head.

The back of my neck prickles; I feel as though someone's watching me. I turn around quickly.

There's no one there.

I shouldn't get my hopes up about the photographs. Grandad always says I should manage my expectations. But if I had a choice between forgetting everything over the past few days, or being hurt from finding the truth, then I'd choose the truth.

Chapter Ten

I've been watching her for weeks and she hasn't noticed. She's too busy living in that head of hers. I watch in the rearview mirror as she gazes out of the window. She's looking around.

I glance over at the pile of pink notepaper on the passenger seat. It's surprising how much meaning can be conveyed in so few words. Will it mean anything to her, to them?

I slide down in the seat of the car as someone passes. I don't recognise him; he mustn't be a neighbour. Streets have gone all Neighbourhood Watch nowadays.

The radio plays 'Norwegian Wood' by The Beatles. My fingers go to the radio – a reflex – and switch it off. Shutting the memories down. We used to listen to that together, didn't we? I can't remember if it was your favourite song, or mine.

Chapter Eleven

Friday, 4 July 1986

Debbie

The oil from Bobby's fish fingers spits from the frying pan; a drop touches my lips. I put my finger on my mouth to rub the sting away.

I can't have imagined Nathan this afternoon. We had a conversation.

'We *have* to see each other,' he said. There must be meaning in that. But why would Monica say Nathan was at work? And if she was so worried about me looking hysterical in the street, why didn't she pull over?

The front door slams shut. It must be ten past five. Bobby's banging his legs against the chair under the dining table. Thump-thump, thump-thump.

'Stop it!'

He doesn't look up, but stops his legs.

It'll take Peter another five seconds to hang up his jacket. Five, four, three, two—

I hear him throw his newspaper onto the settee. He usually says hello.

'Everything okay?' I say, peering through the kitchen doorway into the living room.

'Hmm.' He pulls off his tie. 'I've brought in your flip-flops. They were on the doorstep.'

'What? Again?'

I can feel my heart banging in my chest. Has Monica told him about this afternoon? Has Nathan? I'm sure I had them on after I picked Bobby up from school.

'Oh,' I say. 'They probably slipped off again when I was getting the pram in.'

'It didn't look like it. They were placed together, just outside the front door – like someone had put them there like that.'

'How odd. Did Monica ring you?'

He looks at me, wrinkling his nose. 'Are you being serious?'

Bobby must've seen my flip-flops slip off, picked them up. Or I might've put them there before I closed the front door. That could've happened. Monica must've mistaken my flip-flops for bare feet earlier – they must keep coming off without me noticing. Easily done. I'll wear sandals next time I go out.

I don't tell Peter I haven't prepared our tea. Instead I say, 'I thought I'd go to the chippy for us tonight. A treat for you – after working so hard.'

I sound like my fifty-two-year-old mother.

I should've become a Career Woman. I heard that Michelle Watkinson from college flew to the Bahamas last year, first class. Though she probably has to put up with letches feeling up her arse as she pushes the trolley up and down the aisle. She hasn't spoken to me since I had children. And I haven't put make-up on since Annie was born, so I wouldn't be any good at her job.

I'm stuck, in limbo.

I don't know why I'm trying to appease Peter anyway. It wouldn't hurt him to offer to cook tea once in a blue moon. But I'd never say that. What if he knows something? What if he can read my thoughts?

73

'Hmm,' he says, again.

I interpret that as: *You've done nothing all day. The least you could've done is stick a Fray Bentos in the oven and some chips in the fryer.*

'I'll make you a cup of tea while you think about it,' I say.

He goes straight to the baby; she's lying on the blanket on the living-room floor.

'Hello, my little angel,' he says.

I fill the kettle, roll my eyes at the wall, and immediately feel guilty for it. I put a bowl of beans in the microwave and turn the dial. It's handier than I thought it'd be. It pings, and I burn my fingers taking the bowl out. Peter's already sitting in his chair at the table.

'Had a nice day, have you?' His tone is neutral.

'Well, you know. Been stuck in the house for most of it.'

'You should get yourself out and about.' He leans back in the chair. 'If I had the day to myself, I'd be out there. Spot of fishing, trip to the park.'

Day to myself? I want to shout. If I had the day to myself, I wouldn't choose to be inside all day. But I don't want to appear ungrateful.

'But you don't even fish.'

'I'd take it up, probably.'

'You can't take a baby fishing.'

The kettle clicks off and the beeper sounds in his pocket.

'For God's sake,' he says, the chair nearly toppling behind him as he gets up to use the phone in the hall.

I pour hot water into the mug with *Mr Tea* on it.

When did we become people like this? We used to laugh about friends who turned into their parents. We said we'd never be like that when we had kids. We said we'd go out all the time, cook nouvelle cuisine, and listen to records. Trisha over the road is always zipping about here and there. They've got a car seat for their precious Tristan and they've been to Marbella twice since she had him. *And* she has highlights. They've got the money, I suppose. She's got a white Ford Escort cabriolet that she loves showing off. It's a C reg; Peter says that's only last year's. She's went back to work at the hairdressers' when her little one was seven months. I heard her shouting about it outside to her friend. It's exhausting just thinking about work.

I dump three sugars into Peter's mug.

His face is red when he comes back into the kitchen. He's breathing hard through his nose.

'What's happened?' I say.

'I've got to go back in. The alarm's going off in the shop and there's nobody else answering their bloody phone.'

'Have a sip of tea before you go.'

I grab his cup from the counter and hold it out to him.

He frowns. 'I haven't got time for that.' He flicks his wrist.

The cup flies out of my hand and smashes onto the floor. Tea splats like paint from a tin. For a moment, we lock eyes.

He shakes his head, turns around and walks out, slamming the front door behind him.

I've managed to get both the kids asleep at the same time. It might only last a few minutes. Peter still isn't home. I hope he doesn't come back while I'm watching *EastEnders*. Since I became pregnant with Annie, I've become obsessed with soap operas – especially this new one. They empty my brain just enough.

A few minutes after the opening titles, the key goes into the front door. I press pause. I don't want him to think I've just been lounging around. He comes straight into the living room – without hanging up his jacket – just as I'm getting up. He glances at the telly.

'I didn't know this was on on a Friday.'

'I taped it.'

He takes off his jacket and flings it onto the opposite couch.

'Everything okay?' I say.

I cleaned up your mess and swept your favourite mug into the bin.

He slumps onto the settee. I look at him, and I don't think I know him at all. He can't have been at Woolworths for nearly three hours – it doesn't take that long to turn an alarm off. His eyes aren't meeting mine. He's not usually this secretive – perhaps he's planning something. I glance around the room. He might've been watching me while he was out. I've seen those hidden cameras on *Game for a Laugh.*

'I'm tired,' he says. 'All these broken nights.'

'Oh,' I say, narrowing my eyes. 'I'm sorry. I didn't realise you woke up too. You always seem so fast asleep.'

He waves his hand. 'Never mind.' He sits up. 'I'm going to book a holiday – or rather, I was hoping you could do it. It'll get you out of the house for a bit. I can get some brochures this weekend. We can get one of those last-minute deal things. You could let your hair down.'

I want to tell him it's a ridiculous idea, but all I say is, 'We can't go with a newborn. It's a stupid idea.'

'No, it isn't,' he says. 'These first few weeks are the easiest – she won't take much looking after.'

'Easiest for who?' I whisper.

'They always sleep at this age,' he says. 'I was thinking. We could ask Nathan and Monica to come. Leo could keep Bobby entertained. It'll be fun.'

'I don't know if a holiday's such a good idea. Anyway, wouldn't it be better just the four of us? Me, you and the kids. Annie's so young, she might keep everyone awake.'

'We don't have to share accommodation . . . though that would make sense financially. She'll be sleeping soon, if Bobby's anything to go by.'

I feel the urge to scream and laugh hysterically in his face.

'And,' he continues, 'I was thinking of going abroad. We've not been anywhere hot together before, have we? And it'll be something to look forward to. I've seen loads of last-minute deals on Teletext.'

'Hmm. I'll speak to Monica about it tomorrow.'

The thought of going on an aeroplane makes my stomach churn. I've always hated heights.

'Ha!' he says, leaning forward. 'I know what you're like: if you're not keen on something, you go quiet, hope it gets forgotten.'

I open my mouth to speak. He gets up quickly.

'I'll give Nathan a ring now.'

'But it's twenty to nine – you might wake Leo.'

My mother would never telephone anyone after eight o'clock at night – nor would she answer it. 'If it's an emergency,' she says, 'then they know where we live.'

'It's fine,' he says, getting up and turning on the hall light.

'Don't talk too loud,' I say, 'or you'll disturb the kids.'

My heart thumps as I hear him speak. I want to listen in and hear what Nathan says in reply . . . or grab the receiver out of Peter's hands and talk to him myself.

Why is he being so stubborn about a holiday? It's not like him to be this impulsive, or sociable. I turn my ears off, and only switch them on when he's preparing to say goodbye.

'I'll get Debs to give you a bell when it's arranged.'

Me? Why is he suggesting I ring Nathan?

'Okay then,' he says down the line. 'Will do. Bye, Monica.'

I stand up quickly.

'You were talking to Monica?'

He shrugs as he walks into the living room.

'Yeah. Nathan was out.'

'Where?' It comes out of my mouth before I think.

Peter wrinkles his nose. 'I don't know. I didn't think to ask.'

He's the least curious person I know. 'Why didn't you pass the phone to me?'

'Because it was my idea . . . and Monica *is* my friend too.'

Don't I know it. He looks so pleased with himself.

'I'm making a brew,' he says, walking into the kitchen. 'Do you want one?'

'No. It'll only keep me awake. Think I'll head upstairs, early night.'

'Night then,' he shouts, above the sound of the kettle.

I switch off the telly, which was frozen on Lofty behind the bar at the Queen Vic. Poor Lofty, always taken advantage of . . . being messed around by Michelle. I used to think that about Peter, but now I'm not so sure. Maybe he's not so predictable after all.

My hand's reaching for the switch in the hall, when I notice a pink envelope on the doormat. It's no one's birthday, I think, as I bend down to pick it up. Didn't Peter notice it when he came in?

There's no name on the front. The flap isn't stuck down; it's tucked inside. I open it and take out the piece of paper. There are only six words. I hold on to the wall to steady myself.

I know your dirty little secret.

Chapter Twelve

Anna

I wait until Sophie has gone to bed before I mention Debbie. I didn't want to confuse her by talking about another grandmother – who she thinks has passed away. How am I going to explain to her that Debbie *is* alive after all?

'Don't get your hopes up,' says Jack – words I have heard many times – while he pours himself a glass of white wine.

'I'm not,' I say. 'But the woman behind the counter said photos usually come out well, even after all that time.'

I grab my laptop and take it into the living room. I still don't know what to say in my reply to Debbie. It is too important to just fire off a few words when I have a whole lifetime to write about. She won't be expecting a message from me, but I doubt Monica or Dad have replied yet. They would have told me if they had, though I'm not sure of anything these days.

'Just ask to meet,' says Jack, reading my mind. 'You don't have to write an essay. If she is who she says she is, then you'll find out soon enough.'

Perhaps it is as simple as that. There is a tiny part of me – self-preservation, again – that tells me not to give too much away in an email. She must earn the right to hear my news. The least she could do is meet me.

I click on the email forwarded by Dad. I already know her words off by heart, but I still read it. '*The memories of shells and sweet things . . .*' No one else could know about that.

I type out the reply before I can think about it, and press send.

I look up and flinch. Jack is standing just centimetres away from me.

He laughs.

'You were off in dreamland then.' He hands me a piece of paper. 'These are a few of the private investigators we use at work. The other partners hire them to find people for court summonses. One of them might be able to help if you don't get a reply. Tell them to charge it to my account.'

'What makes you think she won't reply?' I say. He shrugs. I look at the list. 'So, are these PIs like Magnum?'

'Er, no. Unfortunately not. They're more likely to drive a Volvo estate than a Ferrari.' He laughs at his own joke.

I settle back into the sofa. Some names to research; it makes me feel useful. I've never spoken to a private investigator before; they must lead such exciting lives.

'They'll probably jump at the chance of this job,' says Jack. 'They're usually sitting in a car for eight hours at a time, pissing into a coke bottle.'

'Oh.'

'I'm just nipping down to the shop for more wine. Tough case at the moment.'

'But it's Friday night.'

'If I can get this done, I can relax for the rest of the weekend.'

'You can't drive – you've already had a glass.'

He tuts. 'I'm walking to the offy on the corner.'

It's what I hoped he'd say.

As soon as I hear the front door shut, I race up the two flights of stairs to Jack's office in the loft. *Tough case*, my arse. He's a conveyancing solicitor, not a human rights lawyer.

There's no door to open – the whole of the loft is his work space. Three walls are hidden by bookcases filled with leather-bound books I'm certain he's never read, and sports trophies from his university days. There's a sofa bed to the left and a large mahogany desk under the roof window. The blue screen of his laptop is reflected in the skylight. If I'm quick enough, the screensaver won't have kicked in yet. He's protective over his passwords.

I slide onto his chair. His Facebook account is open. I click on the messages tab, but there are none. Not even the link to our old house for sale that I sent him last week. I check the archive folder. Still nothing. I must have at least fifty messages archived in mine. He must have deleted every one. Who does that? Especially someone who professes to hardly ever use Facebook.

Francesca was the name of the woman who signed her name at the bottom of the letter. I go to his friends list, my hands shaking. Jack might only be minutes from walking through the door.

He only has fifty-nine friends. She's not hard to find. I could have looked on his friends list from my account. Francesca King. Even her name sounds glamorous. She has long chestnut-coloured hair and her photo looks professionally taken. I click on her profile, and jot down everything I can see in her *About* section. *Partner at Gerald & Co, Winckley Square, Preston.* She works across town from Jack. I want to look through her posts and photos, but I don't have time.

I tear off my notes from Jack's pad, scrunching the paper into my jeans pocket. I click back to his news feed. As I put both my hands on the chair arms to get up, a red notification appears over the message icon. He has it on silent . . . of course he does.

I should leave it. If I read it, he will know – there's no way of marking them as unread.

But I can't stop myself.

A sharp intake of breath as I read the words.

Have you told her yet?

I look to the sender. It's not Francesca King, but a name that is vaguely familiar: Simon Howarth. Where do I know it from? I thought I had met all of Jack's colleagues, but they aren't the most interesting of people – I can't remember all of their names. It can't be a relative of Jack's; he's an only child, as are both of his parents.

The front door clicks shut. I race down the loft stairs and go straight into the bathroom. I stand behind the closed door. The kitchen is directly below me; I bet he's pouring another glass of wine. I hear him put the bottle noisily into the fridge.

If he sees my face, he'll know what I've been doing. I flush the toilet and run the taps, waiting until I hear him tread the stairs.

I have a lot of research to do.

The information I found about Francesca King was the same limited details from her Facebook account. On her firm's website – no win, no fee ambulance chasers – was a notice for a drop-in consultancy clinic on Monday nights. I wouldn't have the bottle to face her – what if she'd seen the picture of Sophie and me on Jack's desk at work?

After firing a quick email to several of the private investigators, I slam my laptop shut.

Jack probably won't come down for the rest of the evening – too busy in the company of wine and Facebook. It's ridiculous really. Why aren't I saying anything to him?

Because of what I did six years ago.

He had to get me out of the mess I'd got myself into. It wasn't about him cheating, it was about me, chasing ghosts. It happened before, when I was at college, but Jack doesn't know about that. It's not like that now: this isn't stalking, per se. Everyone looks at what their husbands and partners are up to online, don't they?

Anyway, I have proof. I took a picture of the letter on my phone. Jack would be the first to say it: you can't argue with evidence.

I look in on Sophie before I go to bed, as I do every night. She looks so angelic when she's asleep; I imagine all children do. Debbie would have seen me sleeping as a baby. Did she think I was an angel, or an inconvenience? Before now, she was a ghost – I had idolised her, exalted her – thought she disappeared through no fault of her own. I believed it must have been something really awful for her to have left us. But if this email *is* from her, then I should accept that she *chose* to leave us.

If I found her after all this time, I'm not sure I'd even like her.

Chapter Thirteen

Monday, 7 July 1986

Debbie

When I worked, I hated Mondays. I'd spend the second half of Sunday under a cloud of dread, eating chocolate and watching videos from the corner shop. My colleagues weren't bad people, but being estate agents turned them into arseholes. I'd had dreams of being a fashion designer – leaving home, going to art school and pondering Andy Warhol soup cans, floating about in chiffon and sandals. But I should've known I wasn't good enough for that life. Dad said I was lucky to get a job at all. 'Get any job you can,' he said. 'That'll show Thatcher. She wants us to disappear into the woodwork like cockroaches.'

The trouble was, everyone thought estate agents were cockroaches too.

The office is a distant memory. Now, Mondays are the same as any other day. Peter's at work and Bobby's in school and gone is the pressure of playing happy families. Annie won't mind if I sit and cry all day or if I don't get out of bed and just stare at the ceiling for hours. As long as she's fed and changed, she's fine.

Today, though, I have a job to do: book a holiday I don't

want to go on. It took too long to get out of the house, but we made it. It's a job in itself, but Annie is fast asleep in her pram.

The sun is shining and I'm not in the mood for it. Sunshine is for barbecuing with friends, spending the day at the beach; being happy. I want the weather to match my mood and never stop raining. I keep thinking about that note on the pink paper. I hid it in my knicker drawer. I thought about it at night when the noise of the day had faded. Who would send a letter like that to someone? I haven't got a dirty little secret. The more I thought about it, the more I reasoned that it wasn't for me. What if it's Peter who has the secret? Without a name on the envelope, I could pretend it didn't exist. That doubt means I can forget about it. For now.

Peter didn't stop going on about the bloody holiday all weekend. He got some brochures on Saturday, and dropped the same ones off with Monica. The prices are ridiculous. What's wrong with going to Wales like we always do? I tried telling him how much we'd save staying in Britain.

'In a year,' I said, 'we'll have enough for a deposit on a house. Property prices'll go up soon.'

He rolled his eyes and said, 'Working as a secretary in an estate agency doesn't make you a property expert. Anyway, what about what happened to Kevin? We have to make the most of things. You never know when your last holiday's going to be.'

Kevin Jackson was Peter's assistant manager at Woolies. He was only twenty-three when he was killed in a motorbike accident three months ago. Saturday was the first time Peter had mentioned him since the funeral.

The travel agents is a twenty-minute walk away, and the high street is quiet right now. I take my time; it's just after eleven and the deadline of the three thirty school pick-up isn't looming as much. There's an advert in Mrs Abernathy's shop for a weekend sales assistant, but I know what Peter will say: 'Family time is important.' His dad worked nearly every weekend when Peter was growing up. They're barely on speaking terms now, even though Peter's mother passed away three years ago, and his father only lives in Lytham. I can't face Mrs Abernathy after last week, anyway.

A dandelion clock passes through the air in front of my face. My uncle Charlie used to call them fairies. 'Catch them in your hand, make a wish, then let it go on its way.' Sometimes my wishes came true, which always surprised me. I doubt they would now.

I let go of the pram and try to clasp the clock between my hands.

Missed it.

I don't take my eyes off it; it floats on the breeze. If I could just catch it, I could wish for things to get better.

'*Go on, grab it.*'

I can't tell if that voice is inside, or outside, my head.

'I'm trying, Charlie,' I say.

I swipe again. It wafts down and down until landing perfectly still on the ground. It was meant for me.

'I've got it, Charlie,' I say, feeling the fluffiness of it in my hand. I close my eyes to make a—

A car horn sounds.

I turn around.

I'm in the road.

A car's coming straight for me. I look at the driver. I feel like I know everything about her as our eyes meet. My feet won't move. I'm going to die.

A hand grabs the top of my arm. I trip up the kerb and onto the pavement. The hand is still holding me. I look up the arm, up his body until I reach his face.

'Nathan.'

'What were you doing in the middle of the road?'

I look at the woman behind the wheel; she shakes her head at me and drives off.

'I don't know . . . I saw a fairy and . . .'

'A fairy?'

He frowns at me. He has that same look Peter gives me when I put sugar on my chips instead of salt. Please don't let Nathan look at me that way too.

'No, no. Not a real fairy . . . one of those dandelion clocks. You know?'

He lets go of my arm. 'I guess. You could've got yourself killed.'

'I didn't realise.' I look around me. There are people standing a few feet away – more on the other side of the road, just gawping at me. 'I . . . I thought it was quiet.'

The people on the street begin to wander off – it's not a big drama after all.

Why didn't I feel the step down from the kerb? I left Annie on her own again.

The car horn must've woken her. She's crying, but the sound is muffled, like she's in another room. How long has she been crying?

My cheeks burn.

I look down at my feet and my shoulders relax slightly.

At least I have my sandals on.

Nathan and I are sitting opposite the travel agent's assistant. Her hair is bleach blonde and curly. It's held in a scrunchie at the side of her neck. I used to do my hair in the morning, too. I want to tell her that I wasn't always this dowdy.

'So, Mr and Mrs Atherton—'

'No,' I say for the second time. 'I'm Mrs Atherton and this is Mr Bailey. We're booking for both of our families.'

She raises an eyebrow. She'll soon believe us when we list four adults and three children, but who cares?

I look at the wall behind her. There's a picture of a cruise liner floating on turquoise-blue water. What would it be like to jump from that ship? Would it hurt, or would I go unconscious before I hit the sea?

'I bet there'll be nothing to do there,' I say to Nathan outside. 'It'll be full of blokes in nylon tracksuits and football shirts.'

'Didn't have you down as a snob, Debs.'

I sigh. 'I'm not. I just don't think I'm up to it. I only had a baby a couple of weeks ago. New mothers don't just swan off on holiday.'

'You're not that new.' He winks. 'Come on, cheer up. It'll give us something to look forward to. We could spend some time catching up – it'll be like old times. And with us sharing an apartment, it'll be so much cheaper. I didn't think we'd go on holiday at all this year. We're meant to be on a budget.'

'Good luck with that,' I say. 'Monica won't even buy a tin of baked beans less than thirty pence because it doesn't have the right label on it.'

He shrugs, frowning into the distance. I'm always saying the wrong things.

'Do you think we'll get under each other's feet?' I say. 'What if Annie doesn't sleep?'

'Then we'll all leave you to get up with her.'

'Yeah. Nothing new there.'

'Hey. I was joking.'

We start walking in silence. Annie's beginning to get wriggly – it's nearly time for her next bottle. It must be lunchtime because men in big suits and flashy ties are rushing around, tutting at Annie's pram as though I shouldn't be using the pavement between twelve and two. God forbid they miss a precious second of sitting in the pub with a pint.

'Shouldn't you be at work?' I say.

He goes to look at his watch, but it's not there.

'Good point.'

He bends down to say goodbye to Annie.

'Before I forget,' he says, standing up. 'You mentioned your uncle Charlie . . . when you were looking for fairies.' He puts a hand on my shoulder. 'Is everything okay with you, Debs?'

Nathan and I had just got together, nearly eleven years ago, when my uncle died. He and I were really close. It made me needier than I usually was. Perhaps Nathan liked that – perhaps he thinks I'm *still* like that.

'I don't know,' I tell him.

He lets his hand drop away from me.

'You know I'm here if you need to talk.'

'I can't talk to you,' I say. 'I should be talking to Peter.'

He looks at the pavement. 'Do you think we made the right choice?'

'What do you mean?' I say, but I know what he's talking about. But it was another lifetime. There's no point thinking about it now.

He opens his mouth, but he's already said enough. I pull my handbag-strap higher onto my shoulder and grip the pram.

'Bye, Nathan.'

Peter's been in a good mood since I told him the holiday's booked. He brought chips back from the chippy and it's not even Friday. He's offered to put Bobby to bed, which is probably for the first time ever, and said he'll take us to C & A in town to get holiday clothes. I should be excited. I've never been abroad. But I think about all the things that could go wrong: the plane; Annie in the heat; that I won't be as jolly as everyone wants me to be. I might ruin it for everyone. I keep thinking about the note that came through the door. I couldn't mention it to Peter; it would only spoil his mood.

If the holiday had been arranged two years ago – a year ago, even – I'd be bouncing around, picturing sandy beaches, buying so many clothes – that we couldn't afford – along with miniatures of every toiletry I could think of, giant beach towels, and inflatables for the kids. I'd be ringing Monica every five minutes, asking her to order me things from her catalogue, and exchanging promises of babysitting while we were away.

But I was a different person then, and I don't know how to climb my way back.

I lie and rest my head on the settee, listening to Bobby running around upstairs whilst Peter chases after him with his pyjamas. He let Bobby stay in the bath for forty-five minutes. The boy must be freezing.

Finally, I hear Bobby's bed springs as he jumps onto his duvet. He'll be all clean and cuddly. I should be the one hugging him, but I suppose it'll do Peter some good to learn.

It's eight o'clock at night and Trisha's husband over the road is still playing loud music, showing off that they've got a four-foot-wide garage. It can't even fit their car in. I'm surprised Peter doesn't go out and ask him to turn it down. Actually, I'm not. I think he's a bit intimidated by Dean.

'Debs!' Peter's shouting down from the landing.

I know what's coming.

'Can you ask Dean to turn it down?'

I don't know why he thinks I'm braver than he is. Perhaps he doesn't care that he's about to send his very own wife out to talk to the local perv.

'Does that mean I get to miss the holiday?' I shout up to him, standing at the top of the stairs. 'Have a peaceful week here on my own?'

He frowns and shakes his head, and I feel like I'm the child again.

I stick my feet into my flip-flops, which I regret as soon as

I shut the front door behind me: it's windy and blobs of freezing-cold rain drop on my toes. It's July, for God's sake.

Dean looks up from the Ford Cortina he's tinkering with on the roadside. Wham!'s 'I'm Your Man' is playing from tiny speakers in the open garage; a Samantha Fox calendar is nailed to one of the concrete walls inside. He's such a cliché. He wipes one of his screwdrivers with a cloth already covered in oil. He looks at his tool and winks at me. Good God. I almost retch. He's wearing one of those ghastly new shell suits in pale blue. Ugh.

'All right, Deborah?' His voice reminds me of Boycie from *Only Fools and Horses*. He puts it on though.

I never know how he's going to behave towards me. When we first moved in, he mistook my friendliness as a come-on, leaning towards me for a kiss at our first and only street barbecue. I pushed him away of course, but these days he can either be civil or downright nasty.

'Do you mind turning your radio down, please, Dean? Peter's putting Bobby to bed.'

'Is he now?' He sits on his car bonnet like he's Kevin Webster. 'Don't let Trish hear you say that. Don't want her indoors getting any of those ideas about men doing women's work.'

'Trisha's out, isn't she? Anyway,' I say. 'It'd be much appreciated.'

He turns and walks slowly towards the garage, swinging his hips as he goes. He probably thinks I'm looking at his arse.

Oh shit – I am. I turn around quickly.

'Hey,' he shouts. 'Tell Pete not to blank me next time I see him in town.'

I look behind me. He's not angry; he's smiling. 'Yes, will do.'

'And that friend of yours – Margaret, is it? Him and her were thick as thieves. Not surprised they didn't see me. I'd keep my eye on those two if I were you.' His eyebrows go up and down.

I try and smile back, but it comes out as a grimace. 'It's Monica,' I say. 'Her name's Monica.'

I run back into the house, and shut the door. I kick off my flip-flops, my heart pounding. He must know something – or he's seen something.

Why would Peter be meeting up with Monica in town? He hasn't mentioned anything.

It must be Dean who sent the note.

But not to me, to Peter.

Chapter Fourteen

Anna

Jack must have slept on the sofa bed in his office upstairs last night, and then left before I woke, because he wasn't in the house this morning. There was no note. Usually he would scrawl something on a Post-it, or make a silly message with the fridge magnet letters. But nothing today. I'd fired off a quick text, asking if he was okay, but I probably won't get a response until lunchtime.

Jack said he'd be more relaxed this weekend, but he was the same. We took Sophie to an indoor play centre on Saturday, even though it was sunny – it's her favourite place – but Jack constantly checked his phone. As soon as we got home at three o'clock, when the rain started, he poured his first glass of wine. I spent the rest of the weekend with Sophie, drawing and making egg cups with her new air-dry clay.

As Sophie and I were leaving for the school run this morning, the landline rang. I almost didn't answer it.

'Anna. It's your grandad here . . . are you there?'

'Yes, Grandad.'

'Ah, good, good. Thought I was on your answerphone-majiggy-thing. I won't take up much of your time, love, I just wanted to ask if you'd mind popping over this morning. I've some of your mother's things I wanted to show you.'

'Oh, okay.'

'I'll tell you more when you're in front of me. Bye now.'

I rang Isobel, put on my croakiest voice, and told her I was taking the day off.

Thirty minutes later, with Sophie safely in school, I pull up outside his house. Robert's car is here too. I hadn't realised what Grandad was going to show me was that important – or that my brother would be here. I have left Robert countless messages on his mobile and he still hasn't got back to me.

Grandad's lived in this house most of his adult life. He married Gran when he was twenty-one and I'm sure everything inside is the same as it was in 1986. I think he stays here so Debbie would know where to come back to, with everything frozen in time so she would feel at home.

It's Robert who answers the door. He glances at me and walks back down the hallway.

'Are you all right, Robert?' I follow him into the living room. 'Robert?'

He's sitting in the chair next to the television, looking sideways at *The Jeremy Kyle Show*.

'Don't let Grandad see you've got that on,' I say. 'You know what he thinks about it.'

He grabs the remote control.

'We should go on it,' he says, switching it off. 'They'd have a field day with our family.'

He isn't smiling. He folds his arms across his chest. The sleeves of his tweed jacket are stretched at the shoulders – he must have had it for years. He dresses like a man twenty years older. His once-auburn hair has more flecks of grey than red, and there are deep frown lines across his forehead that I've not noticed before.

'Don't you want to know what happened to our mother?' I say.

'I wish you'd stop calling her that,' he says. 'What's she ever done for you, except give birth to you?'

'I . . . I just want . . .'

'Yes, because it's all about you. You're just like her. Have you thought about what this is doing to Monica?'

'Have you seen her? She didn't say much about the email when I went round last week.'

'You haven't seen her since last week? She probably thinks you've abandoned her . . . after everything she's done for you.'

'It's only Monday.'

I sit on the edge of the sofa, still in my coat, and glance at the painting of Jesus on the wall above the fireplace. He's always staring at me. His eyes are meant to be kind, but His chest is open, and a giant, graphic image of a heart takes centre stage.

'I do appreciate everything Monica's done for me,' I say. 'She's the only mother I've ever known—'

'Well then. We should forget about that email. It's probably some weirdo anyway.'

'But what about the shells?'

'A lucky guess. Everyone keeps shells.'

'Course they don't,' I say, turning my knees towards him. 'I found a roll of film from your memory box.'

'What? Oh that. I thought I'd got rid of it.'

'Are they your pictures?'

'I guess. Probably from the holiday. Grandad gave me an old camera to use while we were there.'

'*The* holiday?'

His eyes burn into mine, before they settle on the blank screen of the television. Why is he acting like he hates me? We've always got on, had a laugh.

It was only the week before last that he came to the bookshop to take me out for lunch.

'Well, I'm honoured that you've graced me with your presence,' I said that day, 'travelling all this way to the lovely town of St Annes.' I followed him out of the door and he linked his arm in mine as we walked.

'Yeah, very funny,' he said. 'I've an ulterior motive, actually.'

I sat opposite him in the café around the corner.

While we waited for our cheese toasties, he said, 'I've got wind that Monica's planning a surprise party for me in a few weeks.'

I zipped my lips with my finger and thumb. He rolled his eyes.

'She knows I'm not forty for a few years, doesn't she? It's not a special birthday.'

'You know how much Monica loves birthdays. She used to make our cakes from scratch. I remember the time she made a house with chocolate fingers and apple slices for the roof.' I looked down at my cup. 'Although that was the year only two of my school friends came to my party. I suppose, at eleven years old, they'd grown out of kids' parties.'

'It was cruel of them, Anna. Gran had just died, and you were really upset – so was I. Kids don't get that sometimes. If I'd still been at the same school, I'd have given them hell.'

I smiled. 'Course you would.'

He shrugged, grinning at me. He never was a fighter.

'Anyway,' I said. 'Monica wants to do something nice for you. Especially after the D. I. V. O. R.—'

'Don't say it like that. It's too much like that song. You can't kick a man when he's down.'

'But *you* ended it with Kerry ... said she had *stunted, intellectually*—'

He held up his hands. 'Okay, okay. That's what I said to you lot.' He looked around the café, and leant closer. 'It was only partially true. Oh God, it's such a cliché . . .'

'What is? What happened?'

I lean forward too.

'She ran off with—'

'The milkman? The postman?'

'It's not multiple choice. Be serious.' He sighed. 'She ran off with a bloke from the gym.'

'Ah,' I said. 'I see.'

He flapped his hand in the air. 'It's not so bad. Did I tell you that Marie Costigan friended me on Facebook last week?'

'Robert, I didn't even know you were on Facebook. Wasn't she your girlfriend at university? The one with the big—'

'Intellect. Yes.'

'I was going to say "hair" . . .'

He shook his head at me, as our lunch was placed on the table. Robert took a bite and opened his mouth while waving his hand.

'Hot, is it?' I said.

I watched him chew quickly before gulping it down.

'Good God, yes.' Robert hardly ever swore; he didn't want it to come out accidentally in front of his students. 'And that's why the party is a no-no. I'd like to take Marie out, make a fresh start.'

'And you don't want to bring her to the party in case she sees what plebs your family are?' I smiled and patted his hand. 'I'll see what I can do, brother.'

But that was last week. The Robert sitting in front of me now, in Grandad's living room, is not the same person as he was just eleven days ago.

'Sorry,' I say to him, breaking the silence. 'I won't show the photographs to you, if you don't want to see.'

'I was six years old, and my mum didn't come back from holiday with us. The last thing on my mind would've been getting some shitty photos developed. They're probably full of lizards and grasshoppers. I can't stand the sound of grasshoppers.'

I take off my coat, and go into the hallway, hanging it on the bannister. Grandad appears at the kitchen doorway, the china rattling on the wooden tray.

'You didn't have to do anything fancy for us. Here, I'll take it for you.' I grab the tray, but he doesn't take his hands away. 'Grandad?'

'Your brother doesn't seem interested in finding your mum,' he says. 'Shall we do this another day? It might upset him.'

I give the tray a gentle tug and he releases his hands.

'Let him decide. I'm sure he'll leave if he wants to.'

He nods and goes back to the kitchen, grabbing a box from the counter. I place the tray on the coffee table in the living room, and Robert pours tea into one of the cups.

The cardboard box in Grandad's hands is the size of a shoebox. He sits on the end of his chair next to the gas fire.

'These are some of Deborah's belongings. I took in most of her things, when your dad – and you two, of course – moved in with Monica and Leo. Her clothes, shoes, you know . . . I've had them such a long time. But I'm old and I can't hang on to things forever. You'd have to clear it out when I'm dead and buried. So, I had a sort out a few weeks ago, before all of this . . .'

Robert's stirring his tea so loudly it's like a ringing bell. I glare at him, but he doesn't notice.

'You're not dying, are you, Grandad?' he says without looking up.

I want to put my hand over his mouth to shut him up.

Grandad's frowning.

'You're not, are you, Grandad?' I say.

He shakes his head.

'Not from anything specific, but I'm not getting any younger.'

Robert looks at his watch. He doesn't trust Grandad's carriage clock; apparently a gadget that old can't be reliable.

'I've got to get back to work soon,' he says. 'I'm lecturing at one. I need to prepare.'

This usually impresses Grandad; Robert was the first in the family to go to university, but it's like Grandad's not listening to him.

'What it is, you see,' says Grandad, 'is that I found her diary. Not a personal one – I mean the days of the week, you know, like a—'

'A pocket diary?' says Robert. He downs his tiny cup of tea.

'Yes, that's right. I didn't want to pry, but I had to look. She's my only child, you see.'

Robert's shifting in his chair. I wish he'd sit still and listen.

'I know, Grandad,' I say. 'It must be horrible not knowing.'

He edges forward in his chair.

'The diary was hidden amongst her – you know – her undergarments, which is why I only found *them* the other week. They were wrapped in a pair of tights.'

'What were, Grandad?' I say.

'The letters. Though God only knows who would send her words like that.' He looks to the painting of Jesus. Gran always did that if she heard or said anything that bordered on blasphemous. 'It was only when I found them, did I remember her talking about them – not long before she left . . . she said they weren't even addressed to her, though – she didn't seem that worried about them. They might not even mean anything . . . kids messing about.'

Grandad picks out a small shortbread tin from the cardboard box – a tartan one that I remember from a few Christmases ago. He lifts it open, and a few flecks of rust from the hinges fall onto his lap.

'There aren't many.'

He hands one to me, another to Robert. I take the letter out of the envelope carefully. It doesn't look as though it's been opened many times; the creases are still sharp.

I know your dirty little secret.

The skin on my arms turns to goosebumps; the hairs stand on end.

'Who would send her something like this?'

'I've no idea, love.'

'Would you mind if I took these home, to look at properly, I've . . .' I was going to tell him about hiring an investigator, but Robert might get cross with me.

'Yes, I suppose. Unless Robert wants to take some too?'

Typical. Robert has barely spoken to Grandad today, he hardly ever comes round, but when he does, he gets treated like a prince.

'What does that one say, Robert?'

'You can read it for yourself. They're probably part of her silly little games,' says Robert, putting his note back into the envelope. 'Anna can take the stuff. Dad probably showed them to the police years ago. Nothing new.'

'I don't think he did, Robert,' says Grandad.

'Don't you want to find her?' I say to my brother.

Robert stands, tossing the envelope into the cardboard box.

'Find her? Do I want to *find her*? Why should I, when I never lost her?' He bends down and kisses Grandad's cheek. 'I can't be part of this any more.' He goes to the door, and turns before he leaves. 'I . . . sorry, Grandad. I'll call round next week.'

A few seconds later, the front door slams shut, making Grandad flinch slightly.

'I'm sorry about that,' I say.

He gets up and walks to the window, folding his arms.

'No,' he says. 'I know what he means. God forgive me for saying this, but she was ever so flighty, so impulsive.'

'But she wouldn't have left on some petty whim. There must be more to it than that.'

Grandad watches Robert from behind the net curtain; my brother rubs his face before getting into his car.

'That's what I thought, love. I hope we find some explanation. If only for the sake of that poor boy.'

What Robert said before, about the lizards and the grasshoppers, is the most he has ever mentioned about that holiday. I have the box of Debbie's letters next to me on the passenger seat. I want to dive in and look through it all, but there are pedestrians going past. I need to be at home, where I can concentrate.

I've been parked outside Francesca King's offices in Preston for forty minutes. Her name is etched on the glass alongside the names of the other partners. I thought that, because it's lunchtime, I'd catch her nipping to the shops for a sandwich. Perhaps it's just me who's so predictable – Francesca probably has food brought to her by one of her minions.

I go to her Facebook profile on my phone, so I can memorise, again, what she looks like. I slouch down in the seat; it would be just my luck to be spotted by my boss, Isobel, or one of the volunteers, when I'm meant to be off sick, even when I'm miles away from the bookshop.

A black cab pulls up alongside my car.

Oh God, I'm halfway down my seat. I push my feet into the footwell and slowly return to the upright position. I need to look to my right. Perhaps it is Francesca who's getting out of the taxi. I chance a quick glance: it's a woman with her back to me. Her hair is long and dark like Francesca's. She pays the driver and turns towards the pavement, passing the front of my car.

It's not her. This woman must be in her late fifties. She's waiting outside the solicitors. I put on my sunglasses, so she can't see me watching her.

Another woman is walking up the road. The same long hair. I think it's *her*. I get out of my car, although I have no idea what I'm going to do. I can't see anything in these glasses – it's too cloudy. I push them onto the top of my head. She is only three metres away. Why did I get out? My face is hot.

'Francesca, love,' says the older woman, kissing the younger one on the cheek. 'Good timing. I've just got here myself.'

It *is* her. And I'm just standing here like a fool.

'Hi, Mum,' says Francesca. She looks at me and smiles. 'Hello.'

'Hello,' I say, like a parrot.

'Are you all right?' She's tilted her head to one side.

'I . . . er . . . I'm looking for a solicitor.'

She laughs a little laugh, like she's Snow White in the Disney film.

'Well, you've come to the right place,' she says. 'If you talk to Adam on reception, he'll arrange an appointment for you.'

'Thanks.'

It would look silly if I just walked away.

The letter, I want to say. *Why did you tell my husband you were forever his? It's not right.*

No words are coming out of my mouth. Francesca's mother looks slightly afraid of me – I've had those looks before, years ago. 'I'll come back later,' I say. 'I've got to get my son.' I pull the sunglasses back over my eyes and get into the car. I know they're looking at me, but as I pull away, I keep my eyes on the road ahead.

Chapter Fifteen

Friday, 11 July 1986

Debbie

Why is night-time so everlasting? It's been seventeen minutes since Annie finally dropped off, but my mind won't slow down. Thoughts are on repeat in my head: of the note through the letterbox; of Nathan; and of Peter and Monica together.

I've seen Nathan twice on our high street in the past week, yet he works the other side of Preston – at least five miles away. It can't be a coincidence. I should've asked him. Too caught up in my own head, that's my trouble. That's what Mum always says.

What were Peter and Monica talking about when Dean saw them? Why meet on their own and not mention it? Tomorrow I'll ask Peter; I just need to be brave. Even though he might lie; I'll be able to tell by the look on his face. The corners of his mouth turn up when he doesn't tell the truth. Perhaps they've fallen in love with each other. Or is that my guilty mind and wishful thinking? No, no, it's not that. I love Peter.

Infatuation: that's all it was with Nathan and me. But what is it now?

'*They can't be trusted, Debbie. You know what to do.*'

That voice again. It was clearly outside my head this time. Definitely.

'What?' I say.

I sit up quickly and look at Peter. His back is facing me. I lean over to look at his face; he's fast asleep.

Mum talks to God all the time, He must reply to her at least some of the time for her to keep doing it, surely.

'You spoke about your uncle Charlie,' Nathan said the other day. I can't remember talking about him in the street, but what if he's trying to contact me? I've heard people talk about voices from beyond the grave – I read it in a magazine a few months ago.

'Mummy!'

The voice makes me jump, but it's only Bobby calling out from his room.

As quietly as I can, I rush out of the bedroom in case he shouts again. I close the door behind me and flick on the landing light.

Bobby's sitting up in his bed, gripping Ted with both hands, his little cheeks wet with tears.

'What's wrong, sweetheart?'

'I got a bad dream,' he says. 'I dreamed a giant man trampled over the house. He crushed you and Daddy and took away me and Annie in his giant hands.'

I kneel on the floor next to him and pull him close to me. 'You know what that was?' I say.

He shakes his head.

'Did Daddy read you *The BFG* before you went to sleep?'

He nods, rubbing his left eye with his hand.

'It was just your dream remembering the story, that's all.'

'But the BFG was a goodie, not a child-catcher.'

'It must be two different stories put together . . . probably *Chitty Chitty Bang Bang*.' I stroke his hair. 'If you lie down and get to sleep now, I bet you have a good dream next.'

I don't want to talk to him too much, else he won't get back to sleep. I keep stroking his hair until his eyes begin to flicker. I kiss his damp cheek and tiptoe to the door.

I feel terrible for forgetting it was his birthday the day before yesterday. How could I have forgotten that? I always remember his birthday's not long after mine – I used to buy his presents with the birthday money *I* got.

I used to.

Who am I turning into? Bobby means the world to me, yet my mind feels only half present.

Thank God Monica made him a cake. She probably wanted to show me up. She'd brought round loads of presents, too, but I can't be angry with her for that.

'Night-night, my brave boy.'

'Mummy,' he says. 'Promise that a big giant won't come and get you and Daddy.'

'I promise, Bobs.' I leave his door ajar and peep through the gap. 'I'm not going anywhere.'

I don't know what day it is, but it's a school day, and it's lunch-time, and I'm at my parents' house: my childhood home. Mum's laid out some sandwiches, French Fancies and Wagon Wheels on posh plates on the coffee table. She's got out the Midwinter dinner service that Dad got from a jumble sale, complete with a sugar bowl and milk jug.

'You hardly ever visit these days,' she says. 'I wanted to make it more of an occasion.'

Dad's been in the loft and got out the baby bouncer; the same one I used as a baby. Annie's lying still on it – she's too small – but blinking her way around the room. Her eyes rest on the picture of Jesus with the bleeding heart. Poor child will have nightmares, like Bobby. I turn her round so she can watch *Rainbow*.

105

'I only gave birth a few weeks ago, Mum. I'm just getting back on my feet.'

If she tells me that she was out painting fences or making scones the day after I was born, I will scream.

'Where's Dad?'

'He's down at the library. He's got his routine now. Job centre every day first thing, then Monday he goes to the market, Tuesdays he . . .'

Oh, Jesus, I say in my head to the picture of His bleeding heart, *Please don't let me end up like this.*

I wait until she's reeled off Dad's weekly itinerary before I say, 'Are you happy, Mum?'

'What kind of question's that?' she says. 'What's happiness got to do with anything?'

'You always seem to be talking about everyone else. You never talk about yourself, or your hobbies. Do you have any hobbies?'

'What would I want to talk about myself for? I'm not the conceited sort. And anyway, I'm nothing special – no one'd want to hear about *me*.'

I pick up one of the fondant fancies and bite all the pink icing off. Mum rolls her eyes at me and smiles.

'Mum,' I say, mouth full of sponge. 'Do you ever wonder if this is all there is? You go to college, leave, get married, have kids. And then what?'

She frowns as she drops a cube of sugar in her tea.

'Sometimes you must accept the burden of what you've been given . . . and I was given your dad.' She takes a sip of tea. 'Anyway . . . Prince Andrew's marrying Sarah Ferguson next week. I suppose you could call that my hobby.'

'Good God, Mum.'

She nods to Jesus. 'He's listening, you know.'

I grab a tiny egg mayonnaise sandwich. I haven't eaten this much for weeks.

'Do you see much of Monica?' says Mum. 'You were always so close, always together.'

'Yeah. Though not much over the past few weeks. I think she's been busy.' Busy talking to my husband, I don't say.

'Well you need your friends,' says Mum. 'That's a mistake I made. I thought I didn't need them after I got married . . . didn't bother keeping in touch. I had this one friend – Sandra Birkette. She was what they called A Right One, but she was so much fun. She dragged me to one of those dances – got me a port and lemon . . . it went right to my head. But that was the night I met your dad.'

'Ah, Mum. You should look her up in the Yellow Pages.'

'I wouldn't know where to start. She moved to Devon, I think.'

'I could look for her for you. It'd give me something useful to do.'

For just a second, I see a small light in her eye, but a second later it's gone.

'Don't be silly, Deborah,' she says. 'You've got enough to do with the children, the house, Peter.'

Hearing it out loud makes me feel pitiful. My essence, my identity, is defined by other people. I've become a shadow. And I don't know what to do about it.

Chapter Sixteen

Anna

I should not be nervous about seeing Monica, but I feel empty in the stomach. I rang the landline, but there was no answer. This is the first place I thought to go after seeing Francesca in the street. I knock on the front door, expecting no one to be in.

'Monica!'

'Hello, love. I saw you sitting outside in your car for ages. Are you okay? Your dad's doing the shopping at Morrisons.' She closes the door behind us and rubs the top of my arms. 'Why are you shivering? It's boiling outside. The weather doesn't know what it's meant to be doing – it was pouring down this morning.'

'I don't feel so well,' I say. 'I'm meant to be off sick.'

She turns into the living room and I follow. She bends down to their wood burner and throws in two more logs.

'How come you've got the fire on?' I say.

'You know how I feel the cold. This living room is always in the shade. What were you doing outside?'

She grabs the throw off the sofa, points for me to sit down, and wraps the soft material around me. I pull it up to my chin, for comfort rather than warmth.

'I don't know,' I say. 'I had to check something, and I haven't seen you for ages. You were a bit distant the last time I saw you. I hope I haven't upset you. Things are strange at the moment. I don't feel right.' I can't stop the tears. I wipe my face on the throw. 'I'm sorry.'

She sits next to me, putting her hand on my forehead.

'Oh, my darling girl.'

She grabs my shoulders and pulls me towards her, wrapping both arms around me. It makes me cry even more, the sobs shake my whole body.

'There, there. You let it out.'

She smells of apple shampoo and rose perfume. Like a delicious fruit salad, I used to say to her. She pulls away from me and takes hold of my hands.

'Is this about the email?'

'Yes. And about Jack. I think he might be having an affair.'

Monica frowns. She's always looked young for her age, but now I notice the deep lines between her eyebrows as though they have been excavated by worry.

'I can't believe that for a second,' she says. 'What makes you think that?'

Heat runs to my face.

'I was looking through his wallet and I found a letter from a woman called Francesca. I checked his Facebook and there she was: long hair, beautiful.'

Monica wipes the hair from my face.

'You're beautiful too, Anna. It's probably not what it seems. Have you talked to him about it?'

I shake my head.

'I can't say I've been through his things. He'll think I've had a relapse or something.'

'A relapse?' I see her eyes flicker; she frowns. 'But that was

109

nothing to do with Jack,' she says. 'He can't expect you to have been through what you have and not be a tiny bit crazy.'

I laugh through my tears.

'I don't think that's a politically correct way of putting it, Mon.'

She shrugs.

'Well, maybe not. But you didn't hurt anyone, it wasn't the end of the world. And anyway – I've had my fair share of being off the wall.'

She says that, but I've never seen her be anything but calm, the voice of reason – the way she is now. She puts her hands on her knees. 'This calls for a cup of tea, I think. And extra sugar.'

I wipe my face with my sleeve.

'You're really spoiling me.'

'Very funny,' she says, standing up. 'All right. I might stretch to a chocolate digestive. That's if your dad hasn't eaten them all.'

She leaves the living room, and I bring my legs up onto the sofa. Sometimes I wish I could move back here and become a child again.

There aren't any photos of Debbie on the mantelpiece, there never have been, not like there are at Grandad's. There's one in the spare bedroom – the room that used to be mine – but it's probably hidden in a drawer now.

I get up and go to the dresser, where all the photo albums are. All the pictures of Dad, Robert and Debbie are in a red-leather book with an imprint of a horse on the front cover. I open the glass door to reach for it, but it's not there.

Monica brings two cups of tea into the room.

'Where's the album?' I say.

'I . . . I was looking at it upstairs. Do you want me to get it?'

I know every picture by heart – there are only twenty-three. There's one of a Christmas day when Robert got an Action Man; another of his third birthday with the hedgehog cake Debbie made. There's only one of me. I'm lying on a quilt at maybe a few weeks old, and Robert is lying next to me, propping up his head with his hand. My tiny fingers grip his thumb and he's looking down at me. One of Debbie's, or Dad's, fingers covers the left side of the picture; it's an orange-and-white blur.

'No, it's okay,' I say. 'I've looked at them loads of times anyway.'

I sit back down on the sofa, and she sits next to me.

'This whole business,' she says, 'it's affecting your dad too. He'll never say it to you kids, but he's been quiet.' She takes a tiny sip of her tea. 'I couldn't tell you this before – not when you were a child, and since then, well, there's never been a right time to bring it up. But for a long time, Peter was in bits. Your gran moved in with you . . . sometimes your dad would just sit at the kitchen table, staring out of the window.'

'For how long?'

She's looking into the wood burner.

'Monica, for how long was he like that?'

She shakes her head back to the present.

'I don't know. About two years.'

'Two years? How come I don't remember any of this?'

'You were only little, Anna. It's why you and your gran were so close. She doted on you. She said she treated you better than her own daughter. She was always honest like that. I still think of her today.'

'I wish I could remember.'

She looks at me.

'Oh, love. You've always been frustrated about not being able to remember the past, but there's nothing you can do about it . . . you shouldn't be so hard on yourself. Sometimes it's better to forget. And the mind protects you sometimes, I think. Like poor Robert. He asked when Debbie was coming home for about a year. Then he just stopped talking about her. The kids at school probably told him she was dead. That poor boy. It had an impact on him when he was growing up.'

I'd love to borrow Robert's memories for a day – or even for just a few moments. Perhaps once I had them, he would feel a burden lifted and he wouldn't want them back; he might be happy then.

'I do feel bad for Robert,' I say. 'But she left me too.'

She rubs my hand.

'I know, I know.'

I look out of the window. Outside, Mr Flowers is trying to grab something with his walking stick again.

'I wonder if he ever manages to pick up what he's looking for,' says Monica. 'It's always at the same time every day.'

'Have you ever offered to help him?'

She turns to me, her eyebrows raised. 'Do you know, I don't think I have.' She frowns again. Sometimes she is so hard to read. Is she thinking about the old man – or is she thinking about Debbie, Dad, or Robert?

'Have you told Leo about the email?'

'I mentioned it briefly when he Skyped on Sunday. But you know what he's like. He's living a whole new life out there, with Jocelyn and the kids . . . he looked bored when I mentioned it, uncomfortable. And his father . . . well, he hasn't been interested in my life since he left.'

'What you said the other day,' I say. 'About things going strange with Debbie. What did you mean?'

'I wasn't myself when you saw me last. I was talking rubbish.'

'No one has ever said anything like that before.'

'Hmm. It was before we went on holiday . . . your mum wasn't herself. But it wasn't just her . . . we all felt a change, I think, a shift in things – me, Nathan, your dad. We never should have booked that holiday. Things would have been so different. I should've been there for her more.'

'Do you know what happened that night?'

'Just bits,' she says, still staring out of the window. 'It's a lifetime ago.'

'What bits?'

She looks at me. 'About her and Nathan.'

Chapter Seventeen

Saturday, 12 July 1986

Debbie

The heat of the sun that shines through the window bathes me in warmth – even though it's freezing outside, in July. I'm wearing my terracotta duffle coat that won't even do up any more.

Monica comes back from the Ladies'. She's still as skinny as she was ten years ago – and she's showing it off in a skin-tight, sleeveless polo-neck dress; she doesn't have to worry about her arms.

'I had a big breakfast,' she says, sitting down opposite me. 'But you go ahead and order. You need to keep your strength up.'

'What do you think I am? An Olympic athlete?'

She flexes her arm. 'More like Supermum.'

'Hardly,' I say, ignoring the implication that I'm built like a brick shithouse. I grab the menu. 'Anyway, I can't do up my coat. I should go on that new cabbage-soup diet.'

'Jesus, Debs. You've just had a baby. Plus, you're only a size twelve.'

I'm closer to a fourteen, probably a sixteen, but I don't say it out loud. Monica's always been slimmer than me. She

114

never ate dinner at school, but says being slender is in her genes.

'So, how does it feel to be free for a few hours?' she says. 'I wish my mum would offer to have Leo – we have to pay a babysitter. Mum must've seen him, what, ten times since he was born?'

'Don't exaggerate, Monica,' I say. 'That's only because she moved back down south.'

She rolls her eyes.

'You see? What kind of grandmother chooses a career over her only grandchild? It's unheard of.'

'At least she sends money to make up for it.'

'True,' she says, smiling. 'But I do envy the way your mum is with your two.'

'Me too.'

'Ha!' She shakes the sugar sachet before ripping it open. 'She's probably mellowed out since we were teenagers.'

'Not towards me, she hasn't.'

This idle chat isn't why I asked Monica to meet me, but I'm scared to say it. Why should I be? She's the closest thing I have to a sister.

'Do you remember,' she says, 'when you told your mum you were staying at mine, but really we were camping with Mark Saunders in his back garden?'

'I'd forgotten about that. I made you come home with me in the morning in case she could tell from my face I was hiding something.'

'You always were a shit liar.'

I smile at her. She was always the best at lying. Most of the time, she'd tell me stories that were so mundane, so ordinary, that I'd wonder why she'd bother to make them up in the first place. But there was one that stuck with me.

'I remember you said Mark Saunders had a crush on me,' I

115

say. 'I made a right fool of myself sending him that Valentine's card.'

The smile vanishes from her face. 'I didn't think I confessed to you about that.'

'You didn't. *He* told me.'

'Ah.' She sips her tea. 'Bugger, that's hot.'

I smile, not hiding my delight. 'You should add more milk.'

She looks up at me. 'Do you forgive me? I am sorry, you know. My mum said it was to get attention.'

'What was?'

'My making up stories. Though it was *her* attention I wanted, but didn't get, so it hardly worked.'

'It got *my* attention,' I say. 'It made me think you were crazy.'

She laughs. 'Only *you* would stick around with a weirdo like me. You're too nice for your own good.'

I look down at my frothy coffee sprinkled with chocolate powder. I dab the milky foam with my finger and put the mixture in my mouth.

'I doubt that,' I say.

'You've not been yourself these past few weeks, that's all.'

Sometimes, it's like she thinks she knows it all, but she doesn't. We sit in silence for a few minutes. It shouldn't feel this awkward.

'Why did you meet up with Peter the other day?' I say.

A redness appears on her neck and works its way up to her cheeks. She puts her palms on the table and leans forward.

'I was going to tell you about that, but you beat me to it. What did Peter say about it?'

'Peter didn't tell me. It was Dean who lives opposite us. He saw you two in town.'

Saying *you two* makes me feel sick.

'Oh, Dirty Deano.' She laughs.

I narrow my eyes.

116

'Sorry.' She sits up straight and looks around the café, but no one's near us. 'Peter phoned me at work . . . said he was worried about you.'

'Worried? Why?'

'He said . . .' She looks around again. 'He said that you didn't seem to enjoy life any more – that you weren't happy. You know what he's like: he's a sensitive soul.'

'It's only three weeks since I had Annie. And anyway, what's happy got to do with anything?'

I look out of the window at the busy road outside. I can't believe I've just quoted my mother.

'It's got everything to do with it, Debs.' She puts a hand on mine.

I want to swipe it from underneath hers. 'It must be the baby blues,' I say. 'That's a thing, right?'

She shrugs. 'I guess. But I thought the blues came a few days after.'

I lift my hand away from hers, using my coffee as the reason. I sip the drink, but it's cold and bitter.

'I think I've been hearing things . . . voices,' I say. 'It sounds like my uncle – Charlie, who died years ago. I know it's not really him. It must be the tiredness. Everyone hears voices from time to time, don't they?'

Monica's mouth drops open, her eyebrows rise. 'I've never heard voices,' she says.

Oh God. I've made a mistake telling her. She'll tell everyone. Peter might get me sectioned. For a moment, the idea sounds tempting: I'll get a break, away from everything.

No. Get a grip, Debbie.

Monica leans back in the chair, as though she's afraid I might take off all my clothes and run around naked.

'What are you smiling at?' she says.

'Nothing. I was just thinking about Annie.'

117

'How many times have you heard your uncle? What did he say?'

'Something about catching a fairy,' I say. Monica's frowning again. 'You know. Dandelion clocks.' I wave my hand. 'Never mind.'

She's never been into all that ghost stuff. I'm sure it was her who moved the glass when we did a Ouija board at secondary school.

'If it happens again,' she says, 'make an appointment with the doctor. They might give you something for it.'

'Something for it?' I pick up the coffee again to distract myself from her staring at me. 'It was probably Bobby talking in his sleep, or someone in the street.'

I feel silly telling her about it. I can see she doesn't believe me. But really, there's not much difference between the two of us: me hearing voices, her being a habitual liar.

'I'll come with you to the doctors, if you're scared,' she says. 'There's nothing to be afraid of.'

There is, I think. They could take my children away from me.

'Thanks,' I say.

But I've no intention of mentioning it to anyone again. She looks at me as though there's something not quite right with me. I suppose that might be true.

Chapter Eighteen

Anna

The waiting room is beige, and the paintings on the wall are beige. I'd expected Francesca King's office to be more modern, minimalist. There's a television in the corner that's switched off. I could do with a distraction.

In the quiet, the conversation with Monica this afternoon at their house runs through my mind.

'What about Debbie and Nathan?' I had asked. 'What happened between them?'

'I can't talk to you before I've spoken to Peter,' she said. 'You might say something to him. I can't have your dad thinking I'm going behind his back. He didn't want you kids to know.'

'Don't you know me? I'd never do that.'

She placed the back of her hand on her forehead.

'I can't see properly,' she said. 'I think I'm getting a migraine. I can only see half of your face. I need to lie down in the dark.'

And that was the end of the conversation. That's what it has always been like – I only get part of the story.

There is another man in the waiting room. Divorce, I imagine. He keeps sniffing and wiping his face with a stringy tissue that's already soaked. I try not to stare; he doesn't notice me anyway.

The door opens. Before Francesca has a chance to come out, the snivelling man leaps from his seat and almost sprints towards her.

What am I even doing here? I don't think Jack believed there was an emergency at the shop.

'At a closed charity bookshop?' he'd said. 'At seven o'clock at night?'

'I think I left the heater on,' I said, putting on my coat. 'If those books catch fire . . . there are flats above it . . . I wouldn't be able to sleep for thinking about it.'

He was smiling at me as I walked into the hallway. I hadn't told him I'd rung in sick that day. Every time I looked at him, I pictured him with Francesca; stroking her hair, her legs, her face. I was almost sick.

But now I'm here, I don't know what I am going to say to her. Is this normal, what I'm doing? Most people would confront their other half, not sneak around visiting his mistress's place of work.

I get up to leave, but her door opens again. Have I been sitting here that long?

The man is still holding the tissue, but his eyes are no longer red.

'She's good, she is,' he says, pointing to Francesca. 'I can't let that bitch of an ex near my children. She's dangerous.'

'Oh, I see,' I say. 'Very good.' My hands tremble as they cling to my handbag in front of me.

Francesca waits until the man has gone, before she says, 'Sorry to keep you waiting. Come on through.' She says it so nicely, I have no choice but to follow her.

Her office has a large metal-and-glass desk. The bookcases either side of it are white and crammed with leather books, like Jack's. His office is mahogany, more traditional.

'We don't have to read them all,' she says, catching me looking at the shelves. She sits down in her bright-orange tub chair. It looks expensive; everything about her does. 'Only when we get an unusual case.'

I look around for photos of her family. If she has children, perhaps she would understand, be considerate of my situation. She might not have realised Jack's married.

But, on second thoughts, why would her being married with children make a difference? Either you're a person who cheats, or you're not.

'My husband's having an affair,' I say.

She doesn't flinch. 'I'm sorry to hear that.' Her tone is gentle; she's frowning. I almost believe her sincerity.

'I think it's with another . . . a colleague.'

She picks up a pen. Should I give Jack's name? Client confidentiality means she can't repeat anything I say.

'You might know him,' I say. 'Would that be a problem?'

'It shouldn't be. Everything stays professional.'

She hasn't asked who it is. She's like the counsellor I used to see: letting me do all the talking.

'I'm not sure I want a divorce, though,' I say.

She puts down her pen, and clasps her hands on the desk.

'If you decide to go ahead, it's best to be prepared by getting your marriage certificate, records of incomings and outgoings, preferably from both of you. Also, details of any pensions, debts. And, of course, a list of your children and their dates of birth.'

'We've only the one.'

She reaches across her desk and takes one of the leaflets from a plastic holder. She hands it to me. *Putting Your Children First*.

The sick feeling that was in my stomach five minutes ago has reached my throat.

A timer on her desk gives a short, shrill ring.

Before she tells me that our time is up, I stand. I have to swallow before I speak.

'My husband's name is Jack Donnelly. Do you know him?'

This is what I came here for. I keep my eyes on her face. She frowns, opening her mouth, but it takes her a few moments to say, 'Jack. Yes, I know him.'

She didn't elaborate on how she knew Jack, but I hadn't expected her to confess, either. She had given me her card, and said to call if I wanted to go ahead. How unprofessional would that be, to represent me while having an affair with the other party?

I take out the card I stuffed into my pocket.

Matthew Smith. Family Law Solicitor.

It's not hers.

I reach my car and get in quickly. I grab an empty crisp packet, just in time, and I vomit into it.

Chapter Nineteen

Monday, 14 July 1986

Debbie

It took us nearly two hours to get out of the house. When I put on my jacket the first time, Annie decided that her feed shouldn't be in her little stomach, but all over me. After only three hours' sleep last night, and nightmares of shadows watching me through the window, I wanted to crawl up the stairs and never come down. But I needed to visit Uncle Charlie. I haven't been since Annie was born.

It's so peaceful here. The only sound is of the wind chimes over the graves of the little ones *gone too soon*. Mum said that Mrs Taunton, one of the more outspoken parishioners, tried to get the teddies and plastic windmills banned from the cemetery. But Father Matthew put a stop to her petition. 'There's enough to protest about these days,' he said, 'without upsetting those poor parents any further.'

I'd like to be buried here. Though that's a bit morbid, isn't it? I'm sitting on a bench facing the row of children's head-stones. They're in front of Charlie's. I know all their names by heart, and every one of them is tended. There are no dead flowers or soggy cards, unlike some of the older ones behind them.

I used to see a woman visiting Albert Jenkins' grave every time I came here at two o'clock on a Monday. It was months between me last seeing her, and her name being added under Albert's – a fresh mound of earth on top. I didn't like to think of her, the woman with a twinkle in her eye, lying under the heavy soil. It didn't seem right. Lilian, she was called. I only found that out from her gravestone. I should've said hello to her, at least once.

Uncle Charlie's grave always has flowers on it. Mum comes every Sunday after Mass, 'To visit them all,' she says. I never met my grandmother or my grandfather. They'd been dead years before I was born. Poor Mum and Charlie, losing their parents so young. My grandfather had been a piano teacher: one of the few little details I know about him because it's so unlike anyone in our family to play the piano. 'It's something only wealthy folk do,' Dad used to say, ''cos they've got too much time on their hands.'

I reach under the pram for the three roses I snipped from the bush in our front garden (probably planted by the people who rented it before us). I leave Annie in her pram, next to the other children and make my way towards Charlie.

I place two on my grandparents' grave, before putting the other stem into Charlie's vase. I wipe the bits of mud from the year of his birth.

'All better now.'

I look around; there's no one else here.

'Now what's all this business of you talking to me?'

There's silence. What else did I expect?

'You're going to get me into trouble. The men in white coats are going to cart me off.'

A breeze blows across my face.

'I'll have to get going, Uncle Charlie.'

I stand and look over to Annie's pram.

There's a man crouching over it. Where the hell did he come from?

'Hey!' I shout.

My feet are unsteady as I run towards her pram. I'm running over graves, whispering, 'Sorry.'

The man stands.

'Nathan?' I blink several times. 'What are you doing here? Why are you dressed like that?'

He's usually in a shirt and tie during the day, but he's wearing a black tracksuit with white stripes down the side.

'I've just been jogging,' he says.

'Oh. You must have run a fair bit – it's miles from your work.'

His eyebrows rise, and he looks at his watch – it's different to the one he wore the other day. He used to love that expensive watch.

'Yes, I suppose it is. Must've got carried away.'

I pull the pram handles towards me. Annie's eyes are open; she's awake, staring at the sky.

'I didn't wake her,' he says. 'She was already like that. You should be more careful, leaving her like that.'

'I was only over there, it's—'

'Hey.' He raises his hands in front of him. 'I was only joking.'

'Hmm.' I get a wet wipe from the changing bag and clean the mud from my hands. 'Did you know I'd be here?'

'What? No, of course not. How would I know that?'

I shrug. 'Did you know Monica met up with Peter in town?'

I don't know why I'm mentioning it – I'm trying to forget about it.

He frowns. 'No,' he says. 'Why would they meet on their own?'

'To talk about the holiday, probably.' I look at the ground. Monica's right: I'm rubbish at lying. 'Anyway. Shouldn't you be getting back?' I look at my wrist, but I've forgotten my watch. 'Oh no, what's the time?'

125

'Three o'clock.'

'I've got to get Bobby in half an hour.'

'I could give you a lift if you want?'

'It's okay. If I walk quickly, I should make it. Bye, Nathan.'

It's difficult to run while pushing a pram. I'm not that far from school, but I like to be early. It feels as though everyone's staring at me. Being unable to use my arms means that I'm panting by the time I get to the gates. Cue the dirty looks from the immaculate mothers. You'd think I was brandishing a chainsaw from the glances I'm getting.

I look down at my clothes. Okay, muddy knees on my jeans from the cemetery, but otherwise nothing inappropriate. Shoes on, top buttoned. My hair's probably a mess, but when isn't it these days?

I reach into my bag for my sunglasses, so I can look at them without them seeing. There are no muddy patches or stains on *their* clothes. Their hairstyles are almost identical – all layered, either in the style of Princess Diana or Farah Fawcett, which says it all, really. They wouldn't know Blondie if she were standing in front of them.

Another member of their clan jogs up to them in her sports outfit, complete with leg warmers and a head band. Bloody hell – she thinks she's Jane Fonda.

I quickly look at my nails as she catches me grinning at her outfit. She actually tuts. I doubt she's run that far anyway; she's not even sweating.

Nathan.

He wasn't sweating either.

No, I'm reading too much into it.

I could give you a lift if you want?

He hadn't been jogging at all.

★　★　★

126

Everything's strange – it's like I'm watching an episode of *Tales of the Unexpected*. When I got home from school with Bobby, Peter was in the kitchen making spaghetti bolognese.

'Someone told me about it at work,' he said. 'Couldn't wait to get started.'

'Obviously,' I said. 'It's not even four o'clock.'

Now, we're sitting around the table at twenty to six, surrounded by every pan and utensil we own scattered on the kitchen work surfaces.

'Well,' says Peter. 'I think I did a good job. I don't know what all the fuss is about with this cooking lark.'

I open my mouth, but I don't say what I'm thinking: that it took over two hours, my plate is swamped with watery liquid from the sauce, and I would've preferred chicken crispy pancakes.

'Well done,' I say, instead. Because that's what I ought to say, because I'm trying to be as nice as he is today.

Bobby's face is covered in red sauce; he looks like he's been in an accident. 'What's for pudding?' he says.

We both look to Peter.

'I . . . er . . . I thought we could have a banana.'

I try not to sigh out loud. 'I'll make some custard to go with it.'

I fill a pan with milk, and press the ignite switch so the gas hob lights with a whoosh.

I look outside through the kitchen window. The back yard looks so grey when it's raining. I wish we had a proper garden.

I jump as Peter puts his hands on my shoulders.

'I know what you're thinking,' he says, looking outside too. 'You're wishing I'd put that washing line up, aren't you?'

I don't think he knows me at all.

I just smile.

★   ★   ★

127

Peter didn't complain once through *Coronation Street*.

'Do you know,' he said halfway through, 'that there's a surge of electricity on the grid at exactly seven forty-five on Mondays and Wednesdays. Do you know why?'

I was already in my nightie, and held a hot-water bottle to my tummy. I'd forgotten how painful it is after birth.

'No,' I said.

'Because, at the EOPO, everyone puts the kettle on. Isn't that funny?'

'EOPO?'

'End of part one.'

He looked very pleased with this.

'I've taped that other one – *Albion Market*,' he says now, as the end credits of *Coronation Street* play. 'I thought we might watch it together.'

'Has someone new started at work?' I say.

'No. Why?'

'No reason.'

I wonder, briefly, what spurred him into watching programmes he's never seen, or to cook from scratch when he's never shown interest before.

I fake a stretch and get up from the settee, my hot-water bottle falling to the floor.

'Think I'll head up for an early night,' I say.

'Already? What about *Albion Market*? Tony Booth's in it, you know.'

If he says *Albion Market* one more time, I'll scream.

'It sounds very . . . fascinating, but I've had a long day.'

'Have you now.'

I don't take the bait. I go over to him and place a kiss on his cheek. 'See you up there.'

'Hmm.'

I haven't got the energy for it. Annie went to sleep two

hours ago. I'll be lucky to get an hour's sleep before she wakes again.

I close the lounge door, and go to check the front door's locked.

There's another pink letter.

Has Dean nothing better to do?

I pick it up and put it in my dressing-gown pocket. I can't be bothered to deal with it right now.

Chapter Twenty

I'd forgotten how cold it is in the North. It's July, but it's freezing in this bed and breakfast. There's a storage heater under the window – why are they always *under the window*? I don't think it's worked since the 1980s. I don't think this place has been decorated since then, either. There's a television on a stand in the corner near the ceiling, so you need to be lying on the bed to watch it. Next to the bed is the window. It's like being *in there* again.

It was the view outside that kept me going – the sounds that leaked through. The rain beating down and the birds singing when the sun came out.

I didn't have to think about when to eat, when to turn the lights off, because those decisions were made for me. I couldn't sleep most of the time. The noises at night were worse than in the day. I pretended to sleep, though. It was easier that way.

I get up from the bed. It's almost ten o'clock.

There are things I must do.

Chapter Twenty-One

Anna

I wish I could have called in sick again, but I think I would be pushing my luck asking Isobel to cover the bookshop again. It has been raining hard for an hour. It's going to be quiet – apart from the people who will use the shop as a shelter on their way to somewhere else. I will have conversations about the weather with every one of them, and answer each person as though they were the first to talk about it.

The rain tapping on the window makes me feel hemmed in, claustrophobic. It's like all the books on the shelves are gathering and closing in around me. It's too warm in here.

Ellen's due in ten minutes. I haven't seen her since she hid the fact she was looking at the missing persons' website. I should be giving her a chance. I always thought I was quite an open-minded person, but I find her presence intimidating.

The breeze from the shop door opening brings welcome relief.

'Grandad!' I get up from my stool. 'I wasn't expecting you to come in today.'

He turns, briefly, to shake the water from his umbrella onto the step outside. 'Typical weather,' he says. 'Can we not have a bit of sun without the rain spoiling it all the time?' He pats the top of my arm and walks towards the back room. 'I can't be stuck in the house today. The walls are starting to talk back at me.'

I lean against the door frame.

He's looking at the rota on the fridge.

'Oh, good,' he says. 'Sheila's not in today.'

'I thought you two got on.'

'Hmm. She never lets me have a go on the till. She sits there all morning, warming her behind on the heater. And she fancies herself as a church-goer, but she only goes for the tea and biscuits afterwards. She sleeps through most of the service on a Saturday evening. I reckon she thinks no one notices.' He hangs up his anorak and flicks on the kettle. He pulls a round tin from a carrier bag. 'I've made some scones for elevenses. Tea's too wet without a bit of cake.'

'You made scones?'

'I've had to keep myself busy, then I don't think too much,' he says. 'Your gran had a notebook with recipes in, but God rest her soul, she wasn't much of a cook. These are Mary Berry's.'

Ellen will be here in one minute, if she's on time.

'Grandad, I forgot to mention there's a new volunteer. She's called Ellen. She's a bit quiet.'

'I don't mind quiet. I can't bear people who go on and on about themselves.'

'Anyway – I don't think it's a secret, but she was released from prison a few months ago.'

'I see.' He folds the carrier bag and puts it in his coat pocket. 'Well, I suppose she's served her time. We all deserve a second chance.'

'Morning.'

Oh God. How long has Ellen been standing in the doorway? Grandad shrugs, and flicks on the kettle again – the water has to be freshly boiled.

'Cup of tea, Ellen?' says Grandad.

'Yes please, Frank. That's very kind.'

Ellen takes off her coat. 'It's okay, Annie. I'm used to people talking about me. You should've heard the things I got inside.'

'Were they awful to you?'

'Only a few. But you learn to stick up for yourself. Or just merge into the background, like I tried to.'

'I'm sorry.'

'Don't worry. It's okay – it's part of who I am. You don't have to be sensitive on my behalf.'

Grandad walks over, two cups of tea in his hands. He puts them on the sorting table before going into the bookshop. 'Now, stop gassing, you two,' he says. 'There'll be customers to serve.' He sits on the stool and drums his fingers on the counter. 'Any minute now.'

'These are the best scones I've had in a long time,' says Ellen.

'I dare say they are, love,' says Grandad.

It's eleven o'clock and the bookshop is quiet, so we're sitting around the sorting table.

'Do you read much, Ellen?' I say, trying to sweep Grandad's insinuation under the table.

'I do,' says Ellen. 'I quite like crime fiction.'

Grandad raises his eyebrows, and takes a bite of scone.

'What's your new flat like?' I say. 'Have you settled in?'

'I'm not in there yet. Next week. I'm in a B & B at the moment.'

'Well that sounds just the job,' says Grandad, no doubt picturing a grand establishment in the Lake District. 'Imagine, having your breakfast cooked for you every morning.'

'It's not like that,' says Ellen. 'I have to be out during the day. And I'm lucky if there's a mini box of cereal outside my door in the morning.'

'Oh, Ellen,' I say. 'That's awful. What do you do all day? What about your meals?'

'I have a wander around the shops. And there's the drop-in centre. They have soup every day.'

'Oh.' I feel ignorant and patronising.

'Really, Annie, you don't have to worry about me. I'm a big girl.'

'If you ever want more shifts here . . . I know it's not the most interesting of places, but—'

'Thank you.' She stands and takes each of our plates. 'And I love coming here.' She places the dishes in the sink and runs the hot tap. 'It's like coming home.'

My grandfather is very good at putting on a brave face. To see him today, mixing with the few customers who came in, you wouldn't know he has been trying to take his mind off his daughter. He usually finishes at twelve, but I think he's hanging on until Ellen leaves, so he can talk about her. They have hardly spoken to each other, which is odd, as Grandad is usually a master of small talk. I've caught him looking at Ellen more than a few times.

He stays seated at the counter as she comes out of the back room with her coat on.

'Are you sure you want to go now?' I say to her. 'You're welcome to stay longer.'

'It's okay. I'm meeting a friend for lunch.' She walks towards the door. 'I'll see you next week – if I don't pop in before.'

The door is only closed for a second before Grandad says, 'How did she know my name?'

'What do you mean?'

'We'd not been introduced, but she addressed me by name.'

'She probably read the rota.'

'But I'm not down for . . . oh, never mind.'

'What is it? Grandad?'

'It's just this feeling I've got – like I've seen her before.'

'She's got the same birthday as Debbie. It's on her CV.'

Grandad narrows his eyes at me.

'You've got to stop saying things like that.' He gets off his stool, not looking at me. He goes into the back.

Why do I keep thinking stupid thoughts? Sometimes I think they won't go away. My counsellor said I should be honest with the people I'm closest to.

'I'm sorry,' I say into the other room. 'You're not going, are you?'

He walks back into the bookshop with his anorak on.

'I'm just off down the road to get us some butties.'

He comes back in soaking wet after forgetting his umbrella.

'Well, that woke me up,' he says. 'I hope you're not still vegetarian because they only had beef or "tuna surprise".'

'I haven't been a vegetarian for over ten years.'

He sits on the stool behind the counter, so I grab a chair from the back and sit in the doorway, ready to jump up in case Isobel comes in. Grandad hands me the tuna sandwich.

'I can't be eating things like that,' he says. 'You never know what the *surprise* is going to be.'

I peel it open. 'I saw Monica yesterday,' I say.

'Hmm.' He swallows his mouthful with a gulp. 'Don't you see her every week anyway?'

'It wasn't Sophie's day there. Anyway, Monica mentioned something about Dad – how he was after Debbie went missing.'

Grandad straightens on the stool.

'She said Gran moved in with us – with Dad and me and Robert.'

He places his sandwich on the counter, using a sheet of paper as a plate. 'Why is she bringing that up now?'

'Because of the email. She wanted me to know why Robert's so upset.'

'But why tell *you*? You've been the only one who doesn't remember. Why is she doing this to you? We gave you the best start without all of this affecting you.'

'But . . . I know, Grandad. You're right. In some ways, I am fortunate I don't remember her . . . but I'd give anything to have a real memory of her in my mind – not just a photograph.'

He pats my knee. 'I understand, love,' he says. 'What exactly did she say?'

'Who?'

He rolls his eyes.

'Monica. About your dad.'

'That he couldn't cope – that he needed you and Gran's help for two years.'

'Two years is exaggerating it a bit . . . as if your gran would let me be on my own for two years. It was more like two months. And it was no bother to your gran. She loved being with you and Robert. Your father lasted two mornings at the school gates before the whispering and glances got to him. He couldn't do it . . . he called them vultures. They'd heard about it somehow . . . thought he'd done away with her.'

'Done away?'

'No smoke without fire. Don't look at me like that, Anna, it's not what *I* thought – it's what those busybodies without anything better to talk about said.'

I hadn't seriously considered that the police questioned Dad, and that strangers thought he might have killed his wife.

'It didn't help that he answered *no comment* to every question,' says Grandad.

'But that doesn't mean anything. Jack says suspects are told to say that.'

'Yes, they are . . . these days.'

Grandad presses his lips together.

'You don't believe he hurt her, do you, Grandad?'

He puts his barely-touched sandwich back in its wrapper.

'No,' he says, eventually. 'But something's not right. I mean . . .'

'What?'

'They got married, didn't they? Peter and Monica. Debbie would've been horrified.'

'You've never said that before. You really think that?'

He takes a deep breath. 'Oh, I don't know. Don't mention it to them, will you?'

'No, I won't,' I say. 'What do you think happened to her?'

'I've been through it hundreds of times in my head. I often thought it was down to us being so strict with her, that we expected too much from her . . . so she rebelled.' Tears gather in the corners of his eyes. He gets up from the stool. 'But I don't know. Something happened that night. She can't have vanished into thin air.'

I almost have to drag Sophie into the photo shop after last time.

'But what if the witch is there again?' she says.

'Shh,' I say. 'She was just joking.'

'It wasn't a funny joke.'

'Anna Donnelly,' I say to the man behind the counter. 'I've come for my photos.'

He raises his eyebrows: I'm stating the obvious.

'The witch isn't here, anyway,' I whisper, as the man goes into the back room.

'*He* could be her,' says Sophie. 'She has magic. And she prob'ly heard you say *witch*.'

The assistant brings out an A3 envelope and pulls out a packet of photographs. He goes through each one and I try not to look at them. I don't want the first time I see them to be in here. He looks at them so unsympathetically, I want to snatch them from his hands and tell him they're mine.

'A couple of them are over-exposed – they've got stickers on.' He shoves the pictures back into the wallet. 'Which means it's not our fault.'

'Right,' I say. 'I wouldn't have asked for my money back.'

He shrugs. 'You never know with people these days. They don't understand the equipment they're taking photos with.'

'A child took these photos, actually.'

'That explains it.'

I grab the envelope. 'Thank you.'

I stand outside the shop. Should I open them here?

Sophie is jumping up and down.

'I need a wee.'

'Can it wait two minutes?'

'No, Mummy. I'm bursting.'

'Come on then.'

We walk quickly to my car, parked around the corner.

Just one. If I could just look at one.

I reach into the envelope and pull out the wallet, my other hand opening the car door for Sophie.

'My seat belt, Mummy.'

'Yes, yes.'

I fasten her in, close the door, and get into the driver's seat.

I glance at the car parked opposite us. I've seen it a few times this week. There's someone in the driving seat, staring straight at me. I narrow my eyes as I lean towards the window. Is it a man or a woman? Whoever it is starts their engine, reverses and speeds off.

'I'm really bursting,' shouts Sophie.

'Okay, love.'

I close my eyes as I quickly pick out a photo at random.

I switch on the ignition and place the rest of the pictures on the passenger seat.

'We'll be home in five minutes,' I say.

I turn over the picture in my hands, my heart pounding.

I lift it up.

It's a picture of a bloody lizard.

'This is the best tea, me old china,' says Sophie.

'*Me old china*?'

She scoops up her beans with a spoon.

'It's cockney. Miss Graham taught us it. Gramps said he'd get me a book from the library.'

'When did he say that?'

'Last time I was there . . . think it was last month.'

'You mean last week?'

'Yeah. It was June then.'

'Did you tell me about it?'

She nods. I feel awful.

I'm missing all of the little things because my head is taken up with the big things. From now on, all things 'Debbie' will have to be talked about when Sophie is asleep or at school.

The photos are still in their packet on the kitchen counter. I keep glancing at them.

No. I'll have to open them later.

'Did you know Monica was born in London?' says Sophie. 'But it wasn't near the bluebells, so she's not a real cockney.'

'I think you mean Bow bells, love.'

At exactly five thirty, the front door opens and closes. Jack hasn't been home on time this week.

He comes into the kitchen. There are bags under his eyes and he hasn't shaved for days.

'Daddy! Me old china.' Sophie puts together the knife and

fork on her plate, slides off the chair and grabs her dad round the waist.

'*Me old china*?' whispers Jack. 'It sounds so strange in her little voice.'

'I think it's the one bit of cockney rhyming slang she's learnt.'

'Oh.' Jack smiles at Sophie – at least, he's trying to; his eyes have no shine.

'I've saved you some fish fingers,' I say. 'Only five-star service here.' I pull the tray out of the oven – the golden crumb is now brown. 'I'll make something else. I haven't eaten yet either.'

'No, no. They're fine. I could do with some comfort food.'

'Elly's invited me to her swimming party,' says Sophie, sitting back at the table. 'Can I go?'

I open her book bag and take out the invitation, attaching it to the fridge with a magnet.

'Of course you can. Daddy'll take you.'

'Why can't *you* take me? You never go with me to swimming.'

'I just don't like the water, that's all. It . . . er . . . makes my hair go funny.'

'But you like water in the bath.'

'That's different.'

Monica had paid for private swimming lessons for me when I was eight years old, because at school I was the only one who would scream if the teacher tried to guide me into the water. 'Poor Orphan Annie,' my classmates would shout, flicking water at me from the pool. 'Boo hoo, boo hoo.'

The teacher would tell them off, of course, but that didn't stop the snide comments.

The nearest I got to the water, during these private lessons, was dangling my feet in, my little knees knocking together as they shook. 'Well, Annie,' Monica said after the third (and last) session, 'we can't say you didn't try.'

'Sorry, Sophie,' I say now. 'But Daddy loves swimming.'

'Hmm.' She pushes her empty plate into the centre of the table. 'Can I go up the apples and pears? Harry in my class showed me how to make Minecraft figures from Lego.'

'Course you can.' Jack sits at the table as Sophie stands and runs out of the kitchen. 'Two phrases she's learned, then.'

Sophie thumps up the stairs as I sit down opposite Jack, handing him a plate with five frazzled fish fingers.

'You look really tired,' I say.

He rubs his eyes.

'I haven't been sleeping well.'

'What can be so bad at work that it's keeping you awake at night?'

'Did I say it was work?'

'The other day . . . you said you had a tough case.'

He cuts a fish finger and it almost snaps in half.

'Did I?' He shrugs. 'That must be it then.'

I take a deep breath.

'If there's something I should know – you can tell me.'

He crunches the food loudly; I try to not let it bother me this time. His eyes focus on the table. Has he even heard me?

'What? No,' he says. 'Where did that come from?'

'You've been distant . . . spending all of your time in your office . . . sleeping there.'

'*You* can talk,' he says.

'Pardon?'

'You've been obsessed with that email. It's just like that woman last time.'

'It's not like last time. This is something real.'

'Is it?'

He stands, and pours the rest of the fish fingers into the bin, slamming the plate onto the counter. He breathes slowly through his mouth.

'Look,' he says. 'I'm sorry. Really, I am, Anna. There's nothing wrong. It's *you* I'm worried about. It's just . . . I don't know why you're getting your hopes up, like the last time – however misguided you were then.'

I look down at my hands on the table; they're shaking. I'm with my husband – my hands shouldn't tremble with Jack.

'One of those private investigators called,' he says. 'Wanting to know if you were really my wife.'

'Why would he do that?'

'It was a woman. And I don't know . . . probably because we're charging it to my firm's account – she might have been ripped off in the past. At least we know she's thorough.'

'What did you say to her?'

'I said you *were* my wife, obviously.'

He grabs the plate and rinses it under the tap.

'What will she be investigating?' he says. 'It's just about Debbie, isn't it?'

'What else is there to investigate?'

'Just checking you didn't have any other long-lost relatives.' He tries to smile again. 'So I can estimate the cost.'

'No. It's just Debbie.'

He rubs my back between my shoulder blades.

'Good, good.' He kisses the top of my head, and walks to the door. 'I've got to do a bit of work upstairs, then I'll try to be back down before nine.'

I don't reply. He doesn't wait for one.

What just happened?

I asked him what was wrong, and he turned it back on me. Again.

But I lied as well. Francesca King must have said something to Jack.

It's not just Debbie I'm going to investigate. It's him as well.

★   ★   ★

It's eight o'clock and there is no sound from upstairs. Sophie is asleep, and I doubt Jack will come down again, so I've laid out Robert's photos on the kitchen table. There are twenty-seven altogether – seven of which are blurred; three of what I assume is Robert's hand, and four of lizards. The rest are pictures of Dad, Debbie, my pram, and Monica with her first husband, Nathan.

The photos displayed in our house when we were growing up were only ever of us five – Monica, Dad, Leo, Robert and me. Two partial families brought together. It's like Dad and Monica wanted to rewrite history: to erase the people who hurt them. I have always had an image of Nathan in my head that is like Dad, only a little bit different. But he is Dad's opposite. Dad is tall with red hair, which is mainly blonde and grey now, and his white skin is freckled. Nathan is also tall, but lean, tanned, and his hair is almost jet black. And he is very good-looking. In one photo, Monica and Nathan are sitting next to each other, leaning back against white plastic chairs. They are smiling, and Monica's head is leaning towards his, with Nathan's arm resting casually on her leg. Understated, yet intimate. Had they just said *cheese* at the command of the little boy taking their picture? They suit one another.

In another photo, Dad is standing at a huge barbecue, with a sausage on a fork in one hand, and a bottle of beer in another. His hair is a shiny chestnut colour and the freckles on the bridge of his nose have joined together to give him a tan. The skin around his eyes is creased as he smiles. It's like he had no worries at all, standing there in shorts and a T-shirt with his family and friends.

Poor Dad.

One of my tears drop onto the picture. I rush to get a piece of kitchen roll and dab it off before it makes a stain. I wipe my face with it and stuff the tissue up my sleeve.

There's a strange picture of green-neon stripes that I can't work out, but the next one is of Nathan kneeling at my buggy.

My feet are resting on his chest; he must have put them there – I was too young to do that myself.

He's smiling at me, this stranger. Though I wasn't a stranger to *him*. He'd known me since the day I was born. It's a peculiar feeling, knowing someone was close to you and you don't recall them at all.

'What happened to you all?' I whisper.

The next photo is of a glass bottle of Coca Cola, but in the distance, sitting at a table, are Debbie and Nathan. They look as though they're about to—

'Talking to yourself again?'

I stand up straight.

'Jack! How long have you been standing there? I didn't think you'd be back down tonight.'

'I couldn't leave you on your own again, could I?'

He has an empty wine glass in his hand, which he takes to the fridge to refill. It's probably the real reason he came downstairs.

'You got them then?' he says, looking down at the table. 'Wow – your brother had a thing for lizards.'

I smile. 'Seems like it. Though I don't think he appreciates them as much now.'

'Oh, I don't know – his ex-wife had a few reptilian characteristics.'

'Very funny. She wasn't that bad.'

I collect the photographs carefully into a pile and place them back into the wallet. 'Have you finished working for tonight?'

'There's nothing that can't wait until the morning. I thought we might watch a film together – try and switch off from everything for one night.'

'All right,' I say. 'I'll try.'

I grab a glass from the cupboard and pour myself a glass of wine. It's the only way I'll be able to forget about anything tonight.

Chapter Twenty-Two

Tuesday, 15 July 1986

Debbie

Two thirty in the morning. I'd forgotten about the tiredness with newborns. How could anyone forget that? I'm so exhausted I could sit and cry. I had to bring Annie downstairs; she won't settle. I've been pacing the living room for forty-five minutes. I tried singing 'Hush, Little Baby', but I couldn't hear my own voice over her screams. It used to work with Bobby.

It's been three hours since her last feed. Hungry. She must be hungry. Again. I thought she'd sleep at least four hours at night by now.

I grab a bottle from the fridge and place it into a jug of boiling water, carrying it back into the living room. I grab the flicker and turn on the telly: teletext is better than nothing. Don't the television people realise that not everyone is asleep after midnight? Not that I'd be able to watch anything, even on tape. Every time I stop pacing the living room, she shrieks.

I check the milk on my wrist. A tiny bit too warm, but it'll do. I put it to her mouth and she starts gulping it down; maybe she likes it hotter.

I fall back onto the settee, trying to concentrate on the words on the telly, but they're blurred. Blink, blink. I can't fall asleep while she's drinking.

It's so quiet at this time of the morning. All the little worries I have in the day double in size and it feels as though they're ganging up on me. Who is making Peter so happy? It certainly isn't me. And for him to cook tea; that hasn't happened for years, not since before the kids were born. He could be planning to leave me. He might leave in the middle of the night. No, that wouldn't happen – he never wakes once he's asleep.

Nathan.

Why was he pretending to be out jogging? Unless he wasn't pretending for my benefit, but so I'd tell Monica. Perhaps they're all in it together. They think I'm crazy and they're planning ways to tip me over the edge.

As I sit up, I hear the crackle of the envelope in my pocket. The note that came last night. I'd forgotten about it.

I hold Annie's bottle in the hand of the arm she's resting on, and take the letter from my pocket. The envelope's not hard to pull apart; it's not stuck down. I flick it open and shake the note from inside. I can see already it has more writing on the paper than the last one.

I place the letter on my lap and unfold it.

You ought to be more careful with that baby of yours – keep her close next time. You never know who's watching.

I throw the letter onto the carpet.

It can't be for Peter – he's not been alone with Annie since she was born. Someone knows what I've been doing – that I left the baby outside the shop, and at the cemetery. I have to tell someone about these letters: Peter, the police.

My heart's thumping. Can Annie feel it?

She's looking up at me; the bottle's empty. Her lovely blue eyes are gazing at my face, trying to take me all in.

'I'll never let anyone hurt you, little girl.'

We both startle as a car door slams outside. I get up to turn the big light off, and tiptoe to the window. I don't know why I'm trying to be quiet – it's not as if anyone outside can hear me.

I place Annie on the armchair next to the window, putting a cushion along the edge of the seat.

I peer through the gap between the curtains.

There's someone standing next to Trisha's car, over the road – a man.

I open the curtains a few inches wider.

He takes something out of the boot and dumps it on the pavement. I stand on my toes, but I can't see anything, except the shine of a bin liner.

I look back to the man.

He's staring straight at me.

I duck down, almost catching my chin on the window sill. He must've seen me – the telly's giving off light; I should've switched it off.

My heart's thumping.

The car boot slams shut.

I wait a few seconds to give him time to leave, before slowly standing up again.

He's next to our gate, just looking at me.

It's Dean.

I can't move. My knees are shaking.

He brings his hand up. What's he doing?

He taps his nose three times. He's laughing at me, shaking his head.

I grab each curtain and pull them together sharply to close the small gap.

'There, there,' I say to Annie as I pick her up, even though she's perfectly fine. I hold her close to me as I climb the stairs.

She doesn't whimper or cry as I place her in the cot.

I wish Peter would wake at least once in the night, just to ask if I'm okay. Tonight, I'd tell him, no. No, I'm not okay.

I try to see things from other people's point of view. In the early hours of this morning, Dean probably thought I was a nosy housewife spying on him in the middle of the night. To him, I'm the crazy one. Did I think he'd killed Trisha and was getting rid of the body? Whatever was in that bin liner wasn't big enough for that.

Trisha's car's not outside this morning. Perhaps I fell asleep and dreamt the whole thing.

'She slept through the night then?' asks Peter, as he eats his toast. He walks into the living room, getting crumbs all over the carpet – not that it'll make any difference; I mustn't have hoovered this week.

'No,' I say. 'She woke three times.'

'Really? I didn't hear a thing.'

'You never do.'

'A bit tired, are we?'

Why can't he accept that sometimes it might be *him* I have the problem with, and it's not just my lack of sleep?

'Yes. I only had four hours' sleep at most.'

'It'll get better,' he says, kissing my forehead.

I wipe off the smear of butter he left on my skin.

'I would've helped get Bobby dressed,' he says, 'but I never know where anything is.'

'It's where it always is.' I don't have the strength to say more about it. 'Dean was outside last night,' I say. 'Getting something out of Trisha's boot. He saw me looking at him.'

Peter laughs. '*Coronation Street*'s got nothing on Dean, eh? Wonder what dodgy scheme he's involved with this time.'

I should've known that it was my imagination. Listening to myself describe it to Peter makes it sounds ridiculously dull – just a bloke going about his business. Not someone watching me, trying to scare me, which is far worse than him sending me notes.

'Peter . . . I've got something to show you. These letters came through the letterbox – I've kept them upstairs. I think—'

'Can we talk about this tonight, Debs? I've got an early meeting in Manchester this morning. Head office is thinking of having a twenty-five-million-pound sale at Woolies this Christmas. I know the company's doing well and everything, but that's just ridiculous. It'll never happen.'

'I suppose it can wait.'

He bends down to rub Bobby's hair; he's watching one of his videos before school.

'Catch you later, kid,' says Peter.

And then he's gone.

I get up and go to the window, watching Peter as he leaves. I should get rid of these old-fashioned net curtains, but they come in handy during the day when Annie's asleep and I want to watch the world go by. Peter's whistling as he strolls down the path and out of the gate. I wonder what it's like to be in his head – to know what being happy in the morning is like. He gets to go out and talk to people – people who answer him back, like he's a proper human being. I try to imagine going back to work and I can't. The feeling still fills me with panic. I'm safe here – with my children. I don't have to dread Sundays and feel the anxiety of mixing with strangers. That's what I tell myself.

'It's finished, Mummy,' says Bobby. 'Can I watch another?'

'What?'

I must remember my children are the important ones in my world. They depend on me.

'Sorry . . . yes. But we've got to leave for school in ten minutes, Bobs. Maybe just a short one.'

I sit on the settee and watch as he picks one of his three videos, ejecting the last, and putting in another. When did he get so independent? While I wasn't looking, I suppose. He's had to fend for himself a bit more now Annie's here. I've nothing to compare it to – it was only me as a child.

The theme to *Thomas the Tank Engine* blares into the living room. All the talk of useful engines reminds me that I can't just sit around being lazy. I go into the hall and grab Bobby's shoes. The letterbox rattles as something's pushed through it. I glance over, but it's just a folded leaflet – not another pink envelope, and I breathe again.

I pick it up from the mat and it drops open.

It's a flyer for Weight Watchers.

Bloody charming.

I look at the top and it has my name written on it in blue ink – the writing's loopy and slanted.

'The cheek of it!' I say aloud.

I open the front door and run to the gate. I look to my right and there's a boy at the end of the street, running away from me. I look to the left. No one else is posting leaflets – why would he just post it into our letterbox?

Dean and Trisha's door is pulled ajar.

God, I hope it's not Dean again.

My feet are stuck to the path. I need to get inside before it opens fully.

'All right, Debs?'

It's Trisha. Looking immaculate as ever. She must've got up at five o'clock in the morning for that make-up job.

'Yes, yes. Just getting the milk in.'

She looks at my hand, which is still holding the scrunched-up leaflet.

'Milkman ignored the note for one more today,' I say.

'Oh right.' She raises her eyebrows, not even pretending to

150

be interested in my boring life. She bends to pick her milk up. 'Have a nice day!'

She's in her own world, that one. Bet she doesn't even know who the Prime Minister is. Though if she does, I bet she loves Thatcher – people who own their own houses always do.

I look at our empty crate. We must be behind on the milk payments again – they build up too quickly. I slam the front door shut behind me and slump to the hall floor. Trisha must be in on it too. I'm sure she used to be nice to me. Didn't she? Or was it fake?

'*You've got to make yourself useful.*'

That voice, again.

'What?' I say. 'Who's that?'

I crawl into the living room. Bobby's already turned the telly off. How did *he* get so useful? He's standing in the middle of the living room, already wearing his shoes.

'Who put them on for you?'

'Me. Monica taught me.'

'Is she here? I think I heard her.'

'Are you all right, Mummy?' He walks over to me. I'm still on all fours. He puts his hand on my forehead. 'You look sad.'

'I'm fine, fine. I think I might've heard the telly.'

I slowly get up, looking behind Bobby, but there's no one there.

'Let's go a bit early,' I say, grabbing my jacket off the settee. I help him into his coat, and place Annie in the pram.

As we walk down the street, I sense someone watching me. Everyone's watching me. People stare at me as I walk past them.

What's happening to me?

I feel a little calmer on the walk home from school. Claire, one of the nice mums, talked to me at the gates. She's pregnant with her third child, God help her.

'What do you do all day?' I asked her.

'This one's a bit of a handful,' she said, tugging on the hand of her three-year-old daughter. 'I just aim to get through the day, keeping them alive until bedtime.' She smiled. 'If you're getting a bit . . .' she leant closer, 'bored or lonely, feel free to pop round for a brew. Think I'm only around the corner from you. I'd suggest one of the mother-and-baby groups, but they're all run by Princess Diana over there.' She nodded to one of the clan, and straightened back up, rubbing her back. 'Nine months seems to take longer and longer each time.'

A new friend is just what I need. Monica's working full-time now, and I can't share my problems with my mother – it'd make her worry even more. The trouble is, though, how much do you confide to someone you hardly know?

I turn the corner onto our road. Trisha's car's back again. Dean's polishing the bonnet. Why isn't he using his own car? I grab the pram handles, intending to turn around, but I'm too slow. He's already seen me.

He stands and watches as I walk the last thirty yards to our gate.

Please don't talk to me, please don't—

'I'm surprised you're up and about so early,' he says, 'after your late-night shenanigans.'

I turn the pram ninety degrees so my back faces our front gate.

'You not speaking today?' he shouts. 'Peter in the doghouse?'

'Trisha not working today?' I say.

'Course. She's always working, isn't she?'

I shrug.

'I've got the day off,' he says.

He's walking towards me. He always has the day off.

I reach behind for the gate, but it's jammed. Come on, you stupid thing.

He's standing just a foot away from me. He leans his upper body towards me. I can smell stale beer on his breath. I close my eyes.

'Please don't hurt me.'

The gate swings into life and bangs against the fence.

I open my eyes as Dean pulls back his hand.

'Hurt you? I'm not gonna hurt you.' He's laughing at me again. 'Tell you something, Debs. When you women have babies, it turns you cuckoo.' He taps the side of his head as he walks backwards into the road.

The stupid, chauvinist bastard. Where's a speeding car when you need one?

He turns his head back and looks at me.

'Boo!'

I wish I hadn't jumped.

He laughs, and mutters something under his breath.

I wrestle the pram through the gate and walk backwards to the door. I'm going too slow.

I pick Annie out of the pram and open the front door, leaving the pram in the garden. I run into the kitchen and get a glass of water one-handed as I hold Annie tight.

I down it in one, but it doesn't help.

I walk into the lounge. There are toys everywhere . . . open video cases and at least three empty bowls of cereal, and four – five – cups, one of which has curdled tea inside, litter the living-room floor. Have they been there long? How have I missed them?

I pack a bag for Annie, grabbing her bottles from the fridge.

I need to get out of this house.

Chapter Twenty-Three

Anna

I'm on my own in the bookshop today, which is just as well as I have a headache from the two glasses of wine I drank last night. When had I become such a lightweight? Jack and I used to drink a bottle of wine each when we started going out. Before marriage, before Sophie.

Jack put on a rubbish action film last night and we sat in silence. There was a time we would have thought the film ridiculous, laughing at the ham-fisted fighting, before putting on something else.

I had glanced at him sideways. He didn't look much different from when we met – perhaps his hair was greyer at the sides, and he had dark circles under his eyes, but he wasn't sleeping properly. That's what he said, anyway.

I kept practising sentences in my head: *I know about you and Francesca, and the letter in your wallet.* But I couldn't get the words out – he would say I was losing my mind. Again. He'd turn something he had done wrong into something *I'd* done. I'd have to get evidence first, and then confront him with it. I should just ask him – tell him I found the letter when I was looking for something else.

154

Why did I keep thinking these thoughts? Jack has never been unfaithful. What happened in the past was all me.

I met Gillian Crossley seven years ago – when I'd only been at the Preston branch of the charity-bookshop chain for a few weeks. I was pregnant with Sophie, and it was the first time I had been in the bakery she worked in; it was only a few doors down from my shop.

She treated me like an old friend. Her cheeks were flushed with the heat of the ovens and her long dark hair was captured in a net that rested on her shoulders.

'Hello,' I said to her. 'I'm the new manager of the charity bookshop.'

'Oh, you must be Annie!' she said the first time we met; her smile was beaming, infectious. 'I heard you replaced Evelyn as manager – *and* that you're a lot nicer than she is.' She winked at me. I didn't tell her that I preferred 'Anna', as it was nice hearing her call me Annie. People always got my name wrong.

I just smiled.

'I bet you like carrot cake, don't you?' she said.

'Yes,' I said, quietly, trying to find my voice. 'I can't eat too much though – I'm trying not to eat for two.'

She grabbed a piece from the display cabinet, wrapped it in a paper bag and carefully twisted the corners shut.

'Here's a slice on me,' she whispered, glancing to the back. 'Don't tell my boss, though. And don't worry about *your* boss, Isobel. She might give you a hard time, but she's like that with everyone . . . even us and we don't work for her.' She put the cake into a carrier bag with my sandwich. 'I love your bookshop – reading and contributing to charity at the same time. Nothing like a bit of escapism. If you ever get any books about Blondie in, I'll buy them. Obsessed, I am.'

I took the bag from her and muttered, 'Will do.'

Debbie liked Blondie, I thought. It was on my list.

I reached for my phone as I left the bakery, and took a picture of her through the window.

It had to be a sign.

Gillian looked about the same age as Debbie would be.

When I got home that day, Jack was sitting at the kitchen table on his laptop.

'There's a woman at the bakery who was really kind to me,' I said to him. 'She's called Gillian.'

'That's nice,' he said.

I doubted he was listening.

Back then, I kept a photograph of Debbie on the phone table in the hallway: close enough to see every day, but distant enough that she didn't look at me when I watched television.

Jack kept typing on his keyboard. I reached into my handbag and took out my mobile.

'Look,' I said. 'I've got a picture of her. Don't you think she looks like the picture of Debbie by the telephone?'

His fingers stopped mid-air.

'You took a photo of some stranger?'

I held my phone towards him. 'She's not *some stranger*.'

He frowned at me.

'What the hell are you on about, Anna? She looks nothing like Debbie. What are you getting at?'

I looked at the picture of Gillian again. Granted, it was hard to tell through the glass of a shop window, but she had the same hair and she was the same height, the same age. And she had called me Annie.

'Just wait till you see her in person,' I said.

He looked at me for a long time before he said, 'I'm not going to see her in person, am I?' He slammed his laptop shut. 'I'm working upstairs. You should get some sleep – you're not thinking straight.'

He looked at my pregnant belly when he said it – as though

all those hormones running through my body were making me say strange things.

'Fine,' I said, taking four slices of bread out of the packet, a block of cheese from the fridge, and a jar of chilli jam up to bed.

That was just the start of it – though I didn't know that then. I hadn't thought anything I said had been out of the ordinary. I'd seen someone who reminded me of my mother. The mother I couldn't even remember.

I shiver, now, as I recall how much worse it got after that.

The shop door opens, and in walks a woman with curly hair and glasses. She looks to be in her late fifties or early sixties. She is wearing a beige raincoat with the belt straps dangling either side. She doesn't even glance at the bookshelves; she strides straight towards me. I get up from the stool.

'Sally Munroe,' she says, holding her right hand out in front of me. 'Private investigator.'

I shake her hand. 'I—'

'You're Anna Donnelly. I would've come to your house but . . .' She walks to the back room, grabbing each side of the doorway and leaning into it as she looks around.

'But what?' I say.

'There was something not quite right about what your husband said to me.'

She comes to stand in front of the counter again, only looking at me for the briefest of moments. Her eyes dart around as though she is looking for something. She glances at the clock and I make sure my mobile is still under the counter should I need to call for help.

'Your husband doesn't usually pop in at lunchtime, does he?' she says.

I look at the clock, too. I can't believe it's twelve thirty already. I've been daydreaming again.

157

'No, he doesn't,' I say, sitting back down on the stool, closer to my phone. Jack mentioned a woman telephoning him at work, but she hadn't contacted me in return. 'I wasn't expecting you. Why didn't you just email me back?'

She leans against the counter. She sighs heavily and relaxes her shoulders.

'Sorry about that,' she says. 'I like to get my bearings before talking about sensitive issues. We can't have any Tom or Dick listening in, can we?'

I shake my head. Did she mean to say that wrong?

'The reason I'm here,' she says, 'is for a preliminary meeting. I need to make sure I can work with you. Some people can be high maintenance – can't be doing with that. Can pick and choose my clients these days.'

She reaches into her massive handbag and pulls out a poly-thene pocket. She takes a sheet of paper from it, placing it in front of me.

'I take it you've read about my services online,' she says, 'and that you're happy with me going ahead with any necessary searches?'

'I haven't actually heard from any of the other firms I contacted—'

'Was it Tommy and Kev you contacted?'

'It might have been – are they the other local ones?'

'Yep. Tommy's in the Isle of Man – will be for another few days, I'd say. And Kev . . . well, no one's heard from him in weeks.' Her eyes drift to the side. 'I should look into that at some point. We might be each other's competition, but still . . .' She blinks and looks back at me. 'So?'

'So?'

She rolls her eyes.

'So, if you're happy to sign this, I'll get working on it for you.'

'Sorry,' I say. 'You didn't mention a form to sign.'

She picks up a pen from the counter and hands it to me.

I look down at the paper.

Confidentiality Agreement.

Jack says I should scrutinise everything that needs signing.

'It just means,' says Sally, 'that I won't disclose to a third party the results of my investigation, unless specified by yourself – and, if it contains any evidence of a crime, that I'll be duty-bound to hand over to the local constabulary.'

Her signature is already on the document.

'You've spoken to my husband.' My pen hovers over the dotted line.

'Yes. I wanted to make sure you were who you said you were – and to make sure funds would be available to pay for my services. I've been let down in the past, you see. And I told him I'd deal with Janet, his secretary, about my future invoices.'

'I see.'

'Is something holding you back?' She speaks so quickly. 'Are you sure you want to dig into all of this?'

Hearing her say it makes me realise that I will be taking my search for Debbie to a different level. I won't just have conflicting things my family have told me – the unreliable memories, their feelings about her tainting the information they gave me.

That is, if Sally Munroe is any good at her job.

'Look,' she says. 'If I don't find anything that's of any use to you, then I'll only charge expenses. It's a personal guarantee of mine.'

I sign the piece of paper, already printed with my name.

She picks it up, blows the ink dry and puts it back into the polythene pocket.

'Very good,' she says. 'Now, as soon as is humanly possible, can you email me everything you have – including any little bits of information you think might be irrelevant? You never know. Then we can schedule a meeting convenient to us both. How does that sound?'

'Good,' I say. But I feel out of my depth. 'I have photos, do you want to see them?'

She fastens her bag and puts on a tweed flat cap.

'Well, of course, my dear! I want to see everything.'

She walks towards the door.

'Wait!' I say. 'You said something before – about what my husband said.'

She looks behind her before saying, 'Yes, that's right.' She frowns and pulls down the peak of her cap so it half-covers her eyes. 'He asked if I'd be investigating anything to do with him.'

'And what did you say?'

'I said, "Of course I won't."'

'Oh.'

'But I didn't mean it,' she says, opening the shop door. 'You're the boss.'

She winks at me, and then she's gone.

I closed the bookshop fifteen minutes before I should have, but there is never a sudden late rush for second-hand books, so I headed over to Dad and Monica's. Sophie is in after-school club until five thirty, so I have at least an hour.

'I can't chat for too long,' Dad says. 'Monica reminded me that we've got a thing on at six.'

'What kind of thing?'

'Some wine-and-cheese evening,' he says, waving his hand. 'Seems we're back in the seventies.'

I'm holding the wallet of photos, and he glances at them as he pulls out a chair from under the table. I texted him after I got them, but he didn't reply. He leans forward, his hands clasped in front of him.

'I don't think we should look at them right now,' he says. 'Monica could be down any minute.'

'So?'

'It might upset her.'

'But aren't you curious? These are photos you've never seen of her.'

'We can meet up another day, we'll do lunch.'

He shifts in his chair, his eyes darting to the door, to the window.

'Since when have we ever done lunch? What's wrong, Dad? You look nervous.'

'Nothing. Well, not nothing. Jack phoned me this morning . . . said you've organised some sort of detective to find your mother.'

'Jack phoned you? But his office is going to be paying for the detective – it was his suggestion. I don't understand.'

'Don't think he's going behind your back again – he was just letting me know . . . thought it might've slipped your mind.'

'But that's what I wanted to talk to you about now. It wouldn't just slip my mind. Since when have you and Jack been having cosy chats about me?'

After all the times Jack said he doesn't believe my dad's version of events, why would he phone my dad? It's just like six years ago, when everyone was speaking about me behind my back.

'It wasn't like that, Anna. He wanted to ask me a few questions about it.'

'What questions?'

'The ones he usually asks me when he's drunk . . . if I remembered anything I might have missed before.'

'Really? God. I'm sorry, Dad. I thought he was asking questions about me.'

161

'It was nothing like that, love.'

'I'll have a word with him later.'

'No, don't, really. It's nothing. I've had to answer questions about it for years.'

I place my hand over his.

'I'm sorry.'

He takes his hand from under mine and grasps it.

'Don't you ever say you're sorry. You've been through enough.'

'Do you think . . .'

'What?'

'Do you think, that if we find Debbie . . . that you'd want her back?'

He flattens his hands over mine; he shakes his head.

'I loved your mother . . . with all of my heart. I probably should've told her that more. I should've done a lot of things, but you can't go back in time. But no, in answer to your question. We'd be different people. I was fond of Monica all those years ago, but nothing ever happened between us when Debbie was alive. Now, I adore Monica. She has treated you and Robert as though you were her own. She's been there for me.' He closes his eyes for a few seconds before opening them again. 'I have to be honest with you, Anna. I really don't think this email is from Debbie. It can't be.'

'Why do you say that?'

'I thought it might've been, at first. But why would she just send an email? Why just say a few lines? It didn't even read like she would speak.'

'Did Grandad tell you that he found letters? Poison-pen letters, they looked like. They were with Debbie's things that he'd stored, from the house.'

Dad withdraws his hands from mine.

'No, he didn't. In those days after she left, when I was on

162

my own looking after you and Robert, I remembered that Debbie tried to tell me something, but I was always too busy to listen. All I thought about then was keeping my job. I couldn't stay at home with you all, even when that was all I wanted to do. I had to pay for the roof over our heads. It wasn't like it is now – Debbie left her job six weeks before she had you, and that was that. There weren't day nurseries in abundance. We were meant to just get on with it. I wish I'd listened to her more. She wasn't herself. Perhaps it wasn't about the money – we should've found a way for her to go back to work. But after Robert had started school, we would've had to think about childcare for the holidays.' He rubs his forehead. 'We should've tried harder, I know that. But, like I said, you can't go back in time.'

'Was it because of me? That she left?'

'No, no, no. Don't ever think that, love. It was everything. I think she missed being with adults. I'd have felt the same.' He places his elbows on the table. 'But if there's a remote chance that this email is from Debbie, then no. We would never be together again. Debbie would say the same, I imagine. What I have with Monica is too precious. She was there for us all when I was at rock bottom. She has a heart of gold.'

'This is the most you've ever said to me about all of this.'

'I know. It's been really, really hard. I've not wanted to burden you with it. And Monica is my wife. I love her. She hasn't treated you and Robert any differently to Leo. I've had to put her first, above the memory of your mother. This is all difficult for Monica. She's always felt guilty about her and me.'

'I love Monica, too,' I say. I take a deep breath. 'I met the private investigator today. She's called Sally Munroe. She's going to start working on the investigation as soon as I've emailed her all the details – including the email Debbie sent us the other week.'

'I don't mean to be harsh, love, but whoever sent that message, sent it to Monica's email address. Why would someone do that? If it were Debbie, she'd contact me, or you or Robert. It might be from some crank again – you don't want to be wasting money on a wild-goose chase.'

'What do you mean, *again*? You all keep saying that, but I don't remember anything specific. Robert wouldn't go into details when I asked him.'

Dad sighs.

'Because he doesn't know the details. It was about twenty years ago. A letter came through the post. Again, it was addressed to Monica, but using her old surname.'

He gets up and opens the cupboard above the fridge-freezer.

'Why didn't you tell me this? Why does everyone keep secrets from me all the time?'

'It was a long time ago, love. You were only ten years old and going through all that bother at school. I didn't intentionally keep it from you. In fact, I don't know why I kept it all these years anyway. I took it from Monica, and said I'd burned it.'

The envelope is white, creased. He doesn't open it, but pushes it across the table towards me.

'Best not look at it now,' he says, looking to the kitchen door. 'You'll have questions, and I don't have time to answer them.'

'Did you take it to the police?'

'Anna, the police wouldn't have been interested.'

'But they were interested when Grandad went to the police all those years ago.'

Dad's face drops. Why do I keep saying things that hurt people?

'That was an awful time,' he says. 'I was at the police station, being interrogated, for nearly eight hours. Their questions were relentless – Did Debbie have any financial problems? Was she having an affair? Had I found out and done something to harm her? – I thought that they knew something I didn't. What if I *had* hurt her, but couldn't remember?'

'But they let you go. I know you wouldn't hurt anyone.'

'They didn't look as kindly on me,' he says. 'It's because Debbie left a note.'

'She left a note? And no one thought to tell me this?'

He stands, the chair squeaking across the floor behind him. 'Anna!'

It's Monica.

I cover the envelope with my hand and slide it from the table and into my handbag.

'I didn't hear you come in. What have you got there?'

She's looking at the wallet of photographs on the table. She's wearing make-up, but there are still shadows under her eyes.

'Just some pictures Robert took when he was a kid.' I feel Dad's eyes boring into me. 'But I'll show you two another time. Dad says you have to get going soon.'

'We do?'

'Yes, Mon,' he says. 'We've got that thing tonight, remember?'

'Oh right, the thing.'

She's frowning at him.

I get up, kiss Monica on the cheek, and walk into the hall.

'I was just passing. I've got to get Sophie from after-school club.'

Debbie left a note. I want to ask where it is. My family has never been honest with me. It's too hard to ask what I want to know. If everything was out in the open, we could have had the answers years ago.

Chapter Twenty-Four

Tuesday, 15 July 1986

Debbie

It's still light outside. Downstairs, I can hear the telly on for Bobby, and Mum announced about five minutes ago that she was feeding Annie. All is well, and I don't have to get up. I can stay cocooned in my old single duvet for a while longer. It's bobbled with age, but I love it.

'Shall we ring him, Frank?' says Mum. 'Let him know they're here?'

'I'm not interfering in their marriage,' says Dad. 'Not unless Deborah asks me to.'

They must know I'm listening. I could always hear the pair of them from upstairs when I was growing up, but they never had anything interesting to say then. The rooms are too small, and the walls are too thin, in this house.

When I look up at the ceiling of my old bedroom, I could be fourteen again. I spot the tiny square I carved into the polystyrene tiles. If I remove it, there'll be the little note I put in there. I can't remember what it says. Probably a poem about being in love or my heart breaking or something equally as dramatic. One day, I'll look at it again.

Monica and I always spent time at her mother's house, mainly because she was always out working, and we could smoke cigarettes in their massive kitchen. Monica seemed so glamorous when she started at our school after she moved up from London. The closest I got to London was listening to the Sunday charts on Radio One. I was surprised she hung round with me, when I came from a council estate.

Our house was always freezing. I used to think it was because we'd run out of fifty pences for the meter, until Dad said it was because of Mum. 'She's having her sweats,' he said. 'It's like she's run a marathon.'

She had her hot flushes for years. It was only a few years ago, after Robert was born, that they stopped. She said, 'Why's it freezing in this house? We can't have a baby in a house that's as cold as a cave.'

Dad just rolled his eyes and got the extra fifty pees from a jar he kept in the cupboard under the stairs.

I turn onto my side. The little stereo Dad bought me is still on the wicker table. He's always loved gadgets – he'd buy anything electronic from the junk shop in town, even if it wasn't working. I used to be embarrassed by how little I had in my bedroom. Monica had a telly, a video – even a crimper and a set of heated rollers she never used. I envied her freedom – the fact her mother was always out – but now I'm glad my parents are always home, always here for me.

It's a shame Monica didn't come here more often when we were kids. Mum would've liked it, I think. If Monica lived here, she wouldn't have been as skinny. Mum shows love with food – even if her combinations are a little strange.

What does Mum do when no one's around? She only seems to do things for other people. I try to imagine her lying on a sun lounger, drinking Cinzano – a cigarette in a long holder dangling from her fingers. The thought of it makes me smile. Mum might be fifty-two, but she looks so much older, with her permed grey hair. She always wears that pale-blue tabard to save her clothes from her daily bleaching of the house. When I'm fifty-two, I'm going to look glamorous. If I fast-forward to then, the kids will've grown, and I won't have any responsibilities.

My old cot is at the end of my bed. Dad must've got it down from the loft. He's painted it pastel pink; last time I saw it, it was a deep blue.

There's a gentle tap on the door: it's Dad. Mum would've marched up the stairs and knocked as loudly as she could.

'I'm awake, Dad.'

The bedroom door opens slowly. He stands at the threshold – hands behind his back as though he were waiting for a bus.

'What time is it?' I say.

'Nearly ten past five. Did you manage to get some sleep?'

Peter'll be walking through our front door at any minute. He'll find an empty house.

'I thought it was later than that. I didn't hear you bring the cot in – you must've been quiet.'

'I got that down weeks ago,' he says, 'when Annie was born. We've been looking forward to you all coming round to stay. Will you be stopping long, love? If you are, then I've got a train set in the loft. I'd love to let Bobby have a go on it.'

I pull myself up to a sitting position.

'Since when have you had a train set?'

He shrugs. 'Since you were five. I bought it one Christmas – only second-hand, like – but you were more interested in the knitting set your mother got you.' He rolls his eyes. 'I thought I'd try and make you a tomboy, but you were having none of it.' He smiles.

'How do you remember about the knitting set?' I say. 'I'm sorry, Dad.'

'Give over. I'm only messing.'

168

He sits on the end of the bed.

'You know, love,' he says. 'You can stay here for as long as you like. It's been quiet since you left home, and what with me getting laid off at Leyland . . . well, I'm getting under your mum's feet. She wouldn't notice me as much with a house full.'

'Thanks, Dad. But we won't stop long.'

His eyes look to the floor. Poor Dad. He always talks like he lost his job at British Leyland a few weeks ago, but it's been four years. It must be so alien to him, not going out to work every day. I don't know how they manage, but you can't ask your parents how they afford to put food on the table.

'Peter won't know where we are,' I say. 'I didn't leave a note.'

Dad leans forward, resting his hand on my foot.

'He's not hurt you, has he?'

'What? No, of course he hasn't. Why do you ask that?'

'When we opened the front door earlier, you almost fell into the hall. You barely said a word . . . you just rushed upstairs and got into bed.'

'Did I? I can't remember . . . but that wasn't long ago. Are the kids okay?'

'Annie's asleep in her pram after her feed, and Bobby went straight to the telly – as usual. Anyway . . . it was like you'd just escaped from somewhere. You were frightened of something.'

He looks at the carpet, which has brown-and-orange swirls, immaculately hoovered every day, even though I'm never here. I used to hate it, but now it comforts me.

'I'm just worried about you,' he says. 'I've never seen you frightened at the thought of being in your own home.'

'You've known Peter for years. He's not like that.'

Dad purses his lips in a tight smile.

Then I remember the other day, when Peter whipped the

cup out of my hands – it smashed into pieces. He slammed the front door.

'Frank!' Mum's shouting from the bottom of the stairs. 'Your tea's on the table. Hurry up or it'll get cold.'

Dad puts his hands on his knees and stands.

'Are you coming down, Debs? She'll have made a plate for you. It'll dry up if it's left in the oven.'

I flop back down against the pillow.

'In a minute.'

Dad walks to the door.

'You should get a microwave,' I say. 'They're like magic.'

'And they cost a small fortune,' he says. 'Anyway . . . your mother can't even program the video. Let's not let her loose on radiation.'

I hear Dad console Mum by saying my dinner won't be ruined. 'I'll have it for my supper if she's too poorly,' he says.

'She's not poorly, Frank. She's just got the melancholy.'

I don't know why they have to talk so loud. I look to the ceiling again. That would've been the perfect time to have told Dad about the letters I've been getting.

I was eleven and I'd just got back from secondary school, and a letter had arrived addressed to me. I looked at it for ages before taking it off the mantelpiece. I never received post and I'd sent a painting to *Blue Peter* a few weeks before. I felt the envelope, but couldn't feel a badge inside. I tore it open, and the note inside listed names and addresses to send the same letter to. If I didn't, I'd have twenty years of bad luck.

Dad grabbed it out of my hand as I read: *If you destroy this letter, someone you know will—*

'I'm not having that,' he said. 'It's one of those chain letters. I read about them in the paper.'

The tears welled in my eyes as he tore it to tiny pieces.

'But, Dad. It says if I destroy it, someone will die.'

He picked up the bits from the floor and scrunched them into a ball.

'*You* haven't destroyed it; *I* have. And no one's going to die because of it.' He went into the kitchen and threw it in the bin. 'If I find out who sent you that, I'll bloody give them what-for.'

I ran to the window to see if there was anyone outside, which was silly as the post had come that morning. There was no villain lurking in the shadows of our estate. But someone had written my name. Did they write it out of fear – to share the burden?

Dad was right, though. No one died. Uncle Charlie had already passed away that year. Whoever is writing to me now, isn't writing out of fear, but hate. I couldn't tell Dad about the notes; it'd only upset him. I've already tried telling Peter, and he wasn't interested.

'There's peaches and Dream Topping for dessert, Bobby,' Mum shouts from the kitchen.

I pull the quilt up over my shoulders, and feel safer than I've done for weeks.

The phone's ringing downstairs. I turn and face the other way. Peter'll get it.

Whispers from the hallway.

I open my eyes, and the wall is in front of me, not our bedroom window or Annie's Moses basket. Because I'm not at home.

Thuds up the stairs.

Mum opens my bedroom door.

'Deborah,' she hisses. 'There's a telephone call for you.'

I fling back the covers and swing my feet onto the carpet.

'He woke the baby,' she says. 'I'll have to unplug it.'

I rub my face.

'How long have I been asleep?'

'It's ten to six.' Not long. She beckons me with her hand. 'Come on, love. He's waiting for you.'

'Hmm.' I get to my feet and follow Mum down the stairs. 'Did he sound angry?' I speak quietly so Peter won't hear me down the telephone line.

'Not at all. Why would he?'

'Mum, who's on the phone?'

We linger on the bottom stairs.

'It's your old friend, Nathan,' she whispers. 'Lovely man. Even asked how *I* was.' She's grinning at me, as though everything is just wonderful. 'I'll leave you to it.' She tiptoes across the hall and closes the living-room door.

It seems I'm living in the twilight zone.

I sit on the bottom step, like I'm sixteen again, and reach for the handset.

'Hello?'

'Debs! Your mum and dad still have the same number.'

'They do. Nothing seems to change in this house.'

He laughs.

'Is your wife there?' I say.

Why didn't I call Monica by her name?

'No. Don't know where she is, to be honest. I thought her and Leo would be here when I got home, but the house is empty.'

'How did you know I was here?'

'I didn't. I phoned yours and Peter's first to see if Monica was there, but there was no answer.' He sighs loudly down the line. 'Is everything okay, Debs? You don't seem yourself.'

I twist the phone cord in my hands.

'I don't know. I just feel . . . different. It's the sleepless nights. Things should settle back down soon.'

'You know I'm here, if you want to talk.'

'Thanks, Nathan. But, like I said the other day, I should be talking to Peter about things.'

'Okay. I know Peter's busy at work at the moment, so the offer's there.'

'Thanks.'

I lean against the wall to my right and rest the handset on my shoulder. Nathan hasn't telephoned me in years. Hearing his voice, and him listening to mine, makes me feel as though I could close my eyes and float to the ceiling.

'We used to talk for hours, didn't we?' he says.

'We did.'

Mum used to walk past sighing loudly, pointing to her watch. 'It's okay,' I'd hiss, my hand covering the bottom of the phone. '*He* rang *me*.'

'We'd listen to your records all the time,' he says. 'Blondie and – what was that song you used to bring round to mine and made me put on again and again? By The Beatles – your dad bought it from a jumble sale or something.'

I smile. '"Norwegian Wood". I haven't listened to it for years.'

'It came on the radio today. It made me think of you.'

I don't know what to say, so I say nothing.

'I think I can hear the car,' he says. 'I'd better go.'

'Okay.'

'Bye then, Debs.'

'Bye, Nathan.'

There's a brief silence before he hangs up. Still, I hold the phone against my ear. It's quiet for several seconds before the angry tone starts. I place the handset back in its cradle, and put my arms around my knees.

The living-room door opens. Mum probably listened in.

She stands at my feet.

'Deborah, love,' she says, towering above me. 'Why are you crying?'

173

Chapter Twenty-Five

Anna

My laptop and the photographs are scattered around me on the bedroom carpet. The letter Dad gave me this afternoon lies unopened in front of me. I won't be interrupted; it's ten o'clock and Sophie is asleep. Jack says he's at work, but I don't know. There is a part of me that is past caring. Everyone lies, don't they? I don't know why I expect so much from people. They always let me down.

Dad seemed angry that I had more questions about Debbie today. Have I exhausted the subject of my mother? When I was a child, I wanted to know everything about her, but this changed as I reached my teens. My curiosity turned into anger. No one else's mum had vanished – why had mine? I wasn't good enough to have a real mother. It wasn't enough that I had Monica. It singled me out, when all I wanted was to be like everyone else.

I cross my legs and pick up the envelope. It's addressed to Monica, written in capital letters. The date stamped is 1996 and the bright-green stamp is priced twenty pence; second class, probably. It came from Eastbourne, Sussex.

I flip it over; the seal is yellow with age, like the paper inside it. The writing is slanted, scruffy.

Monica,
I know what you did. What will everyone think of you if they
knew the truth?
x

I read it again and again.

Why would they think this is from Debbie? There's no signature, and no one has ever mentioned her being in Eastbourne. It must be from a stranger who saw Debbie's photo on the missing persons' website. Grandad put it up there when the site first started.

My laptop pings with an email notification from Sally Munroe.

Yes, send everything you have. I await.

She's straight to the point.

I use my phone to capture Robert's photographs, but most are ruined by the reflections of the main bedroom light. They will have to do.

I place the photo of Debbie and Nathan in front of me on the floor. Their faces are so close together, but I can't read their expressions. It looks like Debbie is frowning and Nathan is saying something to her. I wish I could have been there properly. It might be the last photo of her.

I upload them as attachments, and type out Debbie's date of birth, height, hair colour. I don't know what else would be useful. My childish list of facts is meaningless when searching the world for somebody. How would it help Sally to know that Debbie was terrible at cooking?

I am about to press send when I remember I also need to send her details about Jack. I type in Francesca's name, and the details of Simon Howarth, the man who sent my husband the Facebook message: *Have you told her yet?* I attach the photograph from my mobile of the letter Francesca wrote Jack, and send it before I change my mind.

I feel the adrenaline running from my heart to my feet.

I've sent it. I might finally get some answers.

It is almost ten thirty and Jack still isn't home. I get off the floor, turn the light off, and crawl onto the bed. I lie on top of the quilt – it's too hot to get under.

At times like these, I wish I had a close friend to call and talk about things with. I live in my head too much. But there's no one any more. I have my volunteers at the bookshop, but that isn't the same. I could never call them with my problems; it would be too unprofessional.

I feel so alone.

The voices from the bedroom in the house next door, on the other side of the wall, affirm it. The woman laughs at something her husband has said.

When I was younger, I had imagined my life to be just like hers.

I reach over and flick the lamp off. I turn my head to the side and smell Jack's pillow. It doesn't smell of him, just fabric softener. I can't remember the last time he slept next to me – I wish we'd never bought that sofa bed for his office.

The key goes into the front door downstairs. A few seconds later, the stairs creak as Jack creeps up. The floorboard next to the bedroom door groans as he pauses outside it. He must have seen our lamp light on from outside, minutes before.

'Are you awake, love?' he whispers.

He hasn't called me *love* for ages.

I don't answer. I'm not up to arguing or interrogating him about phoning my dad – as well as all the other things he is keeping from me.

The door handle turns; he pushes it open, and I close my eyes. I breathe in heavily, faking deep sleep.

He sighs, and walks out again.

Chapter Twenty-Six

Tuesday, 15 July 1986

Debbie

It's dark and Bobby should be getting ready for bed by now. I should get up from this single bed, but my body feels like it's made of stone: cold and heavy and no use to anyone. I glance at the record player on my left. A small collection of records lies on the wicker shelf underneath it. 'Norwegian Wood' will be amongst that pile. I'll try to remember to put it into Annie's changing bag before I leave.

A triangle of light on the carpet.

Mum's in the doorway. She comes into the bedroom; Annie's in her arms.

'I'll just put her down,' she whispers. 'Then I'll give Bobby his bath.'

I can't even sit up.

'I'll do it,' I say, anyway.

'You get your rest. And stop talking or you'll wake the little one.'

She wouldn't accept the irony, so I don't argue.

She lays Annie down in the cot.

'Thanks, Mum,' I whisper.

She nods, backing out of the room. When the door shuts the landing light away, I close my eyes.

Annie's stirring.

'Please don't wake up,' I whisper.

I must've been too loud: she whimpers.

I'm useless. Mum probably spent ages getting her to sleep. She's about to cry, I know it.

I will myself to sit up, grabbing my pillow and placing it at the end of my bed. Moving from one end to another has robbed me of the small amount of energy I had.

I put my arm through one of the gaps in the cot and rest my hand on Annie's shoulder.

'I'm here, little one. I'm here.'

Annie's cries feel like they've pierced my ear drum. We've only been asleep for minutes, surely. There's no light under the door. She cries out again, and I leap out of bed to pick her up.

'There, there,' I whisper.

I half expect Mum to rush into the room, with the noise coming from here, but she must be asleep. There are no shouts coming from downstairs, no telly blaring, though it's hard to be sure with Annie screaming in my ears.

I creep onto the landing, avoiding the three places where the floorboards squeak. Annie's still shrieking; she's never slept here at night before. I tiptoe down the stairs, praying Mum's made up a bottle. I can't believe I only just remembered. What kind of mother am I?

They've left the lamp on in the living room. It's a gesture I appreciate, as Dad can't bear wasting electricity. I grab Annie's blanket from her pram near the window, and lay her on the living-room floor. Her little face is bright red from screaming.

'Shh, sweetheart. I won't be a sec.'

I almost cry with relief when I see three bottles lined up in the fridge. Dad must've bought two more from the chemist. I'll have to get Peter to pay him back.

The sound of the gas heating the kettle seems to soothe Annie. I take it off the heat at the first cheep of the whistle. The bottle doesn't take long to warm; Mum only made 4 oz bottles.

Annie gulps it down as I sit in Mum's chair, under Jesus with the bleeding heart. I feel His eyes burning into the side of my face, and I turn away from Him.

She stops drinking after only two ounces.

Screaming again.

I sit her forward and rub her back.

She burps twice, but she's still crying.

How did I end up here, alone in the near-dark at my parents' house, with a baby who hates me? I want to be Monica with her perfect house, perfect life. I want to be Michelle Watkinson, getting to fly on Concorde. They say in the news, it'll be able to carry passengers around the whole world soon. Dad says that plane is beautiful. 'A work of art, she is,' he said. 'If the British can help build something like that, just think of what else we can do in the future.' After working at the Leyland factory, he appreciates design.

'Be quiet, Annie!' I say. 'You'll wake everyone up.'

I try her with the bottle again, but she closes her mouth firmly whenever it touches her lips. I get up and pace the room. That doesn't work either.

'Please, baby. Please do this for me.'

As I walk, my tears fall onto her Babygro.

'I'm sorry, Annie.'

We walk up and down the room. The house is the same size as ours, yet this room feels smaller.

'I'm sorry, sweetie. I can't remember how to do this. Somewhere, there's someone who's totally right. Who wants to do this.'

I want to place her on the floor and run away.

I can't believe I said that to her out loud.

I hope she doesn't remember . . . use it in arguments against me.

My head is killing me – she's so loud.

'*You're ludicrous. You know it, don't you? You're not good enough for her. They're all going to find out about you. And what they think will be right. You're a piece of shit.*'

'What?' I look around the room; no one's there. 'You're wrong,' I say out loud, to the settee, to the wall, to Jesus. 'I *can* do this.'

I've done everything I'm supposed to do, and still she's not happy.

I sit on the edge of Mum's chair. The room spins.

I'm not really here. My body must be lying down somewhere, and it's just my mind living this nightmare. I give my little finger to Annie's palm and she clutches it. Instinct, I read once; not intention. Her skin is soft, warm. The dry creases on her hand are like hardened flakes of candle wax.

The time on the video flashes: 23.15. It's earlier than I thought.

I put Annie, still screaming, into her pram. We could both do with some fresh air; the whole house'll wake if she carries on like this. I grab Dad's jacket off the hook, and back the pram out of the front door.

I take a deep breath as the gentle breeze makes the tears on my face cold. The air outside smells sweeter than it has done for months. I close the gate behind me and am grateful there's no one around. Most of the houses in the street are in darkness – even Mrs Birchill's opposite. She's always been a nosy old cow. She used to tell me off for sitting on our own wall: 'You're staring at me, I know it. This estate's gone downhill.'

I don't even know if she's still alive. I don't pay attention when Mum announces that another acquaintance has popped their clogs. Mrs Birchill was wrong. This estate's all right. Growing up, there were a few of us from round here at the school in the next town, but some of the kids there turned their noses up at us. And then, those from our estate called us traitors for not going to the local secondary school. I felt like I didn't belong anywhere.

The houses are in rows of four. Some are rendered or pebble-dashed – the owners showing off that they exercised their *right to buy*. I miss the time when every house looked the same. Summers lasted forever, and we played outside all day, only coming back when we heard our mothers shout, 'Tea's ready!' We knew our own mother's voice from a distance.

Annie's eyes are wide open; can she see the stars, or is her eyesight not developed enough? I look up, too. There are a few wispy clouds and the stars look so near.

'Aren't they beautiful?' I say to her. She blinks, and I smile. 'I guess that's all I'm getting from you.'

I walk around the whole of the estate. It takes twenty minutes because I walk slowly. I've never known it so quiet. I turn the corner a few streets away from Mum and Dad's. The bench, lit with the harsh, orange light from the lamp post next to it, has only one plank left; the white concrete has been covered with graffiti. I don't remember it being like that. Perhaps Mrs Birchill was right after all.

At the top of the road, there's a car with its engine running. It wasn't there a moment ago; I didn't hear it start or pull up. I begin walking again, slowly, and reach the middle of the street. The car's engine idles. I can't see what make of car it is. I should turn around. It's waiting for me, I know it.

No, no. They're probably waiting for someone to come out of the house they're in front of. But the house has no lights on inside. My hands are sweating, shaking around the pram handle. My legs don't feel strong enough to run.

I stop, turn the pram around. The car engine growls as it starts to crawl along the pavement. I walk faster, glancing at it behind me. The lights are so bright, I can't tell who's driving – or even the colour of the car.

I run, the pram wheels gliding smoothly over the cracks in the pavement. The car goes faster, matching my speed. A right, then another left, and I'll be at my parents' house. There's a short cut through a ginnel.

I look over my shoulder. A man's face is in the driver's window. Dark hair. Is it Nathan?

I look forward again, and turn down another street. The car follows. I'm nearly at the ginnel.

Oh God. It might be the person who sent me the letters. I should've told someone about them, made Peter listen to me. What if this is the end? No one knows where I am. I shouldn't have just sneaked out of the house; I should've left Mum and Dad a note.

I can hardly breathe; I'm running faster now. There's no one else on the streets. Where is everyone? I look down at Annie and she's fast asleep. How can she sleep now? I thought babies were meant to sense the emotions of their mother.

I come to the ginnel. The street light in the middle of it isn't working. I run down anyway – trees towering either side; rotten wooden faces lean towards me. The car lingers at the entrance behind before speeding away.

I didn't check on Bobby before I left. What if the man in the car has taken him? They *all* might have disappeared for all I know. They might be in the boot. I reach the end of the pathway and bend over. I want to vomit, but there's nothing in my stomach.

The car turns down my parents' road.

Oh God. He knows where they live.

It crawls along, stopping a hundred yards from the house,

but I'm closer – only twenty feet from my parents' front door. I push the pram hard over the grass verge before it bounces off the kerb. The wind blows through my hair as I run down the road. The car doesn't move.

In seconds, I reach Mum and Dad's house. My heart's racing; my breaths are short.

Shit. I haven't got a key.

I put my hands into the pockets of Dad's jacket. There are only a few bus-ticket stubs, no keys.

I tap on the door. Oh Jesus. It's me who's going to be waking everyone up, not Annie. I crouch down and check under the terracotta pot. Thank God. Bless you, Mother. I grab the key from underneath and wipe off the dirt.

The car stops outside the house.

I hold my breath and duck behind the pram.

What am I doing? Making the baby a barrier between me and some crazy stalker?

I stand slowly. The car is silver, like ours. It's a battered Datsun, like ours.

My feet are frozen to the ground as the car door opens and closes. The driver walks round the front of the car and stands a few feet from the pram.

'Why the hell have you taken my children away from me?'

He doesn't look the same. His eyes are dark, wide; he looks unshaven, even though he was clean this morning.

'Peter. Calm down. I didn't take the children away. Stop being so loud and dramatic.'

'Loud and dramatic? You're a fine one to talk, aren't you?'

'Shh, you'll wake Annie.'

'Will I now? Why are you walking the streets at this time of night with my daughter? I was on my way round here, and I saw someone who looked just like you, wandering around at nearly midnight. I thought, *No, that can't be Debs – not in the*

183

dark, not when I've been so worried about her. But then you came closer, and it *was* you. What were you thinking?'

'It's not that big a deal. People go for walks all the time. She wouldn't settle.'

'That's because she's not at home. I didn't know where you were. Why didn't you tell me you were here?'

'Didn't Mum ring you?'

His eyebrows are raised, his fists are clenched, and his feet are wide apart. I take a step back and lean against the front door.

'Anyway,' I say. 'What are *you* doing creeping about in the car? I thought it was someone trying to get me.'

'*Get* you? Why would anyone be trying to *get* you?' He's moving his head from side to side. He thinks I'm stupid.

'Keep your voice down. I've been getting these poison-pen letters . . . it's like someone's been watching me – and Annie.'

I almost fall into the house as the front door opens.

'What's going on out here?' It's Dad. 'The whole street'll wake up if you two keep shouting.'

'Sorry, Frank,' says Peter. His face has totally transformed into that of a person who looks calm. 'I had no idea where my family was. I needed to check they were safe.'

'At this time? Why didn't you just phone us?'

'I've been trying since seven – it just rung out.'

Dad rolls his eyes.

'Your mother,' he says, glancing at the sky. 'She must've unplugged the phone. She's been fretting about the baby waking in the night. I told her babies wake just fine all by themselves, but she was having none of it.' Dad pulls his dressing gown around his middle. 'As much as I would love to stand out here and have a chat, I think we should get this little one to bed.'

We all look at Annie, fast asleep in her pram.

Peter nods. 'I'm sorry, Frank, Debbie. You must understand how worried I was. I drove to Monica's, to the hospitals. I thought if you were here, someone would answer the phone . . . Are you staying here tonight, then?'

'Yes,' I say. 'Bobby's upstairs. I'll have to take him to school in the morning.'

He bends over the pram and blows a kiss to Annie, then backs away. His arms hang at his sides; his eyes are wet, dull. Poor man – what am I doing to him? He must've thought I'd left, taken his family away.

'Ring me tomorrow, okay?' he whispers.

I nod, and watch as he gets into the car and drives away.

'Come on, love,' says Dad, taking hold of the pram. 'Let's get you both back in the house.'

Inside, I peel back the pram cover.

'Wait,' says Dad. 'Just come into the living room for a minute, she'll be okay there.'

I follow him and sit on the settee as he gently closes the living-room door. He sits on the chair next to me.

'What are these letters you were talking about? Have you got them with you?'

'Were you listening at the door?'

'Just for a minute. I'm worried about you, love. It's like . . . I don't know . . . like the spark's gone out of you. There's no joy about you any more.'

'I'm just tired and out of sorts.'

'What did they say, these letters?'

I rub my forehead; my temples are throbbing.

'Something like *I know your dirty little secret* and *keep her close*. That sort of thing.'

'How odd.'

'I know. But, Dad, you're not to worry about it – they weren't even addressed to me. And before you ask, I don't have a dirty little secret.'

'I wasn't going to ask that.'

I smile at him. 'Yeah, right.'

'If you get any more, then I'll come with you to the police station.'

'What will they do? It's not illegal to send nasty letters, is it?'

'No, it's not. It should be, though . . . the effect it's having on you.'

I stand and take off Dad's jacket.

'It's not the letters that are affecting me. It's everything, I suppose. I'll get used to it . . . the shock of a new baby and all that. Don't tell Mum about them, I don't want her worrying more than usual.'

I open the living-room door, hang up the jacket, and take Annie out of the pram. I turn to go up the stairs; Dad's standing right behind me.

'I know she wouldn't want me saying this,' he whispers. 'But your mum was a bit like this after you were born . . . with the melancholy.'

'What do you mean?' I whisper back. 'She said she was fine after she had me.'

He shakes his head. 'I don't know what she's told you, but no. She wasn't fine.' He glances up the stairs as though he's scared Mum'll hear. 'I shouldn't say any more. I'm only telling you because it was all right in the end, wasn't it? It'll be the same with you, won't it?'

I take a step up the stairs.

'Yes,' I say. 'Yes, it will.'

But I'm lying. Again.

'Night, Dad.'

Chapter Twenty-Seven

Anna

I'm carrying a box of about a hundred books, and am at the bottom of two flights of stairs. You might have thought I'd be used to lugging them around, working in a bookshop, but my hands are shaking. Ellen's in front of me, carrying two boxes, and not at all out of breath. Why is there never a lift in these places?

'I really appreciate this, Annie,' she says. 'I know it was Isobel who offered your services. You could've said no, I would've understood.'

'It's okay, I don't mind.'

I try not to grit my teeth; this box is so heavy.

'I bet this was a lovely house before it was converted,' she says.

'I bet,' I say, trying not to let the strain of the weight show on my face. 'But you've answered my question about lifts.'

'Your question?'

'Never mind. Let's get these upstairs, shall we?' I walk past her. If I go quickly, my arms should still be able to hold the weight. Thank God it's the last batch. I almost drop the box at her door.

'Thank you so much,' she says, placing her two boxes down. 'That's the lot, I think.'

She looks at her boxes, and I feel terrible. This was only the second trip; she hasn't many things, but I'm surprised how many books she has.

'My sister stored them for me in her garage . . . along with the rest of the stuff I managed to collect before . . .'

'That's nice,' I say.

That's nice? Jesus.

I look at my watch.

'I can take it from here,' says Ellen, 'if you have to be somewhere else.'

'I'm meeting someone in half an hour, but it's only in Lytham.'

I haven't seen the inside of Ellen's flat, having dumped the previous box on the landing.

'Can I get you a cup of tea?' she says. She unlocks the door, picks up a box, and backs in. 'I'll have to set the kettle up, though. Shouldn't take too long.'

'Don't worry about it. If I have a tea now, I'll have to go to the loo as soon as I get to the café.'

It seems I have verbal diarrhoea.

Ellen laughs. 'I know what you mean. I do have a bathroom here, but I'm not sure of the state of it.'

I should stay another five minutes – it won't take long to drive to the café.

'I didn't mean it to sound like that, Ellen. It's just—'

'Stop feeling so awkward around me, Annie.'

My mouth drops open.

'I'm not as violent as they said I was,' she says. 'Not any more, at least.'

She bends over and rips the Sellotape from a box at her feet. I'm waiting for her to say she's joking – smile or something, to cancel out what she just said.

She doesn't.

She picks out a kettle from her box and a Tupperware container. Without looking at me, she says, 'I'll put the tea on,' and walks into a tiny kitchenette off the lounge.

'Okay.'

My feet are glued to the floor. I want to run out of the door, down the stairs and onto the street. The noise of the kettle would mask the sound of my escape.

I jump when her head appears at the concertina door.

'Tea, white, without?' she says, smiling.

I nod; she goes back into the kitchen. I'm reading too much into what she says. As if she would *murder* me – I've just helped her move boxes. I don't think she realised that her comment earlier unnerved me. Perhaps she thought I'd take it as a joke. It's so out of character. Well, from the person she's shown me so far.

'Can I help you unpack?' I shout.

I'll make myself useful, then she won't get any ideas.

Stop being so ridiculous, Anna! It's just Ellen.

But I've only known her for a couple of weeks. I should have asked Isobel what she'd done.

Ellen comes out of the kitchen and places two mugs on the window sill on the other side of the living room. She kneels down next to an open box.

'You can help me unwrap these, if you like,' she says. 'I haven't seen most of this stuff for years.'

My shoes thump the laminate flooring. I crouch opposite her and she passes me a parcel wrapped in the front cover of the *Daily Mirror*. It is yellow with age and dated Wednesday 28 January 1987. The headline reads: *Agony of Mrs Waite.*

'All of this would've been sent to the tip if it hadn't been for my sister saving it for me. I suppose she felt guilty. I didn't think I'd ever see it all again. Not that I've got much, anyway.'

She's holding a wooden picture frame that's been painted yellow, and has dried flowers glued around it.

'My son made me this,' she says, turning it round to show me.

'That's so sweet.'

'You have a little girl, don't you?'

'Yes, Sophie. She's six.'

'A lovely age. Treasure her, won't you.'

I feel the pang of guilt I always get when I think about her, that I don't give her enough attention.

'How old's your son now?' I ask her.

She looks up in surprise. It must be the first personal question I've asked her.

'He'll be forty next week. An important one.'

Her eyes haven't left mine. Why is she looking at me like that? It's as though she's waiting for me to ask more questions. Instead, I finish unwrapping what's in my hand. Another photograph. It's in a silver-filigree frame, the glass is shiny as though frozen in time.

It's of a little boy. He's holding up a Lego construction to the camera, sitting next to a Moses basket.

'That's him,' says Ellen, leaning over the box towards me.

I pass the frame to her outstretched hands.

'What does he do now?' I ask her.

She's stroking the glass of the photo.

'I don't know, Annie. I've written to him three times, but he hasn't replied yet. He doesn't want to know me. He's ashamed.'

'But you might've written to the wrong address.'

She shakes her head.

My mobile phone beeps. I reach into my pocket. A message from Sally.

I'm here.

I get up from the floor.

'I'm sorry, Ellen. I have to go. Are you going to be okay?'

She doesn't get up.

'Of course.' She places the photo on top of the box. 'Are you all right to let yourself out?'

I drive to Lytham almost on autopilot. The little boy in Ellen's photo will be forty soon, but Robert is only thirty-seven on his next birthday.

No. I have to stop these idiotic thoughts. I want to forget I was in Ellen's flat. *I'm not as violent as they said I was.* Why would she say something like that?

I pull into a parking space on the main street, to the annoyance of an elderly man waiting in the opposite lane. I get out and dash to the pavement before he starts waving his fist and shouting at me. I'm a few minutes from the café – one of about fifty in Lytham – so I walk as fast as I can without running.

I have to look twice, but Jack's car is parked alongside the pavement, not far from mine. He often comes to Lytham for work. He asked me this morning if I was free for lunch; I said I was working through. He must've been checking I wouldn't catch him. We were both lying.

I look into the window of the nearest café. He's always lucky with parking.

He's inside, to the left of the counter, sitting alone. I hold up my hand to tap on the window, but stop just in time. There's a half-empty glass across from his cup. He's waiting for someone to come back. If I tell him I'm here, I won't find out who's with him.

'Excuse me, love.'

An elderly couple want to get past; I'm in the doorway.

'Sorry.' I whisper, in case Jack hears me. I pretend to look at the menu in the window.

Oh God, I'm going to see them together. My heart starts

pounding. Instinctively, I grab my mobile from my pocket. If he's with her, I need evidence. If I tell him I know about him and her, then he'll find a way to turn it around – say I was seeing things.

I keep the phone camera close to my chest; I don't want to draw attention to myself by waving it in the air.

Jack looks behind him at the door of the toilets. His companion is no doubt making herself look beautiful. The bitch.

A gust of sea wind blows, and the belt of my mac taps the window. Jack glances up, but I hide behind the menu again. I turn my back to the window. Two women, about my age, walk past, carrying takeaway coffees – heads together, chatting. My stomach tightens. What the hell am I doing, spying on my husband like this, outside a café, in front of everyone? Why can't I be normal like everyone else? If I look back inside and Jack's still alone, I'll just head to my meeting with Sally. I'm already late. She'll think I don't care.

One, two, three.

I turn around.

He's not alone. But he isn't with Francesca, either.

He's with a man.

I'm breathless when I get to Sally's table after running the few streets from the café Jack was in.

'Well, sit down then,' she says, looking up at me. 'We can't have you heavy breathing and scaring the other customers.'

'Sorry I'm late.'

'Only by five minutes. I'm always early.'

'I've just seen my husband.'

She raises her eyebrows. 'Either you've just had a really good time, or you've run away from him.'

I hang my coat on the back of the chair, and pull it out to

sit down. 'Sorry, you don't want to hear about my problems,' I say. 'What did you find out?'

'I'm fine, thank you, Anna. It's so kind of you to ask.' She winks at me.

'Oh God, what's wrong with me?' I say. 'I'm so sorry.'

'I'm just kidding. If it were up to me, I wouldn't bother with hello or goodbye either.'

My hands shake as I get the photographs out of my bag.

'Are you okay?' she says. 'Did you have an argument with Jack?'

I imagine it's in her job description to be perceptive.

'I . . .'

She said the other day that anything said between her and me is confidential. She's virtually a stranger, but I don't want to burden Dad, Monica or Grandad with what is happening with my husband. I already emailed her a copy of the love letter from Francesca, so she already knows part of it.

I tell her about seeing Jack in the café and how he always turns things around, so it seems I'm crazy.

'But why would he want to make out that you're crazy?'

She makes quote marks with her fingers to frame the last word.

'Because I . . . I became obsessed with this woman who used to work near me, a few years ago. I thought she might have been my mother.'

It's too hot in here. I undo the collar button of my blouse. Why am I opening up to Sally? It'll only prove Jack right, won't it? If I tell her about all the things I have done in the past, she will look at me differently – like so many of my so-called friends I don't see any more. I used to time them to see how long it would take to distance themselves from me. Sometimes it would be immediate, others would just not reply to my texts or phone calls. Life is easier without friends anyway, no one can disappoint you.

But I have nothing to lose with Sally – she's being paid to be here.

'Go on,' she says, resting her chin in the cup of her hand.

'I suppose there's always been something there with me, since I was little. I've always known that Monica was Debbie's best friend, that she wasn't my real mother. Sometimes I wish they'd never told me about Debbie, pretended she didn't exist, so I could've led a normal life with a normal family – even just for the first ten, twelve, eighteen years of my life. But everyone was so honest about it all.'

'There's no such thing as a normal family, Anna.'

'There is.' I manage a smile as I dab a tear rolling down my cheek with a paper napkin. 'I met one once.'

I tell Sally about everything I went through before.

I had never been as bad before I met Gillian Crossley. She looked just like Debbie. I convinced myself that she *was* Debbie – that she'd chosen to work nearby to get close to me. I took it too far – started following her home to see if she had a replacement family.

Jack was there for me through all of this, but he didn't know about the ones before. I latched on to teachers, and my counsellor at college. What few friends I had, looked at me differently.

Daisy was my first counsellor. It was a sign, I thought, her having the same initial as my mother, yet she was only about five years older than I was. I thought we were friends. She listened to me for hours (an hour at a time, obviously). She knew everything about me. When I took her presents, she looked pleased.

But when I met her three times in a row at the library on a Saturday morning, she took a step back. 'This isn't a coincidence any more, is it, Anna? You knew I'd be here, didn't you? This has to stop. I'm sorry. I shouldn't have encouraged you. I should've said something the first time I saw you here.'

I only ever saw her in passing at college after that. I was too ashamed to even make eye contact with her. I gradually realised that she knew everything about me because she was paid to; I knew nothing about her, not really.

'I never told Jack about my time at college,' I say to Sally. 'It wasn't that I was embarrassed by it. By the time I met him, I didn't think about it. I lived at home when I was at university – I didn't see anyone from college who knew about it. I spent most of my spare time with Monica. She'd take me shopping, out for lunch.' I give a hollow laugh. 'It was like I was a project for her. She'd taken early retirement from the council offices, so I kept her busy. But in a way, she built me back up again.'

'What changed?' says Sally. 'To make you so transfixed with this Gillian so many years after college?'

'I was pregnant. I suppose expecting a child myself made me question Debbie's decision to leave even more. I felt so close to Sophie when she was growing inside me – an unbreakable bond. How could someone just abandon that?'

The memory of it is still so vivid. The last time I visited the bakery, I was on maternity leave; Dad and Monica had looked after Sophie for the afternoon to give me some time to go into town and browse the shops, but I knew where I really wanted to go.

I stood outside the bakery, waiting for her to come into work. She hadn't been in for days; I'd walked past with the pram. Her colleagues said she was off sick. When I'd pressed them, they said she had a migraine.

But that day was different. Her boss came to the door as I waited on the doorstep.

'What are you doing standing outside again, Anna?' she said, her arms folded in the doorway. 'Gillian's off sick again. You realise all of this is making her ill, don't you?'

'I . . . I . . .'

I stepped back and a huge dollop of rain from the shop canopy landed on my head. I went to wipe it off and realised the rest of my hair was sopping wet. I was standing outside in the pouring rain, soaked to the skin.

I held up a silver picture frame.

'But I thought she might like this,' I said, getting closer to her, trying to get shelter. 'It's a photo of Robert and me when I was two. She won't have seen it before.'

The woman shook her head, went back into the bakery and slammed the door — a waft of warm air from inside hit my face.

'Get yourself some help, Anna!' she shouted through the glass.

Sally's face doesn't react as I finish my story.

'I don't understand why Jack would be horrible to you about that, when surely you needed love, empathy.'

I shrug. 'He's not horrible about it, really. He worries about me. He's very practical, strong. It's why I married him, I suppose. I'm in a good place now — well, I thought I was before all of this . . .'

Sally reaches over and pats my hand.

'While we're talking about Jack, we might as well start there.' She grabs a piece of paper off the empty chair next to her. 'The man who sent Jack the Facebook message: *Have you told her yet?* wasn't that hard to find. But what's interesting is that he had a sister called Francesca.'

'She's married then? Francesca King?'

It is so strange saying her name aloud. It's not just in my head any more: it's real.

'No. Not Francesca King — Simon Howarth's sister never married. Her name was Francesca Howarth.'

A different Francesca.

Oh God, what have I done?

I visited that woman at work – told her Jack was having an affair, hatred in my eyes.

'But, I'm afraid, it's past tense,' says Sally. 'Sadly, Simon's sister died as a result of a car accident. Recently, as it happens.'

She slides over a print-out of an online newspaper article. It's dated three weeks ago.

One person has died and two are injured following a crash involving two cars in York.

A woman, driving a Ford Focus, sustained fatal injuries on the A64, between Copmanthorpe and Bishopthorpe, in the early hours of this morning (Wednesday), and was pronounced dead at the scene.

A man in the second vehicle suffered injuries that aren't believed to be life-threatening.

A cyclist, a man in his late fifties, sustained minor injuries.

Police are appealing for witnesses.

I look up at Sally.

'This wasn't that long ago.'

'That's right,' she says. 'She went to the same college as Jack. If Jack knows her brother, then chances are, he knew her. I believe this is the Francesca we're looking for.'

I glance at the time on my phone. It's one o'clock already.

'Thanks, Sally. That's great. I'm sorry, but I really must go. I'm not supposed to shut the bookshop at lunchtime. I'd like to hear more, but I can't get fired. My boss, Isobel, thinks I'm useless as it is.'

'I'm sure she doesn't.'

I stand, grabbing my coat from the back of the chair.

'Before you go, Anna, there's something I'd like you to ask your family about.'

'What?' I put on my coat, even though I'm boiling hot and the sun is shining outside.

'I spoke to my police contact. Deborah wasn't reported missing until two months after she disappeared. And it wasn't your father who reported it – it was Frank O'Reilley.'

Grandad.

'What? Why?'

'I don't know. It's what you should ask them.' She reaches into her bag and pulls out an estate agent's flyer. 'Also . . . sorry, I didn't expect this to be a rushed meeting, but the house you lived in as a baby . . . the one next door to it's for sale. The woman selling it owns your old house too. I'll arrange a viewing – perhaps we could ask her some information without just turning up on her doorstep?'

I stop my rushing.

'Do you think she'll let me see my old house?'

'I doubt that, but it's worth talking to her.'

Sally stands, holding out her right hand. I shake it.

'Yes. Thank you.'

Chapter Twenty-Eight

Wednesday, 16 July 1986

Debbie

'*She's stolen your children. Get up!*'

Where's Annie? I only closed my eyes for five minutes, didn't I? A voice woke me up. I get out of bed and rush to the landing in Mum and Dad's house. Before I look in the room Bobby's sleeping in, I know the bed'll be empty. Mum and Dad aren't in their room either; their bed's perfectly made.

Nobody's stolen the children. It was just a dream.

I stand at the top of the landing, gripping the railings.

Oh no. It's happening again.

My right arm begins to tingle. I can't move it, but it won't stop shaking – my whole body's trembling.

The ringing in my ears is too loud.

My knees buckle, and I collapse onto the carpet.

I can't breathe.

My heart is about to run out – it's beating too fast for the rest of me.

I'm dying.

My throat feels like it's closing; I shut my eyes.

My breaths are short.

Sick. I'm going to be sick.

There's nothing in my stomach.

Oh God, I can't breathe.

I want it to end; I want everything to end.

But I don't.

I'm on the landing, flat on my back.

Am I dead?

I look at my hand and pinch the skin on my arm.

No.

My poor parents, if they had to find me – what if Bobby had been the first?

Where is everyone? Where's all the noise?

I slowly get up.

There's something seriously wrong with me.

I had blood tests for months before Annie was born, though. They would've picked up something, wouldn't they?

I walk downstairs, holding the bannister tight; my knees are still weak. I feel as though I've been thrown against every wall in the house, yet there are no bruises on my skin.

Sounds of cars driving past outside. Everything's going on as normal. I can't remember what it's like to feel normal.

There's a note propped against the telephone.

Deborah,
Didn't want to wake you. Dad's taken Bobby to school, so I'm taking Annie out for a bit of fresh air.
Mum.

I wish she'd have put the note in Annie's cot.

I'm too ungrateful, I know that. When Annie starts to sleep through, I'll get more sleep myself and then I'll be a better person. I have to believe that, otherwise I'm going to sink into quicksand.

Perhaps it'd be easier for everyone if I wasn't around. I make people angry. I'm not how they want me to be. I'm not who *I* want to be.

Bang, bang, bang.

Someone's at the door.

I get down on my hands and knees and crawl into the living room, even though the front door is made from mottled glass and whoever it is can see me skulk away.

'Debs?' A man's voice through the letterbox.

Oh God, he must've seen me.

I look around the living room: nothing. If I were at home, there'd be an airer full of clothes to hide behind.

More voices at the door. What the hell is going on out there?

A key turns in the lock.

'Just wait there with the pram while I see what's going on.'

It's Mum.

'Deborah! What on earth are you doing on the floor like that?'

She's standing at the living-room doorway.

More footsteps in the hall. Nathan's cradling Annie in his arms. He peers over Mum's shoulder.

I stand quickly, grabbing a cushion to cover the 1950s nightie Mum laid out for me last night.

'I wondered where everyone was,' I say. 'But now that's been solved – seeing as half the people I know are standing right in front of me.'

'I dare say it has,' says Mum, looking at me as though I were parading naked. 'You've a visitor. You might want to run upstairs to make yourself presentable.' She's trying to direct me upstairs by flicking her eyes to the staircase without her head moving.

'Yes, yes, of course,' I say.

I smile and nod at Nathan – who's probably noticed my crimson face – and run two steps at a time up the stairs. I dress in the only outfit I brought with me. After only a few hours' sleep, I feel a bit more refreshed.

It can't be because Nathan's here.

My daughter's safe – that's it too. I hope he's not here on behalf of Peter, to try to convince me to come home.

In the bathroom, I splash water on my face. I look in the mirror as I pat it dry with a towel. I wish I'd brought make-up – I didn't bring anything. I can't even remember the journey here yesterday. I pinch my cheeks like Mum does before church when she thinks no one's looking.

I slowly go down the stairs and take a few breaths before grabbing the door handle to the living room. I want to listen in on what Nathan and Mum are talking about, but all I can hear is the telly.

The pair of them don't even glance up when I walk in. Nathan's long legs, crossed at the ankles, take up half the floor's width as he makes himself at home, and Mum's feeding Annie a bottle in her chair with Jesus above her as a witness. I'm glad Dad isn't here to see the way she's smiling at Nathan. She should be ashamed of herself, and in front of the son of God as well.

'Did you say something funny?' I say to Nathan.

He looks up, pretending to have only just noticed I've come into the room. More likely, he *has* just noticed me. I wish my teenage brain would leave me alone.

'I was just saying to Marion that I could take you all out to St Annes, if you fancied a breath of fresh air?'

Marion? Even Peter doesn't call my mother by her first name – in fact, I don't think he ever calls her anything. And why's everyone so bothered about fresh air? It's overrated.

'And I said to Nathan,' says Mum, 'that I'm going to wait in for your dad, make him lunch. Can you imagine what he'd think if I left him a note saying I've gone off gallivanting with a young man? You and Annie go. I'll be fine here.'

My cheeks are hot again. What's gotten into her? Sending me off on a day trip with another man. She's not this chatty when Peter comes round with me.

'Mum, I'm sure Dad wouldn't mind if he knew you were with Annie and me as well. He might appreciate the house to himself.'

'No, no. I'll stop in. Your dad'll have done two bus journeys after taking Bobby to school and going to the job centre. He'll need someone to come back to.'

'Oh no, poor Dad. I should've taken Bobby.'

'*Poor Dad* nothing. He likes to feel useful.'

'I don't think it'd be right for me to go. Peter might wonder where I am.'

'It's nearly ten o'clock. I plugged the phone back in at six this morning, and there's not been any phone calls. Just go out and let your hair down – it might get some colour in your cheeks.'

'I . . . well . . . if you're sure?' I'm still standing in the middle of the living room. 'But Annie'll be due another feed in a few hours.' I look to Nathan. 'I can't go out for long.'

Mum passes Annie to Nathan; doesn't she trust me with my own baby?

'Don't be silly,' she says. 'I've made a few bottles up for her. Take another two with you. I'll make a flask of hot water.'

My mouth drops open as she hands a bag over to Nathan.

'Are you sure, Mum?' I say, pulling her by the elbow into the kitchen. 'Wouldn't it be better if I stayed here? I don't think I'm well enough to go out.'

'What's wrong with you?' She puts her hand on my forehead. 'Your temperature's fine.' She leans her head towards mine. 'But your eyes look a bit different.' She tilts her head to the side. 'I know I'm usually one for plodding on with everything, but your old friend Nathan's a good sort.' She's blushing. 'I should've

203

taken you out a bit more when you were little. I won't tell Peter if you don't want me to.'

'Mum! That's not a very Christian thing to say!'

'He can't see me in here,' she says, gesturing to Jesus on the wall in the other room.

I lean against the Formica worktop and look out of the window above the sink, then to the sill. There's a broken glass on a newspaper, waiting to be wrapped for the bin. Its glacier-like spikes sparkle in the sunshine. I could just slam my wrist over them – they're only inches away. It wouldn't hurt for long.

I turn to my mother.

'I wouldn't mind if you *did* tell Peter. He's been *off gallivanting*, as you call it, with Monica.'

'Just go and have a nice time. Dad'll pick Bobby up, so you don't have to worry about the time.'

'I suppose.'

At that moment, I realise I have no money on me at all. And the only money I have is the pittance left over from the family allowance and I don't even have my cheque book with me. How far did I think I'd get with no money when I fled the house yesterday? It doesn't matter anyway. Everything feels so pointless.

I feel like I'm in a taxi in Nathan's Sierra, with him in front and me in the back. Annie's lying in her carrycot, the seat belt strapped across it. Nathan's window's open and the breeze is refreshing.

'Am I okay to turn the radio on?' He shouts over the wind.

'Yes,' I holler back. 'Annie's awake.'

If she wasn't, she would be, after all this shouting.

Nathan keeps glancing at me in the rearview mirror. I look to the world outside the window, though we're on the dual carriageway and there are only fields.

'The Chicken Song' comes on the radio. Stupid fucking song; I don't know what all the fuss is about. Memories of my cousin's wedding two months ago flash into my mind. Me, eight months pregnant, sitting in the social club making half a pint of Guinness last two hours, while everyone danced the stupid chicken dance, pissed as farts. Even my mother, who'd had half a glass of sparkling wine, got up, self-consciously waving her hands about like the rest of them. Weddings are shit if you can't drink.

It finally ends and is replaced by 'West End Girls' by the Pet Shop Boys. At last some decent music. I imagine myself in the video, standing moodily next to Neil Tennant, smoking cigarettes. I could've had a different life had I aimed high enough, had I been bothered.

We've been driving for twenty minutes and Nathan and I haven't spoken much. He hasn't explained why he just turned up at my parents' house. Doesn't anyone use the phone any more? Why isn't he at work? It's a weekday, because Bobby's at school.

The sound and movement of the car has sent Annie to sleep. I'm so tired myself, but I can't sleep now. I close my eyes, anyway, and let the wind and the heat of the sun through the window warm me. If it weren't for Annie here next to me, I could be sixteen again – the pair of us driving round the coast in Nathan's fourth-hand Austin Metro.

We've just passed Lytham windmill. Nathan lowers the radio and rolls up the window. He glances at me over his left shoulder.

'I suppose Pete told you he came round to ours last night?'

'Hmm,' I say. 'Mum unplugged the phone. Annie's not been sleeping properly.'

I glance down at her, fast asleep: the irony.

'He said you took off in the middle of the night.'

I roll my eyes. 'Hardly. It was after I picked up Bobby from school.'

I don't tell him I was so scared of being in my own home that I almost couldn't breathe – that I felt that people were watching me through the window, through the walls.

We pass the White Church, where a bride in an ivory meringue is being helped out of a limousine by her dad. *Don't do it*, I want to shout.

'You know I'm here if you want to talk,' says Nathan.

He keeps saying that, doesn't he?

'I should talk to Monica, really. Peter might think it weird if I talk to you.'

Nathan shrugs. 'They have their own little chats, don't they?'

I lean forward, resting my hand on the front passenger seat.

'I thought it was only the one time they met. Have they spoken again?'

'Hang on a sec.'

He pulls up on the road next to the sand dunes and turns off the ignition. He takes off his seat belt, turning to face me.

'On the phone. I've heard them. First it was about the holiday – now he keeps ringing her, asking for advice.'

'Advice? About what?'

He takes a deep breath – his eyes dart around the car before they meet mine.

'You.'

I'm struggling to push the pram through the sand, so I turn it around and drag it.

'I can get that for you, Debs,' says Nathan. He goes to grab the handles, but I elbow him out of the way. I know I shouldn't take it out on him – it's not his fault Monica and Peter are conspiring against me. I shouldn't have to worry about those two at a time like this.

I stop at an area of sand that's far enough away from anyone else.

'Did you bring a blanket?' I say.

He's looking wide-eyed at me. He probably thinks I've gone crazy, like the rest of them do. He pulls out a tartan blanket from his Army & Navy bag, then unrolls it and places it on the sand.

'Do you want me to get Annie out?' he says.

'It's okay.' I pull up the hood to shade her from the sun peeking through the clouds. 'I'll let her sleep a while longer.'

'How many weeks is she now?' he says, sitting on the blanket. He grabs his bag and squashes it into the sand behind him, before laying his head on it, eyes closed.

'Four or five.'

I steal a glance at him while his eyes are shut. Such dark hair. If I hadn't known him since we were teenagers, I'd have thought his hair was dyed that colour. There's a St Christopher chain around his neck. It looks like the one I bought him all those years ago.

I sit down next to him, but not too close.

I look up to the sun and close my eyes.

It wasn't like this after I had Bobby. Everything was easy then. He'd sleep for hours at a time, letting me get myself ready for the day – and he slept through from two months old. But today is the first day in a long time that I've felt halfway human. I wish I could stay here, like this, forever. I might be getting better. I won't need to go to the doctor – I'll tell Monica that it was just lack of sleep, that I've healed myself. I'm a medical marvel.

'What are you smiling at?' says Nathan.

'I was just thinking about Monica,' I say, without thinking.

'Really? You don't mind her talking with Peter?'

I open my eyes to find him looking at me, shielding his eyes from the mid-morning sun. 'I'll speak to Peter about it tonight.'

My stomach feels sick at the thought of confrontation. I

doubt I'll even talk to him. I'm a coward. I don't want him bringing up the fact that I'm failing – as a mother and a wife. If we don't discuss it, I can try to get back to normal without any drama.

I glance at Nathan; he's lying down again with his face to the sky.

'Did Monica mention what they said about me?'

'You should talk to her about it,' he says. 'You know I'm not one for gossip.'

'What? How can it be gossip – I'm right here? You can talk to *me* about me.'

He props himself up, his elbow resting on the blanket, only inches from my arm.

'I know, Debs. It's just that . . .' He takes a deep breath. 'Monica said Peter's been telling her that you two aren't getting along at the moment. He thinks you're *not yourself.*'

'What?'

It's one thing for *me* to think it, but for *him* to say it is another. The thought of it winds me in the stomach.

'I know, I know,' he says. 'It's a shit thing to say about anyone, baby or no baby. And he shouldn't be saying all of this to Monica. I told her I didn't want to hear what Peter's been saying – and you can imagine how she took that.' There's a light smirk on Nathan's face.

'Yes.'

I *can* imagine. There's nothing Monica likes more than to speak badly about others – she doesn't like it when people don't join in with her. She takes it as a slight. A few years ago, she came round on a Saturday afternoon after shopping with Rachel Kennedy, a woman we both went to school with.

'She's just got a promotion at GUS,' Monica said. 'Office manager! Can you believe it? She's twenty-three and she only got one O Level. Thick as pig shit.'

'I'm sure she isn't. She's probably good at her job. She wasn't that bad at school.'

'I can't believe you're sticking up for her. Are you best friends with her or something?'

'Don't be silly, Mon. It's not that I like her,' I said. 'I don't know her.'

She folded her arms and didn't speak to me until she'd thought of someone else to talk about.

'Well,' I say to Nathan now. 'It serves her right. She shouldn't take so much joy in saying bad things about other people.'

'Amen to that.'

Annie whimpers in her pram. Just as I was about to relax.

I jump up and peer over her, but she's still asleep. I look over at the grey sea in the distance, and take off my socks.

'Nath, would you mind keeping an ear out for her? I fancy dipping my feet.'

'Yeah, course. Watch out for the dirty nappies, mind. And don't go walking too far in, Reggie Perrin.'

'Don't tempt me,' I say.

If he knew what was going on in my head, he wouldn't joke about something like that.

The first few steps, where the sand is bone dry, are the trickiest.

A football crosses my path, and a boy of about three or four rushes to grab it. He walks back to his mummy, who's lying on a towel, wearing a bikini. Her bronzed skin is frying in oil, like we're in bloody Marbella and not the lukewarm North of England.

'Mummy, will you play with me yet?' says the little boy. 'You said in five minutes and it's been a million.'

'I meant in ten minutes,' she says. 'And it's never been a million. Stop exaggerating.'

'What's pedgaterating?'

'Give it a rest, Barry.'

I wish I could be that woman. She doesn't care that she's being awful to her son in public because her thoughts are probably kinder, more honest, than mine. I can't let my feelings creep through my mask, though that's starting to slip. My children would be taken away and I'd be alone. As horrendous as it sounds, it's a thought that doesn't fill me with horror.

Shit, Debbie. Stop bloody overthinking things. I want to slap the side of my head, but instead, I grab the scrunchie from around my wrist and pull my hair into a ponytail.

The sand gets firmer as I near the sea. I bend to pick up a perfect ivory shell wedged in it. The sand gets under my finger nails, but I don't pick it out. There's another: a black shell – so thin it might break in my hands. I untuck my shirt from my trousers and use it as a pouch. I could decorate Annie's memory box with what I find.

I kneel when I see a tiny dried-out crab.

Eugh. Horrid, creepy little thing.

I run the pad of my finger on its miniature, smooth shell.

'Sorry, mate,' I say. 'I didn't mean to think that about you.'

I keep walking, closer to the tide. It has a scummy, white foam that I bet you wouldn't find in Tenerife.

I spot a perfect, white, spiral shell. It would look lovely in the centre of the box. I'll have to ask Dad for some proper, strong glue; it looks as though it'll never stay put on the cigar box.

I look down at my collection. I have about twenty shells. That should do it.

As I near the sea, my footsteps leave little pools of water inside them – like mini ponds. I stand at the point where the gentle tide ends, and the scummy water tickles the tips of my toes. I look to the horizon. Southport's just across the water.

Dad used to take me there all the time. Mum never came, though. What did she do, all those times Dad and I went out together? I think of Peter and I can't picture him taking Bobby out on his own – he's always working. Little Bobby, he would've liked that dried-out crab.

I turn and see Nathan lying next to Annie's pram; they're little ants in the distance. I have to get that crab for Bobby. If I find it again, then everything will be all right.

I follow my footsteps, still fresh. I go slowly, scanning the ground. To my right is a couple: a man and a woman; their dog bounding along after a piece of driftwood they've thrown for it to fetch.

I stop when I see it: the perfect little crab, preserved in death like a mummy. How strange must it be to be hard on the outside and soft inside.

Before I reach for it, the piece of driftwood lands in front of me. The dog grabs it in his teeth, taking the crab with it.

'No!' I shout. I stand, folding my shirt to protect my shells. 'You stupid dog! That was Bobby's.'

The woman looks at me, her hand reaching for the man next to her.

'Are you okay?' she says.

'Your dog took my crab.'

The man bends down and takes the wood from the dog's mouth.

'There's no crab here.'

'It's tiny. Really small.'

'Sorry, love. There's nothing here.'

They glance at each other. I know that look: *get away from the crazy lady*. I was on the receiving end of it when I was running down the street after leaving Annie outside the shop.

'You should keep that dog on a lead,' I shout to their backs as they walk away. 'It could kill someone.'

They walk faster in the opposite direction.

Good.

Annoying, happy people.

There are tears forming in my eyes, so I face the sea, briefly, to let them dry. I keep my eyelids open and the salt stings. But that's okay. At least I'm feeling something.

I turn and march towards Nathan and Annie, clutching the collection of shells to my fat, wobbly belly. I feel it as I walk, reminding me again that I'm nothing like that bronzed woman lying only a few yards from me. She still hasn't moved from the ground. With any luck, she'll fry. Poor Barry is sitting cross-legged next to her, making piles of sand.

The ground is getting drier. Nathan is sitting up, waiting for me.

I kneel as soon as I reach the blanket and tip my finds out onto it.

'*She sells sea shells on the sea shore,*' says Nathan.

'Right.'

'*The shells she sells are surely sea shells, so if she sells sea shells on the sea shore, I'm sure she sells seashore shells.*'

'How the hell do you know all of that? It's just a silly tongue twister. It means nothing.'

'From my mum. And it does mean something. It's about a woman called Mary Anning.'

'What?'

He shrugs. 'The Mary bit was from a pub quiz. I only remember her name because we lost the tie-breaker with that stupid question. Who the fuck would know that?'

A passing woman tuts at him swearing.

'Do you ever think about running away from it all?' says Nathan, from nowhere. 'We could go now. There's nothing keeping us here.'

'Very funny,' I say, raking my fingers through the sand. 'Anyway, I haven't got Bobby with me.'

I blush as Nathan smiles. I always take a joke too far.

The clouds have gathered around the sun, and the wind from the sea sends a chill through the air.

'We should go,' I say. 'Dad's picking up Bobby, but I want to be there when he gets back. I don't want them to think I don't care.'

We're travelling back to Preston, and the thought of talking to Peter tonight fills me with dread.

'You're a worthless piece of shit.'

The voice again. It doesn't sound like Uncle Charlie any more. It sounds like me. I should just get used to it – it's only telling me what I already know. I'm in a living nightmare where everything is foggy and dark.

At the beach, I had a little snippet of what normal feels like – just a few hours teasing me about what could've been. My mind feels like it's full of mud, of dark clouds and rain. If I were to just curl up and be left alone, I could dream of another life, far away. Everything would be okay. People around me could get on with their lives and be happier without me in it.

On the radio, Gary Davies is asking a contestant phone-in questions. Nathan has the volume so loud I want to throw Annie's bottle at him.

We pass the sign for Preston. The clouds are greyer, heavier. I don't want to go home – I don't even want to go to Mum and Dad's. I don't want to be anywhere. I open the window, hoping the wind masks the sounds of my sobbing.

Chapter Twenty-Nine

Anna

I park up outside the bookshop after my meeting with Sally Munroe and luckily, there is no queue of people waiting at the door; there is only one person: Robert.

'You not in class today?' I say, slamming the car door shut.

'They're not classes – they're lectures.'

I shouldn't wind him up, but seeing him has cheered me a little. We haven't spoken much over the last few weeks and I have missed him. He still has a frown on his face, though. Even though it's a rare sunny day, he is still wearing a pale-green, cotton scarf – his 'English lecturer trademark', Dad calls it.

I unlock the door and he follows me inside.

'What brings you to St Annes?' I holler as I put my bag and coat in the back. 'Off to play the arcades on the pier?'

'Anna, stop it. I'm not in a joking mood today.'

He sits on the stool behind the counter. It reminds me of two summers ago, when he volunteered here. It was nice to spend whole days with him again, and he charmed the volunteers, fetching them cups of tea.

'You haven't been in a happy mood for ages,' I say, resting my elbows on the counter.

'Do you blame me? What makes you so chirpy today?'

I sigh. 'I'm not really. I've had a shit day, but I'm trying to be cheerful, for you.'

He looks at his hands, resting on his lap.

'I didn't expect you to be so honest.' He glances up at me with a brief smile. 'Sorry for being an idiot the other day at Grandad's. It's just . . . it's just that I remember the last time Monica received a letter that was supposed to be from Debbie. Dad told me he showed it to you the other day.'

'Yes, he did. Why did they think it was from Debbie?' I take a deep breath. 'Did no one ever question why the letter was sent to Monica and not Dad? I mean, if Debbie found out that those two had got married, she should have gone to the police. Dad's committed bigamy.'

'I don't know – probably because it's the same house Monica and Nathan lived in years ago. But Jesus, Anna, *those two*? Whose side are you on? To me, it sounds like you're angry with the wrong people. Dad brought us up – even when his heart was breaking, for God's sake. You've been dreaming about Debbie – this ghost of a mother who you've put on a pedestal. And you know what – I wish she *was* dead. If she *is* alive, she can stay the hell away from me.'

'I'm sorry, Robert. You're my brother – the one person I used to be myself around. Sometimes I forget what you've been through is far worse than what I have. It's just that I've no one to talk to about things. Jack's barely present, I can't talk to Dad or Monica. The only person I've been able to talk to is the investigator – and she's being paid to listen. But I need to tell you something—'

He raises his palms. 'Stop! I don't want to hear any more. Really, Anna. I wish I were you – I wish I didn't remember her, that I could be distant in the way you can be. I want to get on with my life and forget she ever existed.'

215

'You see me as distant?'

He smiles wanly, shaking his head. 'That's what you got from all of that?' He stands from the stool, his eyes on mine. 'You're unbelievable sometimes.' He takes off his scarf and stuffs it in his pocket. 'Go on. What's this thing you want to tell me?'

'Sally Munroe, the investigator Jack organised for me,' – I stretch the truth a little – 'she said that Debbie wasn't reported missing until two months after she disappeared – and that it was Grandad who reported it, not Dad.'

His expression doesn't change. Why isn't he surprised?

He leans forward and rests his arms on the counter.

'Debbie left a note,' he says. 'In Tenerife.'

'I know. Dad only told me a few days ago.'

'I remember it. On holiday, Dad walked around with this piece of paper in his hands for days afterwards. It was the first time I'd ever seen him cry. A few years later, I was rummaging around – I can't remember what I was looking for, batteries probably – and I found it. Just lying in a drawer under all sorts of crap. Why would they still have it? I'd have burnt it . . .'

'What did it say?'

He rubs his forehead. 'God, I don't know. "I'm sorry I have to leave", or something along those lines.' He looks up at me. 'I wasn't . . . I'm not . . . like you, Anna. I didn't want to cling on to everything she ever touched. That's if she *had* touched it. I just put it back where it was. And when I next went to look for it – though I don't know why I'd want to read it again – it'd gone.'

'What do you mean: *if* she had touched it?'

He shrugs and gives a heavy sigh. 'The writing . . . it was all over the place. I don't mean in a child's scrawl or anything like that . . . it was odd. I haven't seen many examples of Mum's handwriting, but it didn't feel like hers. It was on this horrid

216

pink notepaper. It seemed contradictory that this note telling everyone she was going was on such bright paper.'

'Pink notepaper?' It doesn't take long for me to make the connection. 'The letters that Grandad had . . . that Debbie received a few weeks before you – we – went to Tenerife . . . they were on the same coloured notepaper.'

'But you haven't seen the note. You can't know it's the same paper.'

'No. No, I can't.'

I don't mention that he had just called Debbie, *Mum*.

I need to see that note. I know that when I see it, it *will* be the same notepaper.

'I know that look of yours, Anna. I know you want to keep digging, but I'm scared for you, for all of us. If I'm honest, I don't think I want to know. Whatever it is, it won't be good.' He starts to walk away from the counter. 'I don't think Debbie wrote that email you're chasing. Really, I don't.'

I nod slowly. 'Okay.'

'Look, I *am* here for you if there's no one else to talk to. Other people don't know what we're going through – well, they don't know what *I'm* going through . . . *everyone* knows what you're going through.'

He gives a sad smile. He's always been the brave one, the one who tried to protect me from everything. Who's been there for him?

'Shit, I'm sorry, Rob. I've tried to think about what's best for everyone. I've tried to be kind. I've been selfish doing all of this, haven't I? I've hurt you.'

'No, you haven't hurt me, Anna. Stop feeling as though everything's your fault – it's not. And you should stop *trying* to be kind to everyone – you *are* a kind person. You make such an effort in trying to please people, but you should do what's best for you.'

217

He walks slowly towards the door, and I follow.

'That's the nicest thing you've ever said to me,' I say.

'Well, it's true.'

'I know I'm pushing my luck here, but you wouldn't mind if I carried on with the investigator?'

'I'd be contradicting myself if I said no,' he says, turning back into academic mode. He opens the door, lifting his hand in a wave. 'Bye, Anna.'

With the shop empty, I grab the laptop from the back room and open it on the counter. The sky is still cloudless, so it's likely be quiet this afternoon. Isobel hardly ever comes in when the weather is nice: too busy sunning herself in her back garden.

I type in Debbie's name. There are loads of results; Debbie Atherton is not an uncommon name. I sign in to LinkedIn, in the hope I see her face in one of the profile photos. I Google every one with the same estimated age, but I can't find her. It's something I've done countless times before. I don't know why I thought it would be different today.

There are no news articles about her disappearance – I already knew this. I assumed the reason was because it was in the eighties and there was no Internet. I had never queried the fact my dad never actively searched for her. It was always Grandad.

Why hadn't I questioned it? Jack often says I'm naive – he used to think it sweet – but now I feel stupid.

It's now two o'clock and there hasn't been a single customer since I came back. I log in to Facebook and scroll through Jack's friends list again. There is no Simon or Francesca Howarth. I type her name into the Facebook search bar; there are only a few in the UK, but I've no idea where she lived or what university she went to, if at all. Did she still live in Yorkshire? The article reported that her accident happened just outside York, so the chances are high, but the two I find in that area look to be in their teens. I wish I'd had more time to talk to Sally.

Before I left the café, she said that the house next door to the one I first lived in is for sale. I type the postcode into Rightmove, and recognise it straight away; I drive down that road at least once a month. The houses are small two-up two-down terraces, with tiny walled gardens at the front, yards at the back. The inside of next door looks as though it's been untouched for at least twenty years – large sofas and loud carpets. The kitchen is beige-and-brown melamine, but spotless.

My mobile phone sounds. A text from Sally.

Viewing for tomorrow morning okay?

Friday's my day off this week, so I reply yes.

It's not Dad's day to collect Sophie, but I need to see the letter Debbie wrote at the end. I make a call to Sophie's school to tell them not to send her to after-school club. I take the money from the till, quickly balancing it, and lock it, and the laptop, in the security cupboard. The chances of Isobel coming in are slim, but I leave a note on the counter saying I've gone home ill, just in case.

I rarely pick Sophie up from school at the normal time. If she's not at after-school club then my dad picks her up. It's a different world, standing at the school gates. There are a few strays, like me, but most of the parents are in groups of three or four, talking loudly about Marks & Spencer shoes or the new head teacher, Mr Hooper. '*Don't tell hubby I said this, but that Mr Hooper can teach me a lesson anytime.*'

Ugh, *hubby*.

I'm probably jealous. I haven't even seen the new head teacher. Being around these parents makes me yearn to be the same.

Sophie's surprise as she sees me waiting for her makes my heart swell.

'Mummy!' she shouts, running towards me.

At six, she is not yet self-conscious or too embarrassed to show her eagerness in greeting me.

I open my arms and she runs into them, hitting me on the head with her lunch bag.

'Sorry, Mummy.'

'That's all right, love.' I stand, taking her by the hand. 'I thought we could pop and see Grandad and Grandma this afternoon. Would you like that?'

'Er. Okay. But it's not Wednesday, is it?'

'No.'

I feel guilty taking Sophie to Dad's after I promised myself I wouldn't talk about Debbie in front of her. I open the car door for her and she sits on her booster seat. As I pass her the seat belt, my phone vibrates. I take it out of my pocket.

It's a message from Dad.

I hold on to the sides of the car as I take in the words: *Monica's been injured. We're in Royal Preston Hospital.*

Chapter Thirty

Wednesday, 16 July 1986

Debbie

I get home and my dad has already set off to fetch Bobby. Mum's still wearing her tabard as she waves Nathan off from the front step.

'Will you tell Peter you've been on a day out with his friend?' she says as his car disappears around the corner.

'Course I'll tell him. And Nathan was my friend before he was anyone else's.'

Mum tuts and rolls her eyes as she takes Annie out of my arms, and goes back into the house. I drag the pram into the hallway. No matter how old I am, Mum has this special talent for making me feel like a naughty fifteen-year-old.

'What was that for?' I say.

'You two always had your fights.'

'Who?'

'You and Monica. And now you're talking about who was friends with Nathan first!'

'But—'

Mum's already in the kitchen, putting on the kettle. I follow her, and lean back on a kitchen chair.

'Nathan said something to me earlier . . .' says Mum, 'while you were changing upstairs. Are you sure everything's all right between you and Peter? He'd never hurt you, would he?'

'No. What did Nathan say?'

'Oh, nothing. Just something about smashed cups. Ignore me . . . I've probably got the wrong end of the stick.' She takes a bottle out of the fridge. 'He really loved you, Nathan. Didn't he?'

I can't get away from it. I thought coming back to Mum and Dad's would give me a break.

'I'll get back home tonight if that's all right,' I say.

'Course it's all right,' she says. 'But your dad has loved having you all here. I dare say he'll be upset.'

She places Annie in the bouncer on the living-room floor and comes back into the kitchen.

'You will come round next Wednesday for the wedding, won't you? I'll put on a nice spread – it'll save you cooking.'

'Course. Wouldn't miss it for the world.'

'Eh, you sarky thing. This country would be on its knees if it weren't for the monarchy.'

'It's on its knees as it is. And don't let Dad hear you say that about the royals.'

'As if I would.'

She pours hot water into a plastic jug and puts Annie's bottle into it.

'Are you all right, Deborah?' she says, any hint of a smile gone from her face. 'Only I heard you mention to your dad last night about some letters you were getting.'

'Were you listening in?'

She feigns surprise; her hand rests on her heart.

'I don't eavesdrop! You know how sound carries in this house.'

'Well, you'll have heard that I didn't want to worry you then, won't you?'

'I'm your mother. I can't help it — I have to worry. Do you have the letters with you? It might be that creepy neighbour you've got opposite you?'

'Been thinking about it much, have you, Mum?' I smile at her. 'I didn't think you were listening when I talked about him in the past — or Dirty Dean as Monica calls him.'

'I always listen.'

The phone rings in the hallway.

'Get that, will you?' she says, shaking droplets of milk onto her wrist to test the temperature. 'I'll feed Annie . . . seeing as I'll not be getting the chance again for months.'

'Don't exaggerate, Mother,' I shout on my way to the phone.

I pick up the handset. 'Hello?'

'Debbie, it's me.' Peter's voice is quiet. 'I heard you went on a little jaunt with Nathan.'

'News travels fast. I've only been back fifteen minutes. You've been talking to Monica, haven't you?'

He sighs. 'She saw you in his car when she was on her lunch break. And you know what she's like . . . loves knowing information before anyone else.'

'Yes, I do know her. She's been my best friend for over ten years. How could she have seen us? We didn't go through town.'

'She's worried about you.'

'Then why doesn't she speak to *me* about it?'

'She said she tried to, but you started talking about hearing things — voices in your head.'

He whispers the last four words, as though afraid of being overheard.

'What?'

I shouldn't have believed Monica when she said she'd keep that quiet, but I can't believe she actually told him. Even for her, this is one step too far.

223

'I said I was tired . . . that I heard next door, that's all. Why does she have to make a big deal out of everything?'

'I know . . .' he says. 'I told her she was being dramatic . . . overstating things. So you didn't say you heard voices? I told her you would've come to me about it first.'

I don't know what to say to him. I sit on the bottom step of the stairs.

'Debs, are you still there?'

'Yes.'

'You would tell me if you needed help, wouldn't you?'

Scenes flash through my mind: of me confessing I'm not all right, Peter and Monica getting together – of her taking over my life, my children.

I stand and walk over to the mirror. My hair is knotted and dull from the sea air. Shadows line the skin under my eyes. I look a mess, but I don't care.

'Yes, of course I'd tell you.' My voice is flat. I can't fake emotion any more. 'I'm not hearing things. She's making it up. She always was thrifty with the truth.'

There's movement behind me. Mum. She's probably been listening the whole time. I turn around, still holding the phone to my ear.

'Are you okay?' she whispers.

I nod and turn back to face the mirror.

'I suppose,' says Peter. 'Look. Can I pick you up? I've taken the afternoon off. I think we need to talk.'

I tell him yes, and replace the handset. But the last thing I want to do is talk to him.

I sit back on the bottom step.

'Have you ever thought of . . .' I say aloud.

'Thought of what?' Mum stands at my feet, Annie in her arms.

'Nothing, nothing. I'm fine.'

'You're not thinking of doing anything stupid, are you?'

'No, no. Of course not.'

All I can think of is doing something stupid, but to me it makes perfect sense.

Peter and I barely said a word to each other on the drive back home, but Bobby's chatter masked any uneasiness. Now, he's sitting on the living-room carpet in front of the telly watching one of his videos, and Annie's still asleep in the new car seat Peter brought with him.

'This holiday is just what you need, Debs,' he says, putting a mug of milk in the microwave.

'Do you have to microwave everything?' I say.

'We've only got a few days to pack,' he says, ignoring me. 'Did you manage to get Annie's name on your passport?'

He looks at me and holds up his hands.

'Don't worry,' he says. 'I'll see if I can sort it out.'

'I didn't say I wouldn't do it.'

'But you were thinking it.'

'Why do you always presume to know what's in my head? I wasn't thinking about anything.'

'Perhaps that's the problem.'

He says it so quietly I'm not sure I heard him right. I feel like the fight in me has gone, but then, it shouldn't be a fight, should it? I'm still the same person I always was, aren't I? I just do different things with my day.

Looking back at my life only seven years ago, I know I'm a different person. I'd been in my job a year, earning my own money, and I felt I was on the edge of something – freedom, travelling the world maybe. Now, everything feels such a chore; the hopelessness I've felt in the back of my mind has risen to the surface and it's taking over.

I stand straighter, levelling my head with Peter's.

'Nathan said you and Monica have been talking about me.'

He rolls his eyes.

'You make it sound like we're school kids. I've been worried about you.'

'Worried that I've not been making your tea, or doing your washing? Babies take up time and energy, you know.'

The dial on the microwave pings, relieving Peter of the awkward silence. He gives a stilted laugh and gets the mug out.

'Shi— sugar! Why don't they warn you that everything you put in that thing will come out the same temperature as the food?'

'They do,' I say flatly. 'That's why they do special cooking containers. I'm surprised you didn't know that, working at Woolies.'

It's typical of us these days, that whenever we try to have a serious conversation, it always ends up with something domestic. And then it hits me, as I look around our small kitchen: it's spotless. The mess that was there two nights ago has been cleared away.

I've never been domesticated. Mum usually did everything for me when I lived at home, and I went straight from home to living with Peter. We first lived together when we got back from our honeymoon in Wales. I started back at work at the estate agency, and Peter was at Woolworths – he was assistant manager then. I had visions of domestic bliss – of coming home before Peter, tidying around and having a cooked meal waiting for him. But after the first week, I realised it was just so boring.

The dishes began to pile up on the kitchen sides. I'd learn my kitchen skills from watching Mum, but Peter didn't like corned beef mashed with potato and peas. And he said I over-cooked chicken all the time, but Mum always worried about salmonella poisoning – I thought everyone did. So, he bought a freezer. From then on, whoever got home first would put tea in the oven. But then the house fairy didn't magically come and clean up after us.

I got the urge last year to make Bobby a birthday cake, but it looked like a pancake when I got it out of the oven. Luckily, Mrs Abernathy had boxes of cake mix. Everyone had said it was the best cake they'd ever eaten (I'd hidden the box in the outside dustbin).

'You'll have to make this every week,' said Peter.

'Once a year will do,' I said, smiling.

Smiling.

I used to smile.

Looking around our kitchen now, there's not a dirty dish in sight. Peter's been busy.

I turn my back on him and glance at the kitchen clock: only five thirty. Is it too early for bed?

'I know you said on the way back from your mum's not to mention Monica, but she's genuinely concerned about you. And I've arranged for, er . . .'

I turn back around; he's stirring powdered chocolate into the hot milk, clanging the spoon around the mug for longer than necessary.

'What have you arranged? If it's a doctor's appointment, then I can arrange that myself. I'm perfectly fine.'

'No, no. Not the doctor's. A night out with Monica on Friday night. I thought you could let your hair down for a few hours.'

I close my eyes. I suppose that's not such a bad idea. Before I escaped to Mum and Dad's, I felt the walls of this house closing in on me, people watching me. And Monica's tongue is always loose after a few drinks.

'*Nobody loves you. They'd rather you were dead. They're thinking of ways to get rid of you.*'

I open my eyes. 'What did you say?'

He swallows the hot chocolate.

'Nothing. I had my mouth full.'

I'm just tired, that's all it is. Perhaps if I have a few drinks, I'll get a decent night's sleep.

'Okay,' I say. 'I'll go on the night out.'

'Great. I'll let her know.'

I say nothing.

I picture what'll probably happen this evening. Me, putting on a happy face, watching bloody *Albion Market* or whatever it's called, and then going to bed knowing I'll be awake a few hours later. It doesn't even fill me with dread, because I feel nothing.

'If you don't mind,' I say, 'I'm going to have an early night. I didn't sleep well last night.'

I walk through the door to the lounge. Bobby's still engrossed in *Thomas the Tank Engine*.

'But I thought we were okay now?' says Peter. 'How will I do the kids' bedtime on my own?'

He thought we were all right? Did he think that a suggestion of a night out would make everything better? I don't know what planet he lives on.

'It'll be good practice for Friday,' I say. 'Mum made up some spare bottles for tonight – they're in Annie's bag.'

'Wait a sec, Deb.'

I stop and slowly turn around. I'm not in the mood for an argument. I just need to get under the bed covers and lie alone in the dark. I wait for another of his protests, but instead he gets something out of the drawer.

'This came for you yesterday.'

He's holding out a pink envelope. It has my name and address written on it. He's smiling – does he know who's written it?

I don't want it, I want to say. Whoever's writing to me is trying to break me. But I can't tell Peter that.

'Thanks,' I say.

I manage to stop the tremble in my hands as I take the letter. I walk through the lounge into the hall.

'Night, Debs,' he shouts after me. 'Hope you feel better in the morning.'

He talks as though I'm a colleague or someone at the corner shop. Why isn't he intrigued about the letter? I know I would be, if he were to receive one. We hardly ever get handwritten mail these days, people just phone each other. I shut the door to the living room and scrutinise the postmark. *Lancashire and South Lakes*. It's local. This is the first time one of these letters has been stamped. Perhaps it's just a fluke that it's the same colour.

I tear it open.

My hope that the colour is pure coincidence is shattered when I read it.

He wishes you were dead. They're thinking of ways to get rid of you.

I stand for a few moments as I take in the same carefully written capital letters. It's like the words in my head have been printed on paper, but I'm reading them as though I'm a thousand miles away – like it's happening to someone else.

It can't be Dean. I don't know why I even thought it would be. I can't understand why anyone would want to be so mean to me.

Unless they really know me.

Perhaps Peter wasn't curious about it because *he* wrote it.

I can't trust him. He's in on it too. With Monica. I don't think she's ever liked me, not really. But fuck her. I don't care what she thinks of me.

I want to tear the letter into pieces, but I don't. I leave it on the hall table. If it's still there in the morning, then I'm going to collect all of the notes and take them to someone who can help me.

But, for the moment, I haven't the energy to give a shit. Let whoever it is hurt me. They'll be doing me a favour.

Chapter Thirty-One

Anna

I manage to find a parking space in the crammed hospital car park. I switch the engine off, and lean against the seat.

Thank God Jack finished work early and I could leave Sophie at home.

'Did your dad say what was wrong with her?' Jack whispered to me before I set off.

'No, nothing. Just that she was injured and in hospital.'

I was shaking so much my keys rattled as I held them. Jack took both of my hands in his.

'Try not to worry. Shall I drive you there?'

'No, no. I don't want to worry Sophie. I'll be fine.'

I turned to leave, but a thought stopped me.

'How come you're back so early? When I phoned, you were already home.'

'I . . . I just wanted to have a chat. But now's not the right time. Just go – go and see Monica.'

'Oh . . . okay.'

It's bad enough imagining what's wrong with Monica, without worrying even more about my marriage. Oh God. What if she isn't all right? Dad didn't say what happened, and when I tried to phone him, it went straight to answerphone. I get out of the car and walk slowly to the main reception.

I give Monica's name, and almost cry with relief when the man behind the desk says, 'Take the lift to level two, and then through the doors to your right. Bleasdale Ward.'

When Grandad was here three years ago with his knee, it took me at least half an hour to find him, but Monica's is easier to find. I push the hand sanitiser into my palms and spread it up to my wrist.

'Could you tell me where I can find Monica Atherton?' I say to the nurse at the station.

She points her pen to a room only two metres away.

I see Dad straight away, leaning against the window. The curtain around Monica's bed is pulled across, so I can't see her from the doorway.

'Dad!' I walk quickly towards him, trying to walk on tiptoes so as not to disturb the other patients. I don't know why I bother, though, because most of them are chatting away to the visitors milling around them.

It takes a few seconds for his eyes to focus, to recognise me.

'Anna! I didn't expect you to come here. Did I not put that in the text? Where's Sophie?'

'Jack left work early. I had to come – I was worried about Monica.'

She's sitting up in the bed, her eyes closed. Her right arm is in a cast and there are Steri-Strips on her forehead.

'Hey, Annie,' she says, her voice slurred.

'They gave her some pain relief,' says Dad.

I sit on the plastic chair next to the bed; Dad sits on the one opposite.

'What happened?'

'She fell down the stairs at the train station.'

'I was pushed,' Monica says quietly.

I look up at Dad.

'Pushed?' I say. 'Oh my God! Have you called the police?'

Dad purses his lips. 'I think it's the pain relief. I wasn't there, I was paying for the tickets. We were going to go for a day trip to Southport. There were a few other people who saw what happened, but they didn't see anyone push her. Remember when they gave your grandad morphine for his knee? He started talking to your grandmother . . . thought he was about to die too . . . that she was coming for him and after that, he was convinced there were spiders crawling all over him.'

Monica groans. She tries to open her eyes, but the one nearest me, the one with the strips above it, is too swollen.

'She was wearing those ridiculous shoes,' says Dad. 'The ones with the weird tassels on them.'

'I bought her those,' I say. 'And they're pom-poms, not tassels.'

I don't know why I'm taking offence about a pair of shoes at a time like this.

'Sorry, love,' says Dad. 'But they're not very practical.'

'I feel awful now.'

'It wasn't *your* fault, Anna,' says Dad. 'I said to Monica, "They're shoes for sitting down in, not travelling in."'

'Did you?'

He shrugs. 'I suppose living with you two must've rubbed off on me.'

'Pushed,' says Monica.

'You weren't, love,' says Dad. 'But if it makes you feel better, I'll see if the station has CCTV.' He looks at me. 'I really don't think she was pushed.'

I look to Monica: an imperceptible shake of her head.

'Dad, Monica *can* hear you, you know.' I try to whisper, so my voice is lost among the chatter around us. 'Are you sure she's just imagining it? It's not as if she's seeing dead people or creepy crawlies everywhere.'

233

Dad frowns. 'We'll have a better idea when whatever medication they gave her wears off. She was in too much pain to talk before the ambulance came.'

After ten minutes, Monica seems to have fallen asleep.

Dad gets up carefully, so he doesn't scrape the chair on the floor.

'If you can stay for a few more minutes, love,' he says, 'would you mind if I go and grab a coffee from downstairs?'

'Of course.'

He's only been gone half a minute when Monica opens her eyes. She leans forwards, gently smacking her lips together. I reach over for the beaker of water on her cabinet. After taking a small sip, she leans back into her pillow, exhausted.

'So thirsty.' She pats around the bed with her free hand; I put my hand in hers. She squeezes it. 'Darling, Annie. You should find the letters. The truth. Get me some clothes. Use your key.'

'What do you mean, *the truth*?'

Monica closes her eyes again.

'Everything okay here?'

'You were quick, Dad!'

'Was I?'

I take my hand from under Monica's and stand.

'I'm going to pop to yours and get Monica a change of clothes,' I say. 'So you don't have to worry about going back and forth in visiting hours.'

'Are you sure you don't mind?' says Dad.

'No, it's fine.' I walk over to him and kiss him on the cheek. 'I'll see you in an hour or so.'

'Thanks, love,' he says.

Poor Dad.

I don't think he knows as much as Monica.

★ ★ ★

234

It's six o'clock, still light, but the lamp at the far end of their hallway is still on, as always. 'It's the ambience more than the light,' Monica always says; it reminds me of Penelope Keith in *The Good Life*.

Robert said he found the letters years ago, in the junk drawer – the place where all the old phone chargers, screwdrivers, television and microwave receipts are kept. They probably won't have been put back there, but I check it anyway. There are still the same old Nokia chargers that were there years before. I search in the other drawers: tea towels, cutlery, sharp knives. But no letters.

I head upstairs, going straight to Dad and Monica's room. They have fitted wardrobes and drawers along the wall to the left. Monica's clothes are in the cupboard near the window. I grab a weekend bag from the bottom and pull it open on their bed. I look at her clothes; most are unsuitable for a stay in hospital. There are at least twenty dry-clean only dresses, and five silk blouses. I don't think I have ever seen her in a pair of jeans. I go to the chest of drawers near the bedroom door. From what I remember, Monica's things are in the top three. It feels inappropriate to be looking in her underwear, so I just grab a few random items and shove them into the bag.

I open the second drawer and find neatly ironed and folded nightdresses and pyjamas. I take one of each, close the drawer, and grab her dressing gown from the back of the door. She might only be in one night, but you never know. I open the third drawer where she keeps her exercise gear. She's fifty-eight and still does aerobics three times a week. I pick out a pair of what look like yoga trousers and a matching top, still with their labels attached. She might not want to be in her nightwear in front of strangers.

I open the fourth and fifth drawers. Dad's underwear and pyjamas. I kneel on the floor and pull open the bottom drawer.

There are three Clarks shoeboxes in a row at the back. I grab the nearest and take off the lid.

Inside are lots of little packages with Sellotape wrapped round them. *Anna 1992* is written on one of them in Monica's handwriting. There must be seven or eight with my name on. I pick at the tape on one and gently prise off the paper. Inside is a tiny white thing. I take it into the palm of my hand and see that it's a baby tooth. *My* baby tooth. She kept them.

I push the little packages of teeth to one side and pull out the wad of paper underneath. I sit cross-legged as I pick up the first. It's a handmade card with a picture of a woman and a dandelion on the front. *Happy Mother's Day, Monica. I love you. From Anna Bandana.*

Under my words, Monica has written *1993*.

Anna Bandana. I'd forgotten that's what she called me.

Did she mind that I never called her *Mummy*?

Under this are other cards I made her. The dates scribed underneath them end at 1997. Hadn't I written her a Mother's Day card since? My face grows cold with shame.

I remember Dad used to buy her flowers, telling her they were from all of us. 1997 was the year I started secondary school; I had only thought about myself, and the fact my mother didn't want me. But all along, I had Monica. Someone who talked to me about things Dad was too embarrassed to speak about. She stroked my hair when Jason Doherty in Year 10 said I was the ugliest person he had ever seen. 'You're not ugly, Anna. You're beautiful. He probably likes you. They're strange creatures, boys. And we should know, shouldn't we? We live with three of them.'

I lay down the Mother's Day cards, replacing the little packages of teeth on top of them. I place the shoebox next to the other two and lift open the lid of the one next to mine. Inside are identical packages labelled 'Bobby'. I flick the lid of the third, expecting the same, labelled 'Leo', but it isn't.

Inside, there is a pink envelope addressed to Debbie. Underneath it, there are two folded notes in the same colour – the same pink as the awful letters Grandad gave me. My hands shake as I lift them out. I open the first one.

He wishes you were dead. They're thinking of ways to get rid of you.

It is written in identical handwriting to the ones Debbie received. Why does Monica have this one and not the rest?

The other note's folds are worn, as though it's been read hundreds of times. The paper is grubby.

I open it. Robert was right about the handwriting. It's not like the other envelope, but a strange, slurred scrawl.

To my family,
I'm sorry. I can't do this any more. I've tried.
I love you all.
Debbie.

I read it again and again. Is this all she wrote before abandoning her whole family? It's so vague. If she was intending to leave, then why not say everything she wanted to?

I reach into Robert's shoebox. Underneath the Mother's Day cards are birthday cards from age one to six. *Love from Mummy and Daddy*, is written on each of them. Some have been written by my dad, but others have my mother's writing inside. I compare it to the writing on the pink note signed by Debbie.

It's not the same.

Chapter Thirty-Two

She suggested a café I've never been to before, but that wasn't difficult. Smooth FM plays quietly in the background, but I can still make out the song: 'Just the Way You Are' by Billy Joel.

She was already here when I arrived. I didn't tell her what I wanted, but she walks over to the counter and places a black coffee in front of me.

'I didn't mean to,' she says. 'I reached over to say hello and she just fell.'

'She wouldn't remember you,' I say. 'It was too long ago.'

'So, I'm that forgettable?'

'I didn't mean it like that.'

'Is she okay?'

'How would I know?'

'There's no need to be like that.'

'Sorry, sorry. It's just that . . . you could've ruined the whole thing.'

'Excuse me?'

'I'm so close. I'm nearly ready.'

'Why is everything about you?' She leans forward, her eyes

boring into mine. 'You need to remember that I've kept your secret for all of these years. I didn't have to.'

'I know, I know. I said I'm sorry, didn't I?' I run my finger along the rim of the cup, but it's not like glass, it won't make a sound even though I wish it would. 'I'm thinking of confessing – it's been on my conscience for too long.'

'You know I think you're doing the right thing. Perhaps leave out the part where I'm involved, though.'

'I suppose. But they need to hear the whole truth. It's not fair on them. I started all of this – I have to see it to the end. They won't believe me if you don't back me up.'

She shakes her head. 'I really don't understand you.'

'I don't think I understand myself.'

She stands, her coffee barely touched, and puts on her jacket.

'If it all goes wrong,' she says, 'don't come running to me.'

I don't reply; I watch her leave, not looking back.

'Heart of Glass' plays on the radio.

You're following me, aren't you? I try putting my fingers in my ears, but it doesn't drown out the sound.

I push my coffee away and stand.

The bell dings as I open the door. I take a deep breath of fresh air, but there's a scent in the air.

I search for you.

Sometimes I think I see you.

I want to run to you and tell you that I'm sorry. But I can't. Because you're dead.

Chapter Thirty-Three

Friday, 18 July 1986

Debbie

Monica's at the bar, probably asking for another couple of cocktails with umbrellas. They work, these ones. The umbrellas, I mean, not the cocktails (although they work too). You just push the little round bit up and down the cocktail stick, and there you have it: a working umbrella. If you're the size of a mouse. And I'm definitely not the size of a mouse.

Oh God, I should stop smiling to myself.

Shit, I'm pissed.

We've only had two, but I haven't had a drink for months. It feels like years since I've been out like this. From the time we started going to pubs, which was from about the age of fifteen (but don't tell my mother), Monica's always been the one to go to the bar. When I was twenty, I looked about twelve, so I've always handed her the money and she always got me what she wanted.

I suppose I could go to the bar myself, but it's a tradition now. Peter says it's lazy, but I've just had a baby – I'm practically an invalid.

And he's not here anyway, so I can do what I want.

Before I left the house, I went to prepare a few bottles for

Annie, but Peter had already made up four and put them in the fridge. Making me feel useless, again. Since when had he learned how to do all of that? Monica, probably. She must've been giving him lessons. She was probably the one who tidied our kitchen the other day. I won't tell her I'm onto them. Have to keep one step ahead.

If Peter saw me now, I'd tell him that I'm happy.

Right now, at this precise time, in this actual moment.

Time.

I look at my watch. It says eight thirty, though it could be nine thirty.

Ah fuck it, I'm out of the house. I'm me again.

I look down at my crap outfit. Leggings with a baggy grey top that has neon stripes across it. Neon. When did that become a thing? I'm so fat, I can't wear anything decent any more. Monica's wearing a denim skirt and a boob tube. Shit, even three weeks after she had Leo, she was in her old clothes.

I should be thin too by now. I can't remember the last time I enjoyed a meal. I must just stuff it in when no one's looking – including my own eyes. Anyway, it's not all love and roses and Milk Tray. Nathan's still a bit weird about Leo, even after five years.

'I'm Not in Love' by 10cc whines its way from the jukebox. God, it's such a depressing song. I roll my eyes at nobody. Someone should update that machine. We'll have to stick a few fifty-pence pieces in it later. We used to take it over, boring the whole pub with Blondie on repeat.

Monica's coming back. I've got to be sensible now – pretend I can hold my drink. I used to be able to drink Peter under the table, for God's sake.

Sit up, Debbie.

I shuffle my arse to the back of the seat and press my back to it.

'A Slow Comfortable Screw,' she says, setting the drinks on the table.

'First time for everything.' I put the straw to my mouth. 'Hmm, fruity.'

Monica crosses her legs as she sits on the little stool. She bends her body to the table and sucks from the straw without touching the glass with her hands. She must be as pissed as I am.

'Not bad,' she says. 'Though I think I'd prefer half a lager. I'm so thirsty today.'

'You're not pregnant, are you?'

'Since when has being thirsty been a symptom of pregnancy?'

I shrug.

'Anyway,' she says. 'It's so good to have a night out. We haven't done this for years.'

'What do you mean? We went out loads before I got pregnant with Annie.'

'I meant just us two. Like it used to be.'

'I suppose.'

'Do you remember those nights out on the Manx ferry nightclub? I thought we'd live like that forever. Working for the weekends – that's what we used to say. Then we'd meet up again on the Sunday and go to the pictures.'

'It feels like a lifetime ago.'

'Xanadu' sounds from the pub speakers.

'What the fuck is this song about?' I say.

'No idea.'

I want to ask her about her cosy chats with Peter, but I'm worried it'll turn the night into something darker. Every time I look at her, I picture her kissing him. God, I can't look at her any more.

'What's up?' she says.

'Nothing. Just looking at how much this place has changed.'

She looks around, her nose wrinkles.

'It hasn't changed at all.' She lifts her bum, and drags the stool closer to the table, picking up her drink, and throwing the umbrella on the table. 'How is everything?'

'You're as subtle as a brick. Is this why you suggested the night out? So you can report back to Peter with my little secrets?'

She almost drops her drink back down.

'Where the hell did that come from?' she says. 'What do you mean, your little secrets? I wouldn't tell Peter anything you told me.'

'But you told him that I was hearing things, didn't you? I told you in the café the other week. And then you went running to Peter with the latest bit of gossip.'

'Debbie, I swear I didn't tell him. Who else have you told?'

I don't know whether to believe her; she seems so sincere.

'I haven't told anyone else.'

She narrows her eyes. 'Are you sure?'

'Of course I'm sure.'

There's a hesitation in my voice. I don't even believe myself. Did I tell Nathan the other day?

'I know it's been hard for you since Annie was born, being stuck in the house all day. But is there anything else bothering you?'

Her eyes are wide. Is she acting? She was always so good at masking her feelings. Wasn't she? Or was that me? God, I shouldn't drink any more. I look at her again, squinting so I can focus on her properly. She could be lying. It could be *her* who wrote those letters to me.

I grab my handbag and take out the notes, laying them on the table side by side.

Monica bends down so she's inches away as she reads each one.

She scans them again before looking up at me.

'Holy shit, Debbie. When did you start getting these?'

'Only a few days after I got home from hospital.'

'Do you recognise the handwriting?' She picks one up and holds the letter up to her face.

'No. But it's hard to tell when it's written in capitals like that. It could be anyone.'

'Have you told anybody else about these?'

'My dad, Mum, Peter.'

'What did Peter say about it?'

'Nothing really. He didn't seem that interested at all.'

'Has he read them?'

'I . . . I can't remember. I'm sure I gave them to him to read. But he sort of batted me away. I left this one on the hall table the other night, and it was still there the following morning. If he has read it, then he's ignored it . . . he's not mentioned it.'

'How odd. Why didn't you bring it up again?' She holds up another. 'I mean – this one is really creepy. Who does he think wants you dead?'

'What makes you think a man wrote them?'

She puts the letter down as though it's given her an electric shock.

'It's just that . . . Oh, I don't know.' She picks up her drink and throws the straw on the table next to the discarded umbrella and downs the rest of her cocktail in one. She shivers as she places the glass on the table. 'I know a policeman through work. Can I take this one and show it to him?'

She picks up the last one I received. The one that mentions death. I suck up the rest of my drink.

'Sure.'

She folds it back up and puts it in her handbag.

'Are you not scared, Debs?'

244

I lean back against the back of the banquette.

'Should I be scared? I suppose it's made me afraid of being alone in the house, like I'm always being watched.'

'Shit, Debbie. You should've called me as soon as you got them – as soon as you got the first one.'

'But you're in cahoots with them. You'd say I was losing it.'

'What? I can't believe you're saying that to me. I care about you. You're like a sister to me.'

'Perhaps it was you.'

The colour drains from her face.

'What do you mean?'

'It was you who told Peter that I was hearing things.'

Her shoulders relax a little. Her chest rises as she takes a deep breath.

'Okay, okay. Yes, it was me. But it's only because I was worried.'

'I can't believe you lied to me.'

'It was only a little white lie. I didn't want it to spoil our night.'

'Right,' I say, picking up my jacket. 'Right. I understand.'

I put my arms in the sleeves and stand.

'Where are you going?' she says.

'Home. I don't want to look at your smug face any more.' I step aside from the table. 'With your perfect hair, your perfect clothes, your perfect life.'

I turn to leave, but she shouts after me.

'You don't know!' she says.

I stop and turn around. 'Don't know what?'

'My life is far from perfect. I think Nathan's having an affair.'

I shake my head at her. 'Whatever, Monica. You just can't stop lies spouting from that mouth of yours, can you?'

The door slams behind me and the fresh air hits me in the face.

★   ★   ★

It must be just after ten – it's only just going dark and there are still loads of people on the streets. I haven't been out in so long that the taxis aren't in the same place any more. Everything's a mass of lights and sounds. I don't want to be here, but I don't want to go home either. I'll walk it. It'll only take me ten minutes tops. Maybe thirty.

I stand at the traffic lights for ages, while other people cross regardless. They mustn't be as drunk as I am; they're giving me funny looks. Or are they? I wait another few minutes for the lights to change, even though there aren't any cars. Dad says you should never take safety for granted. Green cross code.

I cross and head up the hill. This is going to take me ages. I pull my jacket around me – it's freezing now. Why can't we have summers like they do abroad?

'All right, love?'

I ignore the man leaving the pub to my left. The cigarette smoke billows out of the place. I inhale, and it takes me back to when we had nothing better to do than spend all day in the pub.

There's a hand on my shoulder.

'I said, *All right, love*?'

I turn slowly. 'Oh, it's you.'

Dean. I can't get away from the man.

'That's not much of a hello, is it?' he says.

'Monica should be here any minute,' I say.

'Yeah right. She's a right bitch, she is. I don't know why you don't see it.'

'How come you know so much about Monica?'

He shrugs. 'I've got eyes everywhere.'

I bet you have, you slimy get, I think to myself. 'Anyway, I'd best get on.'

'Reckon you should be at home with your baby at this time of night, don't you?'

I turn and walk away.

'Whatever,' I mutter. 'Caveman.'

'I heard that, you know.'

I start to run – is he following me? I daren't turn around. A bus pulls into the stop across the road; I run towards it.

Dean's laughing to himself. 'As if I'd chase after you, you fat cow.'

People stare at me as I get on the bus. I want to disappear. I shouldn't have agreed to go out – it's safer indoors.

I hand the driver two fifty-pence pieces and sit on the side furthest from Dean. I glance through the opposite window, but he's not in the street any more.

I don't know where this bus is going – it's not even going in the right direction to home.

Why has everyone in this world turned strange? Monica and Peter are conspiring against me, Nathan's following me everywhere (except tonight when I needed him), and Mum and Dad are being overprotective. What changed to make all of this happen? Are other people changing because of me?

I've never felt so alone.

I look at the reflection in the window as the bus starts off, and I see tears streaming down my face. I don't even feel them.

Chapter Thirty-Four

Anna

I am sitting outside the bathroom, leaning against the airing cupboard, listening to Sophie shout and squeal and splash as Jack baths her.

After dropping Monica's bag at the hospital, I just wanted to get home. I didn't tell Dad about the cards and letters I found. I'm meeting Sally tomorrow to see the house next door to our old place, but that will be the last time I'm actively getting involved with this investigation. I need to sort out issues closer to home.

Seeing the Mother's Day cards made me realise I should have appreciated what I had with Monica instead of yearning for someone who didn't even want me.

Sophie tears out of the bathroom in her *Paw Patrol* pyjamas, her hair wet.

'Mummy! You're back!'

'What are you doing creeping about?' says Jack, smiling as he comes out of the bathroom.

'I did shout hello, but you two were making a racket in there.' I ruffle the top of Sophie's hair. 'And I didn't want to disturb all that fun you were having.'

'We pretended,' says Sophie, 'that the water in the empty shampoo bottles was wee.'

'Oh, lovely.'

'It wasn't pretend,' says Jack, winking at me. 'It was real wee.' Sophie wrinkles her nose.

'As if.'

'*As if?*' says Jack. 'Are you six or sixteen?'

'Don't be silly, Daddy. Come on.' Sophie walks into her bedroom. 'Read me a story.'

I get up from the floor.

'You go downstairs,' says Jack. 'Pour yourself a glass of wine. Then we can have a chat.'

He doesn't look me in the eye as he utters the last sentence. He's trying to sound more lighthearted than he feels, I'm sure of it. Jack has never requested a *chat*. In the past, he's always shuddered at the mention of a scheduled *chat*.

'Okay,' I say, as Sophie shouts for her daddy again. 'I'll see you down there.' I turn to go downstairs. 'Hey,' I say. Jack pops his head around Sophie's bedroom door. 'Did you see a car at the end of the street tonight? A red one – a new Honda, I think. I've seen it around a few times recently.'

'Nope,' he says. 'Can't say I've noticed.'

'I must be imagining things.'

By the time Jack gets downstairs, the wine in my glass is warm. Going by his expression, it seems he's looking forward to this talk as much as I am. Does he know that I found out about Francesca – that the girl he was once in love with has recently died? I have a terrible feeling of dread. Perhaps he's beginning to re-evaluate his life now that someone he was once close to has died. Maybe he doesn't see a future with me – thinks that life is too short to be miserable.

'Is that your second?' He points to my glass.

I look down at it. It's still three-quarters full.

'Yes.'

I don't know why I'm lying; perhaps it will make it easier for him to speak freely if he thinks I'm a little bit drunk.

'I'll just get myself a glass,' he says. 'Sophie's fast asleep.'

My heart is pounding. I sit a little straighter on the sofa; smooth my hair down with the palm of my hand. I haven't looked at my face since this morning – my make-up has probably worn off. I tiptoe to the mirror and place my wine glass on the mantelpiece. I pinch my cheeks to bring them colour – I used to see Gran do it, but this is the first time I've tried it and am surprised to find that it works. My lipstick has faded, but there is still a trace of eyeliner on my upper lids – at least my eyes don't look so tired. I really should make more of an effort.

I take a deep breath and a big gulp of wine. I almost retch, finding it hard to swallow. It's too warm and it tastes like vinegar. I have never really liked the taste of wine – I don't know why I pretend to. It's like the Emperor's new clothes, people always—

'So.' Jack's standing at the doorway. He walks over to the chair under the window and sits. 'I think you'd better sit down, too.'

He pats the edge of the sofa nearest him.

He sounds too cheerful for it to be terrible news. Doesn't he?

But as I sit and look at his hands, he can't keep them still.

'So,' he says, again. He takes a long sip of wine and stares at the floor. 'You remember when we first got together . . . you had this thing about asking me all about past relationships and stuff? And I told you that I was with someone when I was at college?'

'No. I didn't think we went into details about that.'

Have I remembered things wrong?

'Okay. I thought we did.' He shakes his head. 'Anyway, that's not the point . . . There was this girl called Francesca. She was only seventeen when we broke up – I was eighteen.' He takes a deep breath. 'It ended badly. She got pregnant and I said I couldn't deal with it . . . I felt like a kid myself at the time. Jesus what a cliché I was. She had a termination . . . she hated me for it. I never saw her after that. I moved to Lancashire for university and never left. We had no reason to contact each other.'

He pauses. He's speaking so pragmatically.

'So why are you bringing her up now?'

'She died in a car accident three weeks ago.'

I reach over to take hold of his hand. He squeezes mine before letting it go.

'The thing is, Anna, is that . . . God this is so hard.'

He puts a hand through his hair.

'Go on.'

My heart is thumping; my legs feel numb.

'Her brother told me that she got together with someone else pretty quickly after I left . . . but really, she was seeing him at the same time she was seeing me . . . You can see where this is going, can't you?'

I think I'm going to be sick.

'Just tell me, Jack,' I say quickly. 'I'm not going to try and guess.'

He takes another deep breath.

'Francesca had the baby.'

'What?'

I put my wine glass down before I drop it.

'She never told me. My parents moved to the south coast when I left – I had no contacts in the area.'

'You have another child?'

'I don't know.'

'What do you mean?'

'When Francesca was in hospital . . . after the accident . . . just before she died . . . she told her brother that the father of her son – it was a boy – was one of two people. The bloke she went out with after me . . . or during, whatever . . . didn't have anything to do with the baby.'

'Oh God, that poor child.'

'He didn't know any different, from what her brother Simon was telling me the other day. Francesca's family have been there for him, thank God.'

The taste of wine lingers in my mouth – I want to spit it out. My face feels hot.

I take a deep breath.

'He's sixteen,' I say aloud, more to myself than Jack.

'I know this is a lot to take in.'

'When did you find out?'

'That he existed – and the accident? Only a few weeks ago. Fran's brother contacted me on Facebook of all places. But you'd just received that email from someone claiming to be your mother.'

'Okay.' I stand. 'Right.'

And I walk out of the door.

Chapter Thirty-Five

Wednesday, 23 July 1986

Debbie

Mum's laid on a cold buffet of vol-au-vents with creamed mushrooms, crustless cucumber sandwiches, and fairy cakes decorated with red, white and blue icing. She's set it on the coffee table, which is quite casual for Mum, considering the occasion. And she's let Peter and me sit on the floor so we've easy access to the food, so it doesn't go to waste.

We're going on holiday tomorrow, and Peter's barely talking to me. It's because I can't remember getting home after the Friday night out with Monica. I must've drunk more than I thought.

'What time did you come home last night?' he'd said, standing over me as I lay in bed on Saturday morning. 'I went to bed at midnight and there was no sign of you. I've been up since six with Annie – I'm knackered.'

'I can't move,' I said, my voice monotone.

I couldn't even lift a hand. How could I tell him that I didn't remember what time I got in? I don't know what I was doing till after midnight. It was only about nine or ten when I left Monica.

'It's ten o'clock, Debs,' he said. 'I've got to go to work. I'm sorry.'

'I can't.'

'I know I said I'd cover the kids for you, but the duty manager's gone home sick.'

For me?

I threw the cover over my head, wanting a hole to swallow me into nothingness.

'I'm sick.'

'You're not sick, you're hungover.'

He whipped the quilt off my head; I brought my legs close to my chest, cowering against the pillow like a wounded animal. I hid my face with my arms. I didn't have the strength to sob, the tears just rolled down my face.

I heard him sigh as he stood next to me. I felt his breath as he crouched before me. His fingers reached through the gap in my arms and brushed the hair from my eyes.

'You didn't used to get this hungover.' He sighed. 'I'll call your mum and dad . . . see if they can come over.'

And they did, God bless them. They stayed until Peter came home from work, but I stayed in bed.

I wouldn't see Monica when she came round on Sunday. On Monday, I got up to pick Bobby up from school, waited until Peter got home, and then crawled up the stairs to bed. Annie was easy to look after. Bottle, nappy change, lie her next to me. She was fine. Tuesday was a repeat of Monday. If my children were still alive, then I was doing my job.

Monica visited again yesterday, Tuesday, evening. I heard her and Peter talking.

'You should call the doctor,' she said. 'It's not normal. It's not like her to be like this.'

Yes, it is, I thought, staring at the bedroom ceiling. It's definitely like me. It's the real me who's been cocooned, pretending, just waiting for the chance to show my real colours.

'She was in a weird mood when she walked out of the

pub on Friday night,' said Monica. 'It was only about ten o'clock.'

'So where the hell was she for all those hours?' said Peter.

They could ask all they want; I didn't know the answer. The last thing I remembered was walking out of the pub. I told Peter I got lost, took the wrong bus. For all I knew that could be true, but it didn't matter where I was. I didn't care what happened to me.

Now he's annoyed because I haven't packed yet and we're leaving tomorrow. It's his day off and we're round at my parents' house. I don't care if I go on holiday taking only the clothes I'm wearing.

'Has it started yet?' Dad's standing at the doorway between the living room and the kitchen.

'Not yet,' says Mum. She turns her bottom so quickly she nearly falls off her chair. 'Have you changed your mind?'

'No, I bloody haven't,' he says. 'Not if that b—' He glances at Bobby running Matchbox cars along the skirting boards. 'Not if that woman's going. I'll be in my office if there's an emergency.'

He means his shed, where he has a sneaky packet of cigarettes and a portable black-and-white telly.

Poor Mum. She loves a royal wedding, but Dad won't watch anything that has Margaret Thatcher in it. The back door slams shut and Mum rolls her eyes, tutting.

'I wish he'd forgive and forget,' she says, as though Dad losing his job was just a falling out of friends.

Peter gives me that look – the one that says, *Your mum lives in a bubble of Jesus and Victoria sponge.*

'Oh, it's about to start,' she says, shifting further from the edge of her seat.

I bet she's dying to sit on the floor to get a closer look at Fergie's dress, but she never would.

'That Elton John,' she says, 'he gets invited to everything.'

★　★　★

It's been on the telly for hours already and they've only just got married. I will Annie to wake up, but she's barely stirring. Was Monica telling the truth when she thought Nathan was having an affair? He's not mentioned anything to me, but then, why would he?

I almost cheer when there's a knock at the door, and jump up from the floor – the most animated I've been in days. 'I'll go,' I say, taking advantage of Mum's abandonment of civility while she's engrossed in *ivory duchesse satin*.

I open the door, and it's Nathan.

'Hey, Debs. Come outside for a bit.'

I blink in the daylight – it feels like I haven't been outside properly for weeks, even though we only arrived here a few hours ago.

'What? Why?'

He beckons me. I pull the door to after clicking the latch on.

He reaches into his pocket and pulls something out. I know what it is before he says anything.

'I got a letter, too,' he says.

He glances around as though looking for someone watching us.

I narrow my eyes.

'Did Monica tell you I was getting letters?'

'Not exactly. I didn't know you got more than one, though – I saw it on her bedside cabinet.'

'What does yours say?'

'Here.' He holds it out to me – his nails are bitten. 'See for yourself.'

I grab it.

Keep your hands to yourself, you dirty bastard.

My cheeks burn with the insinuation of what's been written.

'Do people think we're . . .' I say. 'But we've only ever gone out once . . . everyone knew about that.'

I search for an emotion on his face, but find nothing.

'Monica said she had a contact at the police,' I continue, 'perhaps she should take that one too. What did she say when you showed it to her?'

'I haven't shown it to her. And the police won't care about things like—'

'You haven't shown her? But we haven't done anything wrong.' I glance through the living-room window – Mum and Peter are where I left them. 'Look, I can't deal with all of this – I'm just about managing to get out of bed.'

I close my eyes. I can't believe I'm being so honest with him. I open my eyes again.

'Sorry, Debbie. I shouldn't have come round. I didn't know what to do. I couldn't tell Monica about it . . . she might ask about you.' He goes to put a hand on my shoulder, looks into the window, and puts it down by his side. 'To think someone's been watching us – it's creeping me out a bit.' He starts to walk backwards towards the gate. 'I'll see you tomorrow afternoon. I just didn't want to bring it up in front of everyone and spoil the holiday.'

I don't have the energy to ask why it would spoil the holiday, or tell him that I've been getting the letters for weeks. I watch him as he gets into his big white car and drives away. I want to run after him and shout, 'Don't leave me!'

I go back into the house and close the door behind me. There are cheers from the crowd on telly as Prince Andrew and Sarah Ferguson exit Westminster Abbey. They have everything they've ever wanted now. What would it be like to have a happy ever after?

Chapter Thirty-Six

Anna

I'm sitting in my car, across from the house I lived in as a baby. I arrived early to take in the atmosphere. I have driven down this road countless times and tried to peek in number fifty-seven, but I've never stopped, or walked down this street. I've seen the peach curtains open, closed; the airer in the front bedroom window, but never the occupants go in or out.

I'm not in the mood for this. I lay awake last night, thinking about a child on this earth who might be related to Jack, to Sophie. It all happened years before I met Jack, so I can't be angry about that – he didn't even know himself. I thought about that poor boy who has just lost his mother. The DNA test result will arrive any day now. I'm ashamed to think it, but I hope Jack isn't the father.

A tap on my car window interrupts my thoughts.

'Morning, love,' says Sally, not raising her voice to compensate for the closed window.

I get out, rubbing the tops of my arms. It might be July, but it's freezing. Sally's wearing the same beige mac, but today she's wearing jeans with at least a five-centimetre turn-up.

'Hi, Sally. Let's get this over and done with.'

She tilts her head to one side.

'Are you not feeling up to this? You haven't received any more emails, have you?'

'Actually, no, I haven't. She didn't reply to my suggestion of meeting up, and that was days ago. To be honest, I've had a lot on my mind since.'

'Anything you want to talk about?'

'Not right now.'

A front door slams shut opposite. A man opens a small garage at the side of his house and takes out a toolbox. He's in his sixties, with grey hair and a swagger like he's God's gift.

I look away when he catches me looking at him.

'Well, I never,' he says. 'It's like going back in time with you stood in front of number fifty-seven like that. You look just like my old neighbour. Same long dark hair, pale skin. Pretty too – not that I said that to her face.'

I want to wipe myself clean after feeling his eyes all over me.

'You remember Debbie Atherton?' says Sally.

'Course I do. There's been no one under sixty that's lived there since. Always thought she was too good for round here though, didn't she?' He opens the boot of his car, placing his toolkit inside, next to a bin bag full of women's clothes. 'What's it to you two? You Cagney and Lacey?' He laughs at his own joke, wheezing like he's only got one lung.

'We're just here to view the house next door,' says Sally.

'Ah, yeah. Old Mrs Sullivan, property tycoon.'

He goes into his garage and presses play on a white stereo. Hanging on the wall above it is a 2017 David Beckham calendar. The song 'Gloria' from the film *Flashdance* booms out of the old speakers.

'If it's all right,' shouts Sally, over the music, 'I might come back another time to have a chat to you about Debbie.'

He salutes her. 'Right you are, Columbo.'

She smiles and rolls her eyes at me.

'Come on,' she says, holding me by the elbow and walking me towards number fifty-nine. 'The reason I dragged us both here, is that I've done a bit of research – obviously – and I discovered that the person not only owns the one for sale, but also your old house.'

'You mentioned it yesterday.'

Sally knocks on number fifty-nine and smiles in preparation. It opens slowly, to a woman of about eighty.

'Are you my ten o'clock?' she says.

'We are indeed, Mrs Sullivan,' says Sally.

'Well, come on in then. You don't have to take your shoes off. I keep mine on all the time now. You never know when you'll have to scarper, do you?'

'I suppose not,' I say.

'I was joking, love. They support my ankles. Weak as twigs.'

'Oh, I see.'

For someone who works in a shop, I've never been very good at small talk.

'Who do we have here then?' she says.

'I'm Sally and this is Anna.'

'Right you are. Do you mind if you see yourselves round? Only, I've had three already this morning and I'm feeling a tad delicate.'

Sally purses her lips to stifle a laugh.

'That's fine, Mrs Sullivan. We'll not trouble you for too long.'

We go straight upstairs and stand in the bedroom overlooking the back yard.

'Why are we actually looking round the house?' I say to Sally. 'I thought we were asking about next door.'

'I know. But I didn't have the heart to not have a look round. Plus, I'm nosy.'

'Right, well, let's get back down there. I've got to get home.'

She puts a hand on my arm to stop me from going downstairs.

'Do you want me to keep looking for Debbie?'

I take a deep breath. 'Do you think you're close?'

'I've got a few leads. I've got to go down to Eastbourne.'

'Eastbourne? Where that other letter was from? Why didn't you tell me this before?'

'You said you had lots on your mind. Tell you what, I'll let you know as soon as I find anything while I'm down there. We can catch up when I get back. Okay?'

'Okay.'

I should be thinking that there's hope − a proper lead we've never had before. But another part of me is worried about how she will explain the cost of the trip to Jack's firm. I suppose it could be worse: she could've been travelling to Tenerife.

'She was a beautiful person, your mother,' says Sally. 'I feel as though I'm getting to know her. I'm like that with all the missing people I look for. I suppose some might think that's unprofessional, but I think it helps − to see them for who they were, not just a person in the news. Or *not* in the news, in this case.'

'Thanks, Sally. It's nice to hear someone else say it.'

She did what people always do: refer to Debbie in the past tense. She must know more than she's telling me.

We're still standing on the landing.

'If nothing comes of this,' she says, 'I was thinking of placing something on Facebook − it's actually quite effective these days. Though you have to be wary − violent partners use it to search for vulnerable ex-partners. Always check the source.'

'Will do,' I reply, wondering if she's actually talking to a Dictaphone hidden in her pocket.

I walk down the stairs and I feel as though my head will explode with the enormity of everything. All I can think about is Jack waiting for me at home. He needs my support, but I'm here. I should be the better person, swallow my pride and say that we will deal with anything together: him and me. I suppose Jack is having to do the same.

We shuffle into the hall; we're taking up too much space.

'Thanks for letting us view your house, Mrs Sullivan,' says Sally.

The lady isn't in her chair, but at the window. She's parted her bright-white net curtains, not caring if she's seen by the outside world. We stand at the threshold.

'He insists on playing that God-awful music,' says Mrs Sullivan.

Sally clears her throat. 'I said thank you for—'

'Yes, yes, I heard you.' She drops the net curtain. 'I'm glad I'm moving . . . there's been so much sadness on this street. Even for that one over the road.' She's still looking at the man working on his car. 'Poor Dean.'

Sally and I look at each other with raised eyebrows.

'Had a lovely wife,' she continues. 'Trisha. Though I say lovely, she was rather fond of herself. She took off with a billionaire. No, I'm wrong. It was a millionaire, like the shortbread. Took their little son with her, she did.'

'That's awfully sad,' says Sally. 'What else do you remember about this street?'

'Well, around that time – actually, Trisha left before this – but next door . . . his wife ran away while they were on holiday in Tenerife.'

'Is that what people say?' I say.

'About Trisha?'

'No. About next door.'

She looks at me through narrowed eyes.

'You look familiar,' she says. 'Are you a relative?'

I look to Sally; she shrugs.

'I'm Debbie's daughter.'

Mrs Sullivan's eyes are still narrow, then they widen as she regards me afresh.

'Dear Lord, so you are. You're the spitting image. I bet you get that all the time.'

'Not really.'

'No? How odd.' She shakes her head. 'A terrible thing. I hope you don't think me awful for gossiping – only, it was a pretty big thing that happened on this street.'

Sally steps forward. 'The estate agent told me that you actually own the house next door, and that you're putting that on the market soon. Is that right?'

'It is, love,' she says to Sally, but she's still looking at me. 'Ah, of course. Is that why you're here? Did you want to have a look at next door?'

'I . . .'

'It's a bit of a mess right now. The last tenants left it in a right state. They were six months behind in the rent, but I was held to ransom – they have so many rights, you see.'

'I don't want to put you to any trouble,' I say.

Part of me wants to leave, to not see the house. I wouldn't be able to remember anything anyway. But I suppose we're not here for that; we're here to see if Mrs Sullivan or Dean remembers anything.

Mrs Sullivan grabs a set of keys from a silver cup on her bookcase, and we follow her out of the house. She steps over the small wall dividing the two properties and she opens the front door, pushing it hard against the pile of mail lying behind it.

'I've got cleaners coming in for me next week,' she says.

'Is it still decorated the same?' I ask.

'Good Lord, no,' says Mrs Sullivan.

We follow her into the house. There's a phone on the table

in the hall; the carpet all the way through is brown. Like Mrs Sullivan's house, the only room off the hallway is the small living room, leading to the kitchen.

I was expecting a crack den the way she described it, but all that's been left behind are a few magazines and newspapers on the window sill, and several books on the shelf.

The kitchen is even smaller than the living room.

'We had the units replaced at the beginning of 2001,' says Mrs Sullivan. 'It was overdue then; I dare say it's well overdue now.'

I walk to the sink and look out of the window to the washing line hanging in the back yard. Debbie must have stood here and looked out at the same view. Concrete and a battered wooden gate, under grey clouds and drizzle.

I turn around, my back to the window. To my left is a small dining table under a clock on the wall. I can't picture Dad, with Debbie and Robert, sitting around a table like that. I close my eyes, yet I can't summon an image in my mind. On my right is a row of units – the right wall dominated by a fridge and a washing machine. The place is tiny, claustrophobic.

'I'll take you upstairs,' says Mrs Sullivan, who leads us back to the hall. 'Or rather, you go first – I'll see you up there. My knees are on their way out.'

I'm surprised, given how she manoeuvred over the wall a few minutes ago. I climb the stairs, feeling no connection to this place at all. After driving past it so many times, I thought if I were ever to go inside, I would instantly feel at home. But it feels so cold.

There's a small bathroom at the top of the stairs, a small double room, and a master bedroom at the front of the house. Sally and I go to the window, which is small, considering the room is the width of the whole house.

'My dad used to tinker on his car all the time,' says Sally, looking at Dean over the road. 'I always used to wonder what he actually did, but looking back, he probably used to just love the peace and quiet. Fancy Dean's wife leaving him and taking their kiddy.'

'It happens all the time, I expect,' I say.

It's a sentence that hangs in the air.

'You're not wrong.' Sally pats me on the shoulder. 'Let's hope there's a happy ending for you though, love.'

'Somehow, I doubt that,' I say.

Sally looks at me from the corner of her eye. I wonder if she instinctively knows how a case will end.

'You'll see that this is the biggest room in the house,' Mrs Sullivan says as she enters. She winks at us. 'I'm just practising my spiel. Obviously, it needs a lick of paint in here – you can tell where their pictures were hung.'

'Do you remember much about the time Peter Atherton came back from Tenerife with his children?'

'I remember it all too clearly,' she says. 'I lost my Dennis that spring. Days used to go on forever and I used to spend a lot of time looking out of the window, pretending to watch television. When you hear of something unusual happening, the events around it seem to impress upon the mind.

'I didn't understand what was wrong at first. Just before they went on holiday, there was all this to-do with shouting and whatnot. He used to shout at her all the time. I remember being glad of the peace when they went. The baby would scream for hours before anyone would go to it, the poor little thing.'

My blood runs cold. I hadn't heard this version of the story. I don't know if I want to hear any more. Who would want to learn that no one came to you as a baby?

'Anyway, you don't want to hear about that, dear. I'm sure it's quite common. I used to let mine cry themselves to sleep.'

She flaps a hand. 'Sorry – tell me if I go off on a tangent – I do it all the time. In the end, I was glad when they came back. I missed the sounds of the children – the sounds of life. I'm on the end terrace, you see. Then, after a few days, I realised I hadn't seen the mother out with the baby – it was that other woman . . . what was her name – with the dark hair, slim, dressed well.'

'Monica,' I say. 'Her name's Monica.'

'That's right,' she says conspiratorially – as though I'm not part of this story at all. 'Yes, it was her – she was round there all the time. I don't think she stayed the night though – I would've remembered that. But she hardly had her little boy at all. He must have been at his dad's. Complicated family that one.'

'Did you see her husband, Nathan, at all?'

'That tall, good-looking man? I definitely remember that one.' Mrs Sullivan laughs, but when she looks at me, her smile fades. 'I'm sorry, lovey. I keep forgetting all of this is so close to you. It's strange to think that that little baby was you.'

'So,' says Sally, she's beginning to sound a little impatient. 'Did you see Nathan at all after they came back from holiday?'

Mrs Sullivan frowns. 'No, dear,' she says. 'He wasn't the father of that Monica's little boy, was he? I never saw him again.'

Sally quickly thanks Mrs Sullivan, and takes me by the elbow, almost dragging me out of the house.

'Oh God. This is my fault,' she says. 'I had presumed when you had told me in your first email that *Leo lives in America with his father*, that you were referring to Nathan!' She looks around her as though searching for something. 'I've been lax. I should've asked for everyone's full names – I shouldn't have presumed anything, shouldn't have just gone from who went on the holiday.' She hits herself on the forehead. 'Damn!'

'But what difference would it have made? What's Nathan got to do with anything?'

'Anna,' she says, shaking her head. 'He might have *everything* to do with this.'

Chapter Thirty-Seven

Friday, 25 July 1986

Tenerife, Canary Islands

Debbie

It's two o'clock in the morning and we're finally in the apartment. The journey was as bloody awful as I expected it to be. We were camped at Manchester airport for six hours because Peter didn't want to miss the plane. I'd never flown before and dreaded feeling the same panic I experienced in the house of horrors at the fair a few weeks ago – and that was only a few metres high. Monica and Nathan ordered a lager at the bar as soon as we'd checked our bags in, even though it was only four in the afternoon.

'The only way I'm getting on that plane,' I said, 'is if I'm anaesthetised.'

Monica smiled at me. 'Get this woman a double vodka.'

Peter frowned. 'Do you think you should, Debs?'

'It's either that or I'm not going.'

I prayed he wouldn't mention it taking me days to recover after my last bender of three cocktails.

'We could always inject you with something,' said Nathan. 'Works for B. A. Baracus.'

'If you've got it,' I said, 'I'll have it.' I said it without smiling. Monica's face dropped, her eyes darted around.

Let her feel uncomfortable, I thought. It'd serve her right.

On the flight, even though we'd chosen non-smoking seats, the whole cabin filled with grey, choking fog; my eyes constantly watered. It hid the tears, at least.

Luckily, Annie, Bobby and Leo slept for most of the flight, which was just as well as Peter sat on a different row with Nathan and Monica – who had her nose in *Jackie* magazine like she was fifteen again. I sat between the children, with Annie on my lap. Typical. It was like they'd planned it before we got on the plane.

But we're here at last. I'm wearing a white cotton T-shirt and matching trousers – the type of clothes magazines say you ought to wear 'on-board'. But mine are covered with Ribena splashes and cheesy Wotsits dust.

I glance over at Monica, who's trying to work out how to open the patio doors. I should've worn jeans like her – who'd have thought to wear denim to a hot country? And the way she has her sunglasses in her hair looks effortlessly cool. Well, as cool as someone can look, having sunglasses at night.

The kids woke up grumpy and groggy; I hope they get back to sleep now we're here. The boys are sitting on the dining chairs near the kitchenette, eyes wide and looking dazed. Annie's in a buggy, she can't support her own head in it, bless her.

This place looks nothing like the brochure, but I suppose nothing does. All the apartments look the same from the outside. The block next door reminds me of Preston Bus Station. At least it's clean inside. I refuse to do any housework while I'm here (though I can't remember the last time I did any at home).

'Shall we open this, then?' Peter's holding the bottle of red that was in the welcome pack, which also included a bottle of mineral water, a loaf of bread that looks like cake, and six eggs. Ten pounds down the drain – what a rip off.

I look at the wine and my heart starts to pound. I had two

double vodkas at the airport, and they've worn off, but I daren't have any more. I feel like crawling under one of the beds as it is.

'It's a bit late for me,' I say. 'We have to get the kids to bed.'

By the time I utter the last three words, the rest of them are on the balcony, marvelling at the heat, 'even at this time in the morning'.

Peter and Nathan are still pissed from the flight. I knew I'd be looking after the children, the grown-ups letting their hair down after *working so bloody hard to pay for it*. I'll have a better time with the boys, anyway.

'Come on, kids,' I whisper. 'Let's see if we can get you to sleep.'

There are two bedrooms, and a bed-settee in the living area. Peter and I drew the short straw on that one.

I drag our massive suitcase into the room with two single beds, before taking Annie out of the buggy. In-between the beds, against the back wall, is a white, wooden cot with a mattress that probably has hundreds of different babies' bodily fluids ingrained in it. I place her on one of the beds and unzip the suitcase to find a beach towel to cover it.

'Have you got your PJs, Leo?' I say.

Leo shrugs. It's a silly question, as I can hear Monica exclaiming that there's a barbecue area near the pool; she won't have unpacked yet. I take out two pairs of Bobby's shorts and hand them to the boys.

'It's too hot for proper pyjamas.'

'My daddy took me to Whitby last weekend,' says Leo.

'That's nice, love,' I say.

'Can I phone him tomorrow? He said I can. He said he'd wait by the phone to hear from me.'

'I'm sure they'll have a phone we can use at reception.'

'He'll go to sleep, won't he?'

'Who?'

'Daddy. I don't want him to wait by the phone all night.'

I peel the sheets back on the beds.

'Into bed, boys.' They both jump in and pull the covers up to their shoulders. I sit on the edge of Leo's bed. 'Don't worry, love. He'll have gone to sleep . . . it's the middle of the night. He'll think you're asleep.' He lies his head on the pillow and I bend to kiss his cheek. 'Night, sweetheart.'

I change Annie's nappy on the end of Bobby's bed. Her cheeks are so red – she's not used to this heat. I place her in the cot with her blanket and she looks at the net curtain blowing in the breeze from the open window. There's a sound of a moped in the distance.

A cork pops from the living room and they cheer as though they've never heard one before. God, they can't be starting again this late, can they? They're going to get us thrown out. Perhaps I should encourage them to shout louder.

'Shift up, Bobs,' I whisper. He slides across his bed, and I lie down next to him. There's only one, flat pillow. 'I'll just stay here until Annie goes to sleep.'

'I love you, Mummy,' he says, laying a hand on my shoulder.

'Love you too, Bobs.'

I think Leo's already asleep. He must be used to different beds – his dad has moved house about five times in the past two years. Poor boy. I glance over at Annie, and she's still mesmerised by the curtain – still unable to miss out on anything.

'Night, night, Annie,' I whisper.

But she doesn't even look my way.

I wake to Annie's screams and jump out of Bobby's bed. It's already light outside and I manage to pick the baby out of the cot and whisk her out of the room without waking the boys.

Shit. The three sterilised bottles I packed are in the suitcase back in the kids' bedroom.

Peter hasn't even changed the settee into a bed, and he's sprawled on it with one leg on the floor. Did he assume I'd sleep in the children's room? The sight of him makes the rage reach my chest. I bet he didn't even check on how, or where, I was last night.

The empty bottle of wine is on the coffee table next to him, which isn't too bad between the three of them.

Annie is screaming in my ear.

I nudge Peter's leg with my foot.

'Peter!' I hiss as quietly as I can.

I nudge him again. Annie's cries aren't waking him. I'm tempted to pour a glass of cold water on him, but then I remember him ripping the quilt off me last Saturday morning, and how violated it made me feel.

I strap Annie into her buggy and tiptoe back into the boys' room, taking out the bag of bottles and formula from the already-open suitcase.

I pour mineral water into the kettle and flick it on.

Why hadn't I made up bottles last night? Why hadn't Peter? No, that would never do, would it?

After what feels like hours, I pour the boiling water into the bottle. Oh God, it'll take forever to cool. I fill the sink and place the bottle upright in it.

Still, Annie cries. She's going to wake everyone up. I knew it was going to be like this. It's roasting already in this apartment. I grab the buggy and walk backwards, opening the apartment door and shimmying out of it. As I swing the pushchair round, a cool breeze outside washes over me.

The door slams shut, but I don't care if it wakes Peter.

I don't know where I'm going, but I start walking down the light corridor. I pass three other doors before we get to the lift. We're only on the first floor, but I can't face dragging the buggy down the concrete steps. The lift doors open. Inside, it smells of cigarettes and BO. I press the button for the ground floor and hold my breath until we reach it.

The reception area is small. There's a woman on the telephone who doesn't look up as I go past and out of the glass doors. I walk down the side of the building – there are more apartments along it, their walled seating areas empty, except for the white plastic tables and chairs.

My face is colder than the rest of me, but at least Annie has quietened.

There's a woman walking towards me, a carton of milk in her hands. She's frowning at me. Only a few feet away from me now. Oh no, she's going to—

'Oh, love,' she says. She has a southern English accent; it sounds like she's out of *EastEnders*. 'Whatever is the matter?'

'What do you mean?'

'You seem to have . . .'

She points to my white T-shirt. My eyes follow hers. I'm covered in blood. I touch my face; there's blood pouring from my nose.

'Oh my God. I'm so sorry.'

I pull a blanket out from under Annie's pushchair, holding it against my nose.

'What are you sorry for?' She rubs the top of my arm. 'Don't worry, love. Come with me.'

She takes hold of the buggy, turns it around and pushes it down the path. We pass reception – the woman's still on the phone – and take a right along the other side of the block. She opens an apartment door and ushers me inside.

It's so much bigger than ours. There's a settee and two wicker chairs, plus a portable telly near the double patio doors. It takes me a moment to notice a child of about thirteen sitting on a chair outside – his knees brought up in front of him as he uses them to support the comic he's reading.

The woman pulls out one of the chairs around a large dining table and guides me down.

'How old is she?' the woman says, glancing at Annie in the pushchair.

'I . . . er, just over a month old.'

'I guess it's different these days,' she says. 'I used to count in weeks – until he was at least four months old.'

I don't tell her that people still do, but I can't remember how old Annie is off the top of my head. I'd have to count using my fingers. Is she five weeks in three days or four? I know today is Friday, because the next seven days are pictured in my head like white blocks that'll be shaded black for each one that passes.

'It's not that long ago, surely,' I say, looking to the lad on the patio.

'Oh, he's not mine. He's my nephew. But you're right. My son's nearly nine. Time goes by so quickly when they're young, doesn't it?'

She goes over to the glass doors and pulls across the light curtains. It gives the room an amber glow that mimics the sun.

'Will he not mind?' I say.

'He won't notice . . . he's in his own world most of the time.'

She smiles and walks into the kitchenette, picking out a bright white tea towel from one of the drawers.

'I couldn't use that,' I say. 'I'd ruin it.'

She sits down on the chair next to me.

'Don't worry. I'll just buy a new one.' She takes Annie's bloodied blanket. 'I can wash this for you, if you want – I've got loads of tokens for the washing machine. My Spanish isn't as good as it could be . . . I asked for too many by mistake.'

Now that she's sitting so close to me, I see she's probably about the same age as me. It's her short hair that makes her look older from a distance.

I put the tea towel against my nose. 'I've not had a nose-bleed since I was a child.'

'Stress, perhaps? Or maybe it's the heat. It's probably nothing serious. Don't worry about it.'

'I think it's probably both,' I say, hoping she won't ask any questions about it.

I don't want to tell her that I think I'm either dying or losing my mind. What if it doesn't stop and I bleed to death? Oh God, I can't breathe again.

The woman places a hand on my arm. 'There, there. Don't panic. I've seen plenty of nosebleeds. They usually stop after a few minutes. Take a deep breath in.'

I do as she says. Her voice is soothing; it calms me.

'You're brave, bringing such a young one to Tenerife,' she says. 'Where have you come from?'

'Preston.'

'Oh. I've never been there. We're from the south coast, near Eastbourne.'

She's looking at me as I glance at the balcony.

'I know it's early,' she says, 'but I'm looking after him today. Even though he's probably old enough to look after himself. My husband and my sister have taken my little one to the water park. I can't swim – well, I can, but I'm not a strong swimmer. Doggy paddle mostly.' She smiles, but then the smile drops as she looks at the carton of milk still on the table. 'They're probably having an affair.'

My mouth drops open.

'Sorry,' she says. 'I'm always saying too much to total strangers.'

I take the tea towel from my nose. The blood has stopped.

'Don't worry,' I say. 'It makes a change from thinking about my own problems.'

Annie's been quiet since we got here, but she's starting to

fret. I'm about to say we must go, when the woman says, 'I'm sure them going to the water park is just an excuse for them to spend the day together. She hated swimming when we were kids – more than I did.'

'I see.'

'I'm sorry,' she says. 'It's just that I haven't anyone to talk to. Everyone I know is friends with all of us. It's a bit tricky.'

For the first time since she was born, I'm glad when Annie starts bawling. I stand quickly.

'I'll have to go. Her milk will've cooled by now.'

'Yes, of course.'

She gets up to open the apartment door, and I wheel out the buggy.

'I never got your name,' she says.

'Debbie.'

'Debbie. Right. I'll make sure to get this blanket back to you nice and clean. I'll leave it at reception.' She leans against the door to stop it slamming shut. 'You take care of yourself. I'll probably see you around. I'm Ellen by the way.'

'Bye then. And thank you.'

'No problem.'

I turn and walk away.

She doesn't look like an Ellen.

Chapter Thirty-Eight

Anna

I turn on the car stereo: it's Amy Winehouse singing 'Valerie'. When Jack and I started dating, it played on the radio all the time. He used to roll his eyes when it came on. 'The Zutons' version is far superior,' he said. He was a music snob then. He doesn't listen to music in the house these days.

There's still no news about the DNA test. It's been three days since he gave a sample and, apparently, it might be another two days before we get the result. Well, before *he* gets the result. I thought I knew everything about him. But you only ever know what a person chooses to reveal to you. He never told me his ex-girlfriend was pregnant when they split up. Is that something you would share with your wife?

It's one thing after another.

Yesterday, after we looked around my old house, Sally brought up Nathan as we stood by her car.

'Do you have any idea of what happened to him?' she asked.

'He and Monica divorced, I think. She said he'd moved somewhere down south. Leo barely remembered him . . . he didn't spend much time with him as a kid.'

'Does no one mention Nathan? Have you asked about him?'

'It's not the sort of thing I'd bring up. To be honest, Sally, there's a whole host of things I never ask about. I'm scared of hurting everyone's feelings all the time. I thought my dad and Monica fell in love and then she got divorced. I only knew about Nathan from Robert. There's been no need for Nathan to be in our lives.'

'Okay. I'll let you know if I find out anything else.'

She seemed annoyed at me, and I'm not surprised. I should've drawn her out a family tree – it's confusing even to me sometimes.

'I left my DS at home,' says a little voice from the back seat.

I forgot Sophie was sitting in the back. I'm driving on auto-pilot. I flick off the radio and bring myself back into the present.

'Do you want me to turn around and go back for it?' says my guilt.

'No, it's all right,' she says, with a touch of melancholy. 'I'll probably just watch the movie channel all day.'

'Sorry, love. I'm off next weekend. We can do something fun then.'

'Why is Daddy working on a Saturday too? He doesn't usually work on a weekend when you do.'

'It's just this once. And you love going to Nana and Grandad's, don't you?'

She sighs. 'Yeah.'

We pull up outside Dad's – at least my autopilot didn't take me straight to work. I open the door for Sophie and she hops out.

'I need my backpack,' she says, grabbing it from the back seat.

She leads the way up the path. She's such a little individual. As much as I want her to grow into an independent young woman, I love her just as she is right now.

Sophie knocks twice on the door, but there's no answer.

There's a flap of a hand in the front window. I bend to peer through the letterbox and Dad's walking towards me. He opens the front door as I stand.

'Sorry, sorry,' he says.

I let Sophie go in first, ushering her into the living room before joining Dad back in the hall.

'Everything okay?'

There are sobbing noises coming from the kitchen.

'Is Monica all right? How's her arm?'

I scrutinise his face, trying to read his expression. There are remnants of tears coating his bottom eyelashes. I open the door of the kitchen and Monica's sitting at the kitchen table – an array of papers and letters in front of her.

She stands quickly, ripping a piece of kitchen roll from the holder on the wall.

'Is that the time?' she says, dabbing her cheeks, her make-up surprisingly intact. She puts the tissue into her trouser pocket and sweeps the pieces of paper with her left hand.

'How are you feeling?' I ask her. 'Has the pain lessened?'

'It's okay. The doctor said it'll heal in two or three weeks. It's only a sprain.'

'Shall I take Sophie to work with me? I don't mind – she can help in the back.'

'No, no. I love having her here. She stops me wallowing. I'm a terrible patient.'

'What's this?' I say, picking a pink letter up from the pile on the table. 'I've not seen this one before.'

She snatches it from my hand before I can read the writing.

'Nothing, nothing. Don't worry about it.'

'Are all of these about Debbie?'

She settles the pile into a neat square with her unbandaged arm. She sighs loudly.

'Yes.'

'Why are you crying?' I say.

I sense Dad behind me, not knowing where to put himself or what to say.

'I'm just being silly. Thinking about Debbie and everything else.'

I look down at the top of the pile and there's a photo of Nathan. It's not the time to bring it up, but I need to tell them anyway.

'I went to the old house yesterday,' I say. 'With Sally.'

'Sally?'

'The private investigator.'

There's a slight roll of Monica's eyes.

'I met Mrs Sullivan, who still lives next door. She said she never saw anything of Nathan after we came back from the holiday in Tenerife. When was the last time you heard from him?'

'I can't remember.'

Her eyes don't meet mine. Dad helps her to sit back in a chair.

'He phoned a few times, didn't he?' he's talking to Monica. 'He gave you an address he was staying at.'

Monica nods.

Dad looks at me.

'But you're right,' he says. 'I last saw him the night your mother left.' He sits down in the chair opposite. 'I always thought they ran away together. Did Monica ever tell you that Debbie and Nathan were a couple in their teens?'

'No,' I say, trying to catch Monica's eye again, but she's still looking at the picture of Nathan.

'He wrote a few times,' she says. 'And the odd phone call. But I didn't see him. After seven years of no contact, I divorced him.'

'Have you still got his letters?'

She shakes her head.

'Why didn't you keep them?'

'Because he hurt me.' Her shoulders shake as she sobs. 'And

280

I didn't want to upset your dad. Peter and I – all of us – had already started living together. We'd moved on without the pair of them.'

Monica's mobile phone lights up; it's ringing on silent, the caller unknown.

'Aren't you going to answer that?' I say.

She shakes her head, just staring at it.

It stops flashing. I peer at the screen.

'There are eleven missed calls, Monica. What if it's her?'

'How could she know my number? It could be anyone.'

'Then why not answer it?'

She covers her eyes with both hands, elbows resting on the table.

I glance at the clock; it's already 9 a.m. – I should be opening the bookshop now. I really am going to get fired at this rate.

'But after all this time,' I say. 'I thought something might have happened to her – that she was dead. Why have you kept this from me?'

Dad makes a fist and pounds the table.

'Because it's not always about you, Anna!'

'Right, right.' I blink away the tears. 'Right. I'll phone you later to check on Sophie.'

I walk from the kitchen and dart my head around the living-room door.

'See you later, love.'

She nods, her eyes wide. She must have been listening.

'Do you want to come to work with me?' I say, trying to keep my voice even. 'You can help sort through the books – it'll be fun.'

She shakes her head. 'It's okay. I'll try and cheer Monica up. She's always crying.'

'I . . .' I say, but I can't get into it with her now.

I reach into my pocket – and pull out Sophie's DS. 'Oh!' I

look at it as though it were put in my pocket by magic – I thought the weight was my mobile phone. 'Look what I found!'

Her expression changes in an instant.

'Thanks, Mummy!' She gets up and takes it from my hands, then settles into the sofa next to her little rucksack.

'See you later,' I say. 'Don't forget to ring if you need me.'

She waves, her eyes on the console as it chimes into life.

I say a quiet goodbye to Dad and Monica in the kitchen, but Dad is towering over Monica, his arms wrapped around her. She's not crying about Nathan now. The letter she snatched from me wasn't like the rest – its ink hadn't faded, the creases were sharp. If I were to guess, she received that letter this morning.

I park around the corner from the bookshop and walk as fast as I can. I get my keys out. Ellen is standing outside the shop. She hasn't a coat; her hair has a fine mist of rain on it, like a halo.

'Sorry, Ellen,' I say. 'I got caught up with childcare.'

'That's okay,' she says, but she's biting her bottom lip, her eyes fixed on the ground.

She follows me inside, into the back room, and I hang up my damp coat.

'I'll make you a nice hot cup of tea,' I say.

'Thanks, Annie.'

I fill the kettle and flick it on, wishing, for the millionth time, that she wouldn't call me that. I get the float money from the safe and carry it through to the bookshop. I hold the blue cotton bag in my hands as I collapse onto the stool. I can't stop the tears falling, my breath is taken over by uncontrollable sobs, even though I'm trying to be quiet.

'Oh, love,' says Ellen, appearing at my side. 'Whatever's the matter?'

'Everything,' I manage to say through sharp breaths.

She goes into the back room and, a few minutes later, places a mug of tea on the counter.

'I've put two sugars in,' she says. 'Here, give me that.' She takes the money bag from me and opens the till drawer. 'Just in case Isobel comes in. She can't say we're slacking then, can she?' She winks at me.

'Thanks.'

I put my hands around the warm mug.

'You don't have to tell me what's going on,' she says. 'But it might help.'

She tilts her head to the side. Her tone is so kind that I do – I tell her everything – about Debbie, about Tenerife. I tell her that Jack might have a child with someone else, that my stepmother is hiding something, and my father always takes her side. I tell her that I've barely spoken to my brother these past few weeks, and I used to be so close to him.

When I finish, Ellen gets up from the chair she pulled in from the back. Her eyes are glossed with unshed tears.

'I met someone called Debbie once,' she says.

My own tears have dried.

'What?' I throw a damp tissue into the bin. 'It's quite a common name.'

'I met her in Tenerife.'

'Did you live there?'

'No, no. It was a holiday.'

There's a voice in my head screaming at me; I can't make out the words. It sounds like: *Don't trust her.*

'Ellen,' I say. 'Can I ask you something? I know I said I didn't want to know, but—'

'Why was I in prison?'

I nod slowly, and watch as she puts the coins in their allotted compartments.

She turns to me and says, 'Because I killed someone.'

Chapter Thirty-Nine

When you kill someone, their soul becomes part of your own – you're together forever. Do you ever come to terms with what you've done? Are there different types of killers, or are we all the same?

They'll never forgive me.

I should never have sent that email. I still haven't replied to the one she sent back. What am I supposed to say? Some things are too big to say in so few words. I've learned that now.

Chapter Forty

Sunday, 27 July 1986

Debbie

We're all sitting around the pool, and I'm enjoying a quiet ten minutes while Annie sleeps in the pushchair next to me. She's not taken to the heat – she's like me. The others have started on the cocktails already while Leo and Bobby mess around in the pool. It's only eleven o'clock in the morning for God's sake.

'It's a scorcher today,' says Peter.

'Yes,' I say. 'We know.'

He's said it about fifty bloody times in two days and I bet he doesn't realise. No one else mentions it because they're nicer than I am. Or maybe life is just one long drama where we repeat ourselves against different backdrops over and over again.

I saw Ellen again yesterday, with her nephew. We were sitting around the pool like today when she approached me. She didn't have sunglasses; she squinted and used her hand to shield her eyes from the sun.

'I've put the blanket in the wash, love,' she said. 'I soaked it yesterday. It should be ready for the little one tonight.'

'Don't worry about it,' I said. 'I brought a spare.'

She glanced at Monica lying flat on the sun lounger in a

black bikini – her skin glistening with baby oil, Walkman head-phones on her ears.

'All right for some, eh?' said Ellen, wrinkling her nose.

'She's with me,' I said, with a little too much force. 'She's my friend.'

'Sorry, love,' she said. 'Didn't mean to offend.'

We exchanged an awkward goodbye, and she went off to get a slice of pizza for the teenager dressed in black.

Monica's in the same position this morning, only she's in a neon-green bikini. She hasn't one hair on her body. If only I had the time, the energy or inclination to be bothered with that. I've had the same pair of shorts over my swimsuit since we've been round the pool. I'd wear a wetsuit if I could.

'Are you going in the pool today, Debs?' says Monica, barely moving her lips.

Peter and Nathan don't look up from their card game; they're using pesetas with holes in the middle as poker chips.

'I'm not inflicting my blubber on everyone,' I say. 'I'm fine as I am.'

Monica sits up, removing her headphones. I don't think she has any music playing.

'Blubber? What are you like? You look gorgeous!'

'Hmm.'

'The water will cool you off nicely when it gets hotter later.'

I wish she'd shut up about the bloody swimming pool. But I look at it, glistening in the sun, and wish I could be like everyone else – jump in like Bobby and Leo, not care what anyone thinks.

'Why don't you get a cocktail?' says Monica. 'It might chill you out a bit.'

'I am chilled. I can't be drinking while I've got the baby. Peter's on his second drink already. He never drinks cocktails in England.'

She laughs and swings her legs to the side of the lounger.

'We're all here – everyone can help with the baby.'

'Yeah, right,' I mutter.

'I heard that.' Monica stands. 'And that's why I'm going to get you one.'

Before I can argue, she's sauntered off to the bar at the side of the pool. She returns five minutes later with half a pint of an orange creation.

'I'll never drink all of that.'

'Sure you will,' she says, handing me the deliciously cold glass. She stands over me and I go to place it on the floor.

'No, no. Have a sip.'

I do as she says, my resolve weaker than my mind. I feel the cool drink run down my throat and into my stomach. It leaves a lovely warmth.

'How much alcohol's in that?' I say.

She settles back down and places the headphones over her ears.

'Enough.'

She closes her eyes. So much for her helping with the baby.

I take a longer sip from the straw. Perhaps this holiday would go a lot quicker if I were pissed.

I'm sitting on a stool, leaning against the bar. I'm kind of thinking that the mixture of sun and vodka has gone to my head. But at least I feel more like *me* again. This is what I used to be like: fun. Whatever was in those cocktails has done the trick.

Luckily, I had the foresight to make up a day's bottles for Annie and they're all neatly lined up in the fridge in the apartment – like I'm a proper earth mother, or something.

After the first cocktail – I think there were at least three different spirits in there – I stood up and announced: 'Peter!'

(I was probably as wobbly as I am now.) Anyway, I said, 'Peter! Make that your last drink. You're looking after your daughter for the rest of the day.'

Monica sat bolt upright. Told you she wasn't listening to music.

'Good on you, girl,' she said. 'I'll get us more.'

Peter rolled his eyes at Nathan. Course he did. Though I don't know why they're suddenly so pally – they barely spoke at the airport. But here, in *Tenerife-ee*, they're getting on like a house on wheels – fire – whatever; it's too hot here. Peter gave the rest of his drink to Monica. I should've been pissed off about that, but I wasn't, because she downed it in one, laughed and dragged me here, to the tiniest bar in the world.

Only, it's an hour or so later, and it's not Monica sitting next to me, but Nathan.

'And so, the trouble is, Debs . . .' he says.

I think he's slurring his words more than I am. I'm only half concentrating on what he's saying as I've only got one eye open and it's taking in his face. He's got a really nice face, but he doesn't half go on and on and on.

'. . . don't you think?' he says.

'Yeah,' I say.

I can't be bothered to hear what I missed out on. It'll be nothing.

'Really? You agree? That we should start our own pool bar together in Blackpool?'

I feel my nose wrinkle. 'Eh?'

He turns and sips the rest of his drink, slurping the dregs with a straw.

'Knew you weren't listening,' he says.

He orders two more off the cocktail menu. I grab the drink and swivel on my stool so I can look over the pool. Monica and Peter are playing happy families, but I don't mind. I squint and see that Peter's trying to change Annie's nappy, and I smile to myself. Probably the first one he's changed of hers.

'Bet you've never changed a nappy, Nathan.'

He swivels around too, straw in his mouth.

'Hardly the most attractive of bets, Debs.' He pulls his sunglasses over his eyes. 'And no, I haven't. I've never seen myself with children. I mean, I know I have Leo and everything, but it's not the same. Not when her arsehole ex is ringing up all the time.'

'He's hardly an arsehole. He works at the Gas Board . . . or is it the Water Board? Nothing'll be a *Board* soon, the way things are going. Bloody Thatcher privatising everything . . .'

'Steady on, Debs. No need to get political – we're on holiday.'

'It's Ellen,' I say to Nathan, as subtly as I can.

'Why are you talking with your mouth closed?' he shouts, as loud as he can.

'Because she's right—'

'Hello, Debbie! You haven't met my Alan, have you?'

I shake my head, but the straw's still in my mouth. I clear my throat and sit up straighter. I've got to look more grown-up.

Ellen's wearing a Hawaiian-print sarong, tied around the waist, and a bikini with cups that look like actual giant shells. Someone get that woman a Piña Colada. Nathan lifts his sunglasses, squints and puts them back on again.

Luckily, Ellen doesn't take offence; she's staring at him, tilting her head to the side.

Her face changes when she looks up and sees where her husband's eyes are; they're on the front of my swimming costume. Oh God.

Alan squeezes past Ellen and holds out his hand to me. His dyed-black hair is gelled back, and he's wearing the smallest swimming trunks I've ever seen. I try not to look at them, but he's got his other hand on his hip.

They must holiday often, as both have skin the colour of

cinnamon. I must start wearing sunscreen; Ellen looks older with fewer clothes on.

I shake her husband's hand and it's slick with sweat.

'So this is the delightful new friend you've been talking about, Ellen.'

She looks up to the sky. 'Can't you stop it, Alan, just this once.'

'You've just had a baby, eh?' he says. 'Nice and ripe, then?' He laughs.

I think I'm going to be sick.

'What did you just say?' Nathan places his drink on the bar behind him. 'You can't talk to a woman like that.'

Alan raises both palms. 'I didn't mean any harm. Ellen'll tell you what I'm like . . . a bit of a joker.'

'Bit of a wanker, more like.'

'What did you say?'

Ellen stands between Nathan and Alan. 'We must get going,' she says. 'I'd say let's meet up for a drink later, but I don't think you'd want to.'

Nathan stands, too.

'Course we should.' He lowers himself to Ellen's height. 'We can't have you isolated because of him.'

Ellen beams at him.

Typical. Everyone falls for his charm.

'That'd be great,' she says.

Nathan turns to the bar as they walk away.

'I think I've just sobered up,' I say.

I'm still facing the pool when Ellen turns and walks back towards me, her flip-flops slapping her heels.

She puts her head close to mine. I smile – thinking she's going to say how kind Nathan is.

'You won't do anything about it, will you?' she says.

'About what?'

I look to Nathan, willing him to see this exchange, but he's talking to the barman.

'I've seen it before with women like you,' she hisses. 'Pretending you're everyone's friend and then stealing their husbands from under their noses. I've seen the way you look at my husband.'

I smile at her. Has she been drinking too? I kick Nathan's ankle, but he doesn't look up.

'What do you mean?' I say. 'I've just had a baby. I've never stolen anyone's husband in my life.'

'I saw what you did just then – playing footsie with Nathan. They might not be happy together, but that's no reason to go stealing him in front of everyone.'

'What are you talking about, *not happy*? I'm not trying to steal him.' I slide down from my stool. 'And you're not invited later after all. You're talking crazy.'

She grabs me by the elbow.

'Oh, I'm the crazy one, am I? Not what your friend over there, holding your baby, said last night.'

She walks off as calmly as she walked over.

'Did you hear what that woman just said?' I say to Nathan. I turn to him, but he's already standing next to me.

'Yes,' he says. 'Yes, I did. That is one weird bitch. We've been transported to the set of *EastEnders*.' He passes me another drink. 'Get that down you. We'll not have those two with us for drinks tonight.'

I take too big a sip, and some of the cocktail slips out the sides of my mouth.

'Nathan,' I say, grabbing a napkin and wiping my face. 'You shouldn't call women bitches.'

He laughs and shakes his head at me.

'You're one of a kind, Debs. I'll tell you that for free.'

I'll tell you that for free. It's a phrase my dad uses all the time.

I've a sudden pang to be with him and my mum right now. I've never had a confrontation like that before. My shoulders are tense and my stomach is churning.

I feel out of my depth here.

It's four o'clock and the pool is half empty. The cocktails are starting to wear off.

'Why don't you go in the pool now, Debs?' says Monica. 'There's a spare lilo over there.'

I pick up her Pimms and lemonade, and down it in one.

'Easy, tiger,' she says, laughing. 'You'll drown if you have any more.'

I stand and stretch, leaving my arms out beside me, enjoying the sun on my face. Annie's on a blanket under a parasol, staring at the logo. I take off my shorts.

'I'll take Annie with me,' I say, picking my baby up. 'I read in a magazine once that babies can swim.'

Monica sits up quickly; for a moment, I see two of her. She holds up her hand and shields her eyes.

'Don't worry,' she says. 'Have a break. I'll look after her.'

'Get off. She's mine. I can do what I want with her.'

'Okay, okay.'

I wait for her to say something else, but she doesn't. She's moving from side to side. Or is that me?

I kick off my flip-flops and walk over to the steps leading to the shallow end. The water feels deliciously cool against my scorched skin. I've been missing out on this feeling for days. Yeah, sod what everyone else thinks. Dad says that people are far too bothered about themselves to worry about what I'm doing.

I glance at a woman in her sixties sitting on a plastic chair beside the pool. She's resting her elbows on parted knees, smoking; her skin's like leather.

It's observations like those that make me realise what Dad says is rubbish. I judge people all the time.

No, no. Stop thinking.

Stop thinking, and start doing.

Another of my father's phrases.

I drag the lilo towards me and hold the bar at the side of the pool as I sit in the middle, causing it to sag.

I'm a whale.

But I don't care right now. I hold Annie close to my chest and it takes a few seconds to balance before I lay my head on the soft inflatable pillow. I kick the side of the pool, and Annie and I float away.

'Isn't the sky beautiful, little one?'

There are a few fluffy clouds. I turn Annie on her side, so she can look at the water.

She's so beautiful and she came from inside me. How is that even possible? Everything is so new to her. What must that be like? To wipe everything clean and start again.

'You're perfect, Annie.'

I stroke her downy hair, skimming over the patches of cradle cap. A breeze wafts over us and a plane flies above, leaving its cottony trail in the sky.

'They're off on an adventure,' I say. 'Or going home.'

Just saying the word *home* feels strange – it seems so very far away.

Annie sighs noisily; it's the sweetest sound.

Right now, I am happy. I take in the image of the blue sky and my baby, and close my eyes.

This might be the best I'm ever going to feel.

Sprays of cold water are on my face.

Someone's shaking me.

I'm under water and I take a short breath by mistake.

My feet land on solid ground. I cough out the water from the back of my throat.

Peter's in the pool, standing. He's pulling Annie out from the water.

'What the fuck, Debbie?'

He holds the baby up. She blinks the water from her eyes before letting out a piercing scream.

'What happened?' I say.

'You fell asleep. Jesus fucking Christ. You feel asleep with the baby on you. You—' He cradles the baby into his torso. 'There, there. Thank God you're okay, Anna.' He turns his head. 'She could've fucking drowned, Debbie. You're a fucking liability.'

Peter strides towards the steps and hands my baby to Monica, who's standing at the side – tears streaming down her face.

My feet won't move. What have I done? Peter's words register in my mind. She must've slipped from my chest. I thought I was holding her tight, but I haven't slept properly in weeks. I should be running towards her, shouldn't I? Making sure she's okay.

I feel numb, yet I can feel warm tears on my hot skin. I don't know what's wrong with me. I look down, but I can't see the pounding that's coming from my chest. I feel the pulse on my wrist, yet it's the same as normal.

Why am I just standing here?

Annie's screams echo around the whole poolside. I wade across to the steps and climb them.

I'm not here any more. My body is doing everything for me. I just have to put one step in front of the other and I'll be with my family.

The ground is hard beneath my feet. People are staring at me. I can't let their gaze affect me or it'll consume me.

I reach them at the sun loungers. Annie's still crying. That's a good sign, isn't it?

I kneel at Peter's feet.

'I'm so sorry. I didn't mean to.'

He looks to the side before looking me in the eye.

'It's just as well Monica was watching you both.'

A hand grips my arm.

'I should've stopped you going in,' says Monica. 'It's my fault. You were in no fit state.'

No fit state.

'Calm down, everyone,' says Nathan. 'Debs fell asleep. It's hardly the crime of the century. Everything's okay. The baby's fine. Let's just forget it happened, eh?'

Everyone looks up at him. I want what he said to be true. I want everyone to forget. *I* want to forget.

'Where's Bobby?' I say.

Peter frowns. 'He went to the kids' club three hours ago.'

Monica places a hand on his. Her hands get everywhere. *She* gets everywhere. Where does she get the energy to be so bothered about other people?

She turns to me.

'Don't worry, Debs. It could happen to anyone. It probably happens all the time.'

I look up at Nathan, and he rolls his eyes.

'Nothing *happened*. The baby was in the water for two seconds, tops. Give Debs a break, for God's sake.'

I catch the briefest of glances between Peter and Monica. There's something there I've not seen before. They're ashamed of me. I'm a liability, like Peter said I was. I don't know what to do right now. I need someone to tell me the rules of everything.

Monica picks up a towel and wraps it around my shoulders. It's damp and feels too hot on my skin.

295

Annie stops crying when Peter puts a dummy in her mouth.

'Where did you get that from?' I say. 'Bobby never needed a dummy. I don't want Annie to have one.'

'It was easier. She's been grizzly all day,' says Peter. 'And thank God I introduced it.'

Monica rubs my shoulders.

'It's all right now – Annie's fine. She'll not remember it anyway.'

Peter sits on a plastic chair next to me.

'I'm sorry, Peter. I've been so tired since she was born. I shouldn't have taken her with me in the pool. I'll not make that mistake again. I'm never going in a swimming pool again.'

His shoulders raise as he takes a deep breath in.

'Okay.' He won't meet my eyes. 'I'm sorry for swearing at you. I panicked.'

Monica stands and clasps her hands together like a *Blue Peter* presenter.

'It's half past four. Why don't we head back to the apartment to get ready for tonight's barbecue?'

'Good plan,' says Nathan.

Monica holds out her hand to him, but he holds his hand out to me.

'Come on, Debs. Let's get you inside.'

My eyes flit between them both.

Monica drops her hand and shrugs.

'I suppose she's the one who needs looking after.'

She mutters something at the end of the sentence, but I don't quite catch it. It sounded like *as usual*.

Peter gets up and walks away; Monica follows close behind. She briefly rubs the part of his back between the shoulder blades.

I look up to Nathan. He's still holding out his hand, so I take it.

Chapter Forty-One

Anna

As I stand outside Dad's house to collect Sophie, Ellen's words still ring in my ears. After she said those four words – *Because I killed someone* – I didn't know what to say to her. I've never knowingly met a murderer. I'd often wondered what questions I would ask if I discovered her crime, but in reality, I asked nothing. We were alone in the bookshop. What if she said that it was a random murder, someone who pissed her off?

A customer had come in, breaking the few minutes' silence.

'I'll tell you about it another time,' Ellen said, retreating to the back room.

That time didn't come. Instead, I texted Sally Munroe with Ellen's full name and date of birth, in the hope she will be able to find out more than my failed searches on Google. That's if the information on her CV is correct.

Monica opens the door.

'You look better than this morning,' I say, stepping inside, realising I should've called during the day to check on Sophie. 'Are you okay now?'

'I suppose. I guess I have good days and bad.' She holds the handle of the living-room door and hesitates. 'I loved your mother, you know. She was like a sister to me. I would've done anything for her.'

'I know. You've said before.'

Her mouth drops open, her shoulders sag.

'I'm sorry,' I say. 'I didn't mean to snap.'

But she keeps doing that – blurting out that she loved my mother, talking about her in the past tense. These past few days, Monica has given up pretending to be cheerful. She has never admitted to having bad days before.

Dad and Sophie cheer in the living room.

'Your dad brought down his old computer games.' Monica moves her hand from the door and beckons me to follow her to the kitchen. 'Though *game* might be stretching it a little – it's basically a dot going from side to side on the television.'

She stops at the kitchen sink and turns, leaning against it, folding her arms. The letters and papers are still on the table, alongside the RSVPs for Robert's birthday party. Nathan's picture is no longer at the top of the pile; the most recent letter is.

'Can I read it?' I say.

She shrugs. 'Go ahead.'

I grab it before she changes her mind.

I study the envelope. The postmark is dated yesterday, and the writing is in the same small capital letters as the others.

I take out the letter and open it quickly.

Stop asking questions, or there will be consequences. I'm watching all of you. I know where each and every one of you live.

'What the hell?'

Monica's looking at the floor. When she looks up, her eyes are glistening.

'You have to stop looking, Anna.'

'But you got that email . . . that's what started all of this, not me. I'm just following up on it . . . trying to find answers. It's for everyone, not just for me.'

298

'Can't you see? Since your dad saw that email, we've been coming apart at the seams. Robert's barely been round – he's distracting himself with his work. I doubt he even remembers it's his party tomorrow afternoon.'

'His party . . .? That's not all you're worried about, is it? Some stupid party?'

'It's not stupid to me! I've spent months organising it. I've got all his friends from school, from uni. I've made him a cake.'

She gestures to the kitchen counter. Under a glass cloche, is a massive chocolate cake, decorated with tiny books.

'But he hardly has any friends . . .' I say. 'This isn't the point. Stop detracting from the important stuff—'

'Important stuff? You mean Debbie?' She lifts her arms and drops them as though deflated. 'She's always been the important one to you, hasn't she? You need to grow up, Anna. You have people all around you who love you . . . not some woman who abandoned everyone. It's been over thirty years, love. It was only a few years ago that Peter took her photo off the wall. I feel as though she's been looking over me for all of these years – taunting me for taking over her life.'

'But what if something bad happened to her that night, Monica?' I say, quietly. 'Don't you want to know what happened?'

'She left a note, Anna. It says everything in there.'

'How can you be sure it was her handwriting?'

'Because I recognise it, that's why.'

There are tears in her eyes. Why won't she just tell me the truth? She must know more than she's saying.

'Why did the police give up looking for her?' I say.

'Robert said he told you what happened when we got back from Tenerife.'

'But he was just a child. Grandad said Dad was questioned.'

She turns her back to me.

'We – or rather your grandfather – reported her missing a

few weeks after we got back from the holiday. They came round, asking why Peter hadn't been to them, wasn't he worried something bad had happened to her? He showed them the note. Your gran and grandad confirmed it was her handwriting, but the police still searched the house . . . asked for her passport . . . it was like they were trying to trick us.'

Who would think like that? She's talking about her and Dad as *we* and *us*. Did she label them as a couple even then, or has it morphed into that?

'But she left the note and had taken her clothes and passport,' she says. 'What else were we to think?' She turns around, still not meeting my eye, tears streaming down her face. 'We all lost someone that night, Anna.'

It's only eight o'clock on a Saturday night, but Jack and I have already closed the bedroom curtains on today. For the first time in days, my husband is lying next to me. I can tell he's not asleep; he keeps sighing and changing positions.

He'd only worked in the morning, but had been drinking whiskey since three in the afternoon — he was drunk and silent when I got home with Sophie at tea time. He went to bed as I cooked Sophie's dinner, probably forgetting, in his drunken state, that he'd been sleeping in his office in the loft for the past few days. Perhaps because he confessed, he feels his conscience is clear — that he can share the burden of his problems.

It's Robert's party tomorrow night, yet my thoughts drift between Debbie and Jack. *What if Debbie were alive? What if she were dead? Does Jack have a son?*

I wish I had a sleeping pill or something to make my mind go blank, because I don't have the answers.

My mobile vibrates with a text on the bedside cabinet. I'm tempted to ignore it. Whatever it is, it's bound to keep me from sleep, and sleep is what I need. Sophie is fine, Jack is fine. It can't be anything important.

After ten minutes, I can't sleep for thinking about it. I grab the phone. It's a message from Sally Munroe.

En route to Tenerife after a development. Will contact you when I know more. S.

Tenerife.

It's going to cost a fortune, but it's the most obvious country to search – the place Debbie was last seen alive. I text my reply.

What have you found out? Would rather know ASAP x

She replies seconds later.

I'd rather tell you when I know more. Don't want to cause unnecessary alarm. S.

I sit up. My heart is banging in my chest. I stand and walk quietly out of the room, clutching the phone in my hand. I glance back at Jack and he's on his side, facing the window. I open Sophie's door and she's fast asleep, star-shaped across her bed. I pick up her quilt from the floor and gently drape it across her.

I pull the door slightly ajar and tiptoe downstairs.

The kitchen floor is cold under my feet. It might be July, but it's been cold today. Though that's not the reason I'm shivering.

The possibilities are running through my mind: *Sally's found Debbie, living abroad; she's found someone who knows her; she's found her grave.*

I hold up the phone and dial Sally's number.

She answers after three rings.

'Hey, Anna. Sorry. I shouldn't have texted you. I just didn't want you wondering where I was.'

'What have you found?'

She sighs. 'I didn't want to tell you over the phone. But I contacted the Spanish Consulate to ask if they have any . . .'

301

She stops talking.

'Unclaimed bodies,' I say, finishing her sentence.

'Yes,' she says quietly.

'And they do.'

'Yes. There were hundreds across mainland Spain, but there aren't as many in Tenerife. There are three that were found in 1987 and four in 1988. They've already been buried, but the person I spoke to said they've kept various personal items that were found with the bodies. Sorry . . . I know I'm talking in a blunt way about something so close to you. I might find nothing that's connected to your mother, but we must close this line of enquiry. It's where she was last seen alive.'

I pull my dressing gown around me – I'm still shaking. I sit on the nearest dining chair.

'Let me know as soon as you hear anything.'

'Of course. Try not to think about it too much until you hear back from me.'

'I think we both know that's impossible.'

'I know. I'm sorry. Take care, Anna. Speak soon.'

I end the call and throw the phone onto the table.

It's still light outside and the sun is low in the sky. It should be raining now; it should always rain with bad news.

I take a deep breath.

So, this is how it ends.

She died the night she disappeared.

I should've known that all these years, shouldn't I?

I stand and reach for my memory box and place it on the table, taking out my favourite picture of my mother. I hold it in my shaking hands just inches from my face. Her young face beaming into the camera, before I was born, before her troubles began.

Her twenty-seven-year-old face that's now decomposed, buried in an unmarked grave in a Spanish cemetery. My stomach churns as I picture it. I place the photo face down onto the table. I can't do this to myself.

I'm going to find out what happened to her. Has my father been covering up something for all of these years?

I jump. Jack's standing in the doorway.

'What's happened?' he says.

'Sally's on her way to Tenerife. She says there are unidentified bodies – they've been buried, but they kept the belongings they had on them.' My words flow out too fast. I look up at him. 'I should be crying, shouldn't I? I just can't believe it. Why hadn't anyone checked before?'

He walks towards me and grabs me in a hug. This is all it takes for me to break down.

'Oh, Anna.' He strokes my hair. 'Try not to think too much about it until you hear anything concrete.'

'That's what Sally said,' I say between sobs. 'But it'll be all I think about until she calls back.'

He kisses the top of my head, and goes to the cupboard above the kettle, taking out a bottle of whiskey. He pours large measures into two tumblers, adding ice from the freezer. He hands me a glass.

'It'll help you sleep.'

I take a sip. I've never liked whiskey. It burns my throat as I swallow, but the warmth is comforting. Jack pulls out the chair next to me and sits, taking a large gulp of whiskey. He winces as he swallows, leaning back against the chair.

'Oh God,' I say. 'It's going to cost your firm a fortune for Sally to travel abroad.'

'Jesus, Anna! Don't think about that. The amount of times Gerard has paid to have his mistress followed . . . don't worry about it.'

'Really?'

Jack raises his palms. 'Don't ask.'

'Okay,' I say. 'What if one of those bodies is Debbie's?'

'Then I'll help you get through it. I know it sounds crass, but then at least you'll have closure. You've been living under a cloud for most of your life – you need answers.' He reaches over and takes my hand in his. 'I can't imagine what it's like, wondering where your own mother is. I guess I've tried not to make a big deal about it over the years, but it's only because talking about it makes you so sad. I don't want you to feel sad. You're the most important person in my life. Apart from the little one upstairs, of course.'

He smiles.

'I feel as though I've neglected her over these past few weeks,' I say.

'Don't feel like that. She's her usual happy self. And you're a great mother.' He gently squeezes my hand.

'Shall I phone Dad, tell him what Sally said?'

He shakes his head. 'God, no. Think about how you feel, then times that by a hundred. They were married.' He looks up at me. 'Sorry. I didn't mean to be so frank.'

'It's okay. I know what you mean. You don't still think my dad did something to her, do you?'

He opens his mouth, but closes it. He leans back in his chair again.

'I've known your dad for nearly ten years . . . he's a decent man, I know that. When I say those things, I'm just speculating – it doesn't mean I think them.'

'You're just saying that.'

'I'm not. Shall I be truthful with you?'

'Of course.'

'Over these past years, I can see that your dad still mourns Debbie. It's Monica who's always been slightly strange about it all. Don't you think?'

I look up to the ceiling.

'I suppose,' I say. 'I can't go on thinking about what *might* have happened. But I do think Monica is – or she *and* Dad are – hiding something. I thought whatever it is, was kept from me so I wouldn't get hurt.' I look into Jack's eyes. 'As usual,' – I give a hollow laugh – 'I'm thinking everything's about me.'

'Don't be silly, Anna. You see things from your own point of view – most people are the same. Don't think you're any different. And, anyway, Sally Munroe might find nothing. It might be a wild-goose chase.'

He sips his drink.

There's a few minutes' silence before rain starts to patter on the kitchen window.

'What a strange few weeks,' he says. 'Why does everything have to come at once?'

'I've been thinking that. I'm glad I've got you back.'

He raises his eyebrows. 'I never left. I just didn't know how to deal with everything.' He runs a hand through his hair. 'I hadn't thought about Fran for years. It was always just you, you know. I haven't been pining after her for years. She was a girl I dated for a few months when I was seventeen.'

I nod and take another sip.

'I've a confession,' I say. 'That night, on my birthday, I was really pissed off with you – you came home late and had been out for a meal on your own. I went through your wallet.'

He takes his hand from mine and holds the tumbler with both hands.

'I know,' he says.

'What? How?'

'I found the letter years ago. It was in with my old GCSE certificates, but I never thought to get rid of it – it was a harmless teenage love letter. The day I heard about her accident – the day before your birthday – I dug it out – I don't know why. I guess I wanted to see her last words to me. Then I heard you coming up the stairs and I panicked, put it in my wallet. When I looked at the photo of you and Sophie a few days later, I could see something behind it – I knew I wouldn't have put it next to your picture. I felt such a shit, forgetting your birthday. I had so much on my mind, and then when I saw the letter had moved – I felt so guilty, I couldn't look you in the eye. I couldn't talk to you without feeling bad.'

'I thought you were having an affair.'

'I'm sorry. I should've just said what was going on. But you got that email, and everything changed. I didn't want to burden you with what was going on with me.'

I lift up my glass to take a sip, but I don't think I can stomach it. Jack takes the glass from me and places it on the kitchen counter. I watch as he pours milk into a mug and puts it in the microwave. When it beeps, he pours the whiskey into it and stirs in a teaspoon of sugar. He places the hot mug in front of me.

'That should do it. I saw my mum make it for my dad when I was a kid.'

I take a sip and it's delicious.

'Does it help?' he says.

'A little.'

'Are you still up for Robert's party tomorrow?'

'I have to be. I can't let him down – even though it's the last thing he wants. You're still coming, aren't you?'

'Of course.' He stands up and picks up both our drinks. 'Come on. Let's take these upstairs.'

We're walking up the stairs when Jack's phone pings with an email. We go into the bedroom and he places the drinks on my bedside table. I watch as he opens his mail.

He looks up after reading it.

'It's from Fran's brother,' he says. 'The other man has had his DNA result back.'

I sink onto the bed.

'And?'

'He's asked if I want to know from him or to wait for my own result.'

'What do you want to do?'

'I've prepared myself to hear by post.' He sits down next to me. 'But this will affect us both. I've kept you out of this, as you were going through enough shit, but this is about a child who's just lost his mother.'

I put my arm across his back.

'You know I'll support you whatever the outcome, don't you?'

'I'd hoped that. I didn't take it for granted.'

He leans back on the bed and takes out his phone, and scrolls to a picture.

'This is Matthew, when he was ten. Simon, Fran's brother, sent it to me. He said we looked alike. I can't see it though, can you?'

I take the mobile from his hands and look at the lovely little boy staring back at me.

'It's hard to tell, Jack. I look nothing like my dad.'

I bring the picture closer and see a nose that looks the same as Jack's, the tilt of the head and the closing of one eye in the sun. I've known what it's like for my biological mother to be absent, but Monica has been an amazing parent.

I look into the little boy's eyes: he knew his mother. The pain he must be going through must be unbearable. He must feel so lost. I just hope his family haven't told him about the uncertainty of his paternity. That shouldn't get in the way of the boy's grief.

I hand the picture back to Jack.

'Whatever he needs, we'll be there for him.'

Jack takes the phone, holds it against his stomach. He wipes away the single tear that rolls down his face.

Chapter Forty-Two

Sunday, 27 July 1986

Debbie

Peter's letting me get ready in peace, as he's reserved a barbecue in the gardens at six and he doesn't want me to be late. *In peace.* He means I should sober up, and now I'm soaking in a bath of salty water with bubbles.

I'm an embarrassment to him. Why can't I just be normal? I almost killed our child, for God's sake. I don't want to think what would've happened if Monica hadn't been watching over us. She's our guardian angel, I suppose.

But Annie's fine. That's what I tell myself again and again.

I feel homesick. And I *am* drunk, I think. It's only the afternoon, but people get away with drinking earlier on holiday. Or rather, everyone else does. I shouldn't be allowed near water again. Perhaps that's what he wants now: me to fall asleep in this bath, into an oblivion of salt water and Mister Matey.

Before the swimming-pool incident, Nathan and I drank four cocktails at the bar. He must be able to take his drink, because he's fine. I can hear them all laughing at something he's said in the living area.

There's only a small mirror in this bathroom, above the sink. It doesn't even have condensation it's so hot here. It's almost unbearable. I keep saying that: unbearable. It rolls too easily in my thoughts. I must say it all the time.

My thoughts are everywhere. That's the trouble with peace.

What the fuck was Ellen on about earlier? As if I'd go near her letch of a husband . . . and her thinking she knew my character. She couldn't be more wrong. I'm not interested in anything like that. It's bad enough having the trouble of one husband, without getting into the complications of having an affair. I can't even look after myself.

Peter and Monica are getting on well. Neither have mentioned my problems from home, though they might have talked about it amongst themselves. I'm past caring right now. It's all been trumped by my behaviour this afternoon. I thought Monica wasn't maternal before this holiday – she was only nineteen when she had Leo. She mothered him as though it were a job. But after today, and hearing her now with Annie, she's like a different person. The walls are so thin.

'I'm sure Annie just smiled, Nathan,' she's saying.

'It's probably wind,' says Peter, repeating what my mother said about Bobby at that age.

'Have we got any beers in the fridge?' says Nathan.

The water drips off me like I'm a washed-up whale as I sit up in the bath. The bubbles have slipped off me and my belly is hanging over like Father Christmas's. I prod my white, stretch-marked stomach and my finger goes in at least two inches. I should be bothered about it, but I'm not.

'Hurry up, Debs!' shouts Monica at the bathroom door. 'You've been in there an hour. I need to wash this chlorine off me before we go out.'

'Really? That long? Did you put your watch forward by mistake?'

'What?'

'Never mind. I'll be out in a minute.'

It doesn't matter what time her watch says compared to mine – time is passing the same, isn't it? I used to think like she did – I used to get excited about going out. It's probably because I've got two kids now, and she only has one. That's why she cares about what she looks like. It must be that.

I pull the plug and stand, grabbing the shower rail for balance as I climb out. It must be nice to have a shower – so much quicker. I think this for only a few seconds before realising showering would still be too much of an effort. What's the point of bathing or showering every day if you hardly go anywhere?

I grab the outfit from the hook on the back of the door. Monica must've selected it from my suitcase. It's my favourite baggy black dress and I love her for choosing it for me. She does know me after all.

I dress and look at the top half of myself in the mirror. My hair is frizzy, and my skin is blotchy, but it'll do.

I open the bathroom door and expect a waft of cold, but the air's stifled.

How much would it cost to telephone Mum and Dad from here?

I've been placed on a white plastic chair around a white plastic table next to Nathan and Monica. Peter's happy because he's *manning* the barbecue. He gave me a glass of sangria – almost half a pint. I tried to protest, but he said, 'You deserve a night off after the day you've had.' It's like he's a different person to this afternoon.

Monica's on baby duty. She put a roll of film in the old camera my dad gave Bobby, and gave Leo one of those new disposable ones. They're taking pictures of the floor – God knows what insects they'll find over here. At least it's keeping them quiet. Bobby's such a good boy. I used to call him Mummy's

Special Soldier when he was smaller, but like most things, it passes.

He's been looking at me funny since this afternoon – like he doesn't believe it's really me, that an alien's possessed his own mother. Perhaps that's true.

Oh shit. Ellen's walking over. She's only fifty or so yards away. I slide down in the chair.

'Who the fuck invited her?' I hiss to Monica. 'I told her not to come.'

She follows my gaze.

'Oh. Sorry. I forgot to mention, Peter spoke with them earlier – they almost invited themselves, or rather, she did.'

'That bloody woman's a psycho. One minute she's really nice to me, the next she accused me of eyeing up her perv of a husband.'

Monica turns sharply to face me.

'Are you kidding? Him?'

She turns to look at the vision that is Alan, complete with beer-belly overhang. We could almost be tummy twins.

'*Him?*' I say. 'You're meant to be shocked at the insinuation of *me* having an affair.'

'Yeah, that too,' she mutters under her breath; they're only a few feet away. 'That woman is deluded.'

In an instant, Monica plasters a smile on her face and stands, holding out a hand to the glorious couple. They're matching in neon green – her with a boob-tube dress, and him with long shorts (no T-shirt).

Bobby and Leo come towards us, sniggering. They both take a picture of them. That photo will really cheer me up when I get home.

Alan sits next to Nathan, and Ellen pulls out a chair next to me. She smiles when Peter hands her a glass of sangria.

'Well, isn't this nice,' she says, sitting back, admiring the view of the concrete apartment block next door. She leans towards me. 'Heard about your *Miami Vice* episode in the swimming pool today. It could've gone so wrong if your Don Johnson over there hadn't come to your rescue.'

She's looking at Monica. My mouth drops open. Ellen hated the sight of her yesterday. I feel uneasy just being next to her.

'I was overtired,' I say. 'It's having a newborn.'

'Hardly. You were necking those cocktails back. Still,' – she pats me on the hand – 'we can't all be Wonder Woman, can we?'

'Quite,' I say, sucking my straw. 'I'm more Miss Piggy than Wonder Woman.'

Ellen bends over, and her shoulders shake. It's like she's laughing, but there's no sound.

'Oh, you're a card,' she says.

She raises her head; her face glowing after too much sun.

'Is your sister not joining us tonight?' I say.

She glances at me from the corner of her eye, her smile gone.

'I forgot I told you about her. Don't say anything, will you? You caught me at a bad time.' She sucks sangria through her straw. 'She's babysitting our boy. No more nosebleeds, then?'

'No.'

Monica pushes a sleeping Annie in her buggy away from the table when Alan lights up a cigarette. She leaves my baby a few feet away from us all. Nathan stands and walks over, kneeling in front of her. I watch as he places her foot on his chest and smiles at her. I should warn him that he might wake her, but I don't want to interrupt the moment. I've never seen him like this with a child before.

'You're all doe-eyed watching them two,' Ellen says in my ear. 'Be careful his wife doesn't see. I must say, though, he's a bit of a dish.'

I don't reply. If she continues whispering in my ear like this, I'm going to move.

Nathan stands. He leaves Annie and walks behind me to get to his chair, ruffling my hair as he passes.

'Sorry, Debs,' he says. 'I couldn't resist. She's just the most beautiful baby. She looks just like you.'

The banter between Monica and Alan quietens as Nathan returns to his seat.

Ellen's voice is in my ear again. 'Awkward.'

Thank God Bobby and Leo are walking towards us.

'Can I have a picture, please?' Bobby says to Monica and Nathan.

Nathan leans towards her, placing a hand on her lap. If you saw that, you'd think them a happy couple. But they're not. They've barely spoken today; they've barely spoken all holiday.

They smile their *cheese*, which fades as the boys leave.

Seconds later, Alan's leering over Monica.

'Doesn't Nathan mind all of that in front of his face?' Ellen's lit a cigarette; she takes a long drag. 'I know *I* would. But I'm used to it.' She leans closer again. 'He gives me a slap sometimes . . . when I give too much mouth. Does yours do that?'

'Mine?' The sangria's gone to my head. I look at Peter, and can't imagine him even thinking of hitting me. I shake my head. 'No.'

'You've got a good one there, then.' She takes another drag. 'Shit. I don't know why I'm telling you this – I tell no one, not even my family. You've got one of those faces, I suppose. The way you're sitting there like that . . . it's like you're apologising for fucking being alive.'

I didn't want to engage with her; I didn't want to talk to her, but I can't help it.

'Your husband shouldn't hurt you, Ellen,' I say.

'All the fellas I've been with have. Must be me then, mustn't it?'

My hand reaches over to hers.

'No,' I say. 'It's not you.'

She bats my hand away.

'Don't you start being kind to me. It'll set me off.'

She dabs the back of her hand on the tears in her eyes. Her blue eyeliner and mascara doesn't streak. She must know the right make-up to wear.

'I'm sorry about being off with you at the cocktail bar,' she says. 'I'm allowed to be feisty to other people especially when he's only had a few drinks – and as long as it's not targeted at him. It's when he's had too many that I have to keep my mouth shut.'

Nathan moves his seat next to me; Ellen turns her head to Monica. Alan saunters over to poor Peter at the barbecue.

'Not drinking the sangria?' says Nathan. 'You've still got half left.'

'I've had more than enough booze today.' I smooth the black fabric over my legs.

'One can *never* have enough booze, Deborah.' He downs what red drink is left in his glass, and we sit in silence. I listen in on the women next to me, which isn't hard: Ellen's voice is so loud it echoes.

'How long have you and Nathan been married?' she shouts.

'Two years.' Monica's voice is quieter.

'He's not the boy's father then?'

'No. I didn't marry Leo's father. I was only nineteen when he was born. It was a fling, but Leo still sees his dad.'

'Isn't that modern?'

'That's one way of putting it. It was hard being a single parent, but I stayed at university – my mother paid for childcare. After uni, I managed to get a good job to support us both. I

315

got together with Nathan when Leo was three . . . I met Nathan through Debbie – they went out with each other when they were teenagers. They bumped into each other on the street a few years later, and Debbie gave him my number. I'd met him myself when we were younger, but they spent a lot of time alone . . . I only got to know him properly all these years later.'

'I can see that those two used to have a thing,' says Ellen.

I shift in my seat. They must know I can hear.

'What makes you say that?' says Monica.

My face burns. I shouldn't listen, but I can't help it.

'He does seem rather taken with her, doesn't he?' Ellen's voice isn't as loud; she's leaning into Monica's ear.

'I . . . I don't know.'

Thank God Peter is far enough away. I've only met Ellen a few times, but she's poisonous. I turn to Nathan, thinking he won't have heard a thing, but he's looking at me, frowning.

'What's that silly cow talking about now?' he whispers. He takes my hand. 'Come on. Let's go for a walk, away from that crazy couple.'

'She's had a rough time with that shitty husband of hers.'

'That's no excuse.'

He pulls me up from the chair; it doesn't take much effort as my body is willing, betraying me.

'It's terrible timing, us going for a walk,' I say, glancing at Monica.

She's narrowing her eyes at Ellen. I hope she sees that Ellen's shit-stirring – trying to deflect from her own awful home life.

'I'm just taking your wife for a wander,' Nathan hollers to Peter.

Peter gives a salute with the barbecue tongs. My husband's such a lovely man.

Nathan tugs at my hand until I follow.

'We can't be long,' I say. 'The food'll be ready soon.'

316

He releases my hand and puts both of his in his pockets. I look at his arms. He's always tanned quickly – his skin would turn golden in a conservatory, whereas mine would turn pink, like a pig's.

We walk down the side of the apartment block and out onto the sandy road. Topless men on mopeds whizz past. English tourists, wearing socks and sandals, walk along miserably, laden with carrier bags of food. Probably full of tea bags, baked beans and digestives.

'I found this gorgeous view the other day,' says Nathan. 'I know there are plenty of lovely sights around here, but even though there's a road right next to it, it feels so peaceful. The sound of the waves drowns out the cars. It has a bench, too – perfectly placed. It's not far away.'

We walk in silence, going uphill until we reach a bend in the road. There's an area of dried, yellow grass with a small seating area. Nathan takes my hand and leads me over rocks and stones. About five feet from the bench, there's a drop, with the blue sea below.

'Are we on the cliffs?' I say.

'Yeah. This one's called La Gran Caída.'

We sit on the bench. There are cars speeding past on the road behind us, but the sound of them quickly fades in my ears.

'This is beautiful,' I say.

'I thought you'd like it.'

'What do you mean?'

'You must know.' He's staring straight ahead at the waves, crashing on whatever's below – I can't see from this angle. 'There was only ever you, Debs.'

'But . . . but we're married. To other people! Nothing can ever happen between us.'

He turns his body to face me, raising a leg and resting it on the seat.

'You feel the same, then?' he says. 'I knew it.'

'No . . . I've just had a baby. My hormones are all over the place.'

He puts his arm around my shoulders.

'I can keep you safe. Peter can't.'

'Safe from what?'

'Those letters we've been getting. I know who sent them. I'll stop them.'

'Who sent them?'

He taps the side of his nose.

'Don't you worry about that.'

'Nathan! Stop being weird. What's wrong with you?'

He slumps against the back of the bench, as though I've winded him.

'I'm not being weird. I'm looking out for you.' He turns his gaze back to the ocean. 'And Monica's too busy fawning over Peter to bloody notice anything I do.'

I nod slowly. 'Okay. So *that's* what this is really about. You're feeling neglected by your wife.'

'If anything, it's the other way around.'

I look at Nathan: I loved this man once. But he was a boy then – intense, troubled. He could still be like that now.

'Just talk to her, Nathan. Get everything out in the open. You love each other. Don't waste it all on some idea you have of me. It's not even real. If you lived with me for five minutes, you'd go off me.'

'No, I wouldn't. Before you had Annie, Peter used to rave about how relaxed you were. Monica's so caught up with what everyone thinks of her – the dad she never sees, the mother who doesn't give a shit.'

'Hang on. Before I had Annie?'

'I'm not saying you're a nightmare now,' says Nathan, smiling, 'I'm just saying that I haven't spoken to Peter properly since.'

I lean back against the warm concrete of the seat.

'What does it all matter, anyway?' I say.

'What do you mean?'

I stand. The dress sticks to the back of my legs. I peel it away.

'*See, the only person who loves you is as crazy as you are – you're making him that way. You might as well do your family a favour and leave them in peace. They're better off without you – can you see that now?*'

'Oh, shut up,' I say.

'What?'

Oh God.

I'm replying to the voice in my head.

'Doesn't matter,' I say. 'Let's head back.'

We walk back to the apartments in silence. Only Monica looks up as we get back to the barbecue area. Ellen's standing next to Peter near the barbecue, twirling her hair with her fingers. If she's trying to make her husband jealous, it's not working; Alan's face is just twelve inches away from Monica's, whose chair is backed up against a tree.

'I think you'd better rescue your wife,' I say to Nathan.

'She'll be fine.'

Annie's still in the buggy. Nathan sits at her feet on the grass. I tut loudly at him and walk towards Monica.

'Would you mind taking a look at something for me?' I shout to her.

She stands straight up, and shimmies sideways against the table to escape.

'That sounds interesting,' says Alan. 'Room for a third?'

I narrow my eyes at him.

'You stuck-up bitch,' he says. 'Who do you think you are?'

Nathan gets up from the grass.

'What's your problem? Do you have an issue with women? You can't talk to Debbie like that.'

319

He walks towards Alan, his chest puffed.

'I just did.'

Alan leans over the table.

'Hey, hey.' Peter walks towards them, tongs in one hand and a bottle of beer in the other. 'The food shouldn't be long. How about a bit of music?'

He reaches under the table for his cordless tape recorder (probably got it on special with his discount at Woolies) and puts on 'Club Tropicana'.

Alan sits back down; Ellen sits in the chair next to him. She strokes the side of his face, but he bats her away.

Monica puts a hand on my wrist, and guides me away from them.

'What did you want to show me?'

'Nothing,' I say. 'I was trying to rescue you from that twat.'

'Thanks, Debs.' She frowns at Nathan, who's sitting back on the grass next to the pram, a bottle of beer in his hand. 'No thanks to you,' she says to him. 'He could've attacked me for all you care.'

'Don't be silly,' he says. 'You can handle yourself just fine.'

'What?' She walks towards him. 'He's twice the size of me.'

'Monica, *everyone* is twice the size of you.'

She glares at him, but he looks away.

'Where did you go with Debbie before?'

It's like I'm not standing here, next to them.

'Just a place.'

Why can't he just lie? He's still not looking at her; he's pulling out tufts of grass and flicking them away.

'It's embarrassing,' hisses Monica, 'you fawning over Debbie. Everyone can see it, you know.'

'I don't give a shit what you or anyone else thinks.'

Monica's face is red. She glances at me, her eyes glistening.

'Sorry, Debs,' she says. 'He must really annoy you.'

'Monica! Stop that.' Nathan's looking at her now. He gets up slowly. 'What makes you dictator over everyone? You can't control my feelings. It doesn't matter if I like Debbie. I won't do anything about it.'

'Only because she wouldn't let you.'

The talking has stopped behind us. I turn and see the three of them looking at us, the song has ended. Peter's standing next to the stereo. His head jerks back – he's wide-eyed. He blinks several times before 'Agadoo' booms out from the cassette player. He looks so hurt that I feel a pain in my chest. I walk towards him and reach a hand out to touch his, but he moves it away.

'Do you love Nathan?' he asks.

My eyes meet his.

'Of course I don't. I don't think I ever did, even when we were kids. I've just been a bit lost recently. I—'

'I don't believe you. You've been acting strange for weeks. Nathan's always around . . . that little outing you went on to St Annes . . .'

'I thought you didn't mind about that. Nathan said he mentioned it to you before.'

Peter raises his eyebrows, looking at Nathan, shaking his head.

'You don't have to pretend any more, Debbie,' says Nathan, striding towards me. He takes hold of my hand. 'It's all out in the open now.'

I wrench my hand from his.

'No. That's not right. Why are you making this up? You're deluded.'

He looks up to the sky before looking at me – his eyes slightly bulging.

'Oh, I'm the deluded one, am I? I'm not the one hearing voices.'

It's like he's taken the air from my lungs. I bend over to catch my breath.

'Fucking hell, Nathan,' says Monica. 'What did you say that for?'

My knees buckle, and I fall to the ground.

'Why did you tell him?' I whisper to Monica.

'I thought it would help to try to . . . Oh God, I don't know. I don't know what's happening here. It's not my fault. I've always tried to help you.'

'See.' It's Alan, behind me. He's revelling in this. 'Told you she was a crazy bitch.'

There are footsteps towards the table behind me.

'Just fuck off, will you.' It's Peter.

'What?' says Alan.

'You heard. Get lost. You're not welcome any more.'

'How bloody rude!'

'Alan,' says Ellen. 'We have to go.'

I turn around and Ellen takes hold of her husband's arm, pulling him from behind the table. He shakes her off. I see Bobby and Leo fifty feet away – their cameras pointed at the ground. They haven't noticed the commotion, thank God.

'I was going to leave anyway,' Alan says, putting his sunglasses on, walking down the path. 'Worst barbecue I've ever been to.'

Ellen follows behind him.

Peter's standing there, holding the metal tongs. Annie lets off a piercing scream.

'Well, just great, everyone,' he says.

'I'll see to her,' I say, crawling on my knees towards her. I unclip the straps and lift her into my arms. 'There, there.' I reach under the pram and there's a bottle of milk that's cooled. I take off the lid and place it to her lips. She jams her mouth shut. 'Come on, little one.'

I try again, droplets of milk spill down her chin. It's like she's holding her breath – her face gets redder and redder. I take the bottle away and she opens her mouth with a big scream. I stand and rock her in my arms.

'There, there,' I whisper. I kiss the top of her head and hold my little finger against her tiny hand. She doesn't grab it like she usually does. I walk up and down; still she screams. 'Shh, Annie. It's okay. Everything's okay now.'

The other three are just standing there, watching. Monica shakes her head and walks over to us.

'Do you want me to have a try?' she says.

'No, no. I can do this. I'm her mother.'

'I know, Debs. But you're stressed. She'll be able to sense it.'

'What? I'm not stressed! It's you lot arguing that's upset her. Can't you see that?'

'We weren't exactly arguing. We were only talking.'

I look to Peter, to Nathan.

'You were arguing, weren't you?'

Nathan shrugs.

'We didn't raise our voices,' says Peter.

'Oh, great. You're ganging up on me as usual.'

Annie's face is almost purple as she screams.

'We're not,' says Monica. 'It's just that you're out of sorts—'

'Have you forgotten what you and Nathan were just talking about? It wasn't *me* causing all of this – it was you.'

'But can't you see, you're acting strange right now? You're pacing back and forth so quickly – you're almost shaking Annie.'

Peter lets the tongs drop from his hands.

I stop moving. Is that why I'm breathless? Was I really doing what she says I was doing?

'Here.' Monica walks towards me slowly. Her smile is false, I can sense it, she's nervous – I know her too well. Her hands tremble as she reaches for Annie. 'Just let me see if I can stop her crying.'

I let her take my baby from my arms.

Monica cradles Annie close to her chest. 'There, there.'

She says the same words as I did, but her voice is so calm. I don't think mine was.

It only takes a few seconds for Annie to stop crying.

They're all looking at me again. I walk away, still facing them.

'I tried,' I say. 'You all saw that I tried.'

I turn, and I run.

I'm lying on Bobby's bed as it's the one nearest the window. The breeze makes the net curtain billow like my mother's skirt when she hangs the washing out. I'm so homesick, but not for mine and Peter's home: for my parents' house. Dad always knows what to say to make me feel better. He probably knows because of what happened to Mum after I was born.

I haven't been abroad before – never been on a plane. Had I told Peter that, or had he assumed I had? Mum and Dad couldn't afford foreign holidays when I was growing up, not with Dad being constantly threatened with redundancy. I've been ashamed about it in the past, not wanting to draw attention to our poverty, but everyone probably knew anyway – we weren't the only ones.

Gleeful screams come through the window from the pool. I kneel up and pull across the net curtains. Peter's watching over Bobby and Leo as they jump in and out of the water. Annie's buggy is next to him and he's pushing it backwards and forwards; she must be asleep – I can't hear her crying.

Bobby's made friends already; it's so easy at that age. The temporary nature of life is more visible when they're young.

His hair looks darker when it's wet – it doesn't look as red. Luckily his skin doesn't burn as easily as his dad's and mine.

Just look at him. He's not even wearing arm bands and he's jumping in and out of the pool. And he's swimming! Who taught him that?

I lie back on the bed.

Annie was so distressed at being anywhere near me. Everyone's better off without me.

I sit up and swing my legs to the floor, slipping on my sandals. I stand and lift out one of Annie's blankets, and inhale the smell. But it's the one Ellen washed. It doesn't smell the same. I throw it back into the cot. Now isn't the time to be sentimental, anyway.

I know what to do now to make everything better for everyone.

I walk to the front door of the apartment and take a last look around. I shan't miss it.

I open the door, but there's someone already standing there: Nathan.

He's following me around like death's shadow.

He pushes me back inside and closes the door. He leans against it.

'I thought you'd come back here,' he says.

He presses his hands behind him, against the door, and pushes himself towards me.

'Why are you acting so strange, Nathan?'

'*Me* acting strange? Look in the mirror! You were all over the place twenty minutes ago, and now you're all calm.'

'I haven't got time for this.'

I try to push him aside to get to the door, but he puts his arm across it.

'Look, Debs, I'm sorry. I didn't mean that – saying you're acting strange. It's Monica. It's all her fault, isn't it?'

I stop struggling to get away from him. Standing back, I look at his face. He's usually cool in the heat, but he's dripping with sweat; his sideburns are so wet they've gone curly.

'I've seen how jealous she is of you,' he says. 'How do you think it makes me feel? Realising my wife hates me – that she's in love with her best friend's husband?'

I fall against the wall.

'That's not true. She wouldn't do that to me. We're like sisters.'

'Are you, now?' he says. 'So why have you been fantasising about me?'

'I . . .' I think back to the time when I was pregnant, and just after I had Annie. My head, my hormones, had been every-where. But how did he know? Was I that obvious? 'It was just a silly crush,' I say. 'For God's sake . . . when I was expecting Bobby, I had a crush on the postman.'

He wrinkles his nose. He moves towards me and puts a hand on my shoulder; the other strokes my face.

'I know it's not a silly crush, Debs,' he says softly. 'We were meant to be together . . . childhood sweethearts.'

I take hold of the finger stroking my cheek and push it away.

'We were never sweethearts.'

'But we were in love.'

'We had a great few months, but you wouldn't give me space. You even hated me spending time with my parents.'

He breaks into laughter.

'Jesus Christ, Debbie. Who wants to spend time with their own parents – especially at that age?'

'I was seventeen. I pretended to be street-smart, but I was immature.' I look away from his gaze. 'I probably still am. I'm letting them down.'

'Who?'

Nathan tilts his head to the side. The squeals of delight from the swimming pool float through the window.

'Everyone.'

'It's Monica who made you think you're crazy. She's been telling everyone you've been hearing voices . . . that you've been wandering the streets in bare feet.'

'She hasn't told everyone.'

'You don't understand. She's a lot sneakier than you realise. She gets into people's heads – makes them think she's oh-so innocent, so helpful.'

326

'That's not true.'

'She's really got you fooled, hasn't she? She's played a long game, I'll give her that.'

'I've known her since I was fourteen – longer than I've known you or Peter. She'd never have an affair with my husband . . . or make me think I'm going crazy. What would she gain from that?'

He shrugs and walks to the fridge, pulling out a bottle of beer. He opens the lid with a can opener and drinks almost half of it.

'Ahh. Just what I needed.' He wipes his mouth. 'I know she doesn't love me. She's never home. I don't know why we're still together – it's not as if I'm the kid's father. She's always wanted more children. But I can't be arsed with all of that.'

'*The kid*? You can't call him that. And Monica loves you. She's always saying so.'

'All lies, I'm afraid, Debs.'

He holds my gaze; he's no longer sweating. Nathan always was a good liar. *No, I didn't make silent phone calls to your house*, he said all those years ago. *It wasn't me who threw stones at your bedroom window*.

I thought he'd grown out of lying – that Monica got the better version of Nathan. But she didn't, did she?

'I can't do this any more,' I say.

I go to the door, expecting him to stop me, but he doesn't. I open it, and he doesn't move.

'Where are you going?'

'For a walk.'

'I'm telling the truth.'

'Whatever, Nathan.'

He reaches into his pocket and pulls out a pink note.

'She wrote these letters.'

He's holding the paper in the air. I swipe it from him and put it in my pocket.

327

'I don't believe you.'

'Why would I lie to you?' he says. 'You'll find out the truth soon enough.'

He grabs the top of my arm and pushes me against the wall. He brings his hand up, his thumb and index finger circle my neck.

'Just do it,' I say, closing my eyes.

'Really?'

He pushes his knee between my legs; he raises it.

'No, not that.'

His hand grips tighter around my throat; I open my eyes.

'No!'

He tilts his head to one side.

His other hand rests on the wall above me.

With my right hand, I grab the bottle out of his hand and smash it on the wall at my side; cold beer drips onto my feet.

I bring the jagged glass towards his neck. He takes his hand away from me. He holds both up in surrender.

We turn our heads to face the apartment door as it opens. Monica.

She looks from me to Nathan, her eyes wide.

'What the hell is going on? What are you doing, Debbie?'

I drop the shattered bottle and run out of the open door.

I sprint down the corridor, to the road, and past the row of shops. Tears are running down my face and my lungs burn.

'*Don't stop*,' says the voice. '*Keep running.*'

'I *can't* stop,' I whisper back. 'I never want to stop.'

I must've been going round in circles, because it's dark and I've reached the clifftop Nathan showed me earlier. I flick off my sandals and walk close to the edge.

The rock I'm standing on is only twelve inches long – just

a foot stopping me falling into the water nearly five hundred feet below. The stone is cool under my bare feet.

It's quiet; there aren't many cars going past behind me. It must be late, or early. There's a lovely warm breeze, one you don't get in England when it's dark. If it gets stronger, it might push me over the edge. Hitting water from this height is meant to be like landing on tarmac.

I've always been afraid of heights. What a strange time to conquer my fear. Nathan said this part of the cliffs is called La Gran Caída. Perhaps the name will be imprinted on my soul, alongside Bobby's and Annie's. I thought that when I had children, I'd become a better person. I think I've always had a badness, a sadness, inside me.

Why are my thoughts everywhere? They need to be here. I'm ridiculous, silly; my mother's right. She's always right. I'm useless to everyone. Everyone will be happier without me. Especially the children.

Oh God, no.

I can't think about the children.

They have Peter. I'd only let them down again. What if I were left on my own with Annie again? I might kill her.

They'll forget me soon enough. They're young enough to erase me from their memory.

Breathe, breathe.

I'm surprised by how calm I am.

It's like my mind was coated in tar, but now it's been wiped clean.

I close my eyes.

So, this is how it ends.

I thought I'd be scared if ever I fell from such a height, but if I jump there'll be nothing I can do about it.

The warm breeze skims my face again. I should be with my children right now, lying next to them, watching them sleep.

But I can't. I'm not good enough for them. They'll end up hating me.

Bobby, Annie, you were the loves of my life.

'Debbie! For God's sake, what are you doing?'

Is that the voice inside my head again?

I close my eyes. I don't want anyone to stop me. I just want darkness.

Don't look back. I can't look back.

'Debbie, come away from there!'

Before I have time to think, I'm turning around.

'Oh,' I say. 'It's you.'

'What are you doing so close to the edge?'

I visualise the picture of Jesus my mother has hanging in the living room. It isn't a graphic depiction of His death: it's the Sacred Heart. I can't believe I've not made that connection before: life is eternal. Perhaps it's Him who's been talking to me all along.

'Leave me alone, Ellen. I know what I'm doing.'

She walks closer to me, and my body begins to shake.

Chapter Forty-Three

Anna

I stop the alarm before it goes off. I've barely slept, and when I managed to drift off, my dreams were of my mother.

In the first one, she walked along the edge of a bridge as though she were balancing on a tightrope just inches from the ground.

'Come on, Annie,' she said. 'Come and have a go. It's fun – you'll like it.'

I was older than her. I had wrinkles around my eyes, yet her skin was so smooth, iridescent and glowing in the sunshine.

In the next dream, I was crawling in a ventilation shaft – like the ones in American films where the victim hides. The bottom of it, instead of being made from metal, was dirt. Worms wriggled beneath my hands and knees – their shiny skin catching the shards of light that leaked into the darkness. I came to a junction and took a left, but stopped as soon as my hand became tangled in strands of hair. I pulled my hand away, but it was covered in maggots and ants.

I knew it was Debbie. I didn't have to look further to know her rotting corpse lay before me.

Jack turns over in the bed so he's facing me.

'Did the alarm go off?' he says, his throat croaky.

'No. I was awake. It's Sunday, anyway.'

'Nice one,' he says. 'What time can I sleep till?'

I wish I were more like Jack. He never wakes and thinks of his worries; he just wants to sleep more.

'Whenever Sophie wakes you,' I say. 'The party's at three. I'm going to see Dad before it starts.'

Jack groans. He folds the pillow and lays his head on it.

'I thought we talked about this last night. We said it was best that we wait until we know more.'

'I know it's going to be bad news. I can feel it. I've never felt this before.'

My pillow is damp from tears I must have cried in my sleep. I've never cried for her before – I've always cried for myself.

'Anna,' says Jack. 'Why don't we just forget about everything for a day? A few hours aren't going to make a difference after thirty years.'

I get up and grab the outfit that's hanging on the back of the door.

'I don't think this can wait,' I say, before heading to the bathroom.

The shower is hot on my skin. Every time I close my eyes, I see her face. Soon, I'm going to find out what happened to my mother. It's like every cell of my body has known that this is the moment I'm meant to find out – that I'm ready to hear it.

I step out of the shower. The mirror is steamed up, so my face is blurred. I could be Debbie – it could be her face staring back at me.

I swipe off the condensation, flick on the tap and splash my face with cold water. I grip the side of the wash basin. I want to go back to not knowing. At least there was hope.

There's a knock on the bathroom door.

332

'Mummy, I really need the toilet.'

'Coming, sweetheart. Won't be a sec.'

Thank God for Sophie.

I stand next to the lounge window with a small mirror to check my make-up. The living room is draped in darkness; outside is overcast. My eyes are swollen with shadows that can't be hidden with concealer. What's the point anyway? I slam shut the compact and throw it onto the chair. I rest my palms on the sill.

I don't see anyone watching the house, but there is a red car parked a few doors down. I lean closer to the window, but I can't see if it's a man or a woman in the driver's seat. Whoever it is, is looking in my direction. Can they see me, too?

I rush out of the front door to the gate. The person in the car puts on a baseball cap, turns on the engine and reverses around the corner of the next street. It's a new car – I can't tell the make from here, but it looks like the one I've been seeing these past few days. It speeds off in the opposite direction.

It probably has nothing to do with me. I've probably caught them spying on someone else. But my heart is pounding; I feel like I'm being watched.

I look down the other side of the street.

'Oh!'

Mr Robinson from next door is right next to me.

'Sorry, love,' he says. 'This was posted through our letterbox by mistake yesterday.'

He hands me a brown envelope.

'Thank you.'

'You jumped about ten metres off the ground then, Mummy,' Sophie says as I walk back into the living room.

She's standing on the sofa, looking out of the window.

'Mr Robinson gave me a fright, that's all.'

'I saw a car speed off. They must've been watching F1 like me and Daddy.'

'Yeah . . . they must have.'

I look down at the envelope, and race up the stairs, opening our bedroom door.

Jack has the pillow over his head.

'I think this is it,' I say.

He groans again and takes the pillow away.

He sits up, taking the letter from me.

'I'll open it later,' he says. 'All of this can wait until after the party. We have to be there for Robert.'

'But don't you need to know? What if you have a son?'

He gets out of bed and puts on his dressing gown.

'I need to do it in my own time, Anna.'

He walks out of the room and slams the bathroom door shut.

It took Jack two hours to come out of the bathroom, and another hour to get ready. I watched as he did his hair in the hall mirror.

'Why are you in such a good mood?' I said.

'Because we are forgetting everything for a few hours and I'm practising now.'

He must've read the results, I thought. He must've been digesting the news while getting ready.

I put sparkly gel in Sophie's hair – glad that she's not into plaits, because I would be useless – and all I could think of was the boy who might be Jack's son, although he's almost a teenager now. Would he want to live here? We would have to convert Jack's office into a bedroom for him. It would be a fresh start for all of us. I could move on from Debbie and concentrate on someone else.

But then it struck me how selfish my thoughts were.

This boy has just lost his mother – a mother who he'd grown up with – a mother that was his sole parent. Jack would be a stranger to him. And there I was, planning happy families in my head – trying to fill a hole in my own life.

Now, we're on the way to the party. *No*, I think to myself, in the passenger seat of Jack's car, *I will plan nothing*. I will let other people decide what they want to do. I can't control everything, everyone. I must let go, stop being so anxious. However much I've tried to keep everything together, I can't control everything. Perhaps realising that is what will make me happy.

'There's a good turnout,' says Jack as we pull into the car park of The Continental.

'There must be a lot of customers, too,' I say.

Jack rolls his eyes at me, and I smile.

'Sorry. Yes. It'll be a lovely party for Robert.'

Jack takes off his seat belt and leans over, kissing me on the cheek.

'I have to tell you now,' he whispers, 'my DNA test was negative.'

'What? Why didn't you tell me when you first read the results?'

He gazes out of the windscreen.

'Because I made a big deal out of waiting until after the party . . . I don't know . . . I had to process it all.' He turns, his eyes meet mine. 'You look disappointed. Are you?'

'I don't know . . . perhaps.'

He shakes his head a little, smiling.

'You're always yearning for something,' he says. 'Isn't what we have together enough?'

We both look behind us at Sophie in the back seat, engrossed in a game on her DS.

'This is enough,' I say, looking back at him. 'It's more than enough.'

Jack puts a hand on the door handle.

'So, how about we party like it's 1999?'

'Er, you've been to my family's parties before, right?'

He opens the door. '1999 was a pretty bad year for me, to be honest.'

I playfully slap his thigh before opening the car door.

Jack and I each hold one of Sophie's hands. We swing her all the way to the entrance.

'Can I have a wine?' she says.

'No,' Jack and I say at the same time.

Inside, I scan the place for Robert. I recognise some of his friends from university, sitting round a large table on the left, but he's not with them.

'Hello, Annie.'

It's Ellen, standing at the bar.

'Oh. It's you,' I say. 'What are you doing here?'

'My son gave me a lift. He got back in touch.'

It didn't answer my question. She lives nearly twenty miles away – why pick the same pub? Did I mention that Robert's party would be here? I can't remember telling her.

'Your family's over there.' She points to the other side of the room, a strange smile on her face.

'Thanks, Ellen.'

I turn my back on her and walk over to Dad and Robert. They're standing next to each other, completely still.

'What's going on?' I say. 'Happy Birthday, Robert! Shall we get you a drink? Maybe you could push the boat out and have a vodka.'

They both turn around.

'What's wrong?' I say. 'Are you drunk already, Robert?'

I look behind them. Monica's standing with her arms around someone.

'Monica?'

She turns around, tears and mascara run down her face.
'She came back.'
I look to the person standing next to her.
It's my mother.

Chapter Forty-Four

2 a.m. Monday, 28 July 1986

Debbie

Ellen stops five feet away from me.

'I'm not going to touch you, Debbie,' she says. 'But you need to come away from the edge. This isn't the way to solve everything.'

'You don't know me . . . you don't know what's been going on in my life.'

'I've seen a snapshot. I've seen a husband who loves you, and a best friend that would do anything for you.'

'Well, you've got the wrong picture, haven't you?'

'I don't think so. I'm good at reading people and situations. I've listened to them when you're not there. Monica is really worried about you – she was in tears yesterday talking about you, about how you're like a sister to her. She feels you're slipping away from her.'

'Really? Nathan thinks her and Peter are having an affair.'

Ellen gives a laugh – almost like a cackling witch.

'Haven't you heard the way Peter talks to her? It's so formal, polite.'

'I've never noticed,' I say. 'Monica's right, though. She's been telling Peter and Nathan that I hear things – voices – telling me to do things. God, I can't believe I'm telling you. A virtual stranger.' I give a dry laugh. 'I'm scared to be with my baby. I'll do her real harm next time, I know it.'

'You could see a doctor for that.'

'They'd lock me up. I'd never see my children again, anyway.'

A car screeches to the left – it swerves before stopping. The window rolls down and a man waves a fist.

'*Sal de la carretera, estupido ingles borracho!*'

There's a man, staggering in the road.

I should've guessed: Nathan.

'Oh, fuck off, Manuel,' he shouts to the driver.

He laughs as the man pulls away.

'I knew you'd come to our special spot, Debs. Didn't think it'd take you this long, though. You've been hours.'

He stands next to Ellen, not registering her presence.

'Why are you so close to the edge?' he says.

'Are the children okay?'

'Course. Monica's looking after them – they're fine.'

'Has Bobby asked about me?'

He shrugs. 'Not that I heard.'

I look back into the darkness of the sea. The light of the moon makes it easy to tell where the sea ends and the sky begins. Soon, I'll be part of that darkness. I close my eyes.

'Please,' says Ellen. 'Come away from there.'

'What are *you* doing here?' Nathan's slurring his words. He must've had more to drink after I left.

Everyone's better off without you. You heard what he said.

Why am I waiting? I should just jump.

'So, when are we leaving?' he says.

'What?'

Don't turn around again, I tell myself. Don't.

'I've brought a bag . . . packed our passports, too. I've got some savings . . . from my redundancy.'

'You lost your job?'

He shrugs. 'I lost it weeks ago. I was lucky to get a few quid. Not that Monica knows – she'd have spent it by now. I got up every morning in my suit as usual and didn't come back until tea time. She didn't suspect a thing. I knew it happened for a reason. I've been planning this for ages . . . since we booked the holiday.'

'Planned what?'

'All of this.' He swings his arms around and sways as though he might fall over. 'Okay, well not the bit about you standing on the edge of a cliff.' He frowns. 'What *are* you doing there? You're not going to jump, are you?'

'You're pissed, Nathan,' I say. 'Go away.'

'Go away? But I thought . . . we could go somewhere together. It's what you wanted.'

'I don't want any of this. I want nothing.'

Footsteps are coming towards me. A thud.

I turn.

He's dropped the bag; he's coming closer.

'Don't come near me, Nathan.'

A small rock next to my feet falls over the edge. It takes a few seconds before it lands loudly. No splash – just a crack as it hits another rock.

'That's what would happen to you,' says Ellen. 'No splash. Just you and a rock.'

Ellen notices more than I realised . . . this person I met only a few days ago. I thought she was drunk all the time, but she picks up on the smallest of things.

Nathan grabs my right arm, the one closest to the edge, as I turn to face him.

'Come on,' he says. 'Don't be silly. You heard what she said.'

I yank my arm away, but he doesn't let go.

'Please don't,' I shriek.

Adrenaline pulses through me.

I step back from the edge with my left foot, leaning heavily on it, but Nathan won't let go of me. He goes to put his other arm around my left shoulder, but I push it away.

His foot falters on the edge; his weight pulls me closer to him.

He slips.

'Ahhh!'

He cries out in pain as his left knee lands on a rock ten inches down. He's trying to balance, but he's faltering. His leg gives way and he lands on his elbows – he howls in pain. I grab both of his hands in mine as the rest of his body flails below. Ellen grabs hold of my waist – trying to pull me and Nathan away from the drop.

'Try and climb back up, Nathan!' she says. 'Keep still! Debbie, lie down on the floor. I'll grab your feet and pull.'

I do as she says, but my hands burn.

'I don't know if I can hold on much longer,' he says, his eyes wide, his face contorted in pain. 'I must've broken my arms – they're so weak.'

There are tears in his eyes. We're holding him, but he's too heavy – Ellen's too slight, she has barely the strength to keep me from the edge.

'I don't want to die,' he whispers.

'Pull us back, Ellen!' I shout.

Nathan's weight is dragging me towards him, I feel myself slide slowly along the ground.

'I don't know what to do!' I scream.

Ellen looks behind her. 'There's no one here to help us. I can't hold on much longer.'

'I love you, Debbie,' says Nathan.

He lets go of my hands.

Silence.

I cover my ears – I can't bear to hear what follows.

I lie there for what feels like hours before Ellen sits beside me. I push myself up, onto my knees.

It feels as though something's blocking my throat – I can't breathe.

I try to speak, but instead collapse next to Ellen.

'Here.' She takes off her sarong and wraps it around my face. 'I know it's not the same as a paper bag, but breathe – the carbon dioxide will help you.'

Inhale, exhale.

Slowly, slowly, my breathing calms.

'What happened?' My voice is barely a whisper. 'It was all too fast. I didn't know he was going to let go. Do you think he's all right?'

Ellen shakes her head. There are tears pouring down her face.

'No.'

I crawl forward on my hands and knees, trying to look down at the rocks below.

'I can't see him.'

'You wouldn't want to.'

I put my head in my hands, tugging at sections of my hair. I need to feel something.

'We have to get out of here,' says Ellen. 'He won't be washed away for a few hours. They're going to think we pushed him. People might've seen a struggle.'

I turn around, crawl back, and land next to her.

'Washed away? Oh God. He can't be gone just like that!'

'We have to go, Debbie!'

'I can't go back, Ellen. What will I tell everyone? How could I look Monica in the eyes, knowing I just killed her husband?'

'But you didn't – he fell.'

'But Monica saw me threaten him earlier with a broken

342

bottle – she'll tell the police. Everyone will think I pushed him. He wouldn't have been here if it weren't for me. I can't. Oh God. What am I going to do? What would my children think of me . . . my parents? The shame of it. This can't be happening.'

Ellen reaches over for Nathan's bag. She unzips it.

'He wasn't lying,' she says. 'There's an envelope full of money here. And passports. He even brought some of your clothes.' She looks up at me. 'What a crazy bastard.' She looks back in the bag and pulls out a paper wallet. 'Looks like he was planning on writing to people back at home after he left.'

'Can I see that?'

She hands it to me. Inside are sheets of unused pink notepaper.

'I should've realised,' I say. 'It could never have been Monica.'

'What do you mean?'

'It doesn't matter. I've been so wrong. I'm not right, not for anybody. I need to leave.'

'What? You can't!'

'It's better than leaving the way I planned to. You can see that, can't you?'

'I don't know, Debbie. This is all madness.' She stares at the grass, then rubs her eyes with the heels of her hands. 'What shall I say to your family?'

'Say nothing. Pretend this night didn't happen.'

'You have to let them know where you're going. They'll worry about you.'

I take a piece of the pink paper out of the bag with shaking hands.

'Have you got a pen?'

343

Chapter Forty-Five

Anna

Debbie has her arm around Monica's shoulder. Dad's face is completely white, his mouth open.

'I . . . I thought you were dead,' he says. He walks towards her; Monica stands aside. He touches Debbie's arm. 'Is it really you?'

She nods. 'I'm so sorry, Peter. I . . . I know I shouldn't have come – I didn't want to upset you, you've all moved on with your lives . . . I just wanted—'

'You don't have to say sorry, Debbie,' says Dad. 'I'm just glad you're alive.' He looks at Monica. 'I can't believe it, can you?'

Monica shakes her head, make-up like slug-trails down her face.

'Annie,' says Debbie. 'I'd know you anywhere. I'm so sorry, love. I didn't know whether I was right coming here . . . I . . .'

I run over to her and put my arms around her.

'You were right,' I whisper. 'I'm so happy to see you. I never thought I would. I've been looking for you for years.'

She holds the top of my arms and stands back to look at me.

'Look at you. You're beautiful. You look just like my mother.' She strokes my hair, my face. 'Just look at you.' She looks at

Jack and Sophie behind me. 'And with a family, too. I'm so proud of you.'

They are the words I have wanted to hear from her for all of my life.

Tears flood my eyes; my body is overcome. I fall into my mother's arms.

'I missed you so much,' she says. 'I wanted to come and see you for such a long time. I thought you were better off without me – that the longer I left it, the more you'd hate me.'

'You should have come,' I say. 'I don't hate you – I love you. I'm not angry with you.'

Her tears fall onto my neck.

'Thank you, Annie. That's all I've ever wanted to hear. I love you so very much – I never stopped loving you. Have you been happy?'

'Yes, but I . . . yes. I have.'

She pulls away from me and looks at Robert.

'Bobby.' She holds an arm out to him.

He looks at us all – his eyes glistening.

He runs out of the door.

I glance around the beer garden. Robert's sitting on a wooden bench; he lights up a cigarette.

'I didn't know you still smoked,' I say.

He blows out the smoke, his bottom lip quivering.

'I thought I'd hate her if I saw her again. But . . . I don't. I can't believe it. I just need a moment.' He takes a deep breath and rests his elbows on his legs. 'Do you think she'll still be there when I go back in? I haven't upset her, have I?'

I rub his back.

'You haven't upset her, Rob.' I sit down next to him. 'Shit. I can't believe it either.'

'Did you know she'd be here?'

'No, not at all. I didn't even get a reply to that email I sent.'

'We should get back in.' He flicks his cigarette onto the ground and grinds it with his shoe. He stands. 'Right. I'm ready now.'

I follow him inside.

Debbie's sitting with Monica – they're holding both hands together on the table, both still crying.

Debbie stands when she sees Robert.

'Bobby, love. I'm so sorry.'

He walks slowly to her. He reaches out to touch her hair.

'It's really you, Mum. I've missed you.'

Debbie puts her hands on his shoulders and pulls him towards her.

He lets her – his head below her chin, like he was half the size. For a second, his arms dangle at his side. Then he puts them around her waist.

'My lovely boy.'

A few moments later, he pulls away.

'I'm sorry if I did something to upset you . . . to make you leave.'

'Darling.' Debbie strokes the tears away from his face. 'It was nothing you did . . . it was nothing anyone did. I wasn't very well. I was ill, though I wouldn't have known it then. I felt I didn't deserve to have you. I couldn't take care of myself, let alone you. You deserved better. I love you so much, Bobby.'

'You won't go away again, will you?'

'No, love. No, I won't.'

Jack pulls out a chair for me and pushes me gently onto it. He leans towards Debbie – his arm outstretched.

'Nice to finally meet you,' he says. 'I've heard a lot about you.'

Debbie holds up a shaking hand to meet his. She holds the wrist with her other hand to steady it.

'Sorry,' she says. 'I'm really nervous.'

There's a sound of smashing glass behind us.

Cold liquid sprays over my legs.

Grandad.

He stands amongst the broken shards; droplets of beer drip down the wood panelling.

'Is it really you?' He looks at each of us. 'Is it really my girl?'

'It is, Frank,' says Jack.

The glass crunches beneath his feet as he walks over to her. He brings his hands to her face.

'It's really you,' he says. He strokes her cheeks and her hair. 'It's been so long, love. Are you all right?'

'I don't know, Dad. I'm trying to be.'

He holds her by the shoulders.

'I'm so pleased to see you. I never thought I'd see you again. You're staying for a bit, aren't you? You won't just leave me again, will you? At least give me a phone number I can reach you on.'

Debbie puts her arms on his.

'I'm staying for a while, Dad. If that's okay? If you forgive me?'

He takes her in his arms.

'My darling girl.' He pulls away, wiping the tears from his face with the back of his hands. 'There's nothing to forgive. I'm just so happy you're alive.' He pats her arms, her back, her hair, with his arms. 'You're real, aren't you? You're really here?'

'I'm really here, Dad.'

Dad and Monica are huddled together on the table next to Debbie and Grandad. He has a hand over hers like he never wants to let go of her again. Jack and Sophie are sitting with me, opposite them. Sophie looks at Debbie, then at me.

'You two have the same face,' she says. 'Only yours has a more wrinkles.' She's looking at Debbie, who laughs.

I take in Debbie's face, her hair. She must dye it, because

there are no signs of grey. How long has she been dyeing it? What went through her mind when she did mundane things like that?

'Did you ever think of us?' I say.

'Every second of every day.' She reaches across the table to put a hand on mine. 'I know it's unforgivable, but I wasn't well. I didn't know where I was, half the time. And then there was that terrible accident.'

'What accident?'

'I . . . Did Ellen not tell you?'

'You know Ellen?'

Debbie nods.

'Yes. She got out of prison a few months ago. I thought I'd made the whole thing up in my head, but she tracked me down . . . said I had to make things right. I didn't know if I had the courage after all of these years, but then Ellen found you – she's good with the Internet and all of that stuff . . . she told me where you lived, but I couldn't just knock on your door. She'd done some volunteer work in the past, so she managed to get a position at your bookshop. I hope you don't think that's weird, Annie.'

I remember the feeling of being watched over the past few days – in town, outside my house. It must have been my mother.

'I . . . I suppose not,' I say. 'I've made some questionable decisions myself in the past, so I'm not really one to talk.'

She frowns slightly.

'But I won't go into all of that now,' I say. 'Go on . . .'

'Ellen had been thinking about everything when she was in prison, you see. About what happened with Nathan.'

I shift my chair back a little.

'What happened to Nathan?'

Debbie glances at Monica.

'I need to tell Monica first. If that's okay?'

'And that was why you came back? Not because you wanted to see us?'

'I just needed that push. The longer I was away, the harder it was to come back. I've a lot to tell you. If you want to hear it.'

Jack's looking at me. He reaches over, and I place my hand on his. Sophie, thinking it's a game, does the same – both her hands are on top of ours.

'I've waited a long time,' I say. 'I do want to hear it.'

Chapter Forty-Six

I thought I'd imagined the whole story of that night in my head. I haven't told it out loud before.

Monica's looking at me, frowning. Her eyes never left mine as I told her what happened to Nathan. Dad and Peter were listening silently from the next table. I felt the shame I knew I would feel – my poor dad listening to me describe how I killed my best friend's husband.

'But why didn't you just come to me?' says Monica. 'Tell me what happened? I wouldn't have thought you'd done it on purpose. You didn't murder him, Debbie. It was an accident.' She breaks eye contact, and looks down at her lap; her left arm is in a support bandage. 'Poor Nathan. All these years, no one has been grieving for him.' Tears drip onto her hands. 'I thought you'd run away together – started again.'

'I wasn't in love with Nathan.' I glance at Peter, but he looks away. He's moved on. Some people find it easier than others. 'My mind was in a strange place. I didn't know what was real or not. And after what happened with Annie in the swimming pool, I thought everyone would be better off without me. If I'd been left alone with her again, something worse might've happened.'

Monica grabs a serviette from the table and dabs her cheeks.

'I know this is too late, but I would've helped you, you know.' She leans closer and whispers, 'I never told anyone about the broken bottle. My loyalty was always with you.' She glances at the ceiling, blinking to stop more tears. 'What have you been doing for all of these years?'

I fold my arms around me.

I'd imagined her telling everyone about me threatening Nathan with the broken glass. I'd got so many things wrong.

'I went straight back to England, but on the train and then the ferry. I haven't flown since Tenerife. All the time, I felt people looking at me, was paranoid they could read my mind. If it hadn't been for my passport, I don't think I'd have remembered my name. For days, I wore the same dress as that night. Once I reached Dover, I didn't know where to go. I didn't have the capacity to book a room at a hotel. I found a café I was comfortable in and stayed there. But it came to closing time and I was lost again. I found a bench and couldn't stop crying and that's where the memory ends. Someone must've called an ambulance or something, because the next thing I knew I was in hospital. I didn't know how I got there. The two years were a blur of Valium and Clozapine. I had a bed near the window . . . it had a view of the car park . . . like I was looking into the world through the glass. I could curl up and sleep, but if I wanted to see life, I could just sit up and gaze out of the window.'

Annie and her husband are sitting a few tables down, their heads together, deep in conversation. They're close, I think. Anyone watching could tell he adores her. I'm so glad she found happiness.

'Why did you send that pink note a few days ago?' says Monica.

'I . . . I got scared. I wanted to run away again. But then I realised that I had to face everything. Otherwise you'd never have known what happened. I'm so sorry, Monica.'

She purses her lips, but her eyes still glisten.

'Anna and Robert need your apologies more than I do.'

My beautiful children, now grown-up. I've missed so much. Would it have been best for them to see me at my worst, and grow up resenting me, or let them start afresh without me? Either way, they must hate me.

'Did you hear about Mum?' says Dad, breaking my thoughts.

I turn my chair around and shuffle it towards Dad's table.

'A few months after she died. I'm so sorry, Dad. I'm sorry I wasn't here to help you through it. I couldn't believe it. I thought . . . I thought there was always enough time to come back. I left it too long, didn't I?'

'She thought she was going to be with you . . . at the end,' says Dad. 'It wasn't like these dramatic heart attacks you see on television. She was standing in the kitchen. "I don't feel so good," she said. "I think I must've eaten something off." She was out of breath, but she hadn't done anything strenuous . . . her face was damp with sweat. I grabbed her a chair and sat her down, but she slumped in it . . . said she had a pain in her jaw. That's when I knew. I phoned for an ambulance, and when I went back to her, her face was pale, full of pain . . . I'd never seen her like that before.'

'Oh, Dad. Poor Mum.'

I want to close my ears, put my hands over them, shut my eyes. But I must listen to it. I have to know. It's not cowardice, though, is it? If my mind doesn't work the same way as other people's. One of my doctors told me that. She said it wasn't me being lazy or weak, it was my illness. I've battled through years to believe that.

'What did she say?' I ask him.

I clasp my hands together tightly. I'm right here, I'm listening, I'm in the present. This is real and I'm about to hear my mother's last words.

Breathe in, breathe out.

Everything'll be okay if I just breathe.

'She said, "I'm going to be with our little girl now, Frank."' Dad glances at the smashed glass on the floor to his right before looking back up at me. 'I begged her not to leave me, but she did.'

I put my face in my hands and can't stop the sobs.

'I'm so sorry, Dad.'

He stands and rests a hand on my shoulder.

'There, there, love,' he says. 'You let it all out.' He puts a hand on my head and smooths down my hair. 'I never thought I'd see you again, love.' He kisses the top of my head. 'I'm so happy that you're back. I always knew you'd come back to me.'

I've been away for so many years, yet I feel his love as though it were yesterday that I left. I'm going to spend the rest of my life making it up to him, to everyone.

Chapter Forty-Seven

Anna

Debbie whispered quietly, after speaking to Monica, telling me what happened the night she disappeared. Her eyes were swollen and red from crying.

None of it has sunk in yet. I still can't believe she's alive, but what happened that night . . . it was like she was describing a film she had just seen.

'Didn't anyone look for Nathan?' I asked her.

'His parents are dead,' she said. 'They died years before he did.'

'But that didn't make it right,' I said. 'He deserved to be missed.'

'I know, I know. I made the note sound as though we were about to run off together,' she said. 'I had his passport, clothes.' She couldn't talk about him without crying. 'I was desperate, Annie. I didn't know what to do. He'd written me all of these horrible letters. It was one thing after the other. I had – have – depression. I know that now. It was an awful time.'

'What changed?' I said. I couldn't believe I was so calm, but I knew the enormity of it wouldn't hit me until later. 'What made you contact us?'

'Ellen. She looked for me. I'd read about her in the paper.

Did she tell you that she killed her husband? He was such an awful man. He used to hit her, control her – not that that meant he deserved to die. One day, she lost it. Had a kitchen knife ready. That poor woman. She's been through so much.

'But I wrote back to her because I had to know if what happened that night in Tenerife was real, or just a dream – if my whole life before that had been a dream. It was like myself, my history, had vanished after that night. I barely remembered who I was, my past.'

As she spoke, the only person I could think about was Nathan.

He might've been obsessed with her, but he deserved a life – he deserved to be grieved for by someone.

Now, we're on our way home.

I broke down in tears after closing the car door. I couldn't speak for half an hour.

Jack rubbed my back.

'We won't set off until you're okay,' he said.

I tried to speak, to tell him that it might be ages before I'm okay, but I couldn't.

'What's wrong with Mummy?' said Sophie.

'She's had a shock. She hasn't seen her mummy since . . . well, I don't think she can ever remember seeing her.'

'But Monica's her mummy.'

'Yes, that's right,' said Jack. 'But the other lady is Mummy's biological mother. She was very ill and wanted to get better.'

'What's a biological mummy? Is it like a robot?'

I almost laughed.

I sat up, wiping the tears with my cardigan.

'No, love,' I say. 'But I think that's a talk for another day.' I reached over for Jack's hand. 'Let's go home, shall we?'

We're passing through town and everything looks the same.

Debbie promised to visit me and talk properly. I hope she does – I have to trust that she won't leave again. I want to get

355

to know her — show her the box of things I've kept. I think she'll like that — to know that she was missed, and loved.

Robert talked to her again after drinking four double vodkas. I don't know what he said to her, but I hope he was kind. I hope he saw that she's a person, with troubles all of us have. It wasn't our fault — it wasn't anyone's fault. She thought she prevented us from having an awful life with her, but I wish we'd been given the chance to see for ourselves. But we can't turn back time, can we? Debbie must've known she'd left us in good hands with Dad and Monica.

Just before I left, she gave me a canvas shopping bag, with seven or eight books inside.

'Don't look at them now,' she said. 'But these are my diaries . . . though they might be a little sparse . . . they don't cover the whole time I was away. I thought . . . well, there's nothing in there that I wouldn't tell you. You don't have to read them. It's probably mostly boring stuff anyway—'

'I'd love to read them,' I said. 'Thank you.'

I'm now holding the bag tight, almost hugging it. My mobile phone rings.

It's Sally Munroe.

'Hi Anna. I've got some news, but it's not what I thought it'd be.' She sighs loudly down the phone. 'I found there were two unidentified bodies found on the island. One of those was female, but was aged between fifty and sixty. The other was male. It'd been in the water for about twenty years before it was discovered. They found a silver St Christopher in the skin of his neck. I think it might be—'

'Nathan. Sally, I'm sorry. I should've texted you as soon as I saw her.'

'Saw who?'

'My mother. She was just — there — in the pub for Robert's birthday. Her friend must've told her where the party was.'

'What? Just *there*? I don't understand.'

'I don't understand either, not really. I think she had a nervous breakdown, or post-natal depression, or psychosis, I don't know. I've read so much about different conditions – but no one person is the same.' I look behind me, and luckily Sophie is playing on her beloved game console. 'When they – we – were on holiday, she said there was an accident – that Nathan fell.'

'Has she gone to the police about the accident?'

I don't think so. 'What would happen to her if she did?'

'I don't know,' she says. 'There might be a trial – depends what the coroner says.' There's a brief pause. 'I didn't think it would end like this.'

'No,' I say. 'Me neither.'

'Oh, before I go . . . Ellen wasn't hard to find – she uses her maiden name now. She was sent to prison in 1990 for the murder of her husband, Alan. She pleaded self-defence, but the prosecution went for her.'

'Was it self-defence? No . . . sorry, I shouldn't ask.'

'From what I read in the reports from the time, it seemed so.'

There's too much to take in. I need to sleep, to process all of this.

'Thank you, Sally. For all you've done.'

'You're welcome. My bill's in the post.' She laughs. 'I'm glad it worked out for the best for you, Anna.'

We say our goodbyes, and I throw my phone into my bag in the footwell.

'I still can't believe it,' I say to Jack. 'I started the day thinking my mother was dead, yet she was living in England all of this time.'

'I don't think she's had a happy life, though. Are you okay? It must've been a shock.'

'I'm *still* in shock to be honest.'

Mum said I was lying on her chest while we were on a lilo

in the hotel swimming pool. She fell asleep, and I slipped from her, almost drowning. She asked if there were any lasting effects – was I afraid of water, but I lied. I said no.

She said Monica saved me that day.

I know, I wanted to say. She's been saving me for years.

'I thought Robert would be angry with Debbie,' says Jack.

'I suppose, when you think about it, all that matters is that she's back, she's alive.' The anxiety, that knot in the pit of my stomach that I've lived with for years, has vanished. I look out of the window. 'Thank God she's alive.'

I have been waiting for this moment all day. Jack is reading to Sophie upstairs, and I'm settled on the sofa with Debbie's journals. Some are like school exercise books, others are notebooks with different designs. It might feel as though I'm prying when I read them, like Dad and Monica would have felt listening to the messages I left for Debbie when I was a child. Perhaps if Dad still has the phone, he could give it to her, so she can hear all the calls she missed.

Before reading them all from cover to cover, I flick through the different books. Her handwriting is sometimes neat, at other times, erratic. There's a sentence crossed out too.

12 September 1987

I've been told – or rather, it has been suggested to me – that I should start writing in this journal. I haven't written in a diary since I was about fourteen years old. They assure me no one will read it, that my thoughts will be private, but I don't believe them. It's weird, though, I seem to be able to think a bit more clearly when I'm writing.

I'm in a secure ward – I've been here for nearly a year, under S3 of the MHA (because, apparently, I'm a risk to myself.

~~Which is ridiculous because I'd be doing everyone a favour if I were to succeed.~~ At any time, the police could come in and take me away for what I did last year.

Prison might be better than this place, though. It's so noisy here – especially at night. Everyone must have bad dreams. I know I do. I see his face, so close to mine, as he let go of my hand. When I close my eyes during the day, too. They used to say I shouted his name in my sleep – that I saw people in the corner of the room. 'I hear things,' I told them. 'I've never seen things.' But what if they're right? I could've seen lots of things and they felt real to me. I've no idea, really.

Sometimes, I can't remember what I look like. They're not big on mirrors in this place. Some days I push my food away; other days I eat everything they put in front of me – even taking food others don't want.

I must be fat right now because my clothes feel snug around my belly. I think I was skinny three months ago. When I look down at what I'm wearing, I don't recognise the top and the jeans. No wonder they don't fit properly.

Depression with postnatal psychosis is what they say I have now. At first, they thought I was schizophrenic after I told them God – or my dead uncle – was talking to me. But I don't hear anyone any more.

They won't tell me why that is. They must think they've cured me. They can't explain much, if you ask me, just prescribed different pills after the first time I tried to . . . Well, they just keep giving me different ones. I've no choice.

Give it a few months, they say. 'A few months?' I want to scream. I don't think I have a few months. I've got nothing to live for, and I'm absolutely no use to anyone else. Why don't they let me just do what I want to do? It'd save them a fortune in fucking medication.

359

6 January 1988

I've realised they don't actually read my diary. I've been keeping this one in my packet of sanitary towels (and no one likes to pry in there). To test this, I made up some disturbing thoughts about nurse Adrian and they haven't kept him away from me so far. And that was two months ago.

They say I've been 'doing well' for a few months now — that this new medication must be working after all. (Doing well — what a shit description of a life.) Now they say I'm nearly ready to leave. I'm not under constant obs any more, which is a relief because that was like being haunted.

I don't think I'm ready to leave, but I don't want to be in here any more. I feel so very, very low. Sometimes my thoughts are so dark, I constantly think of ways to end all of this. Which would be the least painful method? I've no blade — they give us plastic cutlery, and we don't get enough pills to save. I want to talk to Karen in the next bed — she's always talking about it — but when I want to speak, she just looks at the picture opposite us. It's the one with the fucking sheep in a fucking meadow. The bastards probably hung that picture there to remind us of what we are.

I'd be able to get what I want outside. That's what I need. To get out and have my freedom. Freedom of choice. Here, I'm like a child being babysat.

Would I do it somewhere no one would find me — or somewhere I'd be found? It's a constant chatter in my head. One that I tell no one about. I'd not want to involve anyone else directly by stepping or jumping in front of their car or train. No, it has to be clean. I wish I could look up ways, talk to people, but there is nothing. The books on our paltry shelf are all stupid novels by privileged people.

What else could I do if I get out of this place? People will know what I've done just by seeing the guilt and shame in my eyes. I won't be able to make friends — you have to be honest with friends, don't you? How could I tell them I'm a mother, but haven't seen my children for nearly a year and a half? Not to mention the fact I killed someone and have misplaced my mind. They'd think I'm a monster. They'd probably be right.

5 November 1990

I've been out for one year, seven months and thirty-two days.

I'm still alive.

The thought of seeing my children is stopping me from doing anything 'stupid' again. Bobby and Annie are out in the world and they are getting older. Soon they will be old enough to want to come and find me. It's a hope I must cling to.

I'm starting a new job tomorrow. When I say job, I mean volunteering in a soup kitchen (not sure they call them that these days). When I went for the interview, it was humbling seeing people without a place to eat or somewhere to sleep. At least I have my benefits, a room (which is pretty grotty, but . . .).

So why do I still feel so fucking low?

Sleep. I need sleep.

Another pill. About the fiftieth bloody pill I've taken today. When will this end?

19 January 1998

I can't believe it. I thought she would live forever. I thought we'd have a chance to meet again. That's been wiped away. I don't know if I can [words illegible] always thought I'd have the time. They'll never want me back now. [words illegible] [words illegible] showed me how to work the internet, and I typed in my mother's name first and her death was what came up!

Six months ago.

Why am I writing in here? I should be going to see my dad. I'm fucking useless.

Useless and I don't deserve to be on this fucking earth.

I'm going to go to the registry office tomorrow to get a copy of the death certificate. It might not even be real. This Internet thing might all be made up – hardly anywhere has it.

My name was listed as her daughter. My children as her grandchildren.

I can't fucking bear it. My mother is dead.

What use is writing when [ends]

24 June 2002

It's Annie's birthday today – she's sixteen years old. I wonder what she's doing to celebrate it. Having a party with all of her friends, I guess. I bet she has loads of friends.

She probably doesn't know I exist. It's easier for them if they never mention me, I imagine. I'm a dark stain they want to blot out. The only thing that keeps me going is the thought that I created two beautiful children and no one can take that from me: the only useful thing that I've done. One day, I might even see them again. Though they won't want to see me. Why would they?

I'm back here again. I didn't get very far, did I?

I still can't believe my lovely mother is dead.

She was so far away, yet I knew she loved me. I hurt her by leaving. I might have killed her. It was her heart, got too much for her.

It's been six years since she died, but I wake up thinking it's just happened.

Why do I keep going? Is it the thought of one day seeing my children again?

It must be.

The theme tune to 'Mistral's Daughter' is blaring out from the communal area. It's fucking annoying and that series is so bloody old! If I knew anyone outside, I'd ask them to bring in 'The Exorcist'. That would give them something to take their minds off their problems. Dad is out there somewhere. Bobby, Annie and Peter, too. How is Monica dealing with Nathan being gone? Does she think we're together living the high life? How much more wrong could she be?

I remember after I had Annie, there was another mum on the ward. We would watch 'Coronation Street' in the lounge. I can't remember her name, though – it began with an S. I bet she's having a good life.

God. I couldn't do it. However hard I tried out there, the memories and the nightmares always caught up with me. They still do. I don't know what I can do to stop them.

I'm seeing a new doctor tomorrow: Jemima O'Keefe. Her first name makes me think of that kids' programme 'Play School' – Bobby used to watch it. I'm going to have to be sensible and keep those thoughts to myself.

Stacy. The woman in the maternity ward was called Stacy.

28 August 2013

Patrick's finished with me.

It's stupid when I re-read that.

I'm forty-nine years old for God's sake.

Talking about a man who's dumped me.

Why do I always write in here when things turn to shit? I've no happy memories written down. It's always about things gone wrong.

It's because of Nathan.

Karma, probably.

Perhaps it's because I don't deserve happiness. I have tried so hard to get better. I even took up jogging. Endorphins, my doctor said.

And I felt great for ages – my longest time yet.

But then Patrick said he couldn't be with someone like me. I didn't open up enough to him.

Every time I laughed I felt guilty: remembering my children I never see; picturing Nathan's face as he fell.

Who'd want to be with a murderer who abandoned her children, anyway?

Not that Patrick ever knew about that. The murderer part, I mean. I'd shown him pictures of my children, but Annie was a baby and Bobby was six. The picture was so . . .

Four years we were together, yet we lived separately. We met at the café I was working in. He had an engineering contract with some technology group – something to do with pumps or hoses or something. God, I didn't listen, did I?

Patrick was so kind. Physically, he wasn't someone I was normally attracted to (though I couldn't be bothered with all of that shit for years), but he was so kind, and he liked me back. He was divorced, had three grown-up children he saw every other weekend. He liked Chelsea FC, cooking for us on a Saturday while listening to Queen ('Still classics, Deb,' he said. 'No one will ever come close to Freddie Mercury.').

Why am I talking about him in the past tense? He's still alive – just not with me.

He taught me to drive, was so patient with me. He said I could achieve anything if I wanted it enough . . . even bought me a car when I passed my test. He was so pleased . . . said I was on my way to becoming the person I could be.

But I already was the person I could be.

He mustn't have been happy with that.

And I wasn't happy with him trying to change me, to fix me. I don't want a carer – I want someone who accepts me the way I am.

I'll never find that person, will I? Maybe I'm too broken.

It's for me to fix, not him.

I've asked for more shifts at the café. I'm someone else when I'm there. I pretend I'm a jolly soul to the customers, and after being on my feet all day, I collapse, exhausted, at night. When I sleep, I dream I'm someone else.

It's like having two lives.

Neither are mine.

At least the nightmares have stopped.

12 December 2016

Blast from the horrible past. I have heard from Ellen. It feels so wrong that she's been in prison for killing her husband, yet I've been free after killing Nathan.

She said it wasn't killing, though.

We didn't kill him.

He fell.

She's so kind. She tells me that it was on her mind for years when she was in there (though she says that, I'm sure she would've had internet in there and known how to contact me before this).

She couldn't believe it when I told her I hadn't seen my family. If it were her son, she would never have let him go.

Easy for you to say, I said.

This whole thing hasn't been easy for anyone, she said. Damn that Nathan, the crazy bastard. Gave me all sorts of confidence.

I have no idea what she meant by that.

30 June 2017

My darling Annie has replied. I was expecting Monica to send a message back, but my original one was probably too cryptic. I had to test the water – needed to know if they'd actually want to hear from me.

Annie's message was only one line (it was amazingly lifting to hear from her), but mine was only a couple. I wish Annie would have told me about her life. I guess that's selfish of me. She owes me nothing. She probably hates me. I know I would if I were her.

I only had half an hour on the computer at the library and there was a queue. I didn't know what to write back.

This B & B is pretty cheap, but it's basic. The television is an old-style portable. I switched it on one night when I couldn't sleep, but the reception was so crap I turned it off.

There are some people who actually live here. I know that feeling. Of homelessness, hopelessness. Never having roots. Simply existing from one day to the next. Not wanting to die, but not having a life either. Such a fine line.

From just flicking through Debbie's words, I don't know if I can read every entry. Those few pages were so raw, so honest. I so wish she hadn't have left that night in Tenerife. We could have made it better for her. Couldn't we?

Chapter Forty-Eight

Present Day

Debbie

It's strange standing outside Monica and Nathan's house, knowing my children were brought up in it. I used to spend so much time here. We – Peter and I – would come round on sunny afternoons to have barbecues in the back garden. Leo and Bobby were so close, but it's not like that now. When I visited Robert yesterday, he said that since they were teenagers, they didn't get on as well. They barely speak now. If they hadn't been made to live together, would it have been different?

But I can't change the past. It is what it is.

Monica opens the door. She's still as slim as she always was – food must be of no comfort to her.

We stand there, just looking at each other.

Her face is so familiar to me, yet different at the same time. She takes me by the hand and pulls me inside the house.

'I'm so pleased you came,' she says. 'I was half afraid that . . .'

'I'd leave again?'

She's looking at me. To her, I've aged so quickly – in an instant, almost.

'Perhaps,' she says. 'Come on through to the kitchen. Peter won't be long.'

'It's so odd hearing you talk about him like that,' I say, following her. 'Wow, this has changed. It's spotless.'

She flicks on the kettle. 'I took early retirement. Can't bear a mess if I've got to look at it all bloody day.'

On the fridge are photographs of Bobby, Annie and her family. I feel a knot in my stomach.

'You can make new memories,' she says.

'Stop being so nice to me, Mon. I don't deserve it.'

'It's not up to me to decide what you deserve – it's up to you.'

I sigh. 'Since when did you get so wise?'

'Since I got so fucking old,' she says.

'You're not old. You look great – you always did.'

She turns her back to me and looks out of the kitchen window.

'I didn't have my eye on Peter the whole time you were married, you know. We were in such a difficult situation . . . we were there for each other. I was always fond of him.'

'I understand,' I say. She turns around. 'Really I do. Who am I to judge?'

'I thought you'd be so angry with me.'

'How could I be? You and Peter have brought up my children. They're a credit to you, they really are.'

'Oh, Debbie.'

She walks towards me, and rests a hand on my shoulder, then embraces me in a hug.

We're still crying in each other's arms when the front door opens and closes.

'Shall I go out and come back in again?' says Peter.

'No, no,' says Monica, pulling away from me and dabbing her face with the back of her hand. 'I'll just pop upstairs . . . freshen up.'

I want to grab her hand and beg her not to leave me alone

with Peter, but I don't. We have to talk. We haven't been alone since I got back.

'I'm sorry,' I say. The words don't seem enough.

He nods slowly. 'I know.' He pulls out a chair and sits, gesturing for me to do the same. 'I should've known there was something wrong, after you had Anna. I've blamed myself every day since you . . . left.'

'You shouldn't have. It was no one's fault. Though it's taken me so many years to realise that.'

'The children have been happy. I won't lie and say there weren't times when they withdrew into themselves as such, but overall, I think we've done pretty well.'

'I know you have. Thank you.'

'You don't have to thank me – they're my children too.' He shifts in his seat. 'What you said . . . about what happened that night . . . you must go to the police.'

'I know,' I say. 'It's what I should have done a long time ago. But I'll visit Annie first, if that's okay?'

'Of course,' he says. 'But just one thing. Anna hates being called Annie.'

Chapter Forty-Nine

Anna

I've been looking out of the window since midday, and Debbie's finally pulled up outside, driving the car that I've been seeing for days. It's a strange thought, but I never imagined she would drive a car. Dad never mentioned her ever driving; she always took the bus. At some point in her life after us, she would have taken lessons, a test. She must have done so many normal, everyday things without us. Like I have done without *her*.

Thirty years is a long time. What sort of life has she had? We didn't get a chance to talk much at Robert's party, but I'm hoping this afternoon I will get some answers.

I open the door to her.

'I never imagined you'd come to my house,' I say to her, as she greets me with a hug. She smells of Dewberry from the Body Shop.

She stands in the hallway, rubbing the tops of her arms – the rucksack she brought is at her feet.

'I'm not cold,' she says. 'I'm really nervous.'

'Me too,' I say. 'Jack's taken Sophie out for a while, but they'll be back soon. I'll make us some tea.'

She follows me through to the kitchen. I prepared the teapot, cups and saucers, a plate of biscuits and cakes, and a jug of milk, hours ago. I've been up since five o'clock this morning. Everything had to be just right.

'Oh, you kept it!' says Debbie, bending so she's eye level with the shell box she made me that I placed on the dining table. 'I remember choosing the shells, but I can barely recall sticking them on the box.'

'Oh.'

'Annie – I mean Anna, sorry. No. I know I did it . . . sorry. All the talking therapy I've had over the years . . . encouraging me to tell the truth . . . it's not always the best way, is it? Oh, fondant fancies!' She picks one up, turning it round in her hand. 'I haven't had one of these for years.'

Her train of thought is all over the place. I always thought we'd be similar people, but we aren't at all.

'Gran told me you liked them,' I say, pouring hot water into the teapot.

'Really?'

Her face drops, and her lips press together when I mention her mother. I shouldn't push the subject.

'Please, have a seat,' I tell her.

I can't help staring at her all the time. I can barely believe she's here. She seems so small, so vulnerable. I feel as though I want to look after her.

I put a cup on the saucer; it rattles slightly. I can't believe I'm so nervous being alone with her.

'Do you take sugar?' I say.

Such a strange question to ask your own mother.

'No thanks.'

She smiles at me; her eyes are glistening.

'This is lovely,' she says, 'isn't it?'

I nod. 'What made you get in touch now?' I can't help

blurting it out. 'I know you said before about Ellen convincing you after she left prison, but . . .'

'She tracked me down a few days after coming out of prison . . . She didn't want me to mention anything about Nathan, though. She was so scared of the thought of going back inside. It took me a few months to find the courage to even send that email at the library. It was only when I looked for Peter, that I found out he was married to Monica.'

'What? You haven't been on Facebook or anything to search for us?'

She shakes her head slowly.

'It was too painful. What would've been the point when I couldn't be in your lives? I know it sounds flaky, what I'm saying, but after so many years of being away, I got used to feeling alone – the feeling of missing everyone as though you were all dead.'

My mouth drops open.

She looks up at me. 'God, that sounds terrible,' she says. 'I didn't mean . . . I . . . I'm not very good at explaining things. I missed you very much, Anna.'

'I missed you too,' I say, looking at her and realising I don't know her very well at all – not the person she is now. I stir my tea, even though it's probably stone cold by now. 'Gran talked about you all the time. She encouraged me to keep a scrapbook about you. Would you like to see it?'

'Did she?' A tear rolls down her cheek. 'I thought everyone would've forgotten about me. Yes please, Anna. I'd love to see it.'

I jump up from the chair and almost run into the living room to get my book of facts about her. I leave the photographs Robert took in Tenerife in the box; she wouldn't want to see them after what happened there.

I hand her the scrapbook; she pushes her cup to one side

and places the book in front, stroking the cover with her fingers. She opens it. My cheeks warm a little; no one has read it before. Those facts were all mine, but they are, actually, all hers.

She laughs. 'I wish I still had those Doc Martens.'

'Grandad might still have them. He kept all of your clothes, well until recently. He's had a sort through them.'

'I don't blame him for having a clear out – I had so many things I didn't even wear.'

'Did you . . . have you ever . . .'

'Met someone else?'

'Yes.'

'There was someone a few years ago – serious, I think, but I guess you have to love yourself before you love someone else, don't you? I suppose I've always believed I didn't deserve happiness.' She reaches over and strokes my hand. 'I'm not going anywhere. You do believe me, don't you?'

The front door opens, and there are whispers in the hallway.

Debbie and I look to the kitchen door, and Jack appears. Sophie's hiding behind him.

'Is that you, Sophie?' says Debbie softly.

My little girl peeks her head around her dad's waist and nods, before retreating.

Debbie points to one of the cakes, and I nod.

'Would you like a fondant fancy, Sophie?' says Debbie. 'They're my favourite.'

Sophie walks to the table and pulls out a chair before sitting down.

'Yes please,' she says shyly.

I push the plate towards her and she picks up a pink cake, biting the icing off from around the edges.

'I used to do that,' Debbie says, dabbing her cheeks with the back of her sleeve.

'I thought you were dead,' says Sophie.

Silence.

Debbie looks at each of us.

'I've been away. I wasn't well.'

'Are you going to stay now?' my little girl says.

'Yes,' says Debbie without hesitation. 'Yes, I am.'

Acknowledgements

A massive thank you to my brilliant editor, Phoebe Morgan, whose insight and support has been invaluable. Thanks too to Sabah Khan, Elon Woodman-Worrell, Elke Desanghere, and the fantastic team at Avon.

A big thank you to my agent, Caroline Hardman and everyone at Hardman & Swainson.

To Lydia Devadason and Sam Carrington, who have read nearly everything I've ever written. Your support and friendship has been unwavering, supportive, and much appreciated.

To WU for the chat and laughter (and . . . er . . . we do talk about writing some of the time . . .).

Thanks to Ami and Dan at Waterstones, Preston, to Steve and Denise at Nantwich Bookshop, and to Tom Earnshaw at the *Lancashire Post*.

Thanks to my mum, Carmel, for the patience in answering all of my questions about the 1980s – from maternity wards to bad food. To Rosemary McFarlane for the advice on Lytham Club days of the past.

Thank you to Janet Dyer and the lovely ladies at the art group for the tea, cake, laughs and support.

A big shout-out to the bloggers for the time and energy you spend reading, reviewing and blogging.

To Dea Parkin at the CWA, to Claire Reynolds, Louise Fiorentino, Alison Stokes. A big thank you for your support.

A shout-out to Chris, Loretta, Oliver, Nick, James, Conor, Sam, Janny, Maralyn, Jackie, Anne, Carolyn, and Caroline.

To my family: Dom, Dan and Joe, who (mostly) allow me to write in peace (the caravan helps).

And last, but definitely not least, thank you to my lovely readers.

Elisabeth Carpenter is back!

The ebook bestseller with her stunning debut novel.

**Looking for your next
rollercoaster read?**

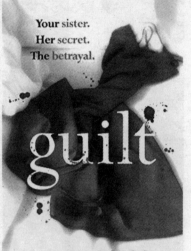
**Look no further. *Guilt* is available in all
good bookshops now.**